THE GHOSTS OF ALTONA

CRAIG RUSSELL

CONSTABLE

CONSTABLE

First published in Great Britain in 2015 by Quercus

This edition published in Great Britain in 2019 by Constable

1 3 5 7 9 10 8 6 4 2

Copyright © Craig Russell, 2015

The moral right of the author has been asserted.

A CIP catalogue record for this book
is available from the British Library.

ISBN: 978-1-4721-3101-0

Printed and bound in Great Britain by Clays Ltd, Elcograf S.p.A.

Papers used by Constable are from well-managed forests
and other responsible sources.

MIX
Paper from
responsible sources
FSC® C104740

Constable
An imprint of
Little, Brown Book Group
Carmelite House
50 Victoria Embankment
London EC4Y 0DZ

An Hachette UK Company
www.hachette.co.uk

www.littlebrown.co.uk

How oft when men are at the point of death
Have they been merry! which their keepers call
A lightning before death.
William Shakespeare
Romeo and Juliet

No man knows till he has suffered from the night
how sweet and dear to his heart and eye the morning can be.
Bram Stoker
Dracula

The existence of near-death experiences is not disputed; their nature is. Many who experience an NDE are left with an overwhelming belief in an afterlife and lose all fear of death. Science views these experiences as powerful and convincing hallucinations triggered by the near-death release of highly potent neurochemicals and intense electrical activity in the brain.

Whatever the cause, whatever their true nature, near-death experiences leave those who undergo them profoundly changed.

Prologue

The sky that day, he would later remember, had been the colour of pewter. When he thought back on it, that was what he would remember, the lack of colour in the sky, the lack of colour in everything. And that he hadn't noticed at the time.

Winter had been half-hearted. That day.

'So why, exactly, are we talking to this guy more than any of the other neighbours?' asked Anna Wolff as she and Fabel got out of the unmarked police BMW. 'Schalthoff has no record . . . never been so much as a suspect for anything and has no dodgy connections that we can find. I just don't get why you get a vibe from him. What is it – some kind of hunch?'

'No such thing as hunches, Anna,' said Fabel. 'Just your unconscious processing information your conscious hasn't got round to putting together. I know something about this guy . . . I just don't know what that something is. Yet.'

'Okay . . .' Anna stretched out the word. 'That makes it clear . . .'

'Bear with me.'

They crossed Grosse Brunnenstrasse and made their way to the apartment building. Like unseen fingers turning pages, an ill-tempered breeze peeled back the damp leaves clinging to the path and tugged at the flyers stapled to bare-armed street-side trees. The face Fabel had got to know so well – big eyes and tousled blond hair above a guileless grin – smiled out from the picture on the flyers. It was that smile, the innocence behind the smile, that had motivated what seemed like the whole population of Altona to join in the hunt for the missing boy. The neighbourhood was full of the flyers: small banners of hope that little Timo Voss would be found alive and well. Everyone was looking to find Timo alive and well. But not Fabel. His job was, and always had been, to find the dead and the guilty, not the living and the innocent. Fabel knew he was looking at the face of a ghost.

'How do you want to handle this?' asked Anna.

'Let's play it by ear. I want to see if we can jangle a nerve. He was just that little bit too scripted the last time.'

As they reached the apartment building, a small woman, coat- and scarf-bundled against the weather, emerged from the main entrance and barged between them. Anna caught the door before it closed, saving them from having to press the entry buzzer.

'It'll be a nice surprise for him.' She smiled.

'Second floor,' Fabel said and he led the way up a stairwell that smelled faintly of disinfectant. When they reached the apartment they wanted, Fabel noticed that the landing, too, seemed to have been recently cleaned. Bass echoes of pop music, drifting down from one of the floors above, haunted the stairwell.

When he pressed the doorbell it made an angry sound, like a bee trapped in a jar. Fabel waited a moment then, when no one answered, he rapped loudly on the door and called out: 'Herr Schalthoff?'

'Maybe he's out,' said Anna when there was still no answer.

'Or working a shift.' But Fabel waited, leaning in to the door and listening.

'I hear movement,' he said quietly. He was about to knock again when the door swung open to reveal a man in his late thirties. Jost Schalthoff, who Fabel knew had worked since leaving school for Hamburg City Council, was still dressed in his work overalls. He was medium height and had an open, pleasant, friendly type of face. Likeable. The kind of face you instinctively trusted.

It was you, you sick murdering fuck.

The thought fell into Fabel's head the instant Schalthoff opened the door. *Little Timo Voss trusted that face of yours but all he was to you was something to be used and disposed of. You took him off the street, did what you wanted and then you killed him.* And in the same instant of clarity, Fabel knew that if they searched Schalthoff's apartment, they would find little Timo.

Fabel could not pinpoint what it had been about Schalthoff's expression that had not been there the first time he had interviewed the council worker. Whatever it was it had instantly triggered his total certainty – something in his expression, something vague and fleeting, in that instant when Schalthoff, who had thought himself now in the clear, saw the police once more at his door. Something more than just guilt.

'We're following up our Timo Voss inquiry, Herr Schalthoff. We have a few more questions, if you don't mind.' Fabel showed his ID and smiled, keeping his tone light and matter-of-fact; Schalthoff tilted his head slightly, his expression dutifully serious. And all the time Fabel knew Schalthoff was the killer, and that Schalthoff knew he knew.

'Of course.' The council worker held open the door and the two Murder Commission officers entered. 'Anything I can do to help. Terrible business . . . just terrible.'

With the door closed behind them, the music from the apartment above was muted to a vague bassline beat. Schalthoff led the two police officers along a short hall to the living room. Fabel scanned as he walked: three doors. Two doors open: small bathroom and toilet, boxroom-cum-bedroom. One door closed, presumably the main bedroom. As he passed the bathroom, Fabel thought he picked up a hint of the same disinfectant odour he had smelled in the stairwell and on the landing.

Two doors open. One door closed.

The living room was clean and tidy and extended into an open-plan kitchen. A picture caught Fabel's eye; it hung on the wall of the hall, just where it opened out into the living area. It was an expensive-looking print of an oil painting, mainly in blacks, dark blues and reds that seemed to combine the abstract with the representational. A hooded and cloaked figure of indeterminate gender stood on the shores of a river. Behind the figure, a riot of shapes and colours suggested some fierce conflagration consuming a city; in the foreground, the figure and the blaze behind it were reflected in the dark, glittering water. The painting had been signed: *Charon*.

The picture looked a little out of place in the apartment – all the furniture was modern and tasteful without being expensive: a well-filled bookcase beneath the window; coffee table; couch and two armchairs. All clean lines. The kitchen counters were uncluttered and populated only by a kettle, toaster and counter-top microwave. Everything functional. Everything in its place. With the exception of the dark print hanging in the hall, Schalthoff's apartment spoke of someone controlled; someone who sought reassurance in efficiency and order. Someone not given to untidiness. To chaos.

But Jan Fabel, who had headed the Hamburg Murder

Commission for fifteen years and had become the Federal Republic's leading investigator of serial killings, knew it was a sham: a carefully constructed fence to enclose the dark, irresistible chaos that churned and roiled deep inside Schalthoff. Something that had to be contained.

One door closed.

'Can I get you a coffee, or something?' Schalthoff made an open-handed gesture of hospitality.

'We're good . . .' said Anna.

'Actually, I could do with a cup of tea,' said Fabel. 'It's so chilly out. If it's not too much trouble.' He cast an eye over the books in the bookcase: horror, the supernatural, a lot of Gothic classics. A brochure for the Altona Jewish Cemetery, which was a monument maintained by the city department Schalthoff worked for, sat on top of the bookcase.

'Not at all,' said Schalthoff smiling. 'Tea, you say?'

'If you have it,' said Fabel. When their host turned to go into the kitchen area, Fabel shot a look at Anna. She caught it and nodded: Fabel was trying to keep Schalthoff occupied.

One door closed.

One door closed but unlocked: all Fabel would have to do was go back into the hall, turn the handle and push. But he had no warrant. And other than an instinct and an opinion that Schalthoff's choice of art and literature jarred with his taste in interior design, Fabel had no probable cause. And that made the insubstantial panel bedroom door as secure as a moat and drawbridge.

Fabel watched as the council technician busied himself in the kitchen. In an unconscious gesture, Schalthoff wiped his palms on his overalls before taking a pale blue teapot from one of the cupboards and rinsing it out under the hot tap. Then he reached up to open one of the wall-mounted units to take out a cup. The pause had been less than momentary: a microsecond of hesitation as his hand had passed one of the drawers.

What's in the drawer, Jost? thought Fabel. *What is it you don't want us to see?* Again, Fabel cursed his lack of a warrant.

'I hope we didn't catch you on the way out.' Anna stepped towards the kitchen part of the open-plan living area, placing herself between Schalthoff and a clear view of the hallway.

'Not at all, I—'

'Do you mind if I use your bathroom?' Fabel interrupted him. It worked. The council worker looked off balance for a sliver of a second, frowned, then wiped clean his expression with a courteous smile. Again, there had been so much squeezed into that sliver of a second.

'No . . . please go ahead,' he said. 'It's at the far end of the hall, nearest the door. To your right.'

Fabel nodded and went back into the hall. The heartbeat pulse from the upstairs music stopped for a moment, before kicking into a different rhythm. Behind him, he could hear Anna affecting a chatty tone.

'There's not a lot we need to ask you,' she said. 'You knew little Timo, I believe?'

'No . . . who told you that?' Schalthoff's tone was even. 'I hadn't heard of him until he went missing. It's sad, really, when you think how close by he lived – just around the corner, really. That's city life, I suppose. Anonymous.'

Fabel knew Anna wouldn't be able to stall him for long. He passed the bathroom, then checked over his shoulder to make sure Schalthoff was still in the kitchen and that Fabel was out of his line of sight before taking the few steps further along the hall to his goal.

He stood before the closed door. If he opened it and found Timo's body, it would be a legally invalid search. For the search to be admissible, he would have to lie and say he thought he had heard a noise, had probable cause to believe Timo was alive and captive behind the door. Except Fabel knew he wouldn't lie.

But if his gut feeling about Schalthoff was right and he and Anna left without looking behind that closed door, there would always be the chance they'd be leaving a still-alive Timo to his fate. He listened. No sounds from behind the door, but he could hear Schalthoff and Anna in the living room: small talk, but now the faintest chord of impatience in Schalthoff's tone.

He placed his hand on the handle.

Please let me be wrong. Please don't let it be me who finds it.

He opened the door.

There was no hint of anything amiss. No captive child, alive or dead. Like the rest of the apartment, the bedroom was clean, tidy, uncluttered; on the spartan side of functional. Bland decoration.

But like the print hanging in the hall and the books on the shelves, there was one discordant note in the bedroom: the wardrobe. Too big for the room, it loomed dark in the corner that got least light, as if trying to hide its bulk in the shadow. Massive, wood-hewn and dark-varnished, it was furniture of the rustic, traditional German kind. In an apartment fitted out with modern, light pieces, the heavy wardrobe looked completely out of place, like a dark forest ghost lost and hiding in the wrong century.

Fabel listened again and could hear Anna talking, dominating the conversation; keeping their reluctant host occupied. But he could only hear Schalthoff as low tones that became lost in the throb of music from an unseen apartment.

A small room. It wouldn't take much searching. And Fabel knew he would search the wardrobe last.

He dropped quietly to his knees and looked under the bed. Nothing. There was nowhere else for a body to be hidden, apart from the out-of-place wardrobe that loomed dark in the corner.

Please let me be wrong. Don't let it be me who finds it.

Three steps took him over to the wardrobe. This was where the chaos was contained, Fabel knew. This was where Schalthoff had hidden Timo's body.

The wardrobe had double doors and Fabel placed his hand on the brass handle of the right door. Turned it.

The door creaked and he checked its opening with his other hand, standing stock-still and listening for the sound of an irate Schalthoff coming along the hall. Instead all he heard was the continuous heartbeat thudding from a flat upstairs and a universe away, and Anna's voice as she continued to stall the wardrobe's owner in the living room.

He gently eased the door fully open.

Please don't let it be me who finds it.

Fabel sighed and wasn't sure if it was out of relief or disappointment: there was no chaos in the dark of the wardrobe, just two suits, a pea coat and three casual jackets hanging neatly. He eased the clothes apart and checked the bottom of the wardrobe: three pairs of shoes, one of work-type boots.

He opened the other side and saw two pairs of jeans hanging inappropriately neatly from hangers; another pair of boots beneath them. Nothing else. No chaos, no horror. No Timo.

Fabel closed the wardrobe doors. It was then he noticed the box.

It was an unsealed cardboard box – the kind movers used – squeezed into the space between the wardrobe and the corner wall. He leaned down, lifted one side of the lid and reached in.

Oh God no. Oh Jesus God no . . .

Fabel stood up abruptly, staggered back. He caught the back of his calf on the corner of the bed, stumbled and landed heavily on the floor. What he had felt inside the box lingered as a phantom on the palm of his hand.

You sick fuck. You sick murdering fuck.

There was shouting from the living room. Through his disgust, his fury, his revulsion, Fabel vaguely guessed that they had heard his stumble and Anna had lost the battle to keep Schalthoff occupied. He didn't care. In that moment he was no longer Fabel the policeman, he was Fabel the father. He just wanted to get to Schalthoff, to grab him, to smash his fist into his face.

He rushed out of the room and down the hall, his mind racing, the phantom sensation of soft curls on a dead child's head burning the palm of his hand.

Anna wasn't arguing, she was yelling. Schalthoff was yelling.

As he got to the end of the hall, Fabel unbuttoned his jacket and reached for where his service automatic rested on his hip.

It all happened in what could have only been a couple of seconds, yet time slowed, stretched. Fabel reached the living room end of the hall and his first thought was *Where did the gun come from?* Then he remembered the drawer. That was what was in the drawer. Not a trophy taken from a murdered child, not some incriminating evidence hastily concealed: a gun. Schalthoff had got around Anna and now stood facing her, his back at an angle to Fabel. The killer's arms were stretched out before him, a revolver iron-clasped in his hands. Fabel could see his profile: drained of colour, features distorted in a tug of war between terror and fury. Anna had one hand raised towards him as if halting traffic, the other held out from her body, poised to go for her sidearm, but frozen in Schalthoff's aim.

They shouted at each other: Schalthoff existential rage; Anna professional commands. Fabel stayed silent, for the moment unseen, reaching for his gun.

It was then that Anna noticed Fabel.

Schalthoff turned to follow her gaze.

Fabel heard three shots, deafeningly loud in the confines of the apartment. Two in quick succession, then a third that sounded different.

The whole world shifted on its axis. Tilted. Shook.

Fabel was on his back.

The universe became the junction of wall and plaster ceiling where the hall entered the living room. He heard screaming and another shot. There was no pain. All there was was the strangest sensation that something heavy and immovable had been dropped onto his chest, stopping his lungs from filling with air. And he was afraid. So afraid. He was afraid because he could not breathe; he was afraid because he could not feel any pain; he was afraid of the pain that was to come.

He's shot me dead. The thought, and the anger with which it burned, penetrated his fear. *I've let everyone down because I let the bastard shoot me dead.*

There was no more yelling. Even the bass beat from the apartment above stopped abruptly. *They must have heard the shots.*

From where he lay, Fabel could see the print on the wall beside and above him. In the midst of his fear and anger a realization dawned on him: *Charon isn't the artist's name, it's who the figure is.*

Anna was above him, looking down on him, blocking out his

universe of wall and plaster ceiling. Her face was filled with fear, panic, and that made Fabel sad. He remembered when she had first joined the Murder Commission, how she had been so edgy and defiant and difficult to manage. So young. He remembered how she had dealt with Paul Lindemann's death on duty, so many years before, and it filled Fabel with a deep sorrow and anger at his own clumsiness realizing that she would now have to deal with his own death. She was talking loudly and urgently to Fabel, tearing at his shirt, pressing down on his chest and adding to the stifling weight.

She was crying. Fabel had never seen Anna Wolff cry.

He thought of Gabi, his daughter. And Susanne. He should have married Susanne. He should have asked her.

He tried to speak. He tried to say *Little Timo is in the bedroom. Don't forget little Timo.* But he had no words. No breath.

Then it came: the pain Fabel had feared. It consumed him, travelled through every nerve in his body like an electric current: white-hot, jangling. He looked pleadingly at Anna, unable to speak, unable to move anything but his eyes. She was using her free hand to make a call on her cell phone, speaking urgently, desperately; choking on her grief and panic. But Fabel couldn't hear what she was saying because the pain now rang in his ears, seared through his head, burned every millimetre of his body, impossibly increasing in intensity. And anyway, it was too late.

Jan Fabel had already begun to die.

2

As Jan Fabel lay dying from his wounds, two things, and two things alone, filled his universe. Pain and fear. His pain reassured him he was still alive. His fear screamed at him that death was imminent.

Then the pain began to fade. There was a moment of intense cold, as if every window and door had been thrown open and winter had claimed the whole apartment. Then nothing.

Fabel knew that the damage to his body was still there, that every nerve would be jangle-hot, but the connection had been switched off: not yet severed, just switched off. The fear persisted, but only for a moment; then even that, too, was gone. He was removed from the machineries of fear and pain, which he now realized were in his body, not his mind. Fabel knew that with each moment his connection to his body was becoming fainter, more tenuous, less important. He was no longer defined by his physical presence.

I *am dying*, he thought without fear or sadness, rancour or concern. And at that moment he became aware of the slow, dark turning of the Earth beneath him.

He was leaving now.

He saw Anna's sad, frightened face start to fade; the picture and the plaster ceiling beyond it fall into shadow. Everything went dark, but not a dark like any he had ever known, not a dark without colour. The full spectrum danced across his vision in gentle glows and vivid flashes.

The world was gone. The world, he now realized, had never truly been there, had never been truly real. This was real, whatever *this* was. Everything he had ever experienced in life had been dulled, muted, out of focus. Now he was experiencing true reality, where everything was sharper, clearer, brighter. He was bodiless, free from form; all around him, in him, through him, the colours grew more intense, more varied: he now saw colours beyond the spectrum, colours he had not known existed. He saw deep within himself; he saw with eyeless clarity the inconceivable beauty of his own existence – spirals of light and energy of which he was made, an endless coiling that was not just himself, but all the generations that had gone before him. He remembered memories that were not his, but had gone into his making. He sank deep into the warm, fathomless ocean of his own consciousness and saw answers to everything that had ever eluded him.

Things happened, thoughts came, visions revealed themselves simultaneously, yet without confusion. There was no sequence because Fabel was, he realized, beyond chronology, outside Time, and everything he experienced was instantaneous.

Fabel, without bodily sensation, to whom a body now seemed an unnatural and distant concept, could somehow sense that he had started to move, and that he was accelerating to a great speed. The light and colours around him became distorted and stretched and he became aware that he was travelling through a tunnel of no substance. A bright light, that would have dazzled had he still had eyes, seemed to fill everything. Jan Fabel felt a euphoria he had never before experienced. A deep, profound, total, indescribable joy.

In that same instant, and without a sense of motion, he found himself elevated above and looking down on Grosse Brunnen-strasse. The rain-damp road glistened and sparkled with overlapping blue flashes from the cluster of police cars and the ambulance that had pulled up outside the apartment building. There was sudden activity as a group of paramedics and police burst out of the main entrance and rushed a wheeled stretcher over to the open doors of the ambulance. An Emergency Service doctor trotted alongside the stretcher, leaning across it and working on the body of a blond man in his late forties. An oxygen mask obscured the patient's face, his shirt had been ripped open and the bright white of the wound pads bloomed dark red as he bled out. Fabel observed the scene with dispassion, disinterest: the body on the trolley had been his, but he now had nothing to do with it, had no further use for it. He watched as they loaded the trolley into the ambulance and Anna Wolff, who had been running behind, clambered in after it.

He remembered, as if remembering a story, how he had once been in the business of investigating deaths, had attended countless murder scenes, and he now wondered vaguely how many of the dead had looked down on him with the same dispassionate curiosity while he had stood over their remains.

Fabel drifted up, further above the scene. He was now high above Altona and was surprised to see how close Schalthoff's apartment had been to his own in Ottensen. Higher. He now saw the whole of Altona and beyond, his sense of sight sharper, further-reaching and more detailed than it had been in life. His vision took in everything around him, in all directions. He was now above the Palmaille and he could see all Hamburg. So much water. Hamburg's element glistered in the night: the lakes of the Binnen and Aussen Alsters; the dark serpent writhe of the River Elbe through the city; the deep harbours of Finkenwerder. He watched the lights glittering along the Reeperbahn, across Sankt Pauli. He could see in all directions at the same time and the whole dark city – from Blankenese to Altengamme; Sinstorf to Wohldorf – sparkled with hard, sharp obsidian clarity.

Fabel understood why he was here, temporarily back from that other place that wasn't a place or a time. He had loved this city so much. He had come to say goodbye.

Suddenly, his view extended even further, reaching out across the low, dark, velvet land beyond the city and taking in the scattered small constellations of illuminated towns and villages.

Again there was a sense of rapid and accelerating motion, of colour and light. Hamburg was no longer below him. Once more, nothing of the world he had known remained. He knew he was back in that place where the laws of physics were completely altered and again Time rushed by and Time stood still. The moment he occupied was both fleeting and eternal.

He was accelerating towards the light that was more than a light. It was the purest white, yet he could distinguish every colour that combined in it. He moved ever faster, yet as he travelled, his entire life played out for him. All of it, every encounter, every sight, sound, smell, touch. He rewitnessed everything he had ever done, everyone he had ever known, every wrong and every right.

As the light grew close, Jan Fabel again felt the most profound joy. It suffused him, filled his being. Dying was beautiful. The most beautiful part of life, he realized, was its end.

His father was waiting for him. His grandparents.

Paul Lindemann, the young officer he had lost to a gunman's bullet and who had haunted his dreams ever since, was there too; but unlike in the dreams, Paul's forehead was unblemished by a bullet wound. Fabel saw little Timo Voss, whose knowing smile made Fabel feel that it was he who was the child and Timo the carrier of great wisdom. There were countless others long gone and Fabel recognized some of them as those he had come to know so well, but only after their deaths: the victims of the murders he had investigated. They all welcomed him, and without speaking – without the machinery of speech – Fabel told them how happy he was to have joined them. And all the time the light that was more than a light grew brighter, warmer, more joyous.

Something burst deep inside him: a hot, burning intense explosion. A vast shadow, like the beat of some broad dark wing, flickered across the light.

'What is happening?' he asked his father.

'It's not time yet. Don't worry, son. It's just that it's not your time yet . . .'

Another burst. This time it came with a surge of intense, searing pain. The light around him dimmed once more. Those who waited for him became shades.

Again. Another searing pain.

Everything around him was gone. A dark rushing. A falling back into the world.

He was back in Hamburg.

Once more Jan Fabel looked down on his body. He knew where he was: the Emergency Room of the Asklepios Hospital in Altona. From somewhere near the ceiling, he watched as a team of four worked on his body. Three stood back as the fourth applied the defibrillator paddles to his chest.

Another burst of dark energy and pain as the current arced up and reconnected him to his body.

The scene he looked down on dulled. The superhuman clarity and range of his vision were gone. The peace and joy he had felt dimmed.

Jan Fabel sank back into the darkness of life.

Part One

Two years later

Part One

Two years later

3

His first thought when he woke was that his wife had left the curtains open, as she preferred to do. His second was that the night sky beyond the window must have been clear of cloud, because a toppled slab of grey-white moonlight lay angled across the carpet beyond his bed. His waking had been into confusion and he raised himself on one elbow and took in the moonlit room, analysing an unfamiliar geometry of shadows, trying to remember if he knew this room, where it was, what he was doing in it.

He struggled to make sense of the dark rectangle in the shadows on the far wall. A painting? And out of the darkness next to his bed, numbers glowed a malevolent red: 01:44. What was this place?

The panic fell from him. He remembered. *I remember it all. I remember everything and I remember that I will soon forget.*

The glowing numbers came from a clock. That's how clocks were made, now. The painting on the wall wasn't a painting but a television set. These days, they could make them as thin as a picture frame.

These days.

He remembered everything. He remembered that his wife could not have left the curtains open because she had died twenty years before. Her face at age thirty, fifty, seventy returned clear in his recall.

He remembered who he was, Georg Schmidt, retired bookseller from Ottensen.

He remembered that he should have died so long ago; that he was old, so very old, and the great weight of his age pulled at him as he eased himself up into a sitting position. He had been dreaming. His dream had been that he was young again and inhabited a world of weaker gravity, where movements were careless, automatic and without thought. Then he realized he hadn't dreamt that: it had been yesterday and he had been awake. His unravelling mind had deceived him into believing he was young again, took fragments of memories and turned them inside out, making him believe the past was the present. He remembered that too: that the palace of memories he had built over nearly a century of life was crumbling, falling in on itself.

And he remembered that moments like this, times in the here-and-now, were becoming rarer, less frequent, less sustained. He had to cling on to each such moment. He had to cling to them because he had an important task to complete before the last threads of his memory finally unwound.

He focused. He brought every part of his mind into that single moment; seized his clarity of thought and clung on to it. He knew where he was: the Alte Mühle Seniors' Home in Altona. Where they kept the old hidden from the young, and today hidden from yesterday.

I am Georg Schmidt, he told himself. I am Georg Schmidt and was there in 1932. I saw it all happen but no one would believe me. I am Georg Schmidt, I live in the Alte Mühle old people's home and my only friend here is Helmut Wohlmann. I am Georg

Schmidt and I play chequers with my friend Helmut Wohlmann every evening and we talk about the old days.

I am Georg Schmidt and I will soon be dead. But, before I die, I must kill Helmut Wohlmann.

4

Frankenstein sat in the cell, in the dark, the night-time ritual sounds of confined men and their keepers resounding through the concrete, steel and brick of the prison. He sat unmoving, a massive, malevolent shadow; something yet darker in the darkness. He had the cell to himself, isolated both from those who would do him harm and those whom he would harm.

Jochen Hübner knew he was a monster. He saw his monstrosity reflected in the mirror, in the expressions of those he caught looking at him; a flash of unease or fear in quickly averted eyes. He was a walking nightmare. The stuff of Gothic tales.

And like most Gothic monsters, he was man-made. Or at least in part man-made. The truth he had learned was that you become that which others hold you to be, that which others tell you you are. Nature may have shaped him, but it had been people who had defined him. A tiny abnormality within – the smallest of growths on the smallest of glands – had been mirrored in huge abnormality without. It had made him monstrous to others, an object to be feared. Mankind had made him: indirectly through its fear and loathing of his appearance, directly through its botched medical science, trying to cure one problem and creating another.

They called him Frankenstein. All called him it behind his

back; few had been foolish enough to call him that to his face. Hübner knew that in the book and the movies Frankenstein was the creator, not the creation, but people were stupid. In any case, the insult had no sting: he *was* Frankenstein's monster. He relished the fear in the eyes of others when they saw him. Especially the fear in the eyes of women. He would never have women's love, would never want women's love, but he could have their fear and their pain. Feed on it. It had been the feeding on it that had brought him to this place.

But soon he would be out of here; he would be free and amongst the women. Amongst their sweet, sweet fear and pain. He would drink it like wine.

Escape had been an obsession when he had first been sent here to Hamburg-Fuhlsbüttel, it had consumed him and he spent every waking hour looking for weaknesses and flaws in the prison's security, scheming and planning flight. But then, as time had passed and he had seen that escape was impossible, the obsession had faded to a concept he carried around with him like a concealed rope ladder, ready to take out and unravel when the opportunity arose.

But it never did.

Even the concept, the idea of escape, had started to fade and he had turned his attentions to becoming master of his new and inevitable reality. Frankenstein set about intimidating and dominating the other inmates, even some of the guards, his size and brutal appearance often enough in themselves to maintain his status. And when more than psychology was needed, he had proven himself capable of a viciousness that shocked even these hardened men of violence. He adapted, but never fully accepted.

He had become involved in activities, had begun to read several hours a day, had even started to take part in social therapy sessions in the faint hope that feigned reform might shorten his term. And it was at the social therapy sessions, in the most unlikely of settings and in the most unlikely of forms, that he found the means of escape. His guardian.

In each social therapy session, one discrete element at a time, it had all been explained to him. The opportunity, the means, the risk. And the risk was huge: before he got his liberty, he would have to pass through a portal more secure than any prison gate. He would have to die, or at least be brought to the very edge of death. And once there, he had to be brought back to life, to consciousness. It had to be timed precisely, to the second; any delay meant he might not be revived, or revived into a brain-damaged, useless state.

It was an acceptable risk: death or moronism was preferable to spending the rest of his life here; both would render him insensible to his surroundings. He knew that if he stayed here any longer, there was no doubt that he would kill one of the others and remove even the remotest possibility of release, or one of the others, or a group of the others, would find the guts to kill him.

He sat and thought of all these things and imagined himself dead. If the plan didn't work and he died, at least there would be peace.

The sounds of prison night-time routine subsided and he turned his attention inward, to his body, his being. He focused on his breathing, counting each breath, fixing his mind on the simplest mechanism of life. One of the social therapy team had taught him meditation skills: a strategy for taking time out from rage. But that was not what he used them for: instead he used meditation to focus all that he was, concentrate the darkness, make denser the malevolence within him. And, most of all, he trained himself to become awake; not to stir from sleep, but to snap out of it in a heartbeat.

He counted his breaths.

When he had his chance, he would have to become fully alert in an instant. He would have to be capable of acting with speed and accuracy the moment they revived him; success depended on him catching them unawares.

Then, and only then, would he be able to feed on the fear of women – and avenge himself on the man who put him here.

They would all learn what it was to suffer.

5

Jan Fabel sat in his car with the engine running, staring at the black-overalled back, emblazoned with the word BEREIT-SCHAFTSPOLIZEI, of the young policewoman who had stopped the traffic. Every now and then she would check over her shoulder to see how far the tailback stretched. She was small, perhaps only 160 centimetres tall, but formless and genderless under the bulked-up, borrowed authority of body armour and uniform. Her riot gear helmet hung hooked on her waistband and she wore a standard service cap, her hair gathered back and tied neatly behind her head in plaits. But woven through the plaits was a narrow, bright red ribbon: a discreet badge of individuality that for some reason cheered Fabel. He had always noticed small things like that – but now he noticed them for their own sake, not just as fragments of a hidden history or telltales of a concealed personality. No longer just as clues.

'Do you want me to tell her to let us through?' asked Anna Wolff, without impatience. Even now, two years on from the shooting, Anna was different around Fabel: quieter, more cautious, less impatient; every interaction wrapped up in a tangle of unspoken thoughts. He knew, without it ever being given voice, that she felt a responsibility, a guilt even, for what had happened. There was no need, he wanted to tell her; and he would. Since the shooting, he had found that he no longer let things go unsaid. At first it had unsettled those around him, who had found him changed. People had been patient with him, indulgent, understanding, sympathetic. But with the same frankness he had told them he didn't need their sympathy.

There had been post-trauma counselling. Psychiatric assessments. He had made clear he hadn't needed that, either. And there had been months of gruelling physical therapy, which he had needed. Really needed.

When he had first come back there had even been a long talk with Police President Hugo Steinbach. Steinbach, who had since retired, had been sincere in his concern for his junior officer. There had been talk of a move to another department and again Fabel's frankness had startled: he had told Steinbach that he knew full well that the Police President didn't really want him to move – nor could afford for him to move – from the Murder Commission; that he understood Steinbach was genuinely concerned, but also simply going through the stipulated Human Resources motions. Fabel had explained that he wasn't some kind of tortured soul, which people seemed to expect him to be, because of the shooting or because he had spent a decade and a half dealing with death. He was content. And he declared himself more than able to return to dealing with the dead.

It had never been mentioned again. By Steinbach or his successor.

Fabel would tell Anna to stop feeling bad about what happened, all right, but later. Later, when the moment was right.

He shook his head. 'We're in no hurry, Anna. One thing you can count on with the dead is they're not going anywhere. Anyway . . .' He nodded towards the fast-approaching reason for the delay: a column of heavily armoured police vehicles thundered towards them and through the junction, like a freight train at a level crossing, causing the small uniformed policewoman to take an involuntary step back. There were several buses laden with riot police, three armoured cars and a water cannon, the column topped and tailed by a blue and silver marked patrol car, blue lights flashing. It looked more like a military deployment than police activity.

'I'm no longer sure if that's the shit or it's the fan,' said Anna. 'This is getting out of hand. You see Wandsbek on the TV last night?'

'Yep.' Fabel had: cars blazing; petrol bombs and police baton rounds arcing through the spring night air.

'Battle zone. And we get stuck in the middle. But if it kicks off today, the May Day riots, Schanzenfest, Rote Flora, Wandsbek – none of that will be anything in comparison.'

'Let's hope it doesn't. I live here. I don't want to see Altona turned into a war zone.' But it would, Fabel knew. The latest estimates were that there would be three thousand far-right extremists marching through the heart of traditionally left-wing Altona, with as many as eight thousand anti-fascists expected to mount a counter-demonstration. As Anna had pointed out, it would all end up with the Readiness Police in the middle and in the spotlight. The Polizei Hamburg's public image was always the first casualty.

And here, in Altona, it all conjured up a distant memory. A very German kind of memory: distant but undimmed. A memory forbidden to be forgotten.

The column passed and once it was completely out of sight, the little policewoman turned and waved them on.

*

One thing Jan Fabel had learned over the years was that the dead waited to be found on pleasant late-spring days like this just as they did in the cold and rain. He had seen blood shimmer in summer sunlight and blot dark in winter snow. There was, he knew, no meteorology for violence. No season for murder.

He had lost count of the number of dead bodies he had seen over the years. There had been those that looked deceptively life-like: as if sleeping, not dead. There had been the sad and pathetic, bodies foetus-coiled in terminal fear and pain. There had been the gut-turning: those pulled out of the Elbe after a week in the water, the foul-smelling flesh fragile and slick like overripe chicken. And then there were those like the one he now gazed down on: the fleshless; the jumbles of bones and the naked grins of skulls. For some reason, despite the skeleton and the skull being the universal symbols of death, Fabel could seldom connect them with anything human, dead or alive, as if their identities had fallen away from them with their flesh. They seemed more objects than anything once animate; anything once a person.

'It's a female, adult.' Holger Brauner grunted as he clambered out of the excavated area. 'Somewhere between sixteen and thirty.'

'Any idea how long the remains have been here?' asked Fabel. Brauner snapped off a latex glove and shook Fabel's hand. The Murder Commission leader and the forensic pathologist had been friends for as long as they had been colleagues. Brauner had found time every day to visit Fabel in hospital in those first crucial weeks of recovery.

Brauner jutted his chin towards a building site across the road. 'There's a new development going up over there. They had to cut this trench here because they needed to reroute the water supply. Just half a metre either way and she may never have been discovered.'

Fabel nodded. The bones lay in a narrow trench that had been cut at an angle across one corner of the car park.

'And I can be very specific about when the body was buried here.' Brauner smiled broadly, which was his habit. Before the shooting, Fabel had always wondered how someone who dealt with the physical reality of death every day could be so cheerful. After the shooting, he understood it perfectly. 'The car park was laid fifteen years ago, and this soil was infill, laid down in preparation. I suspect that the killer knew about the site, dug out the grave, put her in and once he'd covered her up, I reckon he smoothed it all out so no one would notice before finishing the job for him by laying the asphalt. So we have a very clear window . . . March to May 2000.'

'What is it?' Anna Wolff had clearly read Fabel's expression.

'She was twenty-five,' said Fabel. 'Just turned.'

'I'd say there or thereabouts, maybe younger,' Brauner said. 'From the leg bones I'd estimate she was somewhere around one hundred and seventy to one hundred and seventy-five centimetres tall.'

'One hundred and seventy-four.'

Now Brauner looked at Fabel with the same puzzlement as Anna. 'You know who this is?'

Fabel nodded. 'Was she killed by that?' He jutted his chin towards where the skull was caved in on the left side.

'No,' said Brauner. 'That's fresh . . . damage from the digger's shovel. Without soft tissue it will be impossible to pinpoint an exact cause of death, unless we find fractures or blade marks on the bones.'

'Who is she, Jan?' asked Anna.

'Monika Krone. The first case I worked on in the Murder Commission. She was a post-grad literature student. An exceptional student . . . twenty-five years old, beautiful – strikingly beautiful – and fiercely intelligent. She had a great future ahead of her but she walked out of a university party and fell off the world. We never did get her killer. Or find her body, until now.'

'It's a bit early—'

'It's her.' Fabel cut Anna off. 'She went missing from the party on a Saturday night in March, 2000. The eighteenth of March. Like I said, just vanished clean off the face of the Earth.'

'Suspects?'

'Plenty – almost anyone who was at the party. But once we had a chronology worked out, we reckoned she'd been picked at random. Our only solid suspect was a serial rapist on the loose at the time – Jochen Hübner. When we caught Hübner we were hot for him for this, but there was nothing conclusive or even circumstantial to connect him to her disappearance. And there was no evidence that he had ever killed a victim.'

'So why was he at the top of the list?'

'The Sexual Crimes Commission had been after an unidentified serial rapist for a while. He'd been christened "Frankenstein" by the press.'

'Frankenstein?'

'If you ever came face to face with him, you'd understand. And trust me, you never want to come face to face with Jochen Hübner. It was actually his unusual appearance that got him caught in the end. Hübner was – *is* – a monster on the outside and on the inside. He's an offender of breathtaking malice: his hatred of women was astonishing and the Sexual Crimes Commission had red-flagged "Frankenstein" to us as someone whose offending was clearly set to escalate – that it was simply a matter of time before he was going to kill a victim. When we identified Jochen Hübner as "Frankenstein", it seemed reasonable that Monika Krone was that landmark victim marking his switch from serial rapist to serial killer.'

'So do you still think it could have been him?'

'I don't know. Truth is, I have my doubts. Always did. He swore he didn't do it and Hübner was the kind of sociopathic egoist to be proud of his work. Once he was caught, he admitted to all of the rapes, with relish. The lead SCC investigator was a woman and Hübner told her exactly what he had done to each victim in forensic detail – what each had said when they were begging. After his conviction she had to take a leave of absence.'

'Sounds to me like it could easily have been him,' said Anna.

'Perhaps.'

Fabel stared down at the bones in the shallow grave, white against the red-black of the earth, numbered orange forensic markers scattered around her like ancient grave goods. He knew who she was, knew she had lain beneath this grubby mini-market car park for fifteen years, her beauty and her flesh falling from her bones while the living had bustled back and forth with trolleys and carrier bags stuffed with groceries, had squabbled over parking spaces, had shouted at children to be quiet, had cursed as shopping bags had split and spilled, had conducted the meaningless rituals of life. He knew it was Monika Krone in the shallow grave before him, but somehow still could not connect the bones with the person.

The sun broke through from behind a cloud and Fabel turned his face to it.

'I suppose we had better see the next of kin.'

6

The movie was not like the book.

Zombie sat alone in his row. He sat alone because, although this art house movie theatre in Rotherbaum was usually well-patronized, there was a limit to the audience in Hamburg for silent Expressionist movies; alone because he was sitting perhaps a little too close to the screen and should have been three or four rows further back. But this was a monument of a movie and he wanted it to fill his vision; for the slow-moving tectonic plates of Paul Wegener's face, all sharp angles and flat planes, to command his eyes; alone because he didn't want anyone to smell him.

Death, he knew, had a unique odour.

Zombie was not a nickname: a nickname was something given you by others and Zombie had no real connection to others, no solid connection to the world of the living, any more. He was compelled, by the imperatives of his continued but lifeless existence, to interact with others occasionally, but outside the forced ritual of work he kept those interactions to the absolute minimum. Zombie was not even a name: it was a description, a statement of taxonomy. Just like a shark was a fish, like a rat was a rodent, he was a zombie. He had died, but was unburied and did not yet belong with the dead; he was animate, but did not belong with the living. He continued to walk the Earth but was no longer connected to it. And all the time he sought meaning, to understand why he had been condemned to this state of conscious non-being.

He still had favoured places, however. Zombie liked to come to this cinema, he liked the dark and the quiet of his room, and, most of all, he liked to be around graveyards: the homesick pull every unwilling traveller feels.

He still remembered what it was to be alive, though; what it had been like to have had senses: the sight, smell, taste, touch and sound of the world.

When he had been a boy, his family had spent holidays in an aparthotel next to the sea at Cuxhaven. He remembered his excitement – the almost unbearable anticipation – as they had walked along the path to the dunes, and how the sea had promised itself through every sense before yielding to sight: the ozone fuming in the air, the path edged with windswept sand, the sound coming over the dunes of an unseen sea moving against the shore. That was what it had been like to be at the centre of a nexus of senses. To be alive.

He even remembered what it had been like to love; faint echoes of longing, desire, jealousy. The face of the woman he loved, the only woman he had ever loved, remained clear in his recall and the pain the memory brought was the closest thing to an acute feeling he still had.

It was these memories he used to disguise himself when he moved among the living, affecting the empty expression of vitality.

Zombie did still have senses, of a sort. He still saw the world, but it was through the lens of a dead eye, everything muted, dull, vapid. All his other senses were turned down even further:

to the dead-but-walking Zombie the world was an insipid place devoid of taste or odour, except when he caught the occasional whiff of his own corruption, the stench of his rotting flesh seeping through his clothes.

So now he sat alone, in an otherwise empty row that was too close to the screen.

The movie was not like the book.

It was unsurprising that he watched a lot of films about the undead. Most were nonsensical: vampire movies, always camp and comical, had become vacuous teen romances. Zombie flicks in particular were stupid, crass and repetitious: the undead invariably stumbling about clumsily, soullessly, thoughtlessly; sinking blackening teeth into the flesh of the living and turning them to their own creed.

It wasn't like that at all.

No one had ever thought of what it was really like to be dead but still animate, to be at the centre of the experience; what it was like to become the ultimate social outsider. Zombie still ate – vague feelings of hunger stirred occasionally but infrequently – but he ate without savour the food everyone else ate, not human flesh, as the movies would have it. In any case, he ate less than the living and was now stick-thin. People at work – his job one of the many routines he performed to create the illusion of life – said he was wasting away and needed to feed himself properly. But Zombie knew his emaciation wasn't just the result of poor nutrition, it was because he was rotting away. Decaying from the inside out. But he couldn't tell them that. Like when a colleague had joked about Zombie's overuse of cologne, asking if he bathed in the stuff – Zombie could not tell him that it was to mask his corpse stench from the world.

In public Zombie affected the similitude of life: the absurd routines of the living. In private he dropped the pretence, lying for sleepless hours in his darkened room, unmoving, barely breathing, imagining the earthy, wormy rest denied him. But there were two things that persisted from his life: ghost habits. He read books. He watched movies. The films he watched were mainly classics, especially, like this one, classics of German Expressionism. Gothic. Films he watched to understand himself.

The medium of film in itself reflected his condition perfectly. Most of the movies he watched had been made in a time and by people long gone. He had got to know the players – Paul Wegener, Brigitte Helm, Conrad Veidt, Henrik Galeen, Elsa Lanchester, Lyda Salmonova, Olaf Fønss, Emil Jannings – as if they had been his contemporaries, his friends. Like him, they were all dead. Also like him, they were all still animate in death, moving around for his entertainment long after their demise. Monochrome ghosts imitating life across a screen.

But this movie was special: watching it was a quest for self-understanding. This film spoke so eloquently, so perfectly, about Zombie's state of being-nonbeing.

The movie was not like the book.

Zombie had known that before coming to the cinema. He had read the book twice; he had seen the movie more times than he could count. He had enjoyed the book, considering Meyrink underappreciated, even the occasional – but only occasional – equal of Kafka. While the book had stimulated his mind, the movie stirred something deep inside every time he watched it. And he had long considered himself far beyond vital stirrings.

This cinema in Rotherbaum was different, specializing in classic, cult and art films. Unusually for Germany, it screened foreign films wherever possible with subtitles, rather than a dubbed soundtrack. It was important to him to hear the real voices of the actors, not that this movie had voices. This movie was silent, yet it sang to Zombie.

The Golem – How He Came into the World.

Mary Shelley had been inspired to write *Frankenstein* after a visit to Prague and hearing about the legend of the Golem; Wegener's Expressionist on-screen performance as the giant automaton shaped from clay had similarly been the inspiration for every movie Frankenstein monster that followed. Zombie saw his own struggle reflected by Wegener's lifeless, soulless man of mud seeking understanding in a world of the cruelly vital. A dead thing, devoid of a soul, condemned to play a lifeless part in a living world. And like Zombie, the Golem looked on the world of the living with a combination of longing and hatred.

Paul Wegener totally convinced as the Golem: the actor himself had been a giant of a man, nearly two metres tall, and with the additional height of the Golem's huge block boots he towered above the rest of the cast. A monument brought to life.

On the screen, the Rabbi completed the anthropomorphosis of his clay statue by rolling up the sacred word, placing it in the talisman and pushing it into the huge barrel chest of the clay man. Golem opened his eyes. Pale eyes in a grey face moulded from Vltava mud darted from side to side, taking in a world in which they did not belong. A confused birth into a lifeless existence.

It had been like that for Zombie. Waking up in a hospital after he had died, no one believing him when he told them he was still dead, the medicines they gave him, the therapy they insisted on useless. Tools for use on the living.

They had sent Zombie to see a psychiatrist, who had told him about Cotard's Delusion, explaining how, because of trauma, brain injury or lesion, otherwise perfectly rational people believed themselves to be dead. It was made worse in Zombie's case, the psychiatrist had explained, because he had had a near-death experience, which compounded his belief that he had really died.

The psychiatrist had tried to convince Zombie that he was delusional, that he was really still alive. The more the psychiatrist sought to explain, the more Zombie protested, until it became clear that he could perhaps end up losing his job or, worse still, be locked away in an institution for his own safety. Cotard's delusionals often tried to destroy their 'corpses' to liberate the ghost trapped within. So for the first of many times, Zombie faked it: pretending to make progress and accept that he was really alive.

But he knew he was dead, and he had spent months seeking an answer as to why he was being denied his rest. Then it came to him. A slow, hot ember that became the only thing vital and real within him: the need for revenge. He remembered what had been done to him; how he had died. He remembered the knife in his chest that ended his life and he remembered the hands that had held it. This crime, this injustice, had gone unpunished and until he set it right, Zombie would be forced to walk the world as a corpse.

He watched the movie. As the Golem strode, inexorable, relentless, through the jagged-edged architecture of an Expressionist Prague, the guilty and the unjust were crushed between his massive, unfeeling hands.

This, Zombie realized, was what he needed to create: a Golem of his own to do his bidding. An unstoppable weapon of vengeance.

7

The parents were both dead.

Henk Hermann returned Fabel's call to the Murder Commission and told him that Paul Krone had died of a heart attack in 2006, and his wife of cancer two years later.

Fabel remembered them both so very clearly. Herr and Frau Krone had been in their fifties and as unremarkable as it was possible to be, but their earnest, almost beseechingly attentive faces from fifteen years ago – desperately focused on Fabel's every word as he had gone through the routine questions and procedures of interviewing next of kin – were burned in perfect detail in his memory. He had sought to reassure, to encourage hope. Back then, Fabel had still believed that the faces of the missing were not yet the faces of the dead; had not yet come to recognize the telltale elements that distinguished a runaway from a victim, the misplaced from the misused. Back then, he had held all possibilities in his head until a body was found.

Monika Krone's parents were both intelligent, both professionals – he an engineer, she a physics schoolteacher – but they had become innocently, artlessly, desperately helpless in that most primal of crises: a child lost. Fabel had never found their twenty-five-year-old daughter, alive or dead. He had visited them each week, then each month. Then other cases had intruded, other victims' families had turned pleading faces to Fabel.

Fabel remembered their faces, all right. He also remembered a third face, a sad ghost sitting between them who, no matter what she did from then on, would always haunt her parents, be a daily reminder of their pain and loss.

'There was a sister . . .' said Fabel.

'Yep . . . I'm on to it. She's a science teacher,' said Henk. 'I'm digging for a home address or the school she teaches at and I'll call you back or text the details to you as soon as I've got them. I think she still lives and works in Altona.'

The school was in Eckernförder Strasse.

Spring was now yielding to summer and the sky was cloudless. As Anna drove them both across town to the school, Fabel had watched the sun-etched Wilhelmine architecture of Altona slide through the viewing screen of his passenger window. There were police everywhere, black knots of overalls and vehicles gathered at intersections like shadows in the bright sun. Some roads had already been closed off in preparation for the parade. He knew that the route – the hotly debated, protested and negotiated route – would bring the far-right marchers past both the memorial to fallen German soldiers and the memorial to the victims of Altona Bloody Sunday. The original route had been an almost identical path to that taken by the Brownshirts on Bloody Sunday in 1932, but the Polizei Hamburg's objections had been heeded by the city council and a compromise solution found. Even with that, the route was punctuated with potential flashpoints.

It was an undecided thing, that which was yet to unfold that day in Altona. What Fabel had come to believe after he had been shot two years before, was that every day was full of limitless possibilities. Everything could happen and the destiny that seemed certain one moment could change drastically because of the slightest alteration of course: just one decision, a moment's hesitation, or a choosing to go right instead of left and everything changes.

The day he had been shot was an example: there had been a succession of decisions and choices that led to just one of an infinite number of possibilities. If Fabel had stayed in the living room and Anna had gone along the hall, if he had asked Schalthoff what was in the drawer, if he had not asked for tea and the killer had not had reason to go into the kitchen – all of these things had been possibilities left unearthed; pasts and futures left undiscovered. And today, as Fabel watched Altona brace itself, he realized that there were countless possible outcomes to the day.

At the moment, none of them looked good.

On arrival at the school, Fabel and Anna were conducted to a waiting room and informed that Frau Krone was just finishing a class and would be with them shortly. The waiting room was the usual combination of the functional and the brightly informal that tried, but always failed, to look less institutional. Fabel stood at the noticeboard on the wall, examining the hopeful, earnest and purposefully cheerful scraps of other lives: debating societies, environmental projects, after-school activities. Anna sat somewhat stiffly, gazing out of the window.

'You look nervous.' Fabel turned to her. 'Bring back memories?'

'You don't know how right you are. This reminds me so much of my old school. You've no idea how many times I was stuck waiting for the School Director in a room just like this.'

'I can imagine . . .' Fabel smiled. 'A born troublemaker, I'll bet.'

'This sister we're seeing,' asked Anna, 'did she have anything significant to say at the time of Monika Krone's disappearance?'

'Nothing that helped much. The focus was on her because she is the last known confirmed contact with Monika. Monika phoned her an hour after she had left the party.'

Anna was about to say something when the door swung open and a woman entered. Even though he had known what to expect, Fabel was surprised how much her appearance struck him. It wasn't just the beauty of the pale ghost from fifteen years before that hit him. Older, dressed differently, but no less sad. The magnificent blaze of red hair she had shared with her sister had darkened to a rich auburn, had been cut much shorter, as if deliberately muting its impact, and there was a hint of some other colour streaked through it, but Fabel would have recognized her anywhere. The same pale complexion, the same bright green eyes, the same faintly cruel arch to her eyebrows. The same face. Exactly the same face.

Kerstin Krone was, Fabel knew, exactly 174 centimetres tall, exactly forty years old, although she looked younger. And her face was exactly the face that Monika Krone would have had if she too had lived to see forty.

Fabel asked Monika Krone's identical twin sister to sit.

'Is there any doubt?' Kerstin Krone asked when Fabel had finished explaining about the body found under the asphalt of the mini-market's car park.

'It will take time for us to make a definite formal identification—' Anna began to explain but Fabel cut her off.

'It's Monika,' he said. 'I'm sure of it.' Fabel ignored Anna's meaningful look.

'That's that, then,' said Kerstin, emptily. Her pale, slender hands rested on her lap and she sat looking at them for a while. When she looked up again, she was smiling, sadly.

'It's funny,' she said, 'today I was explaining, or at least trying to explain, the Schrödinger's cat thought experiment to a class. Are you familiar with it?'

Fabel nodded. 'I understand the principle. Well, sort of.'

'Schrödinger's cat?' Anna shrugged.

'Erwin Schrödinger came up with it to illustrate the concept of superposition,' Kerstin Krone explained. 'A cat is placed in a sealed box with a vial of lethal poison and some radioactive material. The box has a monitor that, if it picks up any changes in radioactivity, shatters the poison flask and kills the cat. We don't know until we open the box if the cat is alive or dead. So, until we do, the cat is both alive and dead at the same time. Both possibilities. It's only when we open the box and see the cat that the possibilities collapse into a single reality. Do you understand why it came to mind, Herr Fabel?'

Fabel nodded. 'Yes I do. I'm sorry. We've opened the box.'

Kerstin Krone's eyes glazed with tears. 'It's stupid, I know. I mean, I always knew Monika was dead, that something terrible must have happened to her, but I kidded myself there was a chance that she was alive and well somewhere. And it helped. It was silly, but it helped. I kept all sorts of possibilities, no matter how ridiculous or unlikely, alive in my head. Now you've opened the box they've collapsed to one reality. Monika's dead, and that's a fact. When I wake up tomorrow, Monika will definitely not be in the world.'

'It's not at all silly,' said Fabel. 'I understand. I'm just sorry that we don't have better news for you.'

'You're just telling me what I already knew, really. But a little self-deception is a great analgesic.'

'Are you okay?' asked Anna. 'We can come back some other time.'

'I'm fine. If you have any questions, ask them. But the answers will be the same as they were fifteen years ago. Maybe not as clear . . .'

Fabel explained, quietly and clearly, how the finding of Monika's body not only confirmed her death, but added a dimension to the investigation. A new point of reference.

'Someone put her body there. That means we have another location. In fact, it's the only place and event that we can place her killer for sure. There is a history, a chronology to that event: a before, during and after. It's something we didn't have before.'

'But it was fifteen years ago. Who's going to remember where they were and what they saw so long ago?'

'It's a start, Frau Krone. A fresh start. A new lead.' Fabel smiled reassuringly. 'Can we go over it all again?'

Kerstin Krone nodded, but Fabel could see her mind was elsewhere, dealing with the new certainty of a long-suspected reality.

'If you need time,' he said, 'like Commissar Wolff says, we can come back.'

'I'm fine . . .' She looked down at her hands again, and Fabel began the routine deconstruction of long-past events.

'That all got a bit too metaphysical for me,' said Anna when they got back to the car. 'I never was much good at science and was always goofing around in class – one of the reasons I spent so much time waiting in a room like that for the School Director.'

'I knew exactly what she meant by the Schrödinger's Cat thing,' said Fabel. 'It's what we do – open the box for people all the time, remove the uncertainty and with it remove the last shred of hope. I even think of it every time we question a suspect. Another box to be opened to expose someone either as innocent or as a murderer.'

Anna remained quiet for a moment.

'What is it?' asked Fabel.

'I don't know . . . I mean, I know it's all nonsense, scientifically speaking, but the way she talked about pretending Monika was still alive. I thought identical twins had this kind of special bond. I would have thought she would have had . . . I don't know . . . some kind of *instinctive* feeling one way or the other.'

'Telepathy doesn't exist,' said Fabel. 'Whether you're a twin or not. She's just like countless other victims' relatives I've seen over the years, hanging on to any hope, no matter how vague.'

'You're probably right. I didn't really hear anything else of much use.'

'Like she said, they were the same answers she gave fifteen years ago. I just hoped that Monika being found might have jolted some memory into place.'

'She's a striking-looking woman,' said Anna.

'They were both beautiful,' said Fabel. 'Monika Krone had this amazing head of red hair, longer even than her sister's at the time. Everyone we talked to mentioned her hair. Most of them said the same thing: that her hair, her particular type of beauty, her figure and her pale complexion all made her look like she was living in the wrong century. Maybe that's why she was so interested in Romantic and Gothic literature. She even dressed in an odd way. Not a Goth, as such, but more authentically Gothic. Vaguely Victorian – she studied English Gothic literature at Hamburg University.' Fabel gave a small, humourless laugh. 'It's the only murder inquiry I've been involved in where the word "pre-Raphaelite" cropped up in descriptions of the victim. In fact, it was something that stuck with me for a while. She was the kind of woman that men would go crazy for and I seriously pursued the line that she may not have been a random victim, but had been killed by some rejected lover or spurned admirer.'

'And?'

'Nothing. Everyone checked out. She seemed to have been involved with two fellow students, but they both had alibis. And we didn't have a body back then.'

'You know Kerstin Krone was right, don't you? Finding a body after so much time doesn't give us any real new hope.'

'Perhaps not,' said Fabel. 'But Monika Krone has haunted me throughout my career. It's a ghost I'd like to lay to rest.'

'What about Kerstin? No chance she could have done her twin in in a fit of sibling rivalry?'

'You've met her – not the type. Anyway, we checked her out at the time. She was living and studying at the Leibniz University in Hannover. Physics.'

'That's not so far away. Couple of hours by car at the most.'

'We looked into it, of course. Kerstin was with her boyfriend in Hannover the night Monika disappeared.'

Anna nodded thoughtfully. 'We'll never know for sure if Monika died that night or not. She could have been kept somewhere for days before being killed and dumped.'

'She died that night.' Fabel looked surprised by his own statement. 'I don't know why, but I'm sure of that.'

8

Georg wrote it all down in his notebook. He wrote all the important things he remembered, as he remembered them, into his
notebook and locked it away in the desk drawer. His greatest
fear was that he would forget that he had the notebook at all: it
was his testimony, it was his record. It was his memory.

After he had killed Helmut Wohlmann, even if he could not
explain himself, the notebook would do the explaining for him.

After writing out his plan in full, when he was going to do it,
how he was going to do it, *why* he was going to do it, he placed
the notebook back in the drawer. The key to the drawer was on a
chain and after he had locked it, he hung the key around his
neck, pushing it down and out of sight under his shirt. It had
been the first thing he had worked out: even if he forgot about
the notebook, forgot about Helmut Wohlmann and his crimes,
he would still be puzzled as to why he had a key around his
neck. He might lose his memory, but he wouldn't lose his curiosity. He would try the key in every lock in his room – and there
weren't many – until he found it fitted the desk drawer. Then he
would find the diary and read. There he would find his
memory.

He went over to his wardrobe and fingered through his selec-
tion of ties. He did not usually wear a tie, but today he would. He

selected one that he thought would do the job: a nylon mix in the material making it stronger. He wrapped the tie around one hand, then the other, snapping the material taut between them. He tried to imagine Helmut writhing and thrashing as Georg tightened the improvised garrotte around his friend's throat. Helmut had been a big man, physically strong, in his youth and, in a life-or-death struggle, some of that vigour might come back to him.

The tie would be strong enough for the job, decided Georg. But would he?

9

It was such a small piece of news, almost lost, adrift on the ocean of information technologies.

With a logic that only Hamburgers could understand, the *Morgenpost*, Hamburg's morning paper, comes out in the evening and its evening paper, the *Abendblatt*, hits the streets in the morning.

Both newspapers, as well as that evening's edition of TV's *Hamburg Journal*, carried a mention of the discovery of the bones beneath the mini-market car park in Altona. It was reported that the remains were suspected to belong to Monika Krone, the young literature student who had gone missing fifteen years before, although this was still to be confirmed by the Polizei Hamburg.

All the items were unsensational, almost perfunctory. A couple of centimetres of newsprint. Hamburg's attention was elsewhere, focused on the imminent march and counter-demonstration in Altona. The television mention of the body's discovery was squeezed in after an item about the forthcoming inauguration in Altona of a new building named after an anti-Nazi martyr and before the sports results and weather. There was nothing more the media could say until the identity had been confirmed. Brief, factual, unsensational.

But that small scrap of news reached out across Hamburg and for three men – three men leading very different lives in different parts of the city – the news had the impact of watching planes flying into New York buildings.

She had been found.

The ghost of a past that united the three men – and another two as yet beyond the scope of the news – reached out from print and screen and seized them.

The painter stood alone at his easel, a face burned into the canvas of his recall. The architect, as usual surrounded by others, hid his shock in a sleek smile and handsome isolation in a party crowd. The writer sat at his computer, staring at the item on the *Abendblatt*'s online edition, feeling betrayed that his sanctuary of a million words, which he had spent fifteen years constructing, had been destroyed in a single paragraph of disinterested journalism. The past he had spent so long convincing himself to be a fiction had now broken the surface of the real world, shattering his present.

Three men: each alone with memories he could not share with anyone. Memories they could not share with each other, even though the painter, the writer and the architect thought of each other in the desolate wake of the news. They had sworn long ago never to have anything to do with each other again. Three men haunted by the same ghosts; divided forever by the same experience.

But each, in his own way, felt the chill arrival of an overdue reckoning.

10

Hamburg's Police Presidium on the north edge of the Winter-huder Stadtpark was exactly the same age as the Monika Krone case. Fifteen years before, Fabel had been in the middle of the Krone investigation when the Polizei Hamburg had moved head-quarters from a sixties high-rise office block in Beim Strohhause to this custom-built building in Alsterdorf.

The new Presidium – and Fabel still thought of it as the new Presidium – was a six-storey structure that had been built as a cir-cle around a central atrium open to the sky; all the office suites, including the Murder Commission, radiated out as the arms from its circular hallways. From the air, the shape was that of a giant Police Star, the symbol of police forces throughout Germany.

Anna drove the service BMW down into the underground car park beneath the Presidium, parking in one of the Murder Com-mission's allocated spaces.

'Get everyone together for a briefing,' said Fabel when Anna switched off the engine. 'I need to know where we are with case-loads before I start allocating resources to the Krone case. It's a cold case, after all.' He paused for a moment. 'I'd like to take the lead on it myself. I know you've got other stuff on, and you're usually teamed with Henk Hermann, but are you okay working it with me?'

Anna turned to him. There was a cautious, compliant softness in the way she looked at him and again it saddened him. He missed the frank, defiant Anna who had always taken him to task on any decision she didn't agree with. Rank, he had long realized, had been an abstract concept to Anna. But now she deferred to him unquestioningly. It was as if he had survived the shooting, but the old Anna hadn't.

'Sure,' she said. 'No problem.'

They got out of the car. This, decided Fabel, was the moment.

'It's all right, Anna,' he said.

She frowned as she looked at him over the roof of the car. 'What?'

'I just wanted you to know: it's all right.'

'What's all right?'

'Me. Things. Everything.' Fabel closed his car door and leaned his elbow on the BMW's roof. 'I know you've found it hard. Since I came back, I mean. What happened . . . well, what happened was a trauma for you, too. You saw me shot and you killed a man. But I think you still worry about me and I wanted you to know it's all right. I'm okay. *We're* okay.'

Anna seemed to watch Fabel for a while, her expression unreadable. She sighed. 'I go through it in my head all the time,' she said. 'I see Schalthoff begin to turn, like it was in slow motion. I take it apart movement by movement.'

'That's understandable,' said Fabel.

'I hesitated.' Anna broke eye contact with Fabel, looking down for a moment at the floor of the parking garage. 'Going through it in my head . . . taking it apart like that . . . I can see now that I hesitated in firing. I could have shot him before he got off his second round.'

'You don't know that, Anna. You maybe remember hesitating,

imagine you hesitated, when you didn't. You've interviewed enough witnesses to know that people fill in the gaps their memories leave. And what if you did hesitate? I wouldn't want to work with an officer who didn't think twice before ending a life. We're police officers, not soldiers. In any case, I didn't even have my own firearm drawn. If anyone made a mistake it was me. I let my own emotions cloud procedure. I was just so . . .' He struggled for the right word, which refused to yield itself. 'You know, finding little Timo Voss like that. It got to me and it could have cost both our lives.'

Another pause.

'Listen, Anna, there are things I've learned because of the experience I went through. Different ways of looking at things, I suppose. You learn to appreciate what you've got, professionally as well as personally. I know I gave you a hard time when you first joined the team, but that was because I had to control the very energy I recruited you for. I don't want you walking on eggshells when you're around me – not just because it makes things awkward, but because it inhibits your effectiveness. I want you back, Anna. Completely back. If you don't agree with something I'm doing, I want you to tell me. I need you to challenge me again.'

Anna looked at him without answering for a moment.

She nodded. 'Okay. I'll try. It should be easy because you can be a real arsehole sometimes.'

Fabel grinned. 'That's the attitude I like to see, Chief Commissar Wolff.'

Fabel caught up on outstanding paperwork and answered internal emails for an hour before it was time to head to the Murder Commission's meeting room. There was a knock on the door and a woman in her forties entered. Principal Chief Commissar Nicola Brüggemann was Fabel's deputy. A no-nonsense Holsteiner, she was at least one metre eighty tall, and her short-at-the-sides and thick-on-top dark hair added to the masculinity of her look. There was a tall, thin, blond young man with her whom Fabel recognized as Sven Bruns. Werner Meyer, Fabel's longest standing colleague and personal friend, had retired from the police earlier that year and Fabel had had to reshuffle his team. A Frisian like Fabel, Bruns was the newest addition to the team. He had served as a Criminal Commissar with the Polizei Niedersachsen before transferring to the Polizei Hamburg.

'Welcome on board . . .' Fabel stood up and shook hands with the taller man. 'Your timing is perfect, we're just about to have a briefing.'

'It's an honour to have been selected,' Bruns said so earnestly that Fabel smiled. 'I won't let you down, Herr Principal Chief Criminal Commissar.'

'*Chef* will do,' said Fabel. 'We'll get you teamed up and operational, but in the meantime it's a watch and learn set-up. If you have any questions about anything, or any problems crop up, my door is open, as is Principal Chief Commissar Brüggemann's. Okay?'

'Yes, *Chef*.'

The team was waiting in the briefing room. Fabel's second family. Like so many other things, so many previously unconsidered elements of his life, it was something to which Fabel had given a lot of thought since the shooting. People abstracted basic instincts into the most unlikely contexts, passions took the strangest forms. For Fabel, his instinct as a father was one of his most powerful and he had extended and abstracted it into a management style. It hadn't been something conscious or contrived, it was natural; just the way things were with him. He was protective of them, ambitious for them, continuously anxious for them.

The Murder Commission was divided into five teams of two officers each. The senior teams were made up of Chief Commissars: Thomas Glasmacher worked with Dirk Hechtner, Anna Wolff with Henk Hermann. The two Principal Chief Commissars, Fabel and Nicola Brüggemann, oversaw all the investigations on the board and, when there was a particularly high-profile or complicated case, one of them would take personal charge of it. Fabel's own expertise was being requested more and more by other forces across the Federal Republic. He knew the fifth floor – the Presidial Department where the Police President and the senior management of the Polizei Hamburg had their offices – saw Fabel as a poster boy for the Polizei Hamburg. The truth was he found it tiresome to be dragged away from his beloved Hamburg to help track murderers with twisted agendas in Bavaria or Thüringen.

He started the briefing by introducing the new guy, Sven Bruns, who would eventually be teamed up with a senior officer. There were the expected good-natured jokes about there now being two Frisians on the team and Fabel saw some of the tension ease from Bruns's earnest expression. He would watch the new detective, Fabel decided. They had agreed a three month probation and Fabel had explained that there would be no disgrace in moving on afterwards: working constantly with murder was something only a few officers could do, and it was often only after experiencing the reality of it that you found out if you were cut out for it the job.

They ran through the incident board. Contrary to what most

people believed, murder was almost always a sordid and dirty affair; usually the result of drink- or drug-fuelled violence. In reality there were practically no cool-headed and cold-blooded assassins; even the public's movie-influenced image of serial killers was skewed from reality. Serial killers were, for the most part, of below average IQ and acting on the most base of instincts, often impulsively, seeking sexual gratification through the torture and death of others. Those killers who were organized and intelligent were almost always disadvantaged by towering egomania or were otherwise deranged. Or there were the Angels of Death: the medical professionals abusing the trust of others and their licensed access to lethal substances simply to watch the light go out of the eyes of their victims. For many, it seemed, there was wonder in Death.

There were four cases current. Three of them were balefully straightforward: an abusive husband had bludgeoned his wife to death; a youth in his late teens had stabbed another outside a bar in the Kiez; an illegal immigrant had been kicked to death by a gang for no other reason than not being German. The three cases were at various stages of completion and Fabel listened to the progress reports on each. As he did so, he found himself wondering about each victim's leaving of life; whether their experiences had been similar to his.

The fourth inquiry stood apart. Fabel let Anna run through the history of the Monika Krone case.

'Anna and I are leads on this, but I'll need some of you for follow-ups,' said Fabel when she had finished. 'I'll allocate once I have the case plan worked up. Anna, when we're through, could you give me a note of the days you're off over the next couple of weeks?'

'Sure. Why?'

'Just want to make sure I have you with me for a couple of interviews,' Fabel said. It was a lie and he didn't feel good about it. It was a lie because there was one interview he specifically didn't want her to attend.

'Okay,' he said to the team. 'Let's proceed as normal, but remember we may have more cases on our plate by tomorrow morning.'

'The march?' Nicola Brüggemann asked.

'The march. Hopefully there'll be as few injuries as possible, and God knows it would be great if it passed off without incident, but I doubt it. All it needs is one knife brought to the party . . .'

11

The café was in the Schanzenviertel, on the ground floor corner of a chunk of solid and previously grand Wilhelmine architecture now dressed at street level in black-painted stucco and graffiti. In the bright spring sunshine, the café's urban, alternative cool just looked worn, tired and grubby. It suited Zombie perfectly.

Zombie was, as he always was, ten minutes early for his meeting with Alex Schuldhaus, who was perhaps the only remaining voluntary connection Zombie had with the living, and it was a connection maintained purely through necessity.

He always chose to meet Schuldhaus at this café because there were tables outside, which meant there was less chance of anyone smelling his corruption. Zombie also knew – although Schuldhaus didn't know he knew – that his dealer lived in Bartelsstrasse and the café wasn't far for him to come. If you could call Schuldhaus a dealer at all: Zombie knew his former fellow student was no organized-crime figure, and hardly a drug pusher in the professional sense. Instead he was someone who provided a tight circle of friends with weed, and very occasionally something a little more legally challenging. But Zombie was a special customer. Someone who paid over the odds for an already expensive commodity: something very special that he knew made Schuldhaus nervous – noticeably nervous – when carrying. It therefore made sense to make their meet as close to his apartment as possible.

Schuldhaus arrived on time. He was dark blond, tall, rangy and good-looking and wore an outfit of jeans and a Hamburg Freezers T-shirt. He had an old-looking canvas rucksack slung over one shoulder. He was the type who at forty dressed the same way he had as a student; who lived broadly the same kind of life. When they had been at university together, Schuldhaus had been popular and had barely acknowledged Zombie. He didn't hold it against him. Zombie had been the type not to be noticed.

Alex Schuldhaus shook hands with Zombie, a ritual he seemed to insist on following, before sitting down opposite him and ordering a herbal tea. Zombie watched him. His natural liveliness and vigour outshone his nervousness. Schuldhaus smiled a lot. At Zombie, at the waitress, at the world. His perpetual optimism and cheer made him the polar opposite of his customer and Zombie found his vigour nauseating in the same way others would find the presence of a rotting corpse sickening.

'Hi, Martin.' The good-natured Schuldhaus used the name Zombie had had in life, and which he still used in his interactions with the living. He frowned. 'Are you okay? You've lost more weight . . .'

'I'm fine,' said Zombie. 'You got the stuff?'

'I've got it.' Schuldhaus lowered his voice and leaned across the table. 'But listen, Martin, I don't know how much longer I can keep getting the quantities you ask for.'

'Has anything changed? Is there a problem with your supplier?'

'No, it's not that. It's just that this is a risky business. This stuff is a first-schedule drug.' Schuldhaus lowered his voice even further. 'I'm not a criminal, but I could get serious jail time for selling you this.'

'You get paid for your risk, don't you? Or are you asking for more, is that it?'

He shook his head. 'It's not that at all. It's just you use a hell of a lot of it. Listen, I sell stuff to friends to make them happy. Harmless stuff. But this . . . I mean, look at you, Martin . . . you're so pale and thin. I hardly recognize you these days. I just don't want you to end up dead.'

Zombie laughed; so loudly and incongruously heartily that it startled Schuldhaus.

'What? What's so funny?'

Zombie shook his head curtly; how could he even begin to explain his living-dead existence? Instead he said, 'Do you know I died once? My heart stopped beating. They claim they brought me back just in time.'

'No . . . shit no, I didn't know that. What happened?'

'I was stabbed.' Zombie paused for a moment then, with a dismissive wave of his hand said, 'I was in the wrong place at the wrong time – a street mugging. I was stabbed in the chest.'

'Shit, I—'

'None of that's important,' Zombie interrupted. 'The truth is I never did have much of a life. I was the guy no one ever noticed. I was a ghost even back then. But after I was stabbed, as I was dying, I had this . . . this *experience*.'

'What kind of experience?'

'I can't even begin to describe it. It was the most wonderful thing I've ever known. In an instant I forgot all of the unhappiness that had gone before. I was truly, completely happy. Happy like you can't measure in this life. I could suddenly *see* in a way you can't in this life. All of these colours and textures and dimensions I never knew existed. And I could see inside myself too – all of the people who had come before me, like I was looking straight through my DNA or something. I tell you, it was the most incredible thing you could imagine. There is nothing – *nothing* – in life that could be compared to it. As if the whole universe opened up . . .' Zombie paused, lost for a moment in the memory. He shook his head and the temporary animation left him and in his usual dull, matter-of-fact way he said, 'Anyway, that's why I take this stuff . . . Whatever happened to me back then, it takes me back there. Or at least gives me the feeling of being back there. And besides, dimethyltryptamine doesn't kill anyone. It's been around for thousands of years as ayahuasca. You got it?'

Schuldhaus nodded. He sipped his tea and glanced around the other tables. *I'm right*, Zombie thought, *he's not much of a drug dealer.*

'Did you get the other stuff I asked for? The xylazine?' Zombie asked.

'Eventually. It wasn't easy to source, because horse tranquillizer isn't something people normally ask for . . . I mean, it's not like you can get high on that stuff. The only people who use xylazine as a recreational drug are Puerto Ricans. And they call it the zombie-maker. Are you sure you know what you're doing?'

'I know what I'm doing with it, and what I'm doing is my business. Okay, let's have it.'

Clumsily, and so guiltily that anyone watching would probably have guessed the illegal nature of the transaction, Schuldhaus slipped a paper packet from his rucksack and slid it across the zinc top of the table. Zombie casually picked up the packet and put it in his pocket. Equally casually, he handed Schuldhaus a wad of euro notes.

'You should try not to look so guilty,' he said. 'I'll need some more DMT this time next month. You good for that?'

'I'll do my best. What about the xylazine?'

'You've given me all I need. Just the DMT next time.'

Their business done, all Zombie could think about was getting away from the nauseatingly vital Schuldhaus; to get out of the sunlight and back into the shadows. But he had his coffee and Schuldhaus had his tea to finish and the latter always seemed to feel the need to chatter. Maybe it made him feel less like he was simply making money from selling a first schedule drug and more like he was doing a favour for a friend.

'You still living in Altona?' he asked Zombie to fill a silence. 'I hope you don't get caught up with all that shit that's planned. You know, the march and all the crap that goes with it. Fucking Nazis.'

'I doubt it. My apartment is well off the main route.'

'Oh.'

Another silence, then Schuldhaus grabbed onto a passing thought as if he were a drowning man grasping at a lifebelt. 'Do you remember Monika Krone? From university? The girl who went missing?'

Something sparked in the dullness of Zombie's eyes. 'What about her?'

'They've found her body. Who'd have thought, after all these years—'

'Where?' Zombie leaned forward. 'Where did they find her body?'

'In Altona. Not far from where she went missing. It was in the *Morgenpost*. She'd been buried under a mini-market car park, of all places.' Schuldhaus shook his head. 'So what we all suspected all of these years – it's so sad that we were right. You knew her, right?'

Zombie stared at Schuldhaus for a moment, his expression even more empty than usual, his cold gaze making the amateur pusher feel uneasy. An image of a painfully beautiful face with a pale complexion and emerald green eyes framed in a blaze of auburn-red hair came back to his recall in perfect detail.

'Not really,' he said eventually. 'A little.'

They sat in silence for a minute then Zombie, leaving his coffee largely untouched, stood up and said he had to be somewhere. Schuldhaus was clearly making an effort not to look too relieved.

'I'll give you a call next month,' said Zombie. 'When I need more.'

On his way home, Zombie stopped at the S-Bahn station kiosk and bought a copy of the *Hamburger Morgenpost*.

12

Susanne was there when he got home to the apartment.

One of the many things Fabel loved about Hamburg, his adopted city, was its variety. He often thought of cities having definable personalities, but Hamburg was much more difficult to define than most. If anything, it suffered from multiple personality disorder: a constellation of very different identities clustered together in a small space. There were over a hundred quarters in the city, spread over seven boroughs, and each quarter had its own unique personality and atmosphere. The apartment he shared with Susanne Eckhardt was in Ottensen, in the north-west of Altona. Ottensen had once been a town in its own right, independent of the originally much smaller Altona. Over time it had become incorporated into Altona; Altona in turn being absorbed into Hamburg. Despite this history of aggregation, the quarter – just like the Neuenfelde or Schanzenviertel, Pöseldorf or Sankt Pauli, Bergedorf or Wilhelmsburg – had refused with typical North German stubbornness to surrender anything of its unique identity. It was so distinctive that when he had first moved in with Susanne four years before, having given up his own flat in Pöseldorf, Fabel felt he had moved to a completely different part of the country.

Fabel and Susanne had been together for eleven years, the last four of which had been in this apartment. When he got back home, feeling more than a little worn-out, he noticed that Susanne also looked like she'd had a long day. Tiredness etched itself on her face more easily now than it used to and tonight it also tinged her speech: Susanne was originally from Munich and Fabel had noticed how her vowels stretched flatter with fatigue. He had also noticed that she had aged since the shooting: a vague, handsome aging but one Fabel felt bad about, felt responsible for. It was as if his shooting had been a toxic event that had radiated out to contaminate those closest to him. Susanne, his daughter Gabi, his mother. Anna. Each bearing a mark unseen.

Fabel cooked dinner, which he did often, and they ate in the kitchen, chatting aimlessly and, in Susanne's case, a little wearily. Tonight was not a night to eat out in Altona. As he had driven home from the Presidium, he had seen more Readiness Police clustered at intersections throughout the Altstadt. Helmeted, carrying riot shields and with black body armour over their coveralls, they looked to Fabel like the ghosts of Breughelian knights prowling Altona's streets. Storekeepers had pulled down shutters; many had nailed plywood sheets across their windows, as if bracing for the rage of a storm.

Tonight really was a night to stay indoors.

As they ate, Fabel and Susanne skimmed over their respective days – his at the Murder Commission and hers as a forensic psychologist at the Institute for Judicial Medicine at Eppendorf – and not for the first time it struck Fabel how odd it was that they talked about death and killing the way a couple of accountants would talk about balance sheets and tax returns. At one time, he would not have discussed work at home; they had

had an unspoken rule about that. But things were different now. Fabel was different now, his attitude to life less compartmentalized, so occasionally domestic conversations would turn from everyday inconsequences to the twists of mind and deformities of soul that led people to perform acts of violence.

'You're sure it's the same case you worked on back then?' Susanne asked as she poured them both another glass of wine.

'I'm sure. It's funny, when I first worked the case, all those years ago, I knew somehow I'd end up back where I started, eventually – that Monika Krone would return to haunt me one day. I knew I'd get back to it. And now I am.' He shrugged. 'Strange.'

'Not really. It was your first Commission case and it was left unresolved. It makes sense that you'd be left with a feeling of unfinished business. You working it with Anna?'

Fabel nodded. When he finished his mouthful of food he asked: 'Why?'

'How's she doing? I know you were worried about her.'

'I still am. She's having difficulty putting what happened behind her, even after all this time.'

'All this time? It's barely been two years.'

'I'm over it,' said Fabel without rancour, 'I don't know why everyone else can't be.'

Susanne put her fork down. A punctuation point. 'Does everyone else include me? I'm not over it, I'll tell you that. I think about it every day when you go into work.'

'This is Hamburg, Susanne, not New York. Policemen don't routinely get shot at here – what happened to me was the wild exception, not the rule. And that's what Anna has to accept too – she wasn't prepared for what happened because it's not something you expect to happen. Anyway, I know you're not over it and I understand that. But it's different with Anna and me. We have to work together and I don't want her judgement clouded. I've been biding my time ... waiting for the moment to be right before talking to her about it. The moment was right today.'

'And?'

'And I think I got through to her. She opened up to me too. About the shooting, I mean. She feels guilty about it, which I already knew.'

'Do you know something?' said Susanne. 'I always thought you had a bit of a thing for her.'

'Anna?' Fabel said, clearly surprised.

'And I've always said I *know* she has a thing for you.'

Fabel laughed and shook his head dismissively. They fell silent for a while and ate, Susanne's tiredness seeming to overwhelm her.

'When do you have your next session?' she asked.

Fabel laughed. 'You mean the "Club of the Living Dead"? Tuesday.'

'I do wish you wouldn't call it that, Jan. It's not something to be flippant about. Is it helping?'

'It's not meant to help. Or not at least directly. We're subjects, not patients. Lorentz's guinea pigs. His *zombie* guinea pigs.' Fabel held up his hands, clawlike, and made a twisted face. Susanne gave him a look and he dropped his hands and expression. 'I do get something out of it, I suppose. And I guess it's interesting to others who've not had the experience.' He paused. 'How come you've never asked me?'

'Asked you what?'

'What it was like.'

'What what was like?'

'Being dead.'

Susanne looked at him for a moment, something glinting through her tiredness. 'Because you can't tell me. Because you weren't dead. I work in neuroscience, Jan, and that means I know what you experienced wasn't death. Being dead isn't like anything. Being dead is nothing. Exactly that, nothing. You can't experience being dead, because there is no experience to be had. What you experienced was dying, not death. The process, not the event.'

'They said I did. That I was clinically dead.' Fabel affected an expression of mock pride.

'Your heart stopped. You stopped breathing. That isn't death. Those were two physiological events and like I say, death isn't a process, it's a event. You're only truly, *completely* dead with brain-stem death, when the last flicker of neural activity stops. They brought you back before you got to that stage. And if you'd got any closer to it I'd be spoon-feeding you your dinner – a couple more minutes of oxygen deprivation and they'd have brought you back brain-damaged. Any longer than that and you *would* have died. And once you're dead, you're dead, there's no coming back.'

'I'll tell that to my fellow zombies.' Fabel smiled. 'I'm sure they'll be pleased.'

Fabel was stacking the dishwasher when he heard the first sirens. Not too close, but not distant enough. He reckoned they were to the east, somewhere towards Altona Altstadt. Two at first, both coming from the same direction, then a wave of them from another. He switched on the radio and caught the news. The storm had broken, after all.

13

The rage burned in him as he watched the news. Georg Schmidt sat in his room and watched Altona once again fall victim to hate. The Nazi marchers had followed almost exactly the same route they had in 1932. How could that have been allowed to happen? And just like in 1932, the people of Altona had made their opposition known. Why could no one learn from history? Why did we always repeat the same mistakes?

The fury within him concentrated itself, clustering around a specific focus. Helmut Wohlmann. Wohlmann was as responsible for this current carnage as he had been for what happened in 1932. He had helped to create the history now doomed to repeat itself.

Georg Schmidt remembered. It had become a memory stored not in his mind, but in his notebook. Whenever something else came to him, some image from that day, he would add it to his journal. His mind held the pieces, but the notebook held the completed jigsaw. Whenever he needed to remind himself of who he was, what had happened and who was responsible, he read through his notebook.

And remembered.

It all happened that day. A bright, fresh day but otherwise seemingly unexceptional. Except it would be exceptional. Sunday 17 July, 1932.

Later, they would say that everything began that Sunday, that a ball had been set rolling that would crush out eighteen lives during the course of that one day, lead to four innocent men being beheaded a year later and more than fifty million lives lost beyond that. What unfolded that day in Altona would provide the excuse for the Prussian Coup and bring about the end of the Weimar Republic. That bright July Sunday had opened the door to the greatest darkness in the history of Germany, of the world.

It had been another Altona, back then. A cramped, smoky Altona of clustered apartments and terraces, each building with its own small square of yard, each yard with a fruit tree or vegetable plot. It was an Altona of narrow cobbled streets and fuming chimneys. No grand villas here. The people born here had been raised to toil, if toil could be found. This was the heart of workers' Hamburg. Staunchly, proudly, resolutely working-class. Red Altona. Little Moscow.

Georg had been thirteen, but big for his age. His father, like many of the men here, was small, compact, hard-hewn. A man of fifty, Franz Schmidt had become a father late and a widower early. Again like so many in Altona, Georg's father was unemployed but had been a stevedore at the docks, his hands calloused, thick-fingered and rough from rope work.

Georg's father rarely smiled, had little to smile about, but never sought to conceal his pride in his son, who was not only growing tall and broad, but also clever. Nothing seemed to give Franz Schmidt more pleasure than seeing his son come back from the Christianeum library with a book in his hand. Franz

Schmidt had been illiterate until adulthood and it had only been when he had joined the KPD that he had found someone to teach him the basics. It was his duty as a Communist, he had been told, to seize the most important capital of all denied the working classes: knowledge and education. But Franz Schmidt had known it was too late for him; that he probably never would have had the makings of a scholar, whatever social dice had been thrown for him. But his son . . . Georg was bright. Georg not only could read well, he ate books up. He lived in them, through them, for them. And Franz felt true pride swell in his breast every time he saw Georg with a book in his hands or when the boy sat reading to his father or telling him all about the latest book he was devouring. The truth was, Franz Schmidt knew, you were only ever given one life. There was no 'after', there was no better, simpler, purer, happier existence after physical extinction. The great lie of an afterlife for the hard-working, the loyal, the obedient, was just a device employed by church, state and patricians to enslave the masses. In the meantime, everyone was expected to know their place and accept their lot on the promise of something better to come. Franz was no deep thinker, but he knew he had been handed but the one life and that one life had been blighted. But one hope of an afterlife did gleam bright for Franz Schmidt: his son. He could live on through a son who would achieve things, would have a life that was worth living. Georg, his father knew, would go far in the world and Franz was sad only that the boy's mother had not lived to see him grown.

Georg's father had loved to hear the facts that his son seemed to soak up like a sponge, especially those facts about their home quarter: how Altona had started out as a small settlement of fishermen and craftsmen, how it had grown to become the second biggest city in Denmark, envious eyes cast on it by its

German neighbour, Hamburg. How it had developed a very Danish character and became known for its tolerance and its religious and commercial freedoms, attracting Jews and others discriminated against in Hamburg. Even after becoming German and absorption into the Prussian state of Schleswig-Holstein, Altona had kept its individuality and had influenced the liberal and social-democratic policies of its Hamburg neighbour.

But to some, Altona was a symbol of something to be wiped out. A Red Flag to a Brown-shirted bull.

Seven thousand of them had come that day. They zigzagged their way through Altona Altstadt, a brass-band-heralded assault on the city quarter. It hadn't taken long for the first trouble to erupt. The Nazis had shouted inflammatory chants, taunting the Communist Party and threatening Jews and other Altona inhabitants. In reply, Communist Party members had jeered and barracked the marchers. Shouts turned to scuffles and scuffles turned to fights, fists and improvised weapons flying.

Georg had been under strict instructions to stay indoors, his father going out to do his duty as a KPD member and stand up to the fascists. There was going to be trouble, his father had told him, maybe even bloodshed. But it had been too bright and warm a day and Georg too bright and curious a boy and, once his father had left, he had slipped out and followed him at a safe distance.

Georg had navigated through a dense forest of Altonaers, gathered along the route of the march, fenced in by often scared-looking policemen. Eggerstedt, the President of the Polizei Hamburg, was a Social Democrat, but had not heeded Communist Party warnings that allowing the Nazis to march through

Altona would result in a bloodbath. But the political climate had been tense and the Nazis were being appeased, added to which neither Eggerstedt nor his deputy were in Hamburg on the day of the march. His officers, tense and outnumbered on both sides, had been left to deal with the consequences.

Georg had weaved through the crowds, keeping his father just in sight. The jeers and the strident sound of drums and brass swelled in the warm air and, despite himself, Georg felt a thrill.

Then the jeers turned to yells, the tension turned to fury. Georg could now see the marchers, in SS and SA uniforms, and he could hear them too, their full-throated singing of the chant, *Die rote Front schlagen wir zu Brei!* We will beat the Red Front to a pulp!

And it was then he saw Helmut Wohlmann. Wohlmann was four years older than Georg and had been his father's apprentice until recently. After his parents had died, Helmut had lived for a while with Georg and his father and had become like an older brother to Georg. But then, at a time when it seemed like everyone was becoming radicalized, polarized, Helmut had joined the NSDAP. As fervent a Nazi as Georg's father was a Communist, Helmut had moved out and all contact had been severed. And now Georg saw him, brown-shirted, marching with the others.

There was a pulse, a sudden swell and surge as the crowd lurched forward, straining the thin police line. In response, the SA marchers launched themselves at the bystanders, belts wrapped around their fists, using their buckles as weapons.

Georg found himself unexpectedly near his father. Their eyes met and Franz Schmidt looked suddenly scared. He made a sweeping gesture with his arm, shooing Georg away from danger.

It was then that shots rang out.

Two SS men fell to the cobbled ground. One dead instantly, the other screaming for a few moments.

The police looked around wildly, confused, trying to find the source of the gunfire. Then, as the crowd surged forward in fury, fists flying, batons were swung to beat back the wave. First one, then another policeman fired shots at imagined gunmen – the first of five thousand police rounds to be fired that day, most into the crowd.

Georg was pushed forward with the charging crowd and a police baton smashed into his right temple, robbing him of consciousness.

But before the darkness overcame him, one picture was burned into his mind: that of his father clutching his chest and sinking to his knees, and Helmut Wohlmann in his SA uniform standing over him.

After he replaced the notebook and locked the drawer with the key that hung around his neck, Georg Schmidt sat back down to watch the television. He gazed at the screen, suddenly confused about what he was watching.

There was some kind of trouble, a riot. He didn't know where the riot was taking place or who was rioting, and it upset him terribly that he could not remember why this news item should make him feel quite so angry.

14

It would happen now. After so long, Zombie would have his revenge. It was like a starving man anticipating a long-denied feast. For Zombie, that anticipation was a sensation that almost matched the intensity of feeling he had had when he had been alive.

Being dead, he knew he was beyond most of the passions and hungers of the living. But if there was one thing Gothic fiction and horror movies got right, it was that the dead would stir in the name of vengeance to right some ancient wrong. And, just as in Gothic fiction, there was always a catalyst: some event that revitalized long-dead anger and hatred, reawakening a long-dormant hunger for vengeance.

Now Zombie sat in his kitchen, a pack of disposable syringes and two bottles, each containing fifty millilitres of xylazine, lying in front of him on the veneered surface of the kitchen table. It was much, much more than he would need. Picking up a bottle between forefinger and thumb, he held it to the window. His chosen tool for vengeance looked innocuous in the pale light, the clear liquid sleek and viscous in its glass capsule. This was the key that would unlock his Golem. The time would be soon.

Two months before, Zombie had caught a fleeting glimpse

sight of someone in the street. A ghost passing. A small event, but bright and impossible. And a moment around which his plans had slowly coalesced. But it had not been enough to convince him to act. The catalyst for that had been the discovery of the remains, stripped clean of their pale, beautiful flesh, under the asphalt of the mini-market car park. There were connections the police would not have even considered making; they were completely in the dark about what happened that night fifteen years ago, and before they cast light on it, before they tracked Zombie down, he would have fulfilled his mission. He would be avenged. *She* would be avenged.

First he needed his Golem.

Zombie had spent hours puzzling, calculating, researching. He needed to break his Golem free from its bonds, but that was perhaps the most difficult and complicated part of his mission. Communication was all but impossible, transporting the necessary materials was every bit as challenging. The one advantage that Zombie had was not having to worry about leaving incriminating evidence – so long as it didn't lead the police to his door *before* he had completed his mission. Once he had had his revenge, then they could come for him and he wouldn't care.

After all, what could they do to an already dead man?

15

There were people who complained about the luxury enjoyed by convicted prisoners; as if TVs and Xboxes were the sole benchmarks of quality of life. Fabel was not one of those people: every time he had to interview an offender in prison and found himself encapsulated in wall, wire and mesh, he became aware of the crushing claustrophobia of statutory confinement.

Fabel knew that, at the start of his sentence, Jochen Hübner had been an inmate of the controversial Social Therapy Prison in Hamburg-Bergedorf, which dealt mainly with those convicted of sexual crimes. But the Bergedorf facility had been closed in 2004 and the Social Therapy Prison a moved to two brick-built units close to the main prison in Hamburg-Fuhlsbüttel, commonly known as Santa Fu. The prison's Social Therapy Units held some of the most violent offenders in northern Germany, including sex offenders. The units' control and reward system was as much about treatment as punishment and it had seen some spectacular successes.

But not with Jochen Hübner.

In a population of the violent, Hübner had been the most feared. His record of violent assaults on inmates and staff, including the blinding of another prisoner, had resulted in him being transferred here, in 2005, to the maximum security wing of the main prison at Hamburg-Fuhlsbüttel. He was now regarded both as an extreme danger to other prisoners and as a maximum escape risk.

And the idea of Jochen Hübner escaping into Hamburg was the stuff of nightmares.

It was no accident that it was Anna Wolff's day off. Fabel knew it was wrong of him to discriminate against Anna because of her gender, but Jochen Hübner's monumental animosity towards women would mean that Anna's presence would dominate the interview. Instead, needing another officer to come with him, Fabel had asked Henk Hermann to sit in with him. Sit in but say nothing.

'Jochen Hübner's no genius, no evil mastermind,' explained Fabel, 'but he has an uncanny knack of finding ways into your head. And Jochen Hübner is not someone you want inside your head.'

'Do you think he killed the Krone girl?'

'I don't know. Like I told Anna, he's not the kind of ego to allow someone else – even an unidentified someone else – to take credit for his handiwork. But he certainly has the profile for it. I could never understand why he never killed other women.'

Henk and Fabel were led by a prison officer to an interview room. It had one window looking out over the prison gardens and grounds, another between it and the hall they had just come along. It was a bright room, but purely functional, and Fabel could see that both windows, glazed with thick, shatterproof acrylic, were fixed into the concrete of the building and could not be opened. Confinement within confinement. Similarly, the table and benches that occupied the centre of the room were anchored and immovable. Fabel felt himself become slightly agitated but took a breath. He had to be completely relaxed for the interview to come.

'Be warned, Henk,' he said as they took their places at the table. 'Hübner has . . . well, he has *presence*.'

Henk shrugged. 'He's a sick fuck, is all I know, *Chef*.'

Through the viewing window, Fabel saw them approach along the hall: an officer in the uniform of the Hamburg Justice Department and a man so tall only the lower part of his profile could be seen through the window.

The door opened and the two men entered, Jochen Hübner ducking his massive head to pass through the doorway. Fabel sensed Henk Hermann tense next to him. He wasn't surprised: even Fabel, although he had been prepared for it, was once again struck by Hübner's appearance. Fabel reckoned the convicted rapist must have been at the very least 210 centimetres tall. Even with this great stature, his massive head looked oversized, the long black hair scraped back into a ponytail, as if to emphasize the brutality of the features. The impression was of some evolutionary clock having been wound back.

'I see your little friend is taken aback, Fabel.' Hübner's voice was a deep, resonating but harsh baritone as he struggled to angle his legs between the fixed bench and the interview table, like an adult struggling to sit on a child's play furniture. Once he was seated opposite Fabel and Henk, Hübner leaned forward, resting his elbows on the table. In anyone else, it would have been a perfectly normal, relaxed gesture, but Hübner's Easter Island head, with its prognathous jaw and small glittering eyes beneath bulging brow ridges, turned it into an aggression, a threatening invasion of space. He smiled at Henk, exposing gappy, little white teeth that looked intended for a smaller mouth.

Fabel looked across to the prison officer and nodded.

'Press the buzzer when you want him taken back,' the guard said and left. 'Remember, I'll be right outside the door.' There was a metallic clunk as the door locked automatically behind the guard when he left.

'Not what you expected?' Hübner held Henk in his gaze, tilting the mass of his skull and smiling maliciously. Henk said nothing.

'Acromegaly,' Hübner explained, keeping Henk locked in his gaze. 'Maybe Fabel here has already told you. Fucked-up pituitary gland. A benign tumour called an adenoma. It switched my growing back on but for a while slowed down my production of testosterone. They stuck a knife up my nose and cut the fucker out though. Wanna know the funny thing? A real freak this – afterwards I started to produce more testosterone than before. Way too much. The opposite of what usually happens. Something to do with what they call the luteinizing hormone. Anyway, that's what gives me my sunny disposition. Turned me into a fucking and fighting machine.' He widened his grin. 'Got a girlfriend?'

Henk bristled and Fabel cut in before he had a chance to answer. 'We've found Monika Krone,' he said and shot his junior officer a look that echoed his earlier warning about allowing Hübner into his head. The giant across the table caught the look and laughed a deep, cavernous laugh.

'Did you hear me, Herr Hübner? I said we've found Monika Krone.'

'So fucking what?'

'I thought you'd like to know. We've reopened the case.'

'What's that got to do with me?'

'You know what it has got to do with you. You killed her and put her there.'

'Sure I did. I fucked her, strangled her and buried her under a fucking mini-market. There you go, there's your confession. Now fuck off.' Hübner's stone-hewn features twisted in contempt.

'If that's supposed to be a fake confession,' said Henk, 'how do you know that we found her near a mini-market?'

'I follow the Principal Chief Commissar's career with interest.' Hübner turned to Fabel as he answered. No smiling. 'Real close interest. We do get papers in here, you know. I read about it. Just like I read about you getting shot. Nice one. I heard you nearly died. I hope you were scared. Were you scared, Fabel?'

'So you're saying you didn't kill Monika Krone?' asked Henk Hermann. Hübner ignored him, instead splaying his massive hands with their too-long, too-thick fingers on the metal surface of the tabletop and looking at them.

'We placed you in the area of the party the night she disappeared,' said Fabel.

'We went over all this before. You bore me, Fabel.'

'But you were there, weren't you?'

'Like I told you before, I was in the area, yes.'

'What were you doing there?' asked Henk. Hübner looked at him with penetrating contempt, then turned back to Fabel, ignoring the question.

'Thing is,' he said, 'I don't think you think it was me. You're just going through a hoop, aren't you, Fabel? You and the midget here out on a fishing trip.'

'You were there, weren't you?' Fabel asked. 'Watching the party . . . listening to all of that laughter. All of those student girls, laughing and joking and flirting with boys. You don't like clever women, do you, Jochen?'

Hübner deep-rumbled a laugh again. 'Is this the penetrating insight that I've heard so much about, Fabel? Making out I'm intimidated by clever women? Okay, you're right – I hate clever women. I fucking loathe and despise them. I want to make them whine and scream and beg, to do things that make them sick just because they think there's a chance I'll stop hurting them and maybe let them live. Yep . . .' he held the vast shields of his palms up, 'you've got me. I'm a fucking inadequate who makes up for a tiny dick and a small brain by hating college girls.'

'You were there that night, in that area,' said Fabel. 'We know that. I think you were there hunting. You heard the party and you waited until a girl came out on her own. That girl was Monika Krone. You followed her and when you got your chance you snatched her off the street. When you were finished with her you killed her and dumped her body. It's what you had been building up to all that time.'

'This is all you had fifteen years ago. It was fuck all then and it's fuck all now. The only new thing you've got is a body and I'm guessing not much of a body after all this time. Truth is, you never did understand me, did you, Fabel? You still think that I started to kill my victims . . . either this one or others.'

'I know you think you're unique,' said Fabel, 'but you're anything but. There's a pattern to people like you, to your behaviour. A predictable pattern. You would have started killing if we hadn't caught you. What I need to know is if you had already started. So what do you say, Jochen? Did you kill Monika?'

The massive head shook, not in denial but as if in disappointment. 'You don't get it, do you? I didn't kill her or any other bitch. Don't you understand? What I did to them – what I put them through – I don't want them to *die* afterwards. I want them to live. I want them to live long, long lives. Because every day, every single day they live when I'm finished with them, they will remember what I did. What they became. What was done to them. You're too stupid to realize that the worst thing I did to them was to let them live . . .'

16

'Hamburg, throughout its history as a Hanseatic League city, has had an identity unique in Germany. We are, and always have been, about the world, about looking outward instead of inward. About cosmopolitanism, internationalism and global trade. Where we stand now, here in Altona, was for centuries Danish soil. One could argue that Hamburg is as Scandinavian and as Anglo-Saxon as it is German. Traditionally, we have found trading partners in every compass point. In an increasingly globalized marketplace, no city is better placed or has a more appropriate history to seize every opportunity that new technology and new markets offer . . .' Uwe Taubitz, the Principal Mayor of Hamburg, paused for the on-cue ripple of polite applause.

Taubitz was a balding blond man in his late forties, prematurely portly and wearing an expensive Italian suit that would have looked more than just expensive if its wearer had been a few kilos lighter. No one in the audience appreciated Taubitz's skill as a speaker as much as he did himself.

He continued: 'We have seen our beloved old Hamburg become an exciting new Hamburg. Through the bold visions that developed the HafenCity and the waterfront, and other bold steps forward such as this magnificent Albrecht-designed building – the Bruno Tesch Centre – Hamburg has taken the shape the twenty-first century, and beyond, will demand.'

'This speech is going to go on to the twenty-third century,' Tobias Albrecht said under his breath to the beautiful woman with flame-red hair sitting next to him on the improvised stage of the top step leading into the building's atrium. They sat to the side and slightly behind Hamburg's Principal Mayor, who stood at the podium making his speech. 'If he goes on much longer he can segue straight into a speech celebrating the building's tenth anniversary.'

The woman beside Albrecht applauded at another pause. She turned and leaned towards him, pushing a smile into place. 'He's singing your praises – you should learn to be gracious. Why don't you try designing a building to match your ego, Tobias? It would be monumental.'

Albrecht laughed and exposed the bright white teeth of a predator. Despite the sharp, almost harsh geometry of his features, he was an exceptionally handsome man. Tall and lean, with thick, very dark hair swept back from a widow's peak, there was a careless, unintentional wickedness about his expression and the way he moved. Sitting there on the stage, his posture arrogantly relaxed, he looked like a very well-tailored devil.

'If you hate me so much,' he said through his smile, and without malice, 'how come you're fucking me, Birgit, my darling?'

'I ask myself that question all the time. Now shut up and for God's sake try to look modest.'

Hamburg's Principal Mayor finished his speech and Tobias Albrecht and the woman stood up. One of Albrecht's assistants came forward and held out a velvet cushion to Uwe Taubitz. The Bürgermeister took the ceremonial scissors from the cushion and cut the ribbon strung loosely across the glass entrance to the building.

'I declare this fine building – the Bruno Tesch Centre – open.'

More applause.

As previously arranged by the Hamburg Senate's press office, a half-dozen photographers came forward and, issuing carefully deferential instructions, took pictures first of Taubitz on his own, then of the Bürgermeister shaking hands with the much more photogenic Albrecht.

'Could we perhaps have a couple with Frau Taubitz?' asked one of the photographers.

The beautiful, flame-haired woman who had been sitting next to Albrecht took her place for the photo-call, between her husband and her lover.

17

It was a dark house. Dark, large and forbidding. There was also something of the graveyard about it. The old forester's house, two storeyed with a windowed attic, stood on the edge of the Stadtpark woods and was as remote as it was possible to be so close to the heart of Hamburg. The house had stood empty, close-shuttered rather than boarded up, for a year and a half and, as if trying to reclaim it, nature had begun probing with dark green fingers the drive, the paths, the fabric of the house itself. The trees that surrounded all but the road-facing aspect threw the house into shadow.

No one had tended it while the old man had been in the Alte Mühle Seniors' Home which also, ironically, was on the edge of the park and would have been just visible from the house had it not been for the dense, screening swathe of trees. Zombie had not known that his uncle, whom he had never visited and barely knew, had become so old and senile that he'd been moved out to the seniors' home. He had only found out when the old man had eventually died leaving Zombie, as his only surviving relative, to inherit the house.

A property of the size of the old forester's house should have been worth somewhere around half a million euros, and would have been valued significantly higher in a different location, but a challenge to the tax office's generalized valuation, which had been done without an inspection, brought the value down to €350,000.

Zombie had inherited the property six months before but had never moved into it. His initial intention had been to sell it as soon as possible: because he was just a nephew, his inheritance tax allowance was only up to €20,000 and not the €400,000 he would have been allowed – and which would have covered the house's total value – if he had been a son. That left him with seven per cent inheritance tax to pay on the majority of the value of the house. He had explained to the tax office that he simply did not have that kind of money and they had come to an agreement that, so long as he did not move into or rent out the property, he could settle the tax due on sale of the house.

But no one had bought it. The tax office had constantly to be provided with evidence that Zombie was making a genuine effort to sell the house, but its location and forbidding appearance had clearly put buyers off.

It hadn't taken long for the idea to form in Zombie's mind.

The house was perfect. While its unusual, out-of-the-way position had prevented its sale, that same unusual position now safeguarded it against intrusion. It wasn't visible from the main highway unless you had turned into the road leading to the seniors' home, and only one of the minor and less used paths through the Stadtpark ran directly behind the rear garden, which Zombie had deliberately allowed to become overgrown to add to the screen of trees.

Zombie had retrieved the keys from the estate agents, who had until then conducted viewings at their own discretion without involving him. He told them that he wanted to do an inventory of the furniture that was left, for tax purposes, and that from now on they should arrange viewings through him. The truth was viewers were now few and far between, but taking charge of the keys was his way of ensuring there were no unwelcome callers. His main concern now was that squatters or simply vandals would find the place empty and break in. Not that he cared about the house – it was just that, from now on, there would be something hidden in the cellar. Something he didn't want anyone else to see until he was ready.

He had decided that the cellar was the only part of the house he would use. It was too dangerous to use any of the rooms in the main house itself, although he switched the water back on so his guest would have access to a functioning toilet off the entrance hall. The electricity remained turned off, however.

Zombie fitted secure bolts and a lock to the outside of the cellar door. The cellar itself he fitted out with two mattresses to accommodate the size of his houseguest, a store of food, bottled water, toiletries and batteries. Five oil hurricane lamps and four battery lamps provided all the lighting his guest would need. A ribbon of narrow windows ran along the top of one of the basement's walls, looking out at ground level to the front garden and the road beyond it. At night any light, no matter how meagre and even masked by the overgrown garden, would shine out like a beacon in the otherwise lightless forest, so Zombie bought a heavy felt blanket and cut it into strips to black out the windows.

It wasn't ideal, but his guest would not have to remain there long. And, anyway, it seemed fitting that his Golem should dwell under the ground until it was time to strike.

18

Fabel stood at the window of his office, watching the day fade in the sky above the trees of the Winterhuder Stadtpark. He had spent three solid hours going through the file on Monika Krone's disappearance fifteen years before. He had arranged for every witness statement, every specialist report, every photograph to be sent up from the archive. He had a lot of the information literally at his fingertips, a few keystrokes bringing the digitized versions up on his computer screen, but there were other elements he needed that were stored only as hard copy.

In any case, he always printed out the information. Fabel needed to have the detail laid out before him, viewing the chronology and landscape of a case in its entirety and from above.

Monika Krone had had the kind of beauty that seemed to transcend tastes or fashion and which perhaps blinded those who met her to the intelligence and ambition behind it. Those who had known her better had described her as cool and aloof. Her most striking feature had been a head of lustrous auburn-red hair that, combined with her pale complexion and bright green eyes, had given her a look that seemed to belong to some other time.

And it was her remarkable appearance that had caused the greatest mystery. Monika Krone had been a woman you would notice, a face you would remember seeing, yet on the night of Saturday 18 March, 2000, she had left a student party in Altona and had simply vanished from the face of the Earth. It had led the investigation at the time to focus on the minutes immediately after she had left the party. The suggestion had been that Monika had been abducted from the street, bundled into a vehicle. It was the only explanation for there being no further sightings of her.

But that line of inquiry had proved as fruitless as all the others.

There was a knock at the door and Anna entered.

'I heard you took Henk to interview Jochen Hübner.' There was an edge to her voice and she sat down without being asked on Fabel's office sofa. Fabel smiled. Anna – the real Anna – was back.

'It was your day off,' he said.

'Bollocks my day off. You didn't want me there. Do you think a freak like Hübner scares me?'

'I'd be more worried that you'd scare him.' The joke didn't take and Fabel sighed. 'I'm sorry, Anna, but I knew if I went with you, that's all the interview would be about. Put a woman in a room with Hübner and he'd just focus on trying to scare her. He wouldn't succeed with you and I wasn't trying to protect you, I just thought it was the best way of getting the truth out of him.'

'And?'

'And I'm pretty sure I believe him. I don't think he had anything to do with Monika Krone's murder. Which is a pity, because I'd like something to make doubly certain that that monster is kept locked up for the rest of his life.'

Anna nodded towards the files on Fabel's desk. 'Why haven't

you passed that on to the teams? It would save a hell of a lot of time.'

'I'm *forming an overview*.' Fabel used the English phrase. 'There's something I'm not seeing. It's in there and no one saw it the first time. But I can sense it.'

'What kind of thing?'

'There's something about the party, or after the party, that doesn't fit. I don't know . . .' Fabel sighed frustratedly. 'There were sixty-three people at that party. We have sixty-three statements, sixty-three accounts of people's whereabouts after the party, sixty-three statements of knowledge of or relationship to the victim. I can't put my finger on it yet, but there is a disconnect somewhere.'

'What kind of disconnect?'

'Like there's a sixty-fourth person at the party we don't know about. Or that some of these statements don't quite gel, but I can't identify which statements and *why* they don't gel.'

'So you're focusing on the party? I thought the original investigation ruled that out and pointed to a random abduction from the street.'

'And that would bring us back to Hübner, and like I say, I don't think it was him.'

'Jochen Hübner isn't the only sex criminal or woman-hater in Hamburg. It could have very easily been someone else.'

'I know. It's just a hunch I have.'

'You told me once that there are no such things as hunches, just things we already know but haven't got round to realizing we know . . . or some crap like that.'

'Yeah, well, if I remember rightly that didn't end too well for me. But yes, there's something in the detail here and I can't separate it out.' He sighed. 'Monika Krone is this beautiful, intelligent young woman, a student first of Classical Philology, then English Gothic Literature at the University of Hamburg – a highly gifted student, by all accounts. From what we can establish, she had men worshipping her, yet there is no boyfriend. No significant relationship with anyone, not even her twin sister. She is described as distant and aloof, but in a way that seems to add to her appeal, yet her life outside the university and a few social events, like the party on the night she dies, is a blank page. The only thing we really know about her was that she had a passion for all things Gothic.'

'Maybe she was just a private person. Or someone who didn't fit in with the set around her.'

'You've seen her sister. Imagine her at twenty-five. Women like that don't need to fit in with a set, the set fits in with them.'

'So what are you saying?' asked Anna.

'I really don't know. Maybe you're right and Monika was just a private person, but I have a feeling that there was something else going on in her life. Something that she kept from everyone.'

'And you think this something else could be linked to her death?'

Fabel shrugged. 'I just don't know. Anyway, it's getting late. You're right, I should have more eyes on this. I'll split the files between the team in the morning.'

So many things had changed for Fabel; they continued to change. And where he saw that change most was in his daughter's blink-of-an-eye transition from dependent toddler to fiercely independent young woman. It was a change that both saddened him with the burden of lost time and filled him with intense pride. They had always been close, but the shooting two years before had turned up the volume on their relationship, as it had on just about everything else in his life.

Fabel had arranged to meet Gabi that evening for dinner in the city centre. They normally saw each other regularly – at least once a week – although the ebb and flow of cases meant that some at times he was more tied up with work than at others. But he never missed their weekly meal out.

It was uniquely their time. Gabi had always got on well with Susanne and the two had become close, but this small father–daughter ritual was unshared. Something they had always done, just the two of them.

And this was where they usually met. It was a cellar restaurant, below street level at the Alsterarkaden. But because it sat next to the channel of the Kleine Alster, one flank of the cellar was all windows and looked out onto the water and the symbolic white Alster swans that glided across its surface.

The restaurant had an East Frisian theme and they served beers and dishes from Fabel's home region, along with other traditional Northern German specialities. The fact that it was very much a tongue-in-cheek theming made it all the more East Frisian. Fabel had come here often over his years in Hamburg, joking with others about it being his embassy in the Hanseatic City.

Fabel's usual waiter had approached him without his customary cheeriness and had explained that the decision had been taken to close the restaurant permanently. Its doors would shut for good in a couple of months.

'The world moves on, I suppose,' the waiter had said dolefully. 'Things are changing. People aren't interested in traditional dishes any more. They want sea bass and linguine, not eel or herring and potatoes.'

Fabel ordered a beer while he waited for Gabi to arrive and sat watching the swans. Thinking about the restaurant closing made him much sadder than he would have expected. His patronage of this East Frisian outpost in Hamburg had been half-humorous, but the truth was he would really miss coming here. It was also true that Fabel had always had this strange resistance to change: he saw himself as a progressive, forward-looking type in many ways, but this strange attachment to regularity, an inner conservatism, annoyed him. He tended to have established patterns to his life – regular habits and set places – and found it difficult, *uncomfortable*, to shift from them. The odd thing was that since the shooting he had become a much more relaxed person, less rigid in almost every aspect of his life, but this strange attachment to things, places and routines had endured. Perhaps even intensified.

A pretty girl entered through the stone arch of the doorway and waved across to him. She had auburn-red hair, a shade or two lighter and redder than Monika Krone's had been. Gabi Fabel had inherited her hair, complexion and many of her features from her mother, Renate, but her personality was very much that of her father.

She came over, kissed Fabel and sat down opposite him. They chatted for a while, catching up on the week, and Fabel told her about the imminent closure of the restaurant.

'That's a shame,' she said. 'I know how much you like this place. I do too. It always make me think of Gran's.'

'How are things going with your course? You said last week that you were struggling.'

'I'm getting there. An existential flutter, that's all. Just worried that I might be doing the wrong course for the wrong reasons, that kind of thing.'

'And now?'

Gabi shrugged. 'I'm good. Like I said, just a blip. A *brain fart* as the Americans say.'

'It fills me with such pride to see how your studies have broadened your cultural references.' Fabel arched an eyebrow. He tried not to let his relief show too much. Gabi was into her third year as a history student, the same route his studies had taken him. There had, however, been talk of her studying jurisprudence as a route into senior officer-level entry into the Polizei Hamburg. It had been an option that had cost him more than a few nights' sleep. The idea seemed to have faded from her mind.

'Any ideas about what you want to do after uni?' he asked.

Gabi laughed loudly.

'What?'

'My God, *Dad*,' she said. 'I always imagined your interrogation techniques would be subtle to the point of mystical. If you want to ask me if I'm going to join up, then just ask me.'

'Well, are you?'

'No. Probably not, at least. I've been giving it all a lot of thought, especially after the shooting, and I don't think it's for me.'

'Listen, Gabi,' said Fabel. 'God knows I'm relieved that you've changed your mind, but I have to be honest and say that what happened to me is incredibly rare. It's a dangerous job, or at least it can be a dangerous job, but don't think—'

'I don't,' she interrupted. 'It's not the danger, it's the reality I don't think I could handle.'

'I don't get you.'

Gabi leaned forward, frowning, as if forcing a difficult idea into shape. 'I couldn't believe it when you were shot. I couldn't believe that I came that close to losing you. Then I realized that you deal with that feeling all the time, every day. Telling people that a loved one has been murdered, or digging into their grief and the rawest, most secret parts of their lives. Do you know what society is? It's hiding. We build all of these walls and defences to stop us having to face up to our own mortality. Take this restaurant – practically no one here has even seen someone dead. We hide from death. But I bet you can't even tell me how many times you've seen death. Policemen, doctors, nurses, firemen – you are society's caretakers, you tidy it all away so we don't have to face up to it. I don't think I can do that. I don't think I can be a caretaker.'

'Well, I can't say you haven't thought it through.' Fabel paused as the waiter, restored to his usual cheeriness, served their main courses. 'What do you think you'll do?'

'I don't know. I've got lots of time to think about it. I might even do a post grad.'

They spent the rest of the meal talking and laughing about the usual inconsequences. Gabi was one of the few people who shared his particular, often absurdist sense of humour. As they talked, Fabel watched her. She really had grown up so fast and in so many ways.

Things were changing; the waiter had been right.

19

Fabel looked at his watch before starting the briefing. He checked the time against the wall clock: his watch was running fast, again. He shifted the hands to the correct time before calling for quiet.

'Let's get back to the Monika Krone investigation,' he said. 'This is a cold case so I'm afraid that means a lot of catch-up reading.'

He let the groans die before continuing.

'We'll have no involvement in the fall-out from the riots, thank God, and although one right-wing radical is in hospital with serious head injuries, he's expected to pull through and there's already been an arrest. That means I can divide the Krone file between you. I'm taking a different approach to the case this time around and I want you to go through all of the statements and cross-reference them. Anna and I will set up a board and I want you to peg connections between people at the party.'

'But that was done before,' said Thomas Glasmacher.

'No, the last time connections to the victim were sought. This time I want you to ignore Monika Krone and see who was involved with whom at the party. Were there any cliques or sets, that kind of thing.'

'I thought the theory was that her disappearance had nothing to do with the party.' Dirk Hechtner stood leaning against the window sill, looking small and dark next to the burly, blond Glasmacher.

'It was the theory,' said Fabel. 'It maybe still is, but this is an angle I feel was underexplored the last time round. Bear in mind I worked the case fifteen years ago and it was me who originally suggested it was a random abduction . . . a snatch off the street. With the gift of hindsight, I'm just not so sure. Plus there was always that phone call to her sister, an hour after she left the party and during which there was no suggestion of her being afraid or in danger.' Fabel sighed. 'Okay . . . We've got sixty-three partygoers: three teams will each take twenty names – Thom and Dirk, Anna and Henk, and Principal Chief Commissar Brüggemann and Sven. I'll take the remaining three myself. I want us to constantly cross-reference, working across teams as connections are established. As well as connections between individuals, I want you to look for interdependencies between the alibis.'

'You think it could have been a group, rather than an individual?' asked Nicola Brüggemann.

'It's possible, but there again at this stage everything and anything is possible. If anyone sees anything that seems even the slightest bit odd or incongruous, I want it red-flagged on the board. Anna, could you distribute the files?' Fabel looked at his watch again. 'I'll catch up with you this afternoon. I have an appointment to keep . . .'

There was practically none of the meaningless small talk that usually oils the gears of a small assembly. And this was a small assembly, only five of them. Small and odd. They were all different ages and completely different backgrounds. Each member of the group had exchanged polite smiles and perfunctory greetings with the others on arrival, but there was little chat amongst them. Fabel was the last to arrive.

There was the young woman who dressed conservatively, despite the black swirls of tattoos that coiled up from the collar and out from under the cuffs of her blouse, and whose nostrils and earlobes bore the fading signs of multiple piercings. There was the medical student, or ex-medical student, who was as much boy as man and whose intelligent, bright blue eyes were set behind spectacles into a very pale face beneath a mop of thick black hair, and who seemed always to radiate contentment. He always smiled. Not forcedly, not broadly, but always just there in the bright eyes and the faint curve of narrow lips.

Between the medical student and the ex-Goth sat another, unexceptional-looking young man, this time in his mid-thirties. He had three children, he had told the group. All with a year's gap between them. Like everything else in his life, it had been a matter of planning: it had seemed important, he had said, to have them close together. One of the many things that had seemed so important once.

The last member of the group was from Blankenese: a late-middle-aged woman with butter-coloured hair who had clearly been pretty in her youth but now struggled with her weight and who tried not to look too prosperous.

And then there was Fabel.

The Club of the Living Dead.

Fabel had used the name once in a quip when talking to Dr Lorentz and he had regretted it instantly, realizing that his irony reflected not just on himself, but on the others. But they had all laughed. From then on, everyone had referred to the group as the Club of the Living Dead. And now they were assembled, waiting for Dr Lorentz to arrive.

'What's the time?' the Blankenese woman, whose name was Hanne, asked without impatience and despite the fact she was examining her wristwatch.

'You too?' asked the unremarkable man, whose name was Josef but preferred Sepp. 'I can't get a watch to keep accurate time, either. Ever since.'

They were interrupted by the door swinging open to admit a tall, thin man who was balding untidily. Fabel noticed that Dr Lorentz's suit and shoes were expensive, but his shirt was definitely chain-store multipack. He was tieless and the open collar of his shirt exposed a too-thin neck. All in all, it was a comfortingly ascetic look, as if the psychiatrist was some kind of plain-clothes monk.

'I'm sorry I'm late.' Lorentz smiled and sighed as he sat down, as if gaining some peace from a backstory of hectic schedules and frustrating delays. He crossed long legs that seemed all bone under worsted and set a heavy ring-bound folder on his lap. 'Let's just recap on where we left off last session . . .'

Everyone sat patiently and listened to the psychiatrist. Patience was an acquired symptom for them all; an after-effect of the only thing that they all had in common. Each had had the same experience. Even that was not so common: the experience had been different, unique, for each of them. The purpose of the Club of the Living Dead was to find the commonalities, the shared elements to the experience. The shared after-effects.

They had all been invited to take part in the group because each of them had had a near-death experience; some through illness, some through accident and, in Fabel's case, through violent intent. At the first meeting, Dr Lorentz had explained that he was a psychiatrist by training, but his particular expertise was as a thanatologist: a death expert. Lorentz and his colleagues were part of a research programme that examined every aspect – medical, physical, psychiatric and social – of the phenomenon of human death. Lorentz's specific area was trying to understand the phenomenon of near-death experiences.

Before the group sessions had started, before he had met any of the others, Fabel had been subject to individual assessment: a barrage of brain scans, encephalographs, blood tests, psychometric testing and lengthy and very personal interrogations. They all had.

It had been explained from the very beginning that the project was not about helping the members of the group, but understanding their experience. However, Lorentz had added, it was hoped that they would each benefit from the exchanges in the group sessions.

The strangest thing Fabel found was how relaxed he was about talking about himself, something that would have made him very uncomfortable before. Lorentz had from the outset taken a special interest in Fabel, clearly because of his unique perspective as an investigator of death who had himself come close to it. Fabel had felt the need early on to explain to Lorentz that while he was happy to discuss every other aspect of his life, the sensitivity of his work meant that he could not discuss anything to do with it. Nor had he wanted the others to know the specifics of his work within the police.

Fabel was to come to realize that he was not the only member of the group who had been keeping something hidden. During this particular session, it emerged that Ansgar, the youthful but pale ex-medical student, was dying. His near-death experience, he explained, had been brought about by the tumour that was spreading tentacles through his brain.

'I call him the Explorer,' Ansgar said, almost with affection. 'Technically, he's a glioblastoma multiforme.'

Fabel noticed that Lorentz did not look surprised or pass comment: he would have known, and kept confidential, Ansgar's medical history.

'How long have you had it?' asked Fabel.

'Six months, more or less. They grow quickly, this type of tumour. I was always in the top two per cent of my class at medical school, but I started to get headaches and found it increasingly difficult to concentrate. Then, after the seizures started, I was diagnosed. The anticonvulsants they put me on didn't seem to work and then I had this massive seizure. I knew it was coming, I kept having déjà vu and this weirdly buzzed feeling. I can't remember the seizure itself, of course, but it nearly finished me and I had my NDE.'

'Why do you call your glioma your "Explorer"?' Lorentz asked.

'Because that's what he is. Multiform glioblastomas have these tentacle-like projections that stretch into your brain. Probe it. Every time he finds a new area, moves along a virgin axon and stimulates a fresh dendrite, I discover a new element of my mind, a new part of me. I've found myself singing in the most inappropriate of contexts, suddenly understanding questions I never thought to ask myself, smelling or hearing things that no one else can. For a while I even became an accomplished artist, something I could never do before. My Explorer lights up hidden treasures in my brain and, of course, he took me to see Death and showed me how I shouldn't be afraid of it. People feel sorry for me because I'm going to die soon – but the truth is we're all going to die. In the meantime, most people live afraid. I'm going to die unafraid. I know the rest of you understand.'

Fabel watched Ansgar for the rest of the session. He listened attentively but detachedly as others spoke, the constant, gentle smile never leaving the pale, intelligent face. He was, Fabel realized, fading out of life and was doing so in absolute contentment.

That, and Fabel's own recollection of the wonder of a near-death experience, didn't stop him feeling sad and having a sense of a young life wasted.

20

With most drugs, not that Zombie would have known much about any other drug, there was always a moment of contact, a sense of it hitting your system. Dimethyltryptamine wasn't like that at all. *You* didn't change. There was no sense of your body altering or responding to chemical changes; there was no sudden euphoria or opiate rush.

With DMT, it was the world, the universe that changed. Reality, such as it was, wasn't replaced with hallucination, it simply became transparent, overlaid, enhanced. DMT didn't offer an altered state of consciousness, it offered a *true* state of consciousness. Zombie had long ago realized that the drug opened up every level of reality. All of the contradictions and complications of the universe that everyone from philosophers to quantum physicists had sought to resolve suddenly became simple and visible. When he took DMT, spacetime was no longer an abstract theoretical concept, Zombie could *see* it, feel it, experience it.

It had been a challenging time for Zombie. So much planning, so many things to set in place. But vengeance was taking a form he had not expected and those who had remained unpunished for so long were now being brought to account.

He was in a place he needed to be. DMT responded to your

state of mind. It gave you eyes to see all types of reality, to restore all types of memory, to fold time in on itself. But it also amplified whatever state of mind you were in. DMT brought wonders but, Zombie knew only too well, it could also bring horrors.

For Zombie, it opened the gates to exactly the same kind of experience he had had when he died.

He had, of course, read up on the literature. The theory was that the human pineal gland produced dimethyltryptamine naturally, and that it was responsible for the creation of dreams and the regulation of states of consciousness. The psychiatrist who had been giving him therapy had told him that many endocrinologists believed that, at the point of death, the pineal gland pumped an overdose of dimethyltryptamine into the body, offering a hallucinatory release from the reality of death, the rest of the endocrine system flooding the dying person's body with endorphins, creating euphoria and eliminating fear. According to this theory, near-death experiences of hypersenses, out-of-body perspectives, brilliant light and complete joy were all simply a form of super-dream created by pineal gland secretions and a storm of neuro-electrical activity.

But Zombie didn't believe that. He didn't believe that at all. It was one of the reasons he had stopped his sessions with the psychiatrist. That and the fact he had been pressuring Zombie to take part in his stupid study.

And anyway, the theory didn't hold true with Zombie. For a start, he was dead. He had already crossed the threshold and bodily functions played no role in his consciousness any more. He was a ghost: a mind independent of a body but trapped in one. How it was that the physical taking of a drug caused such dramatic changes in that ghostly consciousness was something that Zombie chose not to question.

It was time for him to enter his vault.

His apartment had roll-down metal shutters on the windows, the type more common in southern Germany for shutting out the brightest of the midday sun. With the shutters closed, the apartment was in total darkness except for the single candle he had lit and which now sat on the floor. For Zombie, this was his vault, his mausoleum: a place he could pretend he had found the final rest so far denied him.

Zombie lay on his back, his head propped on the cushion and turned to the side so he could focus on the candle flame. There were noises from outside – the living going about empty daily rituals – and Zombie shut them out, focusing on the flame and nothing else.

But the sounds came back to him, except this time he was not annoyed. Instead of background noise, he suddenly found he could hear every level with absolute clarity. He heard a woman complaining to a friend about her job, about her boss. He heard a child whiningly beseeching its mother for another sweet. He heard two adolescents talk crudely about a girl they knew. He heard a thousand different conversations and listened to them all. But it wasn't a sequence of discussions, they were all happening at the same moment and Zombie could attend to them all. It was a symphony of voices from across the city.

He listened and at the same time heard other layers of voices. The past and the present were overlapping and the long-dead of Hamburg told their story. It was an experience with DMT that Zombie was well acquainted with. For millennia, this had been exactly the reason tribes in the Amazon had taken ayahuasca: to connect with the dead and commune with their ancestors.

The universe was changing, opening up.

Zombie watched the candle flame. The blue, yellow and white in the flame became blues, yellows and whites. The simple form of the flame became a geometry of vast complexity and dimension. He could see the patterns of heat and light normally beyond the visible spectrum; he could also see the origin and the future of the flame, every moment of its existence overlaid in one.

The room broke into patterns of light and colour, kaleidoscope-like. He felt the presence of his father and his grandfather, and others beyond them. They were not there as distinguishable identities but as essences – elements of Zombie's own being.

He was floating. He was now above the floor, and in an instant above his own body, above Hamburg, above the world. The universe erupted into colour and light.

The angels came for him. They had no form, or no fixed form, but were constantly vibrating, scintillating geometric shapes that continuously folded in on themselves, then folded out, like endless Möbius loops of energy. The angels, as always, had no faces, no features, no eyes, yet Zombie always knew their intentions. He knew without them having to speak that they were his guides. He also knew that, as with every experience like this, he must go where they led.

He moved through time and space without moving. He knew he was still in his apartment, but he was also, in the exact same moment, somewhere else, sometime else.

No. He tried to tell the angels with his mind. *I don't want to go there. I don't want to be here.*

It was the Place of Broken Stones. The place he had died. The place he had been murdered. He begged speechlessly for the angels to take him away, not to put him through it all again, but they told him it was he who decided where they should be; he who had brought them to this place.

He saw the others.

Suddenly, he was back in his body, but not his body that lay on the floor of his apartment, not his fifteen-year-dead body. The body he now occupied was painfully, horribly alive. He was being held down on a stone in the Place of Broken Stones. It was happening again. The others were playing their parts again.

I don't want to be here, he screamed silently. He looked up into the night and saw deep, deep into the universe. The same folding, unfolding, eternal geometry filled the sky. He could still see that, but was in a mortal body.

This was where, when and how he had died.

The angels were gone.

Some presence, vast and dark and all-consuming had entered the Place of Broken Stones and the shockwave of its arrival had driven out the angels and any other being of light and energy. He felt it grow near, like a movement of chilled air.

She was above him now. The Silent Goddess. Death. She looked down on him with ice eyes and he was overwhelmed by her beauty and her fearsomeness. The Silent Goddess who takes all lives, from the smallest to the greatest. The Silent Goddess who had been part of the universe since its beginning: the destroyer of worlds and stars, the feeder on energy and life. She was naked and he felt desire mingle with his terror. She had come for him.

He felt the world beneath him shudder and crack asunder. Fire surged up through the spaces between the stones, burned his body.

She raised her sword above him and he could see every layer of the blade's making, the folding of steel in on itself over and over, the metal furnace hot then plunged cold.

Please no! He begged for the life he now felt once again, the sensations in his limbs, even the sweet pain. *I don't want to be dead again.*

The sword arced diamond brilliant in the light of the flames, down and into his chest. He felt it all in unimaginable detail: he felt the blade shear through skin, bone and cartilage; sever artery, vein, capillary; slice through muscle fibre, nerve and organ. His agony was complete, filling every dimension of his being.

He tried to scream but it drowned in a gargle of frothing blood. The Silent Goddess smiled at him, malevolently, beautifully. She leaned down towards him and assumed normal human size. She pulled the blade from his chest and a new wave of pain surged through him. He felt her cold flesh against his cooling flesh as she lay on top of him. She kissed him, her lips and tongue crimsoned with his coughed-up blood.

Zombie died again. He died in the same way he had before. The angels came back and he thanked them, said he understood why he'd had to go through it once more.

Just like the first time he died, Zombie became bathed in a warm, golden light. He was free of his body, free from the pain of flesh. He had become a being of no substance, just like the angels, and could see he was made up of endless, scintillating strands and spirals of pure energy. He was high above his body, looking down on it, and felt no confusion that he was looking down at it both in the Place of Broken Stones and in his own apartment.

All of his family waited for him, the dead generations of it. The light grew in intensity and with it Zombie's joy. He was finally going to be free. He was going to be amongst the dead, where he belonged, and free of his imprisonment amongst the living.

Zombie, now beyond time, spent only a few seconds but also an eternity in this shining place. He had no sense of leaving it, but, as the drug wore off, he drifted into a deep, dreamless sleep.

When he woke back in his apartment, back in his unburied, still-moving corpse, Zombie rolled over, turned his face into the cushion he'd rested his head on, and stifled the sobs that racked his body.

21

Georg Schmidt knew he had something very important to do but, just at that moment, couldn't remember what it was. Whatever it was, it was something huge and frightening and unpleasant, because he felt an inexplicable fluttering in his chest and a knot in his gut. That was what his life had become, recently: a left-luggage locker for feelings detached from their source.

Some instinct also told him that what he had to do had something to do with the past. That in itself wasn't strange, because the past now seemed to dominate his present, 'then' frequently disguising itself as 'now'.

Georg's history seemed jumbled and confused and he found himself relying more and more on his notebook journal: in his mind the memories were dim, distant, vague ghosts, yet the notebook returned them sharp and clear into focus.

But his recollections were full of contradictions and paradoxes: things he thought he remembered experiencing were, when he thought them through, really just things he must have read or heard about. Third-person memories became first person; first-person experiences were recalled as third-person accounts. Sometimes, instead of a single memory recalling an event, multiple memories conflated so that the perspective changed. For example, he remembered marching on a sunny day, the crowds around him hostile and jeering, then he remembered being in the crowd, shouting and jeering at the marchers.

Georg Schmidt had something important to do, but couldn't remember what it was.

His father.

The sudden thought of his father focused him for a moment; drew in the scattered fragments. He remembered seeing Franz Schmidt clutching at his chest and falling to the ground. More shots ringing out. People screaming. Blood bubbling on his father's lips as he tried to say something, his dying voice inaudible above the tumult.

Helmut Wohlmann, who had once been his father's apprentice, who had been like a brother to Georg, his face drained of colour beneath a brown SA kepi.

Now Georg remembered. That's why he had a key on a chain around his neck.

Unlocking the drawer, he fished out his diary, where he kept his memories stored, and read through it again. Georg Schmidt had something important to do and now he remembered what it was.

He took the tie from his wardrobe, rolled it up into a coil, and was about to stuff it into his pocket when he checked himself. He went across to the chest of drawers and rummaged around in first one then another until he found what he was looking for. The tie, he had remembered, might need too much strength.

He opened the clasp knife he'd taken from the drawer, ran his thumb along its cutting edge then, snapping it shut and slipping it into his pocket, picked up his chequers set and headed for the door.

22

It had been more than a week since Monika Krone had come back into the world. Her remains had been transferred to Butenfeld, the mortuary at the Institute for Judicial Medicine in Eppendorf, but they remained silent, refusing to yield any forensic evidence of how, where and when she had died. All the pathologist could say was that the pH of the soil in which Monika had been buried had been such that soft tissue would have decomposed within a year, and that DNA other than that captive in bone would have similarly been destroyed quickly after burial. Only one thing was confirmed: based on a comparison with a sample from Kerstin Krone, the DNA extracted from the remains' femur was a match. A perfect match: identical twins had identical DNA.

In the Murder Commission, the case board Fabel had set up for the Krone inquiry started to take shape. Names were connected and interconnected by pins and threads of different colours. Patterns emerged of friendships, of sexual intimacy, of rivalries and animosities, most of which had probably been forgotten at more than a decade's distance. But there was nothing to be seen, other than an unconnected void at the heart of it all that represented Monika Krone: her presence conspicuous as an absence.

Monika had been active in a lot of clubs and societies. She had been a keen swimmer and a regular at the pools of the Alster Schwimmhalle, as well as a leading member of Gothic and Romantic literature societies. Though no artist herself, Monika had had an interest in art, particularly pre-Raphaelite and art nouveau, and had even modelled for students at the University of Fine Arts in Uhlenhorst.

The picture that emerged was of a young woman connected to many, close to none. Over the years, Fabel had seen how often the strikingly beautiful were the loneliest of people: their physical perfection setting them apart, making them unapproachable, even shunned and loathed.

But he was not at all sure that the isolation of the comely was what he was looking at here: it was as if Monika sought acquaintance but shrank from intimacy. She was part of any number of sets of friends, sometimes the focus of them, but never seemed deeply involved. There was one in particular: an odd assortment made up from students at the university, but in very different disciplines. Others had described them as a very exclusive clique. From the descriptions of them, Fabel had at first thought they were some kind of Goths. But they had, by all accounts, been more sophisticated than that. The focus of the group had been a shared taste for classical Gothic literature.

He didn't think looking into the group would lead anywhere in itself, but it might cast some additional light into the corners of Monika's last days and he took a note to get someone onto it.

Fabel visited Kerstin, Monika's sister, twice more. Each time was to see if he could coax out some extra detail about her twin, but again all that emerged was the picture of a closed-off, aloof young woman who had confided little in anyone.

It was a Saturday evening when Fabel took Susanne out for dinner in her favourite restaurant in Ottensen, along from the Fischmarkt and with huge picture windows that looked out across the Elbe. From their table they could see the inverted silver egg-box of the water treatment works, floodlit silver and blue on the far side of the river. As they ate and chatted, the vast, silent bulk of container ships slid by smoothly and silently causing the velvet waters beyond the window to sparkle with fractured reflections of the dock lights. Not for the first time it struck Fabel how much beauty there could be in industry. It was also one of the things he loved about Hamburg: the sense of things passing through, of connection with a much wider world. Susanne had been brought up in Munich, locked in by the fastness of Europe. Fabel had been born and brought up in Ostfriesland, on the North Sea coast, and could never imagine living more than a few kilometres from the sea.

As they ate, Fabel discussed the case, explaining to Susanne how he still felt discomfited every time he talked to Kerstin, aware he faced the older mirror image of the victim of the murder he was investigating.

'If her sister was the great beauty she appears to have been,' Susanne arched a dark eyebrow as she lifted her wine glass to her lips, 'then Kerstin must be very beautiful too.'

'I can't say I've—'

'Oh no you don't . . .' Susanne laughed. 'Don't say you haven't noticed.'

'Okay, I've noticed. She is very striking. But that's where the similarity ends. Kerstin Krone is totally different from her sister in personality.'

'Do you know what I think?' Susanne put her wine glass down. 'I think this case has burrowed its way into you more than you know or admit. You've always said it's your job to get to know the dead . . . that's how you've always approached every case, using that little historian's brain of yours to bring the dead back to life and understand them. But Monika Krone was your first major case and you never could crack open her personality. It's not just her death that has remained an enigma all these years. I think you fell a little in love with this mystery woman fifteen years ago.'

'Is that a professional opinion? Or personal?'

'A bit of both.'

'There's only one woman I'm in love with,' Fabel smiled.

'Oh yeah? I bet it's some dumpy, florid-faced blonde Frisian lass from your past. Probably called Femke or Swaantje or something equally fetching.'

Fabel reached over and took Susanne's hand in his.

'I want to get married,' he said.

Susanne looked startled for a moment. She smiled a little nervously then said, 'What does Swaantje have to say about it?'

'I'm being serious, Susanne. I want us to get married.'

Susanne drew a deep breath and straightened in her chair, her expression suggesting she was processing something she would never have anticipated.

'Wow,' she said eventually. 'I don't know what to say. I mean, I really don't . . .'

'Listen, Susanne, I don't want an answer now, I just want you to think it over. You don't even have to answer at all, I just wanted you to know how I feel.'

'But why? I mean, why now?'

'I've been thinking about it for the last two years. Ever since . . . Well, you know since what. Things have changed for me. I know you have noticed that. I'm not saying that my feelings towards you have changed – it's not that at all – it's just that I see things differently now and I value the things that are important to me more than ever. And the two most important things in my life are you and Gabi.'

'But we've been happy the way we are . . .'

'I know. That's not what I'm saying. If things don't change – if you don't want them to change – then that's fine. But when I thought I was dying, I regretted never having asked you to marry me. I couldn't stand the idea that I'd be dead and you wouldn't know how I felt about you.' Fabel shook his head. 'I know I can be a bit buttoned-up. That I *was* buttoned-up. But life's too short to leave things unsaid.' He shrugged. 'So I've said it.'

'Thanks, Jan.' She leaned across the table and kissed him. 'I'll need to think about it.'

'Like I said, I don't need an answer if you don't want to give one.' He smiled and raised his glass. 'I just wanted you to know how I feel. In any case, if you turn me down there's always Swaantje . . .'

23

He had been given his instructions in great detail: the exact day, the exact time. Jochen Hübner – Frankenstein – knew that getting the timing exactly right meant everything; not just the difference between continued imprisonment and freedom but between life and death itself. Hübner – who had never relied on anyone, who had never put his trust in anyone – found himself having faith in the stranger who had delivered the means of escape. His guardian. There was something in his guardian's eyes that Frankenstein had recognized as the same dark hunger for revenge he himself felt.

The guardian had promised Frankenstein freedom – from captivity and to do whatever he wanted to whomever he wanted. Only one thing was asked in return: that for a short time Frankenstein would serve his liberator, carry out his bidding. That he would kill those whom the guardian chose he should kill.

Timing.

Santa Fu – Hamburg-Fuhlsbüttel prison – offered its high-security prisoners more room than other prisons. Frankenstein's cell was modern, clean and spacious – he was housed on the floor that had the biggest cells, each with its own screened-off shower.

It was nearly time for the doors to be opened for the morning.

Frankenstein checked his watch, ridiculously small and fragile on his thick, heavy wrist: 5.56 a.m.

At six a.m. the door would be opened for *Lebenskontrolle*: the morning ritual where a guard opened the door and called in 'good morning'. A response, even a held-up hand, meant the prisoner was alive and well.

He leaned into the door and strained to hear approaching footsteps, but could hear nothing. Most of the guards wore rubber-soled shoes and the prison rules meant they were instructed to open the cell doors quietly. You could lock a man up for the rest of his life, apparently, but it was inhuman to give him a rude awakening.

He had to time it perfectly.

As his guardian had told him to do, Frankenstein went to the wall of his cell furthest from and facing the door. He took the disposable hypodermic from under his pillow and gripped it between his teeth while he slapped a vein on his forearm to the surface. A moment's hesitation: he looked at the vein, a dark cable beneath his pale skin. He had taken it on trust that the fluid in the hypodermic had been what his guardian had said it was.

They would be at the door in a minute, maybe less.

The doubt lingered. What if Hübner's strange guardian was really a relative of one of his many female victims? What if the dark hunger for revenge Frankenstein had recognized in his guardian's eyes was really directed at him? What if, instead of a means of escape, the syringe was full of poison?

He heard muffled voices from along the hall. Thirty seconds.

It didn't matter, he decided. Frankenstein had already made up his mind that death would be just another form of escape. He jabbed the needle into the vein and felt his arm chill as he squeezed the dose into his system.

The effects started right away, just as his guardian had said they would. Frankenstein had been instructed to conceal the hypodermic immediately after taking the dose.

'You've got to hide it while you still can,' his guardian had told him. 'Under a pillow or behind a book. Somewhere that's quick. And near – once the drug kicks in you'll find it difficult to move. Don't worry about it being easy to find. All that matters is they don't find it until you're out of the prison and in hospital. When they get to your cell, you will still be on your feet but barely conscious. That's the way the drug works. You will look like shit – no colour in your face. If you can remember, grab hold of your left arm as if it's really hurting you. They'll believe you're having a heart attack.'

It was working just like Frankenstein had been told it would. He felt like he should be falling down, but his legs had turned into stone pillars, keeping him upright but unmoving, rooted to the ground.

The sound of a key in the lock of his cell door. One clunk. Second clunk. Two sliding bars to go. He still had the syringe in his hand.

He forced himself to focus, shaking his huge head in an attempt to clear it, then leaned over and dropped the disposable syringe behind the pillow on his bed.

Everything decelerated. The world beneath his feet turned more slowly, the air around him became thick and viscous. He grabbed his upper left arm with his right hand, but couldn't remember why it was he was to do that.

The door opened and from a million miles away, a voice said good morning.

'Help . . .' Hübner gasped his rehearsed lines. 'Help. I can't breathe. My chest . . . I think it's my heart.' It would be on

Frankenstein's record, his guardian had told him, that his acromegaly condition predisposed him to heart problems.

He could no longer talk. No longer think. But he was still standing.

There were now uniformed shadows at the door; dark blue ghosts shouting something at him. He wanted to ask them who they were, where he was, who he was, but his tongue and lips were too massive and heavy to move.

As the world faded to black, one thought, one instruction, remained burned into his mind: when he awoke, he had to do so the way he had practised. Totally and immediately.

He couldn't remember why, but he knew his life depended on it.

24

'Well,' said Nicola Brüggemann in contralto tones as she leaned into Fabel's office. 'We can't say this isn't a varied job. Nothing like something unusual to get the day started.'

'What have you got?' Fabel smiled and beckoned for her to come in and sit down. Brüggemann was Fabel's deputy, despite holding the same rank as him. She had given up the director-ship of the Sexual Crimes Commission to join his team and he had been very glad of her expertise. The Kiel-born detective also had a dry Waterkant humour that Fabel appreciated.

'The Alte Mühle Seniors' Home in Bahrenfeld,' she explained, 'has had a murder. The victim is a few days short of a hundred and the suspected perpetrator is ninety-six.'

'You are kidding me . . .' said Fabel.

'I kid you not. We've got uniforms and forensics on their way. I would have thought murder would have seemed a little redun-dant at that age, but who knows? Maybe the motive was sexual jealousy. Who do you want assigned?'

Fabel keyed up the duty roster on his computer. 'I'll take it with Anna.'

'Okay.' Brüggemann laid the call sheet on Fabel's desk. 'But you better hurry, in case the suspect makes a run for it . . .'

The Alte Mühle Seniors' Home looked like no other old people's home Fabel had ever seen. It was in Bahrenfeld, still officially within the Altona city borough, but set off the main road and facing into the dense forest of Altona Stadtpark. The only other building Fabel and Anna had passed was the old forester's house, which now looked unoccupied and forlorn, the woodland around it threatening to reclaim it.

If there had indeed, as the name suggested, once been an old mill on the site, it was long gone and the building that had replaced it could not have been more than a few years old. The thing about the Alte Mühle that struck Fabel most was the way it presented a curving, blank, windowless wall to the road, as if turning its back on the city. The lack of windows gave it a solid presence and its self-conscious architecture made it look more like a massive sculpture set against the curtain of forest.

Following the drive, Fabel came round to the front of the home and saw that, where the rear wall had been all brick, the park-facing side was all windows and balconies. The semicircle of the building was made complete by a curving fence, about a metre and a half high, which in turn would be concealed from the home by a dense evergreen hedge.

'Shit . . .' said Anna as they approached the gate house. 'I've never seen a high security old people's home before.'

Once Fabel's police ID had been checked, they were admitted to the courtyard of the home. There was a black mortuary van and two marked police cars parked in the centre.

To Fabel, it was surreal. The main building extended to five storeys and looked like a residential apartment block. Each flat had its own balcony and the only thing that looked slightly strange was that the balcony railings were higher than normal. The ground floor of the building was given over to what looked like normal shops: a convenience store, a hairdresser, a news-agent, a small sit-in restaurant with a takeaway counter next to it. There were three small, single storey buildings set in the courtyard, which itself had been laid out as a park. One, closest to the main building, was set up as a café-bar, the second sold fruit and flowers, the third was a tobacco kiosk. Most bizarrely of all, a bus stop and shelter sat next to the kiosk.

'It's a Dementiaville . . .' said Anna. 'I didn't know there was one in Hamburg.'

'A what?'

'A Dementiaville . . . that's what people call them. Not the official name, obviously. It's the latest thing in caring for dementia patients. The idea is they can lead as normal lives as possible. Feel less institutionalized, I guess.' She nodded towards the bus stop. 'They set up these for the wanderers. The first place a confused patient will go is a bus stop or an S-Bahn station, usually to go home to a house or apartment they haven't lived in for decades. They set up these dummy bus stops so they can collect them and guide them back.'

Fabel scanned his surroundings. 'How do you know so much about it?'

'I do read, you know. The Cheeseheads came up with the idea.'

'The Dutch?'

'Yeah,' said Anna. 'And the Swiss are into it. Cheeseheads however you look at it. I would have thought if they'd wanted to make elderly Dutchies feel at home then they should have built them like budget campsites. Or just driven them in caravans up and down the outside lane of the autobahn at fifty kilometres an hour.'

'Now, now, Frau Commissar Wolff.' Fabel nodded in the direction of the main building. 'Shall we?'

As they neared the main entry, a young uniformed policeman with the shoulder flashes of a police chief master approached them.

'I'll take you up,' he said.

'Who's in charge of the scene?' asked Fabel as they walked in.

'Frau Doctor Koppel.'

Fabel nodded; Marta Koppel had joined the forensics team six months before as Holger Brauner's deputy.

The uniformed cop led them through the main hall, where they were met by a balding man around forty. He introduced himself as Christof Pohl, the Director of the seniors' home. Pohl was casually dressed and wore no name badge to identify him.

'This is a terrible thing,' said Pohl. 'I can't imagine how this has come to happen.'

'Was there any trouble previously between these two residents?' Fabel asked.

'Quite the contrary – Herr Schmidt and Herr Wohlmann were companions. Friends. And neither had been in any way aggressive towards other residents or staff.'

Fabel could see from Pohl's expression that he was sincere.

'Would you like me to take you up?' asked the home's Director.

'We're good,' said Fabel. 'The officer can take us from here, but I'd like a word with you before we leave, if that's all right.'

'Of course . . .' Pohl pointed to a reception desk that looked like it could be an information point in a mall or an airport. 'If you ask for me there they'll show you to my office.'

As they made their way through the building, Fabel became aware of both the deliberately uninstitutional appearance of the seniors' home, apart from the obligatory fire doors and statutory notices on the walls, and how chronologically vague its decor was: everything was neutral, cream and beige tones, furniture that made no absolute statement of period. He felt as if he could have been in any decade from the 1960s until the 2010s, and guessed that that had been the intention. No shock of the new; nothing jarring for the wandering consciousness to bump into.

'Fuck me . . .' he heard Anna mutter. 'Hell is eternity in a mall.'

A flustered-looking woman in her sixties – too young, he thought, to be a resident – came bustling up to them.

'Are you here about the deliveries?' she asked, frowning.

Fabel smiled. 'I'm sorry, I'm not.'

'Oh,' she said, casting an eye up and down the uniformed policeman. 'I thought you were here about the deliveries.'

A younger woman came up and, smiling reassuringly, took the confused woman gently by the shoulders and guided her away. The younger woman's professional demeanour marked her as a member of staff, but Fabel noticed that, like Director Pohl, she wore no uniform or name badge to identify her.

They took the lift to the third floor and the young policeman showed them to a suite of rooms guarded by another uniform.

When they entered, Fabel and Anna slipped on the plastic overshoes and latex gloves handed them by one of the three forensic technicians working the scene.

The room looked remarkably normal. Only the discordant presence of the white-coveralled forensics team marked it as a murder scene. The decor was the same shade of bland as the rest of the home and the pieces of personal furniture, pictures on the wall, books and items on the shelves did little to personalize it. In the centre of the room an old man sat, chin resting on his chest, in an armchair in front of a games table on which lay a chequers board. There was no hint of violence, no signs of any kind of struggle. Instead, the old man looked for all the world like he had dozed off mid-game. One hand hung at his side and this was Fabel's first immediate clue that the old man was dead, not sleeping: it had already begun to take on the purple-blue hue of post-mortem lividity, the fingers swelling as blood, no longer moved by an active heart, let gravity pull it to the lowest points in the body.

A young woman in white forensics coveralls was kneeling beside the body, carefully examining the dead man with fingers sheathed in blue latex. She stood up and pulled the mask from her face when she saw Fabel.

'Good morning, Herr Principal Chief Commissar,' she said, her very formal German slightly tinged with an Estonian accent.

'Good morning, Frau Doctor Koppel. Cause of death?'

Marta Koppel smiled and stepped towards the body and, cradling the crown of the old man's head in one surgical-gloved hand, his jaw in the other, eased his chin up from his chest. With the victim's head tilted back, Fabel could see a cut in the old man's throat, roughly nine centimetres wide and slightly diagonal. It gaped dark and, sickeningly, mouthlike, with the movement of the old man's head. There was little blood around the wound and what there was was pink and frothed.

'Old people don't have as much blood, I suppose,' said Fabel.

'Their blood volume is decreased, sure,' said Marta Koppel. 'But that's not why there's so little blood. From what I can see the carotids, internal jugular veins and oesophagus were all just missed and no more. Complete but slightly transverse transecting of the intertracheal membrane between the first and second tracheal rings. The old guy didn't bleed to death, he suffocated because his windpipe had been cut.'

'I see . . .' Fabel again imagined the process of someone else's death and wondered if the old man had shared the same experience, had had the same dreams Fabel had known two years ago. Hypoxia, he knew from years of dealing with the dead and causes of death, was a peaceful way to die, once the initial panic had passed.

'The suspect?' Fabel asked the uniformed cop who had led them up.

'He's been moved to another room, until his own has been processed. We've got someone with him.'

'No one's processed him?'

'He's been through forensics,' said the young policeman, 'but we don't know what to do with him, Herr Chief Commissar. You really have to see the state he's in to understand.'

'There's no doubt that he was the killer?'

'He was found with the body and with the knife in his hand. He was just sitting opposite the victim when they found them both.'

'Okay,' said Fabel. 'Lead the way.'

The unoccupied suite of rooms where Georg Schmidt was being held was further along the same corridor from the murder victim's apartment. Again it was decorated in a uniformly inoffensively era-indistinct way and Fabel began to feel vaguely claustrophobic. A small, bird-like old man sat on the sofa, dressed in the same type of white coveralls as the forensics team, his feet in white rubber boots. His hands were in constant movement, resting on his lap for a moment but finding no peace and fluttering from lap to armrest, up to touch his face and back to his lap. Behind their rheumy glaze, his eyes too had a fearful intensity and when Fabel entered the room with Anna, he saw the old man give a start. It was clear he was very afraid.

A uniformed officer was sitting in a club chair, at the other side of the room from the old man, and stood up when Fabel and Anna entered. Fabel nodded and the uniform left them alone with Schmidt.

Fabel sat down next to the old man, Anna pulling the chair vacated by the uniform across the room and sitting opposite them.

'You know that we are from the Polizei Hamburg, don't you, Herr Schmidt?' asked Fabel. He kept his voice calm and quiet, and not just because of the man's advanced age: Fabel had comforted many murderers immediately after the act of killing. Post-homicide shock, fear, confusion and disbelief were more common amongst killers than the public thought. Very often murder was as desperate and ill-conceived an act as suicide.

The old man didn't answer but instead searched the white coveralls for pockets that didn't exist.

'I have them here, sir,' he said, his voice light, high, tremulous. 'I beg your pardon, I'll have them in a minute.'

'Have what in a minute, Herr Schmidt?' asked Anna.

'My papers . . .' explained Schmidt and frowned at her, as if confused as to why a woman would be there, asking him for his papers. 'I have them somewhere.'

Resting his hand on Schmidt's arm, Fabel stopped the old man's searching. He had seen this before too, on the few occasions he'd had to deal with this generation. A generation for whom the police was something to be feared, to be obeyed.

'It's all right,' he said. 'We don't need to see your personal ID. Herr Schmidt, do you remember what happened?'

Schmidt seemed suddenly to become aware of his lack of pockets; he looked down at the white coveralls.

'My clothes. They took my clothes. Why did they take my clothes? And my key . . .' His right hand moved to his neck, as if checking for something.

'Don't worry about that just now, Herr Schmidt. What I really need you to tell me is what happened with Herr Wohlmann, and why you did what you did. But before you say anything, I have to tell you that under Article 136 of the Federal Criminal Procedure Regulations, you have the right to remain silent. Do you understand?'

It was as if he hadn't heard Fabel, but a light came on in his eyes as some other thought fell into his mind. 'The march . . . I remember the march. I had to do something because of the march.'

'Which march?'

'The one through Altona. The trouble. There was a riot.' He paused and frowned, then grabbed at the frayed end of the thought. 'I don't want any trouble.'

'The riot?' asked Fabel. 'Did you see the riot on television?"

Schmidt's frown deepened, as if trying to make sense of what Fabel had asked him. 'Yes,' he said eventually. 'That's why I had to do it. Because of the riot. Because of what happened. The shootings . . .'

'There were no shootings,' said Anna.

'. . . all those people dead.'

'But nobody—'

Fabel stopped Anna with a gesture of his hand.

'You mean Altona Bloody Sunday, Herr Schmidt?' he said. 'Nineteen thirty-two? Has that got something to do with Herr Wohlmann?'

'It began it all. It all started then. It wasn't right. It just wasn't right. I had to put things right, before it was too late . . .'

Fabel saw the focus fade, thoughts evaporating in the air. He made several attempts to get Schmidt back to the here-and-now, or at least the here-and-now he had occupied a moment ago and which offered some hope of an explanation of an inexplicable event. But it was useless. Schmidt sank deeper into a confusion about where he was and what he was doing there.

After a while, Fabel gave up.

'We need to get a full psych assessment,' he said to Anna. He turned back to Schmidt. 'We'll leave you in peace just now,' he said. 'Then we'll have someone take you to the hospital to have you checked out.'

Schmidt nodded, but Fabel could see he didn't understand.

'Goodbye, Herr Schmidt,' he said as he got up to leave.

'Can I have my clothes back now, please?' Schmidt looked up at Fabel with earnest, watery eyes. 'It's time for me to play chequers with Helmut . . .'

On the way out, Fabel and Anna called in to see Christof Pohl, the home's director. Pohl could offer no ideas as to why mild-mannered, gentle Herr Schmidt had slit his friend's throat with an old fishing clasp knife.

'As I said before,' he explained. 'They were friends. They spent a lot of time together and seemed to have a lot in common.'

'Did they know each other before?' asked Anna. 'I mean, before moving into the home?'

'I really don't know for sure, but I certainly got that impression. They were both Altona born and bred. Maybe in the war . . .' Pohl suddenly looked sad. 'What will happen to Herr Schmidt now? Will you lock him up?'

'Normally we would take him to the Presidium for question-ing. But given his advanced age and his confused state of mind, we'll transfer him to the secure psychiatric wing at Ochsenzoll instead. He'll be clinically assessed there as to whether he's mentally capable to be charged under the Penal Code, which, frankly, I doubt. I have to say it is a very strange and very sad case. Is there anything about your set-up here that could have been some kind of, well, trigger?'

'This whole place is conceived and designed to remove as many triggers for distress as possible, Herr Fabel,' said Pohl. 'Dementia very often leads to confusion and fear. Any aggression stems from feeling isolated in a frighteningly unrecognizable environment. What we have here in the Alte Mühle is a bubble. At one time it was considered best clinical practice to force patients to engage with reality, with the here-and-now. But all that does is confuse and upset them. What we try to do here is to offer as natural and independent a life as we can. All of the shops and cafés you see here are run by members of the care staff, all of whom wear ordinary, day-to-day clothes. Patients go shopping, meet each other for coffee, have their hair done, have meals out. If, in his or her mind, a patient is unaware what dec-ade it is, or if they believe they are somewhere other than the Alte Mühle, then we let them alone . . . so long as they're happy that is. If their memories or confusion causes them distress, then of course we intervene.'

'That's all well and good,' said Anna. 'But what about when they start sticking knives in each other?'

'We don't accommodate aggressive or violent patients. We're not geared up for that and never have been. Should a patient become aggressive towards staff or other residents, then, regret-fully, we have to pass them on to a facility better equipped to deal with them.' Pohl shook his head sadly. 'But there was never any question of that with Herr Schmidt – he has always been an unfailingly pleasant and courteous resident. I can assure you, this has come as a complete shock to us all.'

25

'Take these things off.' Heiko Goedecke invested his tone with as much authority as he could muster. The young emergency physician in the Asklepios Klinik Nord often found it necessary to invest his tone with authority: he was small, slender and had a thick mop of dark hair that made him look a decade younger than his thirty-two years. This time, however, his decisive tone was as much to convince himself as anything: the truth was, unconscious and near to death as his patient was, Goedecke was tempted to leave the handcuffs in place.

He looked down at the unmoving figure on the trolley, its ankles and shoeless feet jutting out over the end. As a physician, Goedecke knew what he was looking at: a severe case of acromegaly and gigantism, probably the result of a pituitary gland tumour or disorder. The outward appearance had nothing to do, he told himself, with the character within. Except this character had been brought in handcuffed and heavily guarded.

But as a normal creature of instinct and despite his professional assessment, Goedecke felt he was in the presence of a monster, something less, or more, than human. The features on the huge, stone-hewn face were oversized, heavy and coarse; the brow was massive, the heavy supraorbital ridge like an overhang above the closed, small, sunken eyes. The jaw was huge too, as were the sharp, angled planes of his cheekbones. The oxygen mask sat unevenly on the bulky features, gaps all around it, as if someone had tried to force a child's mask onto an adult face. It felt to Goedecke like he was looking at a living palaeontological specimen – some monstrous predecessor who had no place among modern men. He turned and saw his nurse also staring down at their patient, equal disquiet clear in her expression.

'Take these off,' he repeated. 'Now.'

'This is a very dangerous man,' said the prison officer. Two had come in the ambulance and the other now stood guard at the door. 'He's handcuffed for good reason.'

'This man is dying or close to it. He is no danger to anyone. I need to examine his chest without hindrance. If you don't take the handcuffs off immediately and my patient dies because I can't work on him, I will officially name you as a contributory factor in his death.'

The prison officer sighed, came over to the trolley and unfastened the handcuffs.

'Thank you,' said the young doctor. 'A suspected heart attack, you say?'

The officer nodded. 'About six this morning. He complained about not being able to breathe, and pains in his chest and arms. He was still conscious when we got to him but then he collapsed.'

The doctor and the nurse wired their patient to the monitors and the doctor listened for a heartbeat.

'This doesn't look like a heart attack to me. Although he's enormously hypertensive and there's serious arrhythmia and bradycardia.'

The prison officer shrugged.

'It means his blood pressure is through the roof and his heart rate is incredibly slow and irregular. He's going to go into arrest if we don't give him the right treatment right away.' Goedecke frowned. It was all consistent with the acromegaly: arrhythmia and cardiac failure were a common cause of death with sufferers; but Goedecke's instincts as a doctor told him something didn't quite fit. 'Is there any way your prisoner could have had access to drugs like ketamine or xylazine?'

'Not that I know of,' said the prison officer. 'It's always possible, of course, but he's in high security and his cell is turned over regularly.' He nodded towards the prone giant on the trolley. 'As soon as he starts to come to, we get the cuffs back on. Like I said, this is one very dangerous character.'

'*If* he comes to, which is doubtful.' The young emergency doctor turned to the nurse and had just started to give instructions when the alarm on the heart monitor started to sound.

'He's going V-fib . . .' The doctor started compressions, his flattened hands child-small and slim on the huge barrel of Frankenstein's chest. He frowned as he watched the fluttering trace of ventricular fibrillation on the monitor. His giant patient was within seconds of going asystole. And once he flatlined, there would be no getting him back. 'Take over compressions . . .'

The nurse pushed down on the chest while the doctor charged the defibrillator. He set the charge to 200 joules.

'I'm going to shock him, but I want you to keep compressions going between. If we don't get him started on the second jolt, I want you to prepare three hundred milligrams of amiodarone and adrenalin. Clear!'

The nurse stood back. 'Clear.'

The vast body barely twitched from the jolt of electricity. A spike on the monitor, a moment of normal sinus rhythm, then back to V-fib. Goedecke was losing him. He increased the level to

350 joules and held the paddles out from his body, waiting for the recharge whine to change to the ready signal.

'Is he dead?'

Goedecke ignored the prison officer. 'Clear.'

When the nurse acknowledged and stood back he reapplied the paddles to the huge chest. This time there was more movement as the electricity pulsed through the body. The stone-hewn face remained motionless. Goedecke experienced a moment of inappropriate black humour as he thought of the irony of a physician trying to bring a monster like this to life with jolts of electricity. Perhaps there was already an angry mob of torch-wielding villagers surrounding the hospital.

When he checked the monitor, he saw a moment of heart rate turbulence, then, after what seemed an age, the restoration of normal sinus rhythm. He told the nurse to set up an intravenous drip to start delivery of 500 milligrams of adrenalin as well as getting some beta-blockers into the patient's system.

After a while of watching the monitor, Goedecke turned to the prison officer. 'Once he's stabilized, we'll move him to intensive care. He's not out of the woods yet. Far from it.'

'When will he be able to be moved back to the prison hospital wing?'

'Not for a while.' Goedecke went over to the emergency room's wall phone and called the intensive care unit.

There had been dreams. Such strange, dark, frightening, happy, wonderful dreams. He knew instinctively that he had been standing on the threshold that separated the living from the dead. He had turned back from that and now he stood on a second threshold, the one between light and dark, between the dreaming and the awake world. But for a moment he hung there.

From somewhere above and distant, he watched himself. He saw himself as he had been as a boy: quiet, gentle, clever. He watched his twelve-year-old self, standing shirtless and patient, while his mother talked to the old doctor. He had always thought of him as the old doctor, his memory preserving the perspective of a twelve-year-old, but seeing him now, he realized the specialist could only have been in his early fifties. Jochen remembered this visit. He recognized the room. It had been back when he had still been normal, just. Before Jochen Hübner had become Frankenstein.

But the signs had already started.

At the time, Jochen hadn't known why his mother had taken him to the doctor, a specialist in Barmbek, but he had guessed it was something to do with the way he had started to grow faster than the other boys. And he had noticed other changes. His voice had become deeper. Too deep. And his hands and feet had hurt him. They too had started to become too big, too quickly. He had been a clever boy, full of academic promise, but all young Jochen had wanted was to be a footballer, to maybe play for Sankt Pauli one day. But the school coach had told him that, while Jochen was clearly highly skilled, he simply lacked the on-pitch aggression of a winner. And anyway, he had started to become clumsy of late. Uncoordinated.

He watched himself, the doctor, his mother. He knew he had something important to do in the awake world but, for the moment, he was content to watch as the doctor measured his younger self's hands, his feet; the length of his legs. He knew he was watching ghosts: his mother had been dead for a long time and the doctor longer still. But it was nice to see his mother again. To hear her voice.

And it was nice to see himself not a monster.

The dream was gone. There was a light above him, white, hard and sharp. And with it came pain. In his chest, in his arms, in his head.

He felt dizzy and sick and his heart started to race. Something beeped in harmony with his heartbeat.

'They will inject you with epinephrine – adrenalin,' his guardian had told him. 'To regulate your heart rate. It will also help you wake quickly and will make you stronger. You will feel a rush. That is when you have to wake. That's when you have to escape. It all hangs on that.'

Goedecke waited on the phone until he was connected to the admissions office. He arranged for Hübner to be admitted to ICU and for two orderlies to come and assist with the transfer.

'I want to get the handcuffs back on him,' said the prison officer.

Goedecke shook his head. 'There's too much risk of him hurting himself. But we can use medical restraints that will do the same job without risk of injury.' He turned to the nurse. 'Can you dig up some secure restraints?'

When the nurse left the room, the prison officer moved closer to Goedecke.

'There's something you should know about your patient. Something that should go on his notes. He is a danger to women – well, he's a danger to everyone, extremely and unpredictably violent. But the thing you have to be aware of is that he is very specifically a danger to women. An extreme danger. If he's going to spend any time in the hospital we'll need to notify the Polizei Hamburg. I'm sure they'll want to put an armed guard on him to support the JVA prison officers.'

'What did he do?'

'You don't want to know the details, but his victims will never get over what was done to them. Trust me, he looks like a monster for whatever medical reasons, but the fact is he doesn't just look like a monster, he *is* a monster. What's behind the appearance is much worse. We need him to be as secure as possible. In the meantime, we'll go through to intensive care with him. I'll go and tell my colleague.'

The prison officer went out into the hall.

Goedecke, suddenly alone with his unconscious patient, felt distinctly uneasy. He checked the monitor again. Heart rate normal. No arrhythmia. He frowned again. It was too good, too swift a recovery.

Goedecke leaned over to examine his patient, peeling back an eyelid to check pupil dilation.

Both eyes opened.

The young doctor found himself looking directly into the small, black eyes of his patient, glittering cold under the beetling brow. He turned to call the prison guard who was still out in the hall. Or at least he thought about turning to call the prison guard – the body on the trolley moved so fast that he caught Goedecke between decision and commission. Frankenstein's arm shot out and up like a loosed harpoon, the vast hand fastening itself around his neck. The young doctor tried desperately to scream, to shout for help, but no sound came from the squeezed-shut throat.

Frankenstein swung his legs off the trolley and sat up, his hand still clamped around the boy doctor's throat. First casting a look to the double doorway, he leaned the mass of his face into Goedecke's, his small dark eyes locked on the young man's.

'This is your decision,' he hissed, his voice quiet but still resonant. 'This could be your time – the place and the time you die. Is that what you want?'

Goedecke tried to shake his head but could only manage tiny movements. His eyes pleaded for his life.

'If you make a sound,' said Frankenstein, 'then I will snap your neck. I either leave here free, or everyone dies. Everyone.'

He let go of Goedecke's neck. The young man backed away until he came to rest against the hip-high wall unit in the corner of the emergency room.

'Is there another way out of here?' Frankenstein asked, tearing off the monitor pads from his chest and the IV drip from his arm.

Goedecke shook his head, his eyes filled with the terror that the wrong answer would cost him his life.

'Stay.' Frankenstein pointed a huge finger. He was still wearing his sweatpants and he grabbed the white plastic bag that hung at the bottom of the trolley. He took out his T-shirt and sweatshirt, but both had been cut through to get them off his unconscious body. He scanned the room: there would be nothing he could steal that would fit him. He saw some blue surgical scrubs hanging by the door. He grabbed the top and pulled it over his head, but, even though it was sized extra-large and was meant to be a baggy fit, he couldn't wriggle into it.

He would have to go bare-chested. Frankenstein was not the kind of figure to go unnoticed at the best of times, but stripped to the waist he would draw the attention of anyone who so much as glanced at him. He needed to get out as quickly as possible. His guardian had predicted that he'd be taken to the emergency department of the Klinik Nord. Three, maybe four doors and he would be outside the hospital. A 100 metre sprint and he'd be out onto Tangstedter Landstrasse. He just hoped that his guardian would be there, waiting, like he'd promised.

But there were still the JVA prison guards. And one would be back in the room at any moment.

Frankenstein turned back to Goedecke, who still cowered in the corner.

'I'm going now,' he said. 'I may kill people to get away. If I find out that you raised the alarm after I left, I'll hunt you down and kill you slowly. You understand?'

The shaking Goedecke nodded dumbly, nursing his bruised throat.

Frankenstein looked around the emergency room for something, anything, he could use as a weapon. He went over to a metal tray that sat on the unit by the window. The scalpels looked ridiculously small in his huge hands.

The door swung open. Frankenstein lunged forward, expecting it to be the prison officer, but it was the nurse returning. She was tall and blonde, about thirty, her pale blue eyes wide with terror as she stared at Frankenstein. She had padded leather restraints in her hands but let them fall.

He didn't check his momentum but closed the gap before the nurse could scream. The fear. The sweet fear in her eyes. He grabbed her, looping an arm around the small of her back and pulling her into him, his other hand clamping her mouth. He stared into her eyes, now glossed with tears and terror. He held her for a moment, savouring her fear, feeling himself grow hard against her. She felt him and the terror in her eyes deepened. He laughed.

He pushed her away and held her at arm's length, his hand still clamped over her mouth. There would be time enough for that. Time enough for them all, later. He raised his other fist, drawing it back. She would go out like a light, but she'd be haunted by this moment, maybe for the rest of her life. It would be a memory he could leave her with. Frankenstein paused, his fist poised ready to smash into the young woman's face. He turned to Goedecke and smiled.

There was shouting.

Frankenstein turned to see two shaven-headed men in JVA

prison officer uniforms. One could only have been about 175 centimetres tall, the other 190, but both were solidly built. The first officer through the door was the smaller of the two and Frankenstein threw the nurse at him as if she had been a doll. Without rushing, he walked forward, shoved the nurse to one side and grabbed the prison officer's head, holding it between his hands. The officer screamed as Frankenstein stabbed his thumbs deep into his eyes before slamming the back of his head against the wall. The second officer was on him now, trying to prise him away from his colleague. Frankenstein let the first officer drop and slammed his elbow into the mouth of the second. He felt the grinding of teeth breaking and the wetness of blood on his elbow and he spun around to seize the prison officer by the throat, pinioning him against the wall and slamming his free fist over and over into the blood-smeared face.

Now. He had to move now.

Frankenstein reckoned that neither officer was capable of giving chase, and the doctor and nurse were frozen by their terror, so he made his break. He rushed out into the corridor, which was luckily empty of people, and started towards the main hallway that led to the exit. As soon as he appeared in the hallway, a dozen heads turned in his direction. He ignored them and bustled towards the exit, knocking over two people.

A cop.

Frankenstein saw the blue uniform with the red and white Hamburger Tor shield on the upper arm. He avoided eye contact but could see the officer get up as he approached.

He kept his eyes locked on the doors, but as he drew near, the police officer stepped into his path. Frankenstein snapped his gaze into the cop's. He could see the uncertainty in the policeman's eyes, and the fear. Frankenstein was shirtless and shoeless.

And he was what he was. The cop was not to know what had happened in the emergency room, but Frankenstein would look just wrong to him. He looked wrong to the world.

He saw him look at his sweatpants. Prison blue. Unlike the JVA prison guards, the police officer had a pistol on his hip. He would have to be dealt with. Getting the gun from him would be too troublesome: he knew from experience that Hamburg police holsters had an anti-snatch design, allowing only the wearer to draw the weapon.

Frankenstein shifted course by a fraction of a degree. And headed directly for the cop.

'You're in the right place.' He smiled, his teeth small and gappy in the huge mouth. He saw the policeman's hand drift to his hip and he slashed downwards with the edge of his huge hand. His target had been the cop's throat but he missed and the blade of his hand smashed into his chin and jaw. The force threw the officer sideways and his shoulder hit the wall, bouncing him off it and back into Frankenstein's hands. He could hear screams from behind him, near the admissions desk. He held the police officer by the elbows, pinioning his arms to his body and denying him the opportunity to draw his weapon. The side of his jaw was already swelling and his mouth looked twisted. Frankenstein realized he had dislocated his jaw and grinned.

The cop was stunned, eyes unfocused. That was no good. He had to know. He had to feel everything. Frankenstein shook him violently and his head wobbled for a moment before he locked his eyes once more with his attacker's.

'You're in the right place, I told you that. You're going to need a lot of treatment.' Frankenstein smiled again. As if he were swinging some stone war club, he tilted his Easter Island head back before ramming it forward, full force, slamming his massive brow into the policeman's face. He heard bone crack, felt something solid yield beneath his forehead. The screaming behind him increased. He let the policeman drop onto the polished hospital floor, bleeding heavily from his nose and mouth, making a low, half-gargled moaning sound. Frankenstein had to be sure the cop couldn't draw his weapon when he had his back to him. Drawing his right knee up, he stamped down twice, his heel finding its target of the policeman's temple. The moaning stopped. All movement stopped.

Frankenstein left him lying and ran for the door, people scattering as he burst out into the open.

The air was cool and fresh like water on his skin. He ran as fast as his huge bulk would allow. An ambulance was parked and a man in a red and white emergency service parka looked like he was going to challenge him, so Frankenstein barged into him, knocking him to the ground and stamping on his face with the heel of his shoeless foot.

There was a large arch that had been the main entrance to the hospital compound when it had first been built. Frankenstein knew there was no point in slowing to a walk – nothing he could do was going to make him inconspicuous, so he ran through the arch and out onto the main road.

Tangstedter Landstrasse was too busy a thoroughfare for the pick-up, his guardian had told him. Ignoring the traffic, he ran straight across the road, a car screeching to a halt and narrowly missing him. The other side of the road offered the cover of a screen of trees and once behind them he ran parallel to the road before cutting up past some high-rise apartment blocks.

Behind the apartments, just as he had been told, was a residential area with houses lined along cul-de-sacs. The end of the third cul-de-sac was Frankenstein's goal.

'Look for a white panel van,' his guardian had told him. 'It will have a small black and red FC Sankt Pauli sticker on the rear door. It will be unlocked. Get straight in the back and shut the door behind you. But *do not* get in if anyone can see you. The street has to be clear.'

'What if they don't take me to the Klinik Nord?' Frankenstein had asked.

'Then you'll be dead,' his guardian had said.

The van was there, just as his guardian had promised it would be. Frankenstein was approaching it from the grassed area and would not be seen from the houses. He opened the back door of the van, climbed in and dropped with a resonating metallic thud onto the floor.

'Are you okay?' A voice came from the front of the van. Frankenstein nodded.

'Any problems?' the guardian asked.

'A cop. Had to deal with a cop. He could be dead.'

'But no one's following you now?'

'No. But they'll be looking soon. They'll come soon.'

'Then we had better go.'

In the driver's seat, Zombie checked the side mirrors for any sign of the police. When there was none, he started the engine and drove off at a relaxed pace. As he did so, he smiled.

Now. Now, he had his Golem.

26

The van had been stopped for several minutes before the back door opened and Zombie pulled back the tarpaulin Frankenstein had used to hide himself. Frankenstein felt sick and his head pulsed with the most intense headache he had ever experienced.

'It's okay, everything's clear,' said Zombie. 'But get into the house as quickly as possible and wait for me. I'll park the van at the back and out of sight.'

Seeing him again, and in the context of the outside world for the first time, Hübner was struck by Zombie's appearance. In the prison, Herr Mensing – as Frankenstein had then known Zombie – had always worn the same clothes: a white shirt, the too-big collar of which sat like a tie-fastened yoke around the stick of a neck, a blue pullover and grey slacks. The outfit always looked like it had been hung over the back of an unupholstered chair rather than worn on a body. Every time Frankenstein had had a session with him, he had noticed how bird-frail and pale the social therapist looked. To start with, Frankenstein had assumed he was terribly sick, cancer, most likely. But that, he came to realize, was not the ill that ate away at Mensing. The other thing that had struck Hübner was that despite the fact he could have so easily and so quickly crushed the life out of Herr

Mensing, there had never been the slightest hint of fear in the social therapist's eyes.

Here, outside the prison and dressed in a black parka, jeans and a T-shirt, Zombie looked even smaller, frailer, paler. Between them, Frankenstein realized, they were about the easiest couple of travelling companions for witnesses to take note of and remember.

So Hübner did as he was told, but as he hurried to the door of the old house, he took in as much of his surroundings as he could. It was all still new and fresh to him: the world without bounds, without walls, gates and locks and he wanted to drink it in. Here, though, it had a bitter taste: the forest seemed to hem them in and crowd in on the house, which itself was old and looked somewhere between a home and a municipal building. All the window shutters had been closed and the house looked grey, dark, unwelcoming. There was a small portico around a heavy, traditional herringbone-pattern wooden door. It was unlocked and yielded to Frankenstein's touch. He stepped into a dark hallway that was empty of furniture, the floor grey with a patina of dust and what looked like rat or mouse droppings. A heavy-banistered wooden stairway led up into the shadows of the upper floors. He leaned a naked shoulder against the banister and breathed slowly to try to ease the thumping in his head and a profound swell of nausea.

'What is this place?' he asked when Zombie returned from parking the van in the rear courtyard.

'Somewhere safe, where no one will look for you.'

'But I mean, what *was* this place?' Frankenstein's voice resonated deep and dark in the empty hall.

'It was the old forester's house. It was owned by the City Parks Department, but they sold it off. My uncle bought it – he was the last forester to live here and the city let him have it at a knock-down price.'

'So where is he? Your uncle?' Frankenstein's nausea swelled again.

'Dead. He left me the house. Follow me . . .'

He led Frankenstein to the back of the hall and unlocked a door. Beyond it stairs descended to a cellar. Zombie started down but Hübner stopped dead, swaying slightly.

'Wait . . . I need a toilet,' he said between controlled breaths.

'Behind you . . .' Zombie nodded toward another door off the hallway. Frankenstein only just made it, dropping to his knees in front of the toilet bowl. His massive body convulsed as he vomited, voiding everything in his gut, then retching several times more.

When he came back out into the hallway, his massive face was as bleached of colour as his guardian's.

'It's the after-effects of the drugs, the adrenalin and the shock,' explained Zombie. 'It'll pass. The xylazine in your system should help, it's actually also used as a nausea suppressant and anti-emetic. Drink this.' He handed Zombie a bottle of water. 'And follow me down into the cellar.'

The strange thing about it was that Frankenstein could see that Zombie had made an effort to make the cellar as comfortable as possible for him. There was a large box filled with provisions, plastic-wrapped blocks of bottles of water and two cool-boxes. The bed was two mattresses dressed in clean, new-looking bed linen. Next to the bed was a pile of paperbacks, some pornographic magazines and two cartons of cigarettes. In one corner sat another box with batteries, toilet roll, and toiletries; in the other sat the cool-boxes. Hübner's inspection revealed that one cool-box was filled with cartons of fruit juice, and smiled when he saw the other contained enough beer for him to relax with, not enough for him to get drunk. This was carefully calculated hospitality.

There were clothes neatly folded on the bed: a pair of jeans, four shirts, two sweaters as well as underwear and socks, still in their plastic store packets. A huge pair of boots sat in front of the bed.

'I got all of this stuff on the internet,' explained Zombie. 'I didn't want to arouse suspicion by going in person into a store where it would be obvious they weren't for me. I hope everything fits.'

Frankenstein nodded. 'Thanks.'

Zombie ran through the house rules. Like everything he had asked of Frankenstein, they were requests, not demands, but he had made it very clear that every rule was there to prevent Frankenstein's recapture and the consequent collapse of Zombie's plans.

With a whole house lying empty, Frankenstein did not understand why he insisted he spend almost all of his time in the cellar. But that was the way Zombie wanted it, so he complied. It was a new experience for Hübner: to have someone whom he respected, whose bidding he was happy to do. Zombie had explained to him that once he had done what he asked of him, he would be given his turn to wreak revenge on those who had wronged him. Zombie would do everything he could to help him but, he had explained, he might not be able to as the police would probably have him by that time.

'You should be comfortable,' said Zombie. 'It's only temporary, but necessary. No one will find you here and without any sightings of you, the police will assume you have escaped the city, perhaps even Germany. The most important thing is that you stay out of sight. Only go up to the hall when you need to use the toilet and even then you'll need to check there's no one walking nearby. This house is supposed to be unoccupied. Dark and silent.'

'I've got it,' said Frankenstein. Then, after a moment: 'They will question you about the escape, you know that, don't you?'

'Yes, I know that. I'm prepared for it. They'll question any of the staff at the prison who had regular contact with you. Because I was only there two days a week, it'll take some time before they get to me.'

'And what you've said you want to do – you understand you won't get away with it. They'll catch you, eventually. You know that too, don't you?'

'I know they will,' said Zombie. 'In fact that's what I'm counting on.'

Part Two

Part Two

27

She had been found. After all these years, she had been found. The thought had haunted him every day and every night since the news had dropped into his world, shattering it. And, tonight, it had echoed its way through a bottle and a half of red wine and an empty stomach.

Detlev Traxinger drank alone. His partner and business manager Anja Koetzing had left for the evening, having gone through the coming week's viewings and arrangements for the new exhibition at the end of the month. All through the briefing, Traxinger had sat there nodding, taking in nothing, agreeing to everything. All he could think about was the fact that they had found her, after fifteen years.

After Anja had left him alone in the studio, he had opened up the wine and assiduously applied himself to the task of getting as seriously drunk as possible as quickly as possible. Now, Traxinger stood in the centre of his vast studio, converted from an old machine works, and felt more alone than he had ever felt, even during the last fifteen years. He stood and drank, willing himself into a drunken oblivion where he might, just might, be able to stop thinking of her.

They had found her.

He put the glass down and looked at his hands. They were

farm labourer's hands: big, thick-fingered, clumsy. Not the hands of an artist. It had been God's joke – God or Fate or Genetics or Nature – to give him the eye and soul of an artist and the ham fists and sausage fingers of a farm labourer. And now, even though he was only forty-one, years of drinking and drug-taking had added an old-man tremor to the clumsy hands.

What he saw in his artist's mind, the farmworker's hands failed to execute. It wasn't as if the art he generated was bad, and it certainly had attracted both a following and a handsome income; it was just that it never quite matched the perfection of image he had in his mind.

Traxinger looked up from his hands and stared out through the floor-to-ceiling windows of the converted factory, out over the water of the Elbe that glistened like wet oil paints in the early evening light. A ship drifted by: a dark silhouette against the curtain of a deepening sky. Without seeing it, he watched it slide past and finished the glass of wine in two deep draughts. He was somewhere else, his mind removed from the present. A dark place of broken stones; that night, fifteen years before.

They had found her.

He refilled the drained glass, emptying the bottle and opening a new one, preparing for a continuous drift into drunkenness. He left the freshly opened bottle sitting on the studio table, next to carefully arranged paints, linseed and turpentine, and taking the refilled glass with him, made his way through the studio, the entrance hall and the exhibition space. When he reached the storeroom, he unlocked the door, reached in and switched on the lights. Canvases were arranged in double-height, slide-out storage racks. So much work. And so much of that work would never be seen by anyone else. He didn't even let Anja Koetzing come in here alone.

He made his way to the far end of the storeroom, past the rows of work that would eventually be displayed, to the last ranks – the work that would never be displayed.

Setting his wine glass down on the concrete floor, he reached up to the rack on his left, to the canvas stored at the very back, and pulled it out. He tugged at the sheet covering it and it slid free.

She gazed down at him. Beautiful, cold, cruel, magnificent. It had been the best painting he had done of her, and it caught so much of her essence, but again the thick-fingered farmer's hands had let down the perfect vision, the complete and faithful recollection of her that lived in his head.

His secret, hidden muse. His goddess.

She stared down at him from the canvas, silently mocking the emptiness of the last fifteen years of his life. He reached up to the rack opposite, pulled out a second canvas, and the two pictures sat side by side but a universe apart. The second painting was his self-portrait. His hands hadn't failed him here: a perfect reflection of hidden stains, marks and scars. His corruption, his venality and the wastefulness of fifteen empty but soiled years returned his gaze with rheumy eyes.

Traxinger sat down next to his wine glass on the concrete floor and stared at the side-by-side portraits. He started to cry.

After a while, when his tears and his wine glass had both been drained, he pushed the paintings back into place, locked the storeroom and made his way back through to his studio. It was the only place in his life that had any order, an island of organized thought in an ocean of chaos. But tonight, he would break a rule and get drunk there and sleep on the dust-sheet-draped couch.

He refilled his glass to the brim and again drained it as if drinking water. The extra alcohol hitting his system muted the feeling that there had been an odd aftertaste, despite it being the same wine as the last bottle.

He heard a noise behind him.

28

Birgit Taubitz watched him sleep. The bastard even did that handsomely. She had met Tobias Albrecht at a Hamburg Senate official dinner, held in the restaurant in the cellar of City Hall. The second she saw him, she loathed him; she also wanted him with a hunger she hadn't known before. He had been polite, charming and respectful, but she had seen the same hunger, and the same loathing, in his eyes when he looked at her. Two of a kind.

Tobias was the kind of man that had never known a woman to turn him down, much in the same way that Birgit was the kind of woman who could make a near slave of any man she chose. There were other men more handsome, and other women more beautiful, but they both, in very different ways, had something extra in their looks: a classical, dark wickedness that the good were invariably drawn to. But they had been drawn to each other, and it was the kind of volatile, unstable but delicious chemistry they both knew could not last and would probably end very badly. And it was that very danger that added to the intensity of their lovemaking.

Birgit had been married to Uwe Taubitz for ten years. She had seen in him the kind of bland, generic appeal that Germans liked in their politicians. To start with, she had seen Taubitz as a potential Chancellor, and he had become Hamburg's Principal Mayor at only forty-three, but it soon became clear that his political ambitions extended no further than Hamburg's city limits. Some blandness, it appeared, was more than skin deep.

Tobias, on the other hand, was the type of man she had always kept at arm's length. There was nothing bland about him: he was egotistical, arrogant, and probably genuinely bad. His jet-black hair with its widow's peak, his aquiline, predatory good looks and his tall lean frame had defined him: his conceit was at times astounding and as she got to know him, as much as anyone could get to know Tobias Albrecht, she realized he had styled himself as some kind of latter-day Byron. Self-consciously, deliberately and occasionally tediously wicked.

But he was also the best lover she had ever had.

She had been sleeping with Albrecht for eighteen months, their relationship carnal: purely, simply, deliciously carnal. There was never any talk of Birgit leaving her husband for Tobias; such ideas would be ridiculous, if they ever were to occur to either of them at all. Theirs was a relationship that had no future. It was about their bodies, their youth and their sexual vigour. There was no talk of love. There would be no growing old together. No companionship.

As Hamburg's principal Bürgermeister, Uwe Taubitz's social duties were onerous, a burden often shared with his wife, but there were innumerable media events, dinners, openings, presentations and ceremonies that he attended alone, meaning she had all the opportunities she wanted to meet with Tobias. It sorrowed her – though not often and not much – when she thought of her husband's genuine distress that he had to spend so much time apart from her.

Birgit slipped out of the bed and went over to the window.

Albrecht's apartment was a penthouse in a building he had designed himself. The building was only eight storeys high: Hamburg was a largely low-rise city, regulations prohibited anything near the city centre that would dominate the spires of the four churches, the Nikolai ruin and the city hall, which everyone used as landmarks to navigate by. However, Albrecht's penthouse had a commanding view across the waters of the Elbe. The architecture and the interior design of the apartment were a perfect reflection of its designer: it was impeccably tasteful, cool, sophisticated and informed by all the right cultural influences. And, ultimately, it was soulless: as empty of any sense of being a home as Tobias was empty of any sense of being a real human being.

The living space, kitchen and dining area were all open plan, but the ceiling was double height. Original pieces of art were strategically positioned to work with the architecture and emphasize geometries, rather than for their own merit. There was one discordant note, though: the only truly personal touch that didn't fit with the colour scheme or style theme of the apartment: a painting that looked completely out of place.

It was both well-executed and vulgar; combining a modern use of colour with a heavily Gothic reference. On first sight, the painting looked to Birgit like the kind of artwork death-metal bands would use for album covers – and totally out of keeping with Tobias's taste. She recognized the artist as Detlev Traxinger, confirmed by the monogram 'DT' at the bottom of the canvas. It was a life-size nude of a woman standing in a graveyard, her pale, moonlit body framed by writhing ivy and acanthus – more than framed, Birgit realized; it was as if the dark, glossy vines and leaves were seeking to envelop her, to claim her pale flesh and pull it back into the earth. The woman in the painting possessed great beauty, but a cruel, frightening, commanding beauty – a more perfect beauty than Birgit's. There was something about the figure that made Birgit think it had more than a little to do with death.

But that wasn't what troubled her most. The thing that had drawn Birgit's attention to the picture was the woman's hair: a blaze of rich, thick, auburn-red hair. Hair exactly like Birgit's own.

She now stood in the dark, naked at the window, looking out over the river and wondering if Tobias had only singled her out for his attentions because she reminded him of some other redhead in his past, maybe someone he had had real feelings for, or just some flame-headed ideal which she could never live up to. She would end it. She would end it soon, she lied to herself.

'Are you all right?' Tobias's voice from behind her was still laden with sleep but empty of concern.

'I'd better go,' she said without turning.

'I thought you could stay all night.'

'I'd better get back. You go back to sleep, I'll get a taxi.'

'No, it's okay, I'll run you back.'

Birgit Taubitz nodded wordlessly. They had a cladestine routine: taking the private elevator down to the garage avoided her walking out through the foyer and past the concierge, who might recognize her. She went through to the bathroom and dressed, pushing her auburn-red hair back into order as she looked at her reflection in the mirror.

She repeated the silent lie to herself: she would end it soon.

29

Jochen Hübner's escape was splashed all over the media. Despite the risk of panic, it was the most obvious strategy for getting him back behind bars as soon as possible: his physical appearance was so remarkable that it was the best available tool in recapturing him. Generally, it was difficult for any escaped prisoner to remain at large without detection, but when it was someone as easily identifiable as Hübner, getting his photograph and description into as many places as possible was essential. In addition to his massive, brooding features glaring menacingly from every newspaper, TV, computer and tablet screen, the Polizei Hamburg had run off a thousand wanted posters for display in shop windows across the city.

The police Presidium had also taken the precaution of issuing a very specific warning about the particular danger Hübner represented to women. Again it was a calculated move: on one hand it would spread alarm, perhaps disproportionate alarm, on the other hand it would increase vigilance and that might just save another woman from the kind of ordeal Hübner's previous victims had endured.

Everyone in Hamburg would now be on the lookout for Frankenstein, not least every woman who had to walk down an empty street or turn a dark corner.

But no one had seen him. Not a single authenticated sighting since his escape. There had, of course, been a dozen false alarms: a jumpy Hamburg saw a hulking menace hidden in every shadow, around every street corner. But the fact remained that Jochen 'Frankenstein' Hübner had simply disappeared.

A force-wide briefing was given, but Fabel had also gone through the significance of the giant's escape with his team. Beyond the Presidium's windows, the sky had turned to slate and brisk wind drove globes of viscous rain against the glass. As Fabel ran through the information about Hübner's escape, the massive, rough-hewn face of the serial rapist glowered out from a prison identification photograph. The inappropriate thought occurred to Fabel that all they needed was the brooding weather outside to deliver a few flashes of thunder and lightning for the sake of effect.

'This,' he said in conclusion, 'is a bad, bad bastard. He might just become our property if the young officer he attacked doesn't make it.'

'What's the news on him?' asked Nicola Brüggemann.

'He's in a medically induced coma,' said Fabel. 'There's a chance he's going to die, in which case Hübner becomes our meat, and an even greater chance that if he does come out of the coma, he'll be permanently brain-damaged. Added to that we have four other people injured and traumatized. Hübner will kill without thought to stay on the loose, and may start hunting women for sport at any time. We have to get him back into custody. Whatever else you're doing, whatever the inquiry, I want you to flash his face and description to everyone you meet. We desperately need sightings, and so far there hasn't been a single one.'

After the briefing, he called Nicola Brüggemann and Anna Wolff into his office.

'This is quite a coincidence,' he explained. 'And if you know me you'll know—'

'You don't like coincidences,' they said in unison and exchanged a grin.

'I guess I've said that before,' Fabel said. 'But I don't. At least not coincidences like this. After fifteen years, we find Monika Krone's body. Then, soon after, the chief suspect in her murder makes a carefully planned and orchestrated escape from Santa Fu prison.'

'I thought you didn't like Hübner for the Krone murder?' asked Anna.

'I didn't.' Fabel frowned. 'I still don't. But I could be wrong – and I can't ignore the potential significance of this.'

'But as you say,' said Nicola Brüggemann, 'it looks like this was a carefully planned and orchestrated escape. Could Frankenstein have had enough time to plan and prepare for it in the time between the body being discovered and the escape?'

'I just don't know,' said Fabel. 'But even if Hübner didn't kill Monika Krone, he's escaped and on the loose. Like every other department in the Polizei Hamburg we've got to be on the look-out for him. More than every other department, we have got to hunt him down as a potential serial killer. Before he was caught fourteen years ago, the Sexual Crimes Commission evaluated Hübner as ready to escalate to killing his victims. We've got to make sure that he doesn't get the chance.'

'Do you think he will?' asked Nicola Brüggemann.

'Actually, I doubt it. Hübner told me that he didn't want his victims to die, that that would defeat the point of the exercise. He gets off knowing that they will suffer psychological torment for the rest of their lives. Killing them would be cutting that short.'

For a moment, both Brüggemann and Anna, who had in their careers both seen as dark a side to the human condition as it was possible to see, looked taken aback.

'I hope we get to him first,' said Anna eventually.

Fabel's desk phone rang.

If there was anything in his job Fabel truly hated, it was the VIP murder. He had never understood why celebrity suddenly made murder sexy in the eyes of the media. Fabel's approach to his job had always been very straightforward: the dead deserved equal attention, equal justice, whatever their status in life had been. It was a view he knew was shared by the Polizei Hamburg as a whole, but there was no denying the extra pressure brought on the fifth-floor Presidial suite by an intrusive press if the victim had been well known.

It was a damp, grey Tuesday, the kind of monochrome day Fabel hated because it brought back bad memories of a different season and a different year. The call would not have come in when it did and the sudden death of the painter in his waterside studio would have gone unrecognized as a murder until the autopsy, had it not been for the sharp eyes of a female uniform who had clearly taken her scenes-of-crime training more seriously than most.

Detlev Traxinger's studio and gallery was down by the docks, across the Neue Elbbrücke bridge, looking back across at the city. This was a part of the riverfront still dedicated to industry, heavy and light, and the bright sky was pierced by the up-reaching latticed arms of cranes. It was a resolutely, self-consciously industrial location for Traxinger to have chosen: his declaration of painter as artisan, as manufacturer of art.

Fabel decided to assign the case to Thomas Glasmacher and Dirk Hechtner, but drove down to the scene with them. He also called the Presidium's Press Division and gave what details he could. Detlev Traxinger, it appeared, was a Hamburg artist of some importance and Fabel knew that, before long, the press would be all over the case.

But as he drove with Glasmacher and Hechtner, there was something else troubling Fabel: a vague feeling that he had heard of Detlev Traxinger, but not as an artist; in a completely different context. He parked in the large square of asphalt in front of the building, next to the clutch of marked police vehicles.

'Very post-industrial,' said Fabel as he entered the studio with Glasmacher and Hechtner.

Despite the large size and airiness of the studio, the air seemed fumed with the rich, oily odours of paint and turpentine. Fabel found it a strangely appealing smell. The studio was a vast space and Fabel reckoned it had once been some kind of machine hall. The art of engineering had obviously needed just as copious amounts of light as the art of painting, it would have seemed, and the wall facing the Elbe was almost completely glazed: a web of modernist steel-mullioned windows and transoms holding vast sheets of glass in place. Above them the roof was tented with steel-boned skylights and the light inside the building felt more like outdoor light. Like so much commercial architecture in Hamburg, the converted factory had been the kind of self-consciously modernist cathedral to industry that had sprung up in the fifties, filling the spaces razed by British firebombs. It had been Hamburg's typically restrained expression of West Germany's post-war *Wirtschaftwunder* commercial and industrial boom. Even that bright new life, however, had passed and buildings like this were now being demolished to make way for glitzy palaces of sunrise technologies and global trade.

But the rejuvenation and gentrification of the shorefront and the gleaming futurism of the HafenCity development were yet to finger their way this far and the old factory had survived. It made, Fabel thought, a fine and impressive artist's studio.

The studio was one of two halves to the building, divided by the double-height entrance hall. The other half of the building was given over to an informal gallery. Before leaving the Presidium, Fabel had been told that Traxinger had a manager who occasionally arranged private viewings of his work there for clients who felt it too crudely mercantile to bid for art in auction halls or buy it off the wall of a public gallery. The side of the building now entered was Traxinger's painting and sculpture studio. It was there that the forty-one-year-old artist had been found lying dead.

Everything in the studio other than the grey concrete floor was white: the walls whitewashed and the wooden shelves holding materials recently painted, making the various colourful, easel-mounted canvases stand out in vivid contrast. From what Fabel could see, Traxinger had several works in progress on the go at the same time, each at a different stage of development. There was only one completed and framed painting in the studio. And Detlev Traxinger's body lay in front of it.

Fabel's first impression when seeing the body was that it would have been very easy to believe the artist had simply fallen down drunk. Detlev Traxinger was lying on his back at the foot of the huge canvas, eyes closed, one arm flung out wide, the other resting on his belly. A wine glass lay shattered where it had dropped from the outstretched hand and the spilled wine had stained the concrete floor black-red. Ironically, the most conspicuous thing about the scene was the painting standing tombstone-like at his head. It was so striking it drew Fabel's attention away from the body: it was a life-size portrait of a grotesque, deformed, withered old man who stared out malevolently from the canvas. It wasn't just the disturbing subject of the painting that caught his eye, but the artist's style, which looked vaguely familiar.

He snapped his focus back to the body. Traxinger was a large man: tall and heavily built, his mousy hair unfashionably long. As Fabel knelt down beside the body, he could see the artist must have had in life the fleshy bacchanal presence of someone of lusty appetites. Despite his relative youth, Traxinger's physical appearance, added to the lack of any obvious signs of violence on the body or at the scene, could easily lead to the conclusion that he had simply died of a heart attack.

But when Fabel looked closer, very close, he could see a small stain, slightly darker than the artist's dark red shirt, just above the heart.

'Who was it that spotted this and called us in?' he asked.

'I did . . .' A small, homely woman in uniform with dark hair and with the rank markings of a probationary commissar stepped forward.

'Your name?'

'Petra Moser, Herr Principal Chief Commissar.'

'This is very good work, Frau Moser. Did you spot anything else?'

Petra Moser smiled and crouched beside the body, Fabel doing the same. With a latex-gloved finger she eased open the dead man's shirt to expose an ornate, Gothic-styled tattoo on his chest. The letters *D* and *T* intertwined each other and in turn were encircled by an ornate, twisting wreath of leaves and flowers.

'DT . . .' Moser explained. 'His initials. And it's an acanthus plant, by the way.'

'What is?' Fabel frowned.

'The leaves and flowers wreathed around his initials – it's an acanthus plant. The Romans associated it with death.'

'Appropriate . . .'

'But this is what I wanted to show you . . .' She eased his shirt open further and pointed to a small puncture wound about ten centimetres beneath the tattoo. It was perfectly round and no bigger than four millimetres in diameter. There was no more than a smudge of blood around the wound. 'That's the fatal wound, in my opinion. I know it doesn't look like it, but as soon as I saw it, I thought about Empress Sisi.'

Fabel nodded. Glasmacher, who was standing behind him looming bulkily, asked, 'Who?'

'Empress Elisabeth of Austria,' said Fabel. 'She was assassinated by an Italian anarchist who used a sharpened needle-file to stab her. There was practically no blood and it wasn't until she collapsed and died that they realized she'd been stabbed. And before that, back in the Middle Ages, assassins regularly used similar stiletto-type daggers to kill with little trace. It's the same deal here.'

'It looks like it would take skill,' said Glasmacher. 'You'd have to know what you were doing.'

'And you'd have to get close,' said Moser, the uniformed officer. Her enthusiasm made Fabel smile. 'A single strike, right on target, suggests that there was no struggle. And there are no defensive wounds. Whoever the killer was, I think there's a chance Traxinger knew him.'

'Anything else, Frau Moser?' Fabel stood up from the body.

The young uniformed policewoman nodded to the grotesque painting. 'This looks too staged. Like a tableau. As if the killer was making a point.'

'Could be sheer coincidence that he fell here in front of it,' said Dirk Hechtner. Petra Moser moved around to the side of the painting. The frame sat directly on the concrete of the floor, its back resting against a shelving unit.

'This is a completed, varnished and framed painting, the only one in the studio. Everything else here is at different stages of being worked on. There's a drying rack over there, and a finishing table. Once the paintings are varnished and dried, they're moved out of the studio and into the storeroom over in the other side of the building. I'm sure this picture was moved back here recently.' Moser pointed to some white striations on the grey floor. 'See . . . fresh scratch marks on the concrete just here, suggesting it was moved very recently. Added to which this is an expensive frame – when I saw the drag marks, I didn't think Traxinger would be so careless as to just drag it across the floor, so I took a look behind.' She shone a pocket torch onto the floor behind the heavy picture. Fabel came around and saw four or five small, dark drops.

'Well it's not blood,' he said.

'No. It's wine. Splashes from when he dropped his glass. And unless they defied the laws of physics, there's no way they could have got behind the painting unless it was moved here after Traxinger dropped his glass.'

'And dropped dead.' Fabel nodded. 'Again, excellent work, Frau Moser.'

The small uniformed officer beamed.

'So this is some kind of message . . .' Fabel walked back to the front and examined the painting.

'Call me old-fashioned,' said Dirk Hechtner, 'but it's not the kind of thing I'd have up in my dining room. I'm guessing it was some kind of personal statement by the artist.'

'My God,' said Fabel. 'You're right. It is a personal statement . . . Look, it's Traxinger. Just some kind of withered, old, diseased Traxinger.'

'You think . . . ?' asked Glasmacher, clearly dubious.

'No . . . no . . . I see it now,' said Dirk Hechtner, looking from the dead man's face to the painting and back. 'It's him all right. But why on earth would he do a self-portrait like that?'

'*The Picture of Dorian Gray* . . .'

'Come again?' said Hechtner.

'Never mind, just a reference I think he was making,' said Fabel. 'The real question isn't why he painted it, it's why did the killer place this picture here? What's he trying to say?'

Once he was back at the Presidium, Fabel set in train the machinery of investigation. A current case always took priority over a historical one, so Traxinger's murder took precedence over the Monika Krone case. Glasmacher and Hechtner would need to pull in resources. Henk Hermann would be working the old people's home case, such as it was, on his own, but would have access to the new guy, Sven Bruns, whenever he needed an extra pair of hands. There was something about the Traxinger case that troubled Fabel. He couldn't place exactly what it was, but something turned in his gut when he thought of the artist's style of painting. Added to that, Traxinger's name still seemed familiar, but Fabel was convinced it wasn't because he had heard of him as an artist.

Working late in his office, Fabel had an idea that compelled him to go and look at the Monika Krone inquiry board. He was standing staring at it when Anna Wolff came into the Commission.

'I didn't know you were working late tonight, *Chef*,' she said.

Fabel turned. Anna was wearing jeans, a T-shirt and a leather jacket. It cheered him to see her dressed casually: she had taken to more formal outfits for work and this casual outfit, though more expensive and tasteful, reminded him of the punky look she had had when she had first joined his team. Anna had grown, matured, during her time at the Murder Commission.

'What about you?' he asked. 'I didn't think you were rostered for duty tonight.'

'I'm not. I was just on my way home. What's up?'

Fabel looked back at the incident board, then shook his head. 'Nothing. I just had this weird idea that Detlev Traxinger was one of the people at the party the night Monika Krone went missing.'

'And is he?'

'No. I've been through all the names. He isn't there.'

'It would be a hell of a coincidence if he were.'

'If he were, it wouldn't be a coincidence, it would be a connection. But you're right, it doesn't make sense and anyway he's not on the list of names.'

'Well,' said Anna, 'I'll see you tomorrow.'

After Anna left, Fabel looked again for a man who wasn't there on the Monika Krone inquiry board.

'I'm getting too old for this,' he said to himself before turning from the board, grabbing his jacket from the chair back he'd hung it on, and heading for the door.

30

Werner Hensler sat in his car, parked across the street from the bookstore, and stared at his cell phone. Like everything in Hensler's life, the phone was the most expensive you could buy. The car he sat in cost more than many people would pay for a house; and the house he had driven from to come to the bookstore cost more than some people made in a lifetime. These were the things that defined him, that filled what he knew was an otherwise empty life. No wife, no family, no close friends. There were women – there were always women – but Hensler seemed incapable of forming anything more than the most casual relationships.

Maybe that was why he spent more than half his life being someone else: an assumed identity and an assumed life that perhaps offered more hope of connection with others. This was the life he had now.

He stared at the phone. *Do I call or not?*

Despite its flaws, despite the deficits filled by expensive toys and dressings, it had been a good life. Or at least a better life than he had hoped – because in Hensler's past sat a dark mass so dense that it had taken him more than a decade to escape fully from its gravitational pull.

Do I call or not? He had seen the crowds arrive at the bookstore and there was still a queue outside the door, slowly shortening as his fans squeezed into the venue. Werner knew he had to decide, and decide now, whether he was going to call one of the others.

For fifteen years, he had put the past firmly behind him. All that had changed. The darkness from his past had come crashing back into his life, spilling ghosts out into his perfect present.

He continued to stare at the blue screen of his phone, still undecided about his next step. Should he call? If he did, it would be breaking a promise. More than breaking a promise, it would be betraying a solemn oath. They had all sworn that they would have no direct personal contact with each other from that night on. Obviously, there was always the chance that they would encounter each other professionally or socially, and it would probably be unavoidable, but it was agreed any future acquaintance would be by accident, not design. They must never seek each other out. But Detlev was dead. And the papers suggested that his death was suspicious. It had been a month of shocks, starting with the discovery of Monika's body, or what there was left of it after all these years. And then Detlev had been found dead. It couldn't be a coincidence, could it?

Werner liked to tell himself that there hadn't been a day gone by that he hadn't thought of Monika and what had happened that night, but that simply wasn't the truth. The news that her remains had been discovered had shocked him, not least because he hadn't thought of her for a long, long time. He had a new life – a complete and successful existence that was no longer defined by one night of madness fifteen years before. Now, everything that had happened back then had become like a dream, or even a recollection of one of his own stories. Maybe that's why he hadn't thought of it that much over recent years: maybe he, a creator of fiction, had come to believe that it hadn't really happened, that it had been just one more tossed-away bad plot for a horror novel.

But now it had all become so real again.

The screen of his smartphone glowed up at him, the azure bloom like a swimming pool inviting him to dive in. But whom would he phone first? And once contact had been made, then God knew where it would lead.

He checked his watch. He would be late if he didn't go now.

He switched off his phone, got out of the car and crossed the street.

Werner Hensler stepped into the bookshop and stepped into a new identity simultaneously. An attractive young blonde woman wearing a name badge and a welcoming smile was waiting for him, looking a little too relieved to see him arrive. She shook his hand.

'Thank you so much for coming, Herr Edgar. The audience is waiting...'

31

Thom Glasmacher and Dirk Hechtner didn't protest or even seem surprised when Fabel told them that he wanted personally to take the lead on the Traxinger case. They would remain the case team, he explained, and they would work it together with him.

Officially, Fabel was always the senior investigating officer of all homicides, but his role in most was administrative, rather than investigative. The Hamburg Murder Commission's federal-wide reputation had nevertheless been built on Jan Fabel's very special skills as an investigator. Specifically as an investigator of serial murders. And there had been one element, pointed out by Petra Moser, the young Probationary Commissar, that had set alarm bells ringing: Detlev Traxinger's body had been posed – his grotesque self-portrait set like a gravestone at his head. Only two kinds of killers tended to carefully arrange tableaux: suicides and serials. And if one thing was certain, it was that Traxinger's death was no suicide. Of course, a killer was not classed as serial until he had taken three or more lives in separate events, but the posing and the unusual type of weapon troubled Fabel.

It annoyed him that the press would probably assume his direct involvement would be because of the celebrity of the victim.

The first task Fabel had set Thom and Dirk was the usual establishing of the victim's last movements and contacts, as well as building a complete picture of the people in the artist's life. The last person to have seen Traxinger alive was his business manager, Anja Koetzing. He arranged to meet her at Traxinger's studio.

There was still a team of forensics and police at the studio when he arrived. The body long gone, the immediate scene of death fully processed, tagged and photographed, the studio and its surroundings were now being painstakingly searched for evidence. To the rear of the studio they were looking, almost literally, for a needle in a haystack. The initial autopsy reports confirmed what Petra Moser had suggested: that Traxinger had been killed with a 'Empress Sisi' type weapon. So now rows of uniforms were slowly treading their way through the long, reedy grass that separated the studio from the water, looking for a thin-bladed, needle-type weapon. It had to be done, but Fabel's guess was that the killer had either removed the weapon entirely from the locus or had tossed it as far out into the Elbe as possible. Fabel's money was on the former – if this had been the work of an agenda or serial killer, then the unusual form of weapon would suggest they would keep it for future use. Those who set themselves up as craftsmen of death tended to treasure their favoured tools.

Anja Koetzing was small, slender and, Fabel couldn't help noticing, very attractive. He guessed that she was about thirty-five. She had short dark hair and deep hazel eyes and was dressed in a black skirt suit, white blouse fastened at the throat with a too-large, too-ornate Celtic-style brooch, black stockings and flat-heeled shoes. Her monochrome outfit accentuated the crimson of her lipstick and polished nails. It was a look that was at once very conventional and suited to a business environment, yet indistinctly Goth-like. Her polite smile when he introduced himself did not, as he half-expected, reveal unnaturally long or sharp canines. She stood close to Fabel, stepping into his personal space and looking up at him. He could smell a rich, earthy perfume from her. Fabel took a step backwards.

'I wasn't fucking him,' she said in an even tone, her expression empty.

'I beg your pardon?'

'Detlev . . . I wasn't fucking him. And I never did fuck him, ever. That's the first thing I imagine you want to establish, isn't it? My "relationship with the victim"? I was his partner and business manager – nothing more. We saw each other socially, but that was just because there's a social dimension to so much of this business. Detlev was *so* fucking crap at that. I had to hold his hand at functions, exhibitions and stuff like that. I held his hand but never his dick. I think I've made that clear.'

'Perfectly . . .' Fabel gave a small laugh. 'Thanks for that. It was certainly highly informative and very . . .' he searched for the right word, '. . . *succinct*. I have to say, you don't seem very upset or shocked by your client's death, Frau Koetzing.'

'Of course I'm upset.' Koetzing bristled at the suggestion, her expression darkening. 'What a stupid thing to say. I've lost a business partner and a friend – well, a friend of sorts. But anyone who knew Detlev knew he wouldn't live to draw a pension. He was forty—'

'Forty-one,' Fabel corrected her.

'Forty-one . . . but looked at least ten years older, he never took any exercise except the bedroom sort, drank like a fish, chain-smoked, did God knows what drugs, was overweight to the point of obesity and went to bed with any woman who was in awe enough of his supposed *genius* that they'd overlook the fact that he was a fat, ugly bastard. If some jealous husband or thwarted lover didn't kill him then he'd have ended up doing the job himself.' She paused for a moment, as if reflecting on what had happened. 'But, truth be told, I thought it would be the drink that would get him, one way or another. Not this. Not for someone to stab him.'

'I understand. So, from what you're saying, your relationship was very . . . *functional*. Purely business.'

'The truth is I was fond of Detlev in my own way. I believe that like most egotists, he was probably overcompensating for something. Of course I'd never admit this publicly, but he was an artist of very narrow talents, competent – and thankfully fashionable and bankable – but limited. He was just lucky that his talent fell into a spectrum that sold. He was always experimenting with new forms, but all that did was expose his limitations. He made a big deal of being the tortured artist, I think because he knew he was more tradesman than creative genius.'

'Do you have anyone in mind? In the thwarted-lover-jealous-husband category?'

'Nope. Outside day-to-day business or the work-related social stuff I told you about, I avoided seeing him socially. But I'd trip up over the odd conquest or two. He'd fuck them anywhere and everywhere, except here, funnily enough. A bear not shitting where he eats, I suppose. Detlev was oddly fastidious about this place. He has a place up in Blankenese, quite some shack, I believe, but I've never been there. That's where he did most of his *entertaining*.' She arched her fingers in the air to indicate quote marks around the word.

'So how long have you worked for Herr Traxinger?' asked Fabel.

'I didn't work for him, I worked with him. We were partners in the business. You could say he's truly fucked me now, getting himself killed.'

'A fifty-fifty split?'

'Christ no,' said Koetzing. 'I was worth a lot to him – and he wouldn't have sold a tenth of the stuff he did without me – but he was, after all, the "talent", as he never tired of telling me. I got seven per cent of each sale and a salary of sixty thousand euros on top of that. But the finished paintings were the property of the business, not Detlev's.' She suddenly frowned.

'What is it?' asked Fabel.

'Fuck . . . I've got a motive for having killed him. A really good motive at that.'

'Oh . . .' Fabel laughed again. 'And what would that be?'

'I don't know what you're fucking laughing at,' she protested. 'Under our business agreement, I get the whole thing. He had a couple of ex-wives who he didn't want to get a bean if anything happened to him, so we set this all up as a business, a partnership. As I said, we both were paid a salary from it – Detlev's bigger than mine, obviously – but the work produced, the paintings, became capital assets of the business. Detlev is dead, but the business isn't.'

'But, if you don't mind me pointing out, Herr Traxinger won't be producing any more paintings.'

'Exactly. Which means the value of his work will go up enormously. Or at least it will as soon as I can get the fuck in there and start raising the sticker prices. Detlev was a complete screwup in every respect, except as a painter. He may not have been a great talent, but he made the most of the abilities he had. And he was prolific and very fussy. He would only let me sell what he thought were his best paintings. That means there's two hundred, maybe more, canvases in there. The funny thing is a lot of them are his very best work – he had what he called "personal" canvases that he didn't want to sell. He wouldn't even let me see half of them – but a lot of what I did see was really good. Some of it was pure crap, though, like the one they found with his body. I mean, what the fuck was going on with the whole *Picture of Dorian Gray* shite?'

'So that painting had been moved all the way from the storeroom?'

'Yep. That was a canvas Detlev kept very private. I only saw it by chance and he didn't even like me talking about it, but that was mainly because I kept asking him what the hell he'd been on when he'd painted it. That's one painting I won't be selling. The rest definitely. Now Detlev's dead I can clear the lot and get one hundred per cent of the sale price.' She sighed resignedly and held out her wrists. 'Go on, slap the cuffs on me.'

'I'm not quite ready to arrest you yet.' Fabel smiled. He didn't tell her that Glasmacher and Hechtner had already checked and double-checked her account of where she had gone after leaving the studio and her movements for the rest of the night.

'Why don't you put me in handcuffs anyway?' she grinned, taking a step towards Fabel again.

'Could you show me these canvases?' Fabel asked, making his tone businesslike. 'The ones in storage?'

Anja Koetzing let her held-out wrists drop, shrugged and said, 'Sure . . .'

Fabel left Glasmacher and Hechtner talking to the forensics team leader in the studio and followed Anja Koetzing out into the double-height reception hall. Like the studio the walls were whitewashed to maximize the abundant light and to emphasize the intense colours of the large canvases hanging in the reception, illuminated by the huge tent of skylights. Despite the size of the reception hall, even here the rich, oily aroma of paint and turpentine slicked the air.

'Did Herr Traxinger buy the studio?'

'No, it's rented. I always thought it was too far out of town, but he liked it.'

Fabel examined the canvases in the reception hall. Again there was an odd, unpleasant stirring in his gut. Traxinger's style seemed very familiar, but he couldn't work out why. The artist's use of colour was very striking – deep reds and dark greens, velvet blues – and he was clearly accomplished, but Fabel didn't care for Traxinger's work at all. There was an overdone Gothicism to it, making it almost adolescent. He paused in front of one canvas, a scene of the Gothic Revival spire of the Sankt Nikolai church. In the painting, as in reality, the Nikolai was a shattered ruin. The spire was silhouetted blue-black against a fractured sky of umber, orange and deep red. The effect was to make the sky look like the diffuse but still intense glow of a great fire through lozenges of stained glass; the lead between the panels formed by the dark trails of British bombers. It was a clumsily done metaphor and, Fabel thought, bordering on comic-book art.

'How much would this sell for?' he asked Koetzing.

'That one? About a hundred and fifty thousand euros.'

'How much?' Fabel was astounded and leaned closer to the canvas, as if he had missed something in it. 'But it's only about a square metre.'

Koetzing laughed. She moved over beside Fabel to look at the picture. Again she stood too close. 'We don't sell art by the square centimetre, Herr Fabel. This will sell . . .' she waved a dismissive hand at the picture, 'eventually. What a lot of people don't understand about the art business is that the real money is made by selling prints, and that the prohibitive price of original artwork is to allow us to sell limited-edition prints for what seems a reasonably proportionate price. Before this is bought, I will have sold one thousand numbered prints, each at six hundred euros each. The same goes for the rest of the work, so I stand to make a lot of money. Are you sure you don't want to give me the third degree? I'm sure you could break me . . .'

Despite himself, Fabel laughed again.

'Can I see some of the other work?' he asked.

Koetzing led Fabel through the entrance hall and into the other half of the building. She explained that it had in turn been divided into two areas: a spacious, bright gallery and a darkened storeroom, where the canvases not on display were stored. The gallery was a large, square space, again with light coming in from a river-facing wall that was almost all glass and from a row of wide skylights in the roof. The exhibition hall had been turned into a maze of partition walls designed to increase the hanging space available. Fabel, with Anja Koetzing close behind him, walked around the collection, examining each canvas briefly, feeling he was becoming lost in the maze. There seemed little variation, other than in subject matter, in the works. He guessed that Traxinger had found a formula that sold, a 'brand', and had stuck with it.

Fabel felt something leap in his chest as he looked at the painting. He now was right at the centre of the exhibition and, although it was clearly Traxinger's work, there was a distinct difference in the tone of this picture. As he stood gazing at it,

Fabel felt his heart pick up pace and he was transported back somewhere he did not want to be.

The painting was huge; much bigger than the version he had seen in print form. And seeing the full-size original painting, he could see that which a print could never capture. There was a three-dimensionality to the picture: the oil paint had been applied thickly, sometimes layer upon layer, and Fabel guessed that for much of the work Traxinger had used a palette knife rather than a brush. It was a painting that had been built as much as painted.

'Are you all right?' Anja Koetzing had obviously noticed Fabel's startled expression. He didn't answer for a moment, instead staring at the picture.

'It's the same one . . .' he said eventually, stepping closer and examining the signature at the bottom right of the canvas. 'Exactly the same one . . .'

'The same what?'

Fabel made an effort to pull himself together. 'I've seen this painting before.'

'You can't have,' said Koetzing. 'This was one of Detlev's darlings. This is one of the oldest paintings here, done long before I met Detlev. It's never been out on exhibition anywhere other than here. And see . . .' She pointed to a red dot stuck to the wall next to the painting. 'He marked it sold, even though it wasn't, just so no one would pester him with enquiries. But he was proud enough of it – egotistical enough – that he wanted people to see it here in his collection. There's simply no way you could have seen it.'

'Not this,' Fabel said frustratedly. 'Not the original – I saw a print of it.'

'That's not possible either.' Koetzing was emphatic. 'I would know if Detlev had run off any prints.'

'I'm telling you, I saw it.' Fabel raised his voice slightly, then, taking a breath, controlled himself. 'Listen, Frau Koetzing, I know that I saw this painting – *exactly* this painting – in print form. Believe me, it was in a very challenging situation, one I am never likely to forget.' He leaned forward and examined the word written carefully and delicately in white paint at the bottom of the picture. 'I remember that too. *Charon*. To start with I thought it was the artist's signature. Then I realized it referred to the figure in the picture: Charon the boatman. And I thought the river was the Styx. But it's not. It's the Elbe.'

Fabel took out his cell phone and called Anna, telling her that he needed her to come down to Traxinger's studio right away. When he was finished, he turned back to Koetzing.

'Why did Traxinger title this painting *Charon*? All the others have nothing other than his monogram, his initials.'

'I don't know. Like I said before, Detlev experimented with different forms, different themes. He had this thing where he believed his art fell into distinct areas. He didn't do a lot of alternative stuff, mainly because he refused to sell it later, but what he did was all this kind of thing, overlaying classical or Gothic themes on a contemporary Hamburg. I really don't know why he titled this piece or what significance the character Charon had for him.' Koetzing paused for a moment, frowning something back into her recall. 'There was another painting I saw once. Again I wasn't meant to see it because it was a work in progress and Detlev kept those covered up. It was some kind of historical study of a woman, but she was more outline than anything. I remember seeing he had written a title for it at the bottom, but I can't remember what the title was and I never saw the painting again. I guess he scrapped it or painted over it.'

'Do you know if Herr Traxinger ever mentioned someone called Jost Schalthoff?'

Koetzing looked shocked. 'No ... Christ no. Isn't that the creep who killed that little kiddie in Altona?'

'He never mentioned him?'

'No. Of course he didn't. What on earth has Schalthoff got to do with Detlev?'

'That's where I saw the print. On the wall of Schalthoff's apartment. Ever since I first saw Traxinger's paintings I knew they reminded me of something.' He nodded towards the painting. 'That's it. That's what it was.'

'I just don't see—'

'I'd like to see the other paintings,' Fabel said abruptly. 'The ones in the storeroom . . .'

32

The bookstore event lasted longer than he had thought it would. He was grateful that it had, in a way. Being the horror author Alan Edgar for a couple of hours gave him temporary refuge from being Werner Hensler and from the ghosts that haunted that identity.

The reading had gone well. The Q and A session afterwards had been okay too: nothing too demanding, except for one, well-intentioned but irritatingly penetrating question. Werner knew that his writing, just like his Alan Edgar identity, did not possess the depth for close scrutiny.

The Demon's Devices was the latest in the Alan Edgar oeuvre. Like all of his novels, it was set in America, in a fictitious New England town. The last three novels had been about a centuries-old family of vampires who had settled there and who now struggled between their consciences and their thirst for human blood. Werner's opinion of his own work, or more correctly of 'Alan Edgar's' work, was very clear: it was complete and utter crap. And it sold by the bucketload. Hardbacks, paperbacks, audio books – they all flew off the shelves. E-books too – from whatever e-books flew off.

To start with, his readers, when they came to events such as this, were disappointed to find that the American 'Alan Edgar' was really Werner Hensler from just outside Buxtehude; but as time went by his sales and his fan base grew exponentially, making him one of Germany's most popular authors, although his American-set novels under his Anglo-Saxon pseudonym were never published outside the Federal Republic, Austria and German-speaking Switzerland.

The only mildly awkward question from the audience came from a late-middle-aged woman sitting right at the front, which suggested that she had arrived before the others. The manner in which she posed the question too suggested it had been prepared and rehearsed in advance:

'Why is it, do you think, that we as a society seem obsessed with Gothic horror – with the undead, with vampires, boy wizards, werewolves and zombies? And do you think that your writing is a natural continuation of the works of Poe, Shelley, Polidori and Stoker?'

Werner had smiled his best Alan Edgar smile. 'I think as a society we have always been fascinated with the Gothic, even if that hasn't always been the name we have given it. Our oral and folk traditions, through the stories collected by the brothers Grimm, the Gothic greats you mentioned, the marvellous Expressionist films made here in Germany in the twenties and thirties, even into *film noir* and crime fiction, through to the great horror writers of today . . . there is a clear continuum of expression. The truth is that there always has been and always will be a dark side to human nature. We keep that dark side under lock and key, in some shadowed place deep within ourselves. But the truth is that sometimes we like to unlock the door and peer in. That's what Gothic horror is. What it always has been.'

The answer sounded good, as it always did, every time he

used it. The audience actually applauded. The middle-aged poser of the question beamed as if her cast line had hooked a bigger fish than she had hoped.

Alan Edgar smiled back; Werner Hensler screamed deep and silent. *You stupid, stupid old bitch. Do you honestly think the shit I write is comparable to Poe? Do you think Hollywood movies full of cartoon-computer-effects about boy wizards, zombies, and mopey teenage fucking vampires have ANYTHING to do with classic Gothic literature?* He wanted to scream in her face, to spit her own stupidity back at her. Instead, after the applause, he said,

'Very good question, thank you.'

The woman beamed some more.

It was already getting dark by the time Alan Edgar transformed once more into Werner Hensler. The reason the event had taken so long was the number of books laid before him at the signing desk, always a sign of how successful an appearance had been. He had written a special dedication in the three copies of his work presented to him by the stupid bitch who thought Poe could be compared to *anyone* writing contemporary horror fiction, far less himself.

Poe, he had wanted to tell her, had been his god and his devil, his inspiration and his tormentor. In his childhood, Werner had consumed Poe's work over and over again. His discovery, at thirteen, of *The Pit and the Pendulum* had been like striking the earth and it splitting open to reveal a seam of pure gold. In Poe, the young Werner had found a mind that mirrored his: a labyrinth of shadowed corners and sudden, unexpected dark places. In his twenties, Werner had dreamt of becoming the new Poe but had slowly, inexorably, come to realize that he could never be the great man's equal. Not even close. Poe's mind remained an intricate Daedalean labyrinth of bewildering complexity in which one could lose one's sanity; Werner's mind, in comparison, was a simple garden maze.

The day arrived when Werner came face to face with his own mediocrity. And at least he had acknowledged it, then embraced it. His former friend from university, Detlev Traxinger, had been an almost perfect analogue in the world of visual art: a mediocrity with a talent for making money out of his banality. The difference between them, as far as Werner could see, was that Detlev seemed to believe his own propaganda. Mind you, from the outside looking in, maybe people would think the same about Werner. The truth was that every time Werner completed a novel and submitted it to his enthusiastic publishers, he felt as if he had voided his gut. And every now and again, he would reread Poe to remind himself of his own poverty of genius.

The pseudonym had been his revenge.

It was an obvious reference, a clumsy device, for a horror writer to use Poe's first names, albeit in reverse order, as a nom de plume. Poe had, after all, died wearing another man's clothes and using another man's name. It seemed ironically fitting to Werner that he should put Poe's name, at least in part, to his own brand of predictable, shallow horror fiction, while keeping his own, Werner Hensler, unsullied. One day, he had promised himself, one day he would write something worthwhile. And he would write it under his own name.

As he reached his car, thin needles of rain had started to fall. He had just unlocked the car with the remote fob when he was aware of someone behind him. Before he could turn, an arm looped around his throat, holding him firm. There was a sting in his neck and something cold flowed into his veins. He wrestled free from his assailant, who loosened their grip without a struggle.

Werner turned and thought he saw a face he hadn't seen in such a long time, but the world was already darkening. His legs began to give way and firm hands guided him around to the passenger seat, easing him into the car.

He vaguely heard the driver's door shut and the engine kick into life, but these noises already sounded like he was hearing them from some great distance. He felt himself fall into a deep, lightless, total blackness.

His last thought was: *I am falling into the Pit.*

33

The storeroom, unlike the rest of the studio and gallery, was not flooded with natural light. Shutters had been fitted and closed over the window wall facing the river and the skylights were black-shrouded with blinds. In any case, it was beginning to get dark outside so Anja Koetzing hit a switch just inside the door and angled spotlights flickered into life.

'They're angled to illuminate each painting when you pull it out, but it's really not the best light for looking at pictures. Of course that's not the function here. This is just a store.'

Fabel could see that canvases were arranged in rows in floor-to-ceiling rack units, each unit stacked two rows high.

'You remember the kind of boxes colour slides used to be stored in . . . you know, photographic transparencies?' Anja Koetzing asked as she walked over to the nearest unit. 'Or even the carriage in an old slide projector? Well, the principle is the same, just on a much bigger scale. It means canvases can be stored upright in compact units and we can cram lots into the space – but if you want to look at any one of them, you just pull the sliding tray out.'

'Very clever,' said Fabel. 'Your system?'

'The strange thing about Detlev,' Anja Koetzing said as she went to the first unit, 'is that his entire life was complete chaos.

Everything about it was totally fucked up in a way you could only manage if you were really working at it. But this . . .' She yanked on a metal handle and the first stored canvas slid out, held upright in its metal carriage. 'All of this has nothing to do with me. Detlev planned it, designed it, practically built it. In everything else he was a fuck-up, but with his art, with his studio, he was fastidious to the point of obsession. As you can see, he was very prolific but only chose a few canvases at a time for exhibition and sale. He wasn't prolific because he rushed his work, it was because he was very disciplined with working. A tough guy to figure out.'

'So you say these canvases wouldn't be rotated with the ones on display?'

'Not really. Or at least not all of them. Most of the art in here falls into three categories: a stock of satisfactory work for future sale, the stuff he wasn't happy with but wanted to revisit in the future, and his "alternative" works – different styles and different ideas, mainly what you could say were personal favourites. There are a couple of paintings here that I can't wait to sell, because some of them really are much better than his usual output.'

'And will you? Sell all of these?'

'You bet. Not all at once, and none until the exhibition work has been sold. By that time the Detlev Traxinger brand will sell at a premium. You think I'm a cold-hearted bitch, don't you?'

'I don't make judgements like that, Frau Koetzing,' said Fabel, but the truth was her hard-headedness was beginning to cause him to think about checking her alibi again.

The door opened behind them and Anna Wolff stepped in. 'You wanted me, *Chef*?'

'Frau Koetzing, this is Criminal Chief Commissar Wolff . . . Anna, this is Frau Koetzing. Herr Traxinger's business manager.'

The two women shook hands. Fabel thought he picked up an odd vibe from Anja Koetzing, her smile on the grudging side of perfunctory. The dynamics of inter-female relationships was the one mystery Fabel had never been able to solve, more elusive for him than quantum physics. He shook the feeling off and turned to Anna.

'There's something I need you to see.'

'Shit,' said Anna. 'That's the picture, all right.' She and Fabel were alone, back out in the main gallery area, at the heart of the maze of partition walls. The gallery lights were now also on and a pool of light illuminated the huge canvas. 'My mind was on other things, it has to be said, but I remember it all right.'

'I certainly remember it,' said Fabel. 'I thought it was the last thing I was going to see. But according to Anja Koetzing, it was impossible for Schalthoff to have a print of it.'

'You mean Vampira?' Anna snorted. 'Whether she believes it or not, the print was there on Schalthoff's wall.'

'I don't think she likes you either, by the way,' said Fabel.

'Well she likes you. I'd watch yourself there. She'll have her fangs into you as soon as the sun goes down.' Anna focused again on the painting. 'Why did he sign this painting *Charon*?'

'It's not a signature, it's the subject: the central figure in the painting is meant to be Charon, the boatman who conveyed the dead across the river Styx to Hades. As you can imagine, when I first saw it I thought there was a message in there for me. According to Frau Koetzing, Traxinger liked to experiment with different themes and styles and almost brand them differently.'

He leaned closer and examined the painting. The sight of it still caused a churning in his gut, but he knew he had to get beyond that, to apply professional focus. He could see now that the draped figure was actually dressed in modern clothing: a hoodie with the hood pulled up to put all but the lower half of the face in shadow, a long leather coat over the top and reaching down to the ground. It was cleverly done, creating the impression from a distance of an almost monk-like cowl and habit. He again saw the fire behind the figure, represented in diamond facets of red, amber and yellow. But it was clearer now, seen close up and in full size.

'It's a riot . . .'

'What?'

'The fire. The background. It's a riot. That's supposed to be Hamburg, you can see the spires of the Michel and the Nikolai. Look. And if you look into the shapes behind the figure you can see barricades amongst the flames. The hooded figure isn't Charon, he's a rioter. And the river isn't the Styx, it's the Elbe.' Fabel shook his head in admiration.

'You okay?' asked Anna. 'It must be a shock to see it again.'

Fabel gave a small laugh. 'More a surprise than a shock. It was just so bizarre to see it here.' He examined the figure more closely. The eyes shone out from the shadow cast over the face by the cowl of the hood. Green eyes.

He turned away from the painting. 'We need to find out what connection, if any, there is between Detlev Traxinger and Jost Schalthoff.'

'I'll get onto it, *Chef*. Do you want me to bring Henk in?'

'No, leave him to tie up the loose ends on the old people's home case.'

Walking away from the *Charon* painting, Fabel saw through the vast windows of the former machine hall the sun set over the Elbe. The colours in the sky were not unlike those in Detlev

Traxinger's habitual palette. It had been a good place for an artist's studio.

'Thom and Dirk are still here, in the studio, why don't you update them on what we've got so far,' Fabel told Anna. 'In the meantime, I've some other paintings to look at.'

Anna grinned and nodded to the sunset beyond the glazed wall. 'Sun's going down. If you're going back in there with her, you should maybe get your hands on some garlic . . .'

34

Edgar Allan Poe sat across the writing desk from him. They were in a dark room that smelled of earth and damp. Behind Poe was a wall made up not from bricks, but mossy fragments of stone, inscribed with Hebrew. Werner had no idea how he had got there and for some reason didn't feel the need to ask how the great man had come back to life. It surprised him, but only for a moment, when he noticed that Poe was a handsome man. The darkest hair above a broad, wide, pale brow; penetrating, crystal eyes. Werner, the Poe enthusiast, of course had known that before: that some of the later daguerreotypes of the author had been taken during his darkest period and were far from flattering, showing a sunken-eyed, hollow-cheeked wraith who fitted better with the type of fiction he had written. And, of course, there had been a malicious obituary and post-mortem biography written by Poe's executor, who actually envied the dead man's genius and painted him as a drunkard and wastrel.

'Where am I, Mr Poe?' Werner asked in English.

'My name is Reynolds,' said Poe.

Werner shook his head. 'No it's not, sir. Reynolds was the name you were using on the night you died.'

'My name is Reynolds.' Poe coughed, twice, but his eyes remained unblinking. 'I do believe that I may have the cholera spasms. I was travelling through Philadelphia and there was an outbreak . . .'

'Please, Mr Poe . . . please tell me where I am.' Werner again looked past Poe at the wall of gravestone fragments. 'Are we under the cemetery in Altona?'

'My name is Reynolds. This place knows no geography; it is a place of the inner, not outer, universe. You want to write tales such as mine,' said Poe. 'This is the place whence those tales come.' He gave another unblinking cough and a dribble of blood, so dark as almost to be black, found its way out of the corner of his mouth and down his chin.

'It feels like we are under the ground. Am I dead?' asked Werner.

'Not yet,' said Poe. 'Death and the mind construct great mansions. There are rooms in the mind we occupy before and during death. This is one such room. This is the room you must look into – your own words I believe – before you can write great dark fiction. But do not worry, you will be dead. Soon. And your name hereafter will be Edgar just as mine is Reynolds. There are some fictions that endure through death.'

Werner wanted to protest, to ask more, but Poe began coughing again. Another shiny, black-red dribble came from the lips, but this time it defied gravity and began to writhe, to probe the air with its tip, and Werner realized it was a blood-slicked worm.

Werner tried to scream, but suddenly felt his mouth sealed shut.

Werner Hensler left the drug-induced dream behind and regained consciousness. There was no Poe, no gravestone wall; there was nothing he could see in the darkness.

Werner knew that he was now fully conscious but panicked at the thought that he had lost his sight: everything around him was the blackest dark; so completely lightless that there was no difference between having his eyes open or closed. He could see nothing but, when he thought it through, knew somehow he wasn't blind, just as the total, stifling silence did not mean he was deaf.

He was lying on his back. He tried to move but someone had tied him up so tightly as to rob him of even the smallest movement. His wrists had been bound with tape in front of him and his arms fastened tight to his body by rope. At least he guessed that it was rope from the way it dug into him when he struggled against it. His legs too had been pinioned by bonds that bit into his skin at the ankles, calves, knees and thighs.

He was naked: he could feel the varnished hardness against his skin of the wooden table or bench they had placed him on, and every time he tried to move a centimetre, his abrasively tight bonds would bite directly into his flesh. Something chill ran through him at the idea of his abductor having stripped him as he had lain exposed, senseless, naked and vulnerable.

He tried to call out but was stifled by the tape placed over his mouth. A powerful claustrophobia began to seize him: a primal instinct reacting against being robbed so totally of movement. It took a conscious effort not to lose himself to a blind panic and he concentrated on breathing through his nose slow and easy, trying not to think about his mouth being sealed. *Think*, he told himself, *reason it out*. He peered into the darkness. He thought he could sense a depth to it, imagined he perceived a distant corner, perhaps where walls and ceiling met. He was being kept in a darkened room. Lightproof and perhaps even soundproof. The air in his nose felt vaguely damp. The purpose of his confinement was a mystery; perhaps he had been kidnapped for money and, in another room, his abductors were negotiating a ransom with his publishers. A darker thought: perhaps his abduction had nothing to do with who he was, but was the random act of some madman. Maybe the door would swing open any moment, flooding the chamber with light and torment as his insane captor carried in his instruments of torture.

Again he pushed back down the panic that had once more begun to rise. It was insane. It was all insane. Why was this happening to him? What had he ever done to deserve—

Another black, cold thought took sudden shape in the dark. *No, it couldn't be that. After all this time, it couldn't be that.*

But the thought stayed with him. The face he thought he had seen in the seconds before he lost consciousness came back into his recall. It *couldn't* be that. How could it possibly be to do with what happened all those years ago?

The panic bloomed in his chest. Detlev had been murdered. Monika's body had been found and Detlev had been killed. Now it was Werner's turn. He began to whimper behind his gag.

Calm down, he told himself. *Think this through*. Whatever the reason, whoever was responsible, he had to get out. He had to free himself first from these bonds, as quietly but as quickly as he could – if he could – and then he would come up with a way to deal with whoever and whatever lay beyond his cell.

He had written about things like this. The dark chamber, the bound man reduced to reaching out into his darkened environment with his senses. And, of course, he had read about them too. He tried to push the thought out of his mind that for him, of all the Gothic fiction he had read, Edgar Allan Poe had been supreme. And of all the Poe he had read, that one story had been supreme. Werner had read *The Pit and the Pendulum* both in

German and the original English countless times since his thirteenth year and first encounter with the tale. *Oh God no. Not that.*

The only movement he could manage was in his hands. He balled them into fists and twisted one up towards his head, the other towards his feet, as if there was a pivot through his wrists, then reversed the action: rocking motions that caused the edge of the tape to bite into his skin. The ropes that bound his arms severely restricted the movement of his hands but slowly, painfully, he managed to cause the tape to crinkle and fold back on his wrists, the arc of each rocking increasing slightly each time. The tape still bound his wrists together, but now he could move his fingers to where the rope fastened his upper arms. He couldn't believe his luck when he felt the knot beneath his trembling fingertips. His captor had not been as thorough as he thought.

Somehow he found the patience to work gradually and methodically. His fingers alone had to work joint-achingly slowly, probing, hooking and pulling at the knot of what felt like thick nylon cord that bound him. Twice he stopped and lay perfectly still: once because of something like a noise in a room beyond, the second time because he thought he saw a dim light fleet across the ceiling above him. Were they real sensations or was it his mind seeing and hearing what wasn't there?

Think. For God's sake think it through. Reason.

The room was lightproof and soundproof, he decided. Anything he thought he saw or heard was his mind desperate to fill in sensory gaps. The only thing he was certain of was the damp odour in the air. Perhaps he was being kept in a cellar like the one he had dreamt he had shared with Edgar Allan Poe.

Time was another element that had been locked out of his confinement and he had no idea how long he'd been working at the knot, but he was aware that he now felt hot and was sweating, and his breathing hissed in his nostrils, which added to his feelings of claustrophobia. The knuckles and bones of his fingers ached with the effort and he felt as if his hands were swelling. And still the knot didn't seem to be loosening.

He decided to turn his attention to the gag.

He wriggled and shrugged, working his shoulders and upper arms in an attempt to ease the ropes up his body, even a little. As he did so he craned his neck forward, bringing his chin towards his chest and trying to slide his bound hands upwards to his face. Whoever had tied him up had done so in a way that restricted all movement, in every direction. He rested, then recommenced his wriggling shrugs, grunting behind his tape gag.

The rope nudged upward. Not much, but enough to allow him more movement. He strained forward but still could not reach the gag. More wriggling, more muffled grunting and sweating. The skin on his upper arms felt rubbed raw by the effort, but that in itself suggested movement in the rope.

Another rest. This time, before starting, he let out as much of his breath as he could, forcing it through his nostrils and deflating his chest, making its circumference smaller. He wriggled again and the rope slipped up his body, further this time. Straining his head forward and his hands up, his aching fingers found the edge of the gag. He wanted to rip it off, but his restricted movements meant he could only ease it free.

The tape was off his mouth.

He let out a moan of relief and the still muffled sound of it surprised him. There was no depth to it, no resonance, as if dampened; he had been right, the room must be soundproof. He had thought about calling out for help, but had dismissed the idea: it would only draw the attention of his captor. But if this room *was* soundproof, he could be less careful about making noise as he struggled to free himself.

Another cold, obsidian-black thought coalesced in the darkness. He was clearly dealing with a madman who had God knew what in store for him. What if his tormentor was sitting here, malevolent and silent in the impenetrable dark of this soundproof room? He lay still for a moment, straining through the black silence for any sounds. Nothing.

Keep it together, he told himself, *for God's sake keep it together. There's no one here. Just get on with it and get out.*

He turned his attention back to the knot, now moved higher up his body. He ignored the pain and went back to probing it with his aching fingers. Managing to work a finger into the cord, he felt the knot loosen. He now had it between finger and thumb and pulled frantically, hoping he was loosening, not tightening his restraint. It gave way.

He was lathered in sweat. It slicked his entire body, seeped stingingly into his eyes and pooled stickily on the polished wood beneath his buttocks, shoulders and back. The room had become stiflingly hot and the air stale, but he worked on. The freedom afforded by the loosening of the first cord allowed him work on the second. This time the knot wasn't accessible and he focused on easing the cord up over his sweat-sleeked chest and arms, pushing with his fingers and wriggling so he could shrug his shoulders free.

It took him a long time to loosen then untie the second cord. He still could not reach down to untie his legs, but as soon as his upper body was free, that wouldn't be a problem. Similarly, he would be able to work with his teeth on the tape that still bound his wrists together.

After that, he would be able to move, to explore his cell and find where the door was. He went back to work, thinking about nothing beyond getting loose from his bonds. It took an age of gnawing at it with his teeth before he started a tear in the tape on his wrists. It was exhausting work and once he managed to get the tape off, he rested for a moment, but only a moment, before sitting up to untie the cords that bound his legs.

He hit his head. Hard. So hard that he slumped back, dazed. He had tried to sit up and his head had hit something solid and immovable, right above him. Blood mingled with the sweat that trickled into his eyes.

His consciousness had not even fully returned, his head had not fully cleared, when he worked out what it was he had hit his head on. He began to shake uncontrollably, and his fingers quivered in the lightless air as he reached them up. They found the smooth, hard surface above him. He reached out to the sides, first right, then left. A smooth, hard surface on every side.

The thought exploded in his head, surged and seared through every fibre of his being. He wasn't in a soundproof room after all.

He was in a coffin.

This wasn't Poe's *The Pit and the Pendulum*, this was his *Premature Burial*.

Werner Hensler thrashed wildly, senselessly, hysterically. He was beyond logical thought and had become a creature of fear and instinct. His terror was total, primal, and he began screaming: inhuman, high-pitched, incessantly. It didn't even occur to him that no one would hear him.

That the sounds of his screams would be suffocated to silence by the dense, cold darkness of the earth around him.

35

There was one officer left guarding the scene at Traxinger's studio, which would be kept under lock-down until forensics had completely finished their detailed processing of the whole building. Unlike the way it was portrayed in glossy American TV series, forensic recording of a scene was a boring, dull and tedious process, and one that took a lot of time. Until it was completed Fabel, and anyone else on site, had to wear latex gloves and overshoes. He had told Anja Koetzing that she didn't need to stay and that the studio would be secured once he left. Armed with the keys and the alarm code for the studio and gallery, Fabel worked his way through the canvases in the storeroom, pulling each vertical tray out, examining the painting it held, then sliding it back.

He wasn't entirely sure why he was devoting so much time to the exercise, but suspected it was because the deeper into the storeroom he went, the deeper he travelled into Traxinger's mind. It was an instinct to be followed, and Fabel had become much more a creature of instinct since the shooting.

Some of the paintings were bizarre: horrific dungeon images of ravens pecking the eyes from chain-bound prisoners, or grotesque demons twisting and reaching out from their lairs. Others were ornate, almost pre-Raphaelite depictions of women, almost all either raven- or red-headed and pale-skinned.

Fabel decided to call it a day. He was tired and hungry and Susanne would be expecting him.

However, one of his instincts beckoned. Something urged him to give up his methodical process and go right to the back of the rack. He was leaving and it did no harm for him to see if the paintings at the back were the same kind of stuff as those at the front. There was also the suspicion that here, in the secret vaults of Traxinger's creative consciousness, may be some greater truth about the artist that could perhaps lead Fabel to his killer.

The last sliding unit was much heavier and it took Fabel more effort to pull out. The reason was that instead of two separate upper and lower trays, a single double-height tray held a massive canvas draped in a cloth. As he pulled it out, he could see, close-up, one exposed corner of the painting. Traxinger had monogrammed the picture rather than signed it and the monogram he had used was an ornate interweaving of his initials wreathed in ivy and acanthus leaves and flowers. It was exactly the same as the design he had had tattooed above his heart, and Fabel hadn't seen it used on any of the other paintings. Maybe this painting, too, was close to the artist's heart.

Fabel had to go to the far end of the storeroom to get a stepladder, which he used to reach the top of the painting and ease the protective cloth up and off the canvas. Climbing back down, the cloth gathered into an untidy bundle under his arm, he stood back to look at the painting, illuminated by the angled ceiling spotlight.

He took out his cell phone and once more called Anna.

'Can you meet me back at Traxinger's studio?' he asked. 'Sorry to be a pain, but I've found another connection that doesn't make any sense.'

Anna agreed to come straight away and Fabel hung up.

Afterwards he stood as if hypnotized by the painting. It was a nude of a pale, breathtakingly beautiful young woman with a blaze of rich auburn and red hair. The woman stood in a grave-yard, an arch of ivy and acanthus both framing her naked body and reaching threateningly towards it. Her eyes were bright emerald and held the viewer locked in a cold gaze.

This, Fabel realized, had been Traxinger's masterpiece. His secret masterpiece.

Before turning and going to advise the uniformed officer on guard duty that Chief Commissar Wolff would be arriving soon, Fabel stood for a while longer, gazing at the beautiful face cap-tured in the painting.

Monika Krone's face.

36

The Running Woman was blonde, lithe and pretty. She had her hair tied back from her face in a ponytail that swung and flicked at the air as she ran with the carefree buoyancy of youth and vigour. Her legs were sleek, toned and tanned, her backside full but firm, breasts immobile in a sports bra beneath Lycra. She was the only runner who took this path, the one that ran past the back of the house. He would see her running by at the same time every day, her eyes focused on the path ahead, the world shut out by the earbuds of the MP3 player fastened to her waistband. Frankenstein could almost have set his watch by her, but there was one, always seemingly random, variation to her routine each time. The path ran through the most heavily wooded part of the Stadtpark, walled in and shadowed by the trees. It then emerged into a clearing, a small oasis of sunlight breaking the green velvet shadows of the forest. It was here that the path both turned ninety degrees and split into two for a distance of fifty or so metres before joining together again. One of the two paths again became shielded by trees, the other, running parallel, remained in the open for a while and passed immediately by the edge of the garden. Sometimes the running woman would take one path, other times the garden-side spur. There seemed no pattern to it, but simply decided on a whim.

Frankenstein knew he should remain in the cellar, and he wanted to please his guardian, but it sometimes seemed to him as if he had been liberated from one confinement merely to be delivered into another. So, for an hour each day, at a time he knew it was unlikely that Zombie would call, he went up from the cellar and into the dust and gloom of the grey shell that had once been a home. Most of the time he would simply fold his bulk into a shadowed corner and ease a shutter open just wide enough for him to watch through the window, simply to be able to look out at the forest and the sky. A couple of times he had ventured all the way up to the attic and looked out through the unshuttered windows over to where cars and lorries made their way along the distant main road. But even this he knew was a risk: if someone appeared suddenly to snoop around the house, they would be between him and the cellar, left unlocked and open to prying. Not that the idea of snapping the neck of some snooper bothered him – it was just that he knew it would disappoint his guardian. So, generally, he would come up to use the toilet, go through to one of the ground floor rooms and watch the world through a crack in the shutters.

It helped, but his hunger continued to grow, blossoming dark in the cellar like some black fungus.

One night he had even decided to venture out of the house; sure that there was no one around, he made his way up to the front door and unlocked it with the key Zombie had left with him for emergencies. Frankenstein had stood in the overgrown garden and gazed up at the night sky. He knew he was safe. The darkness, except for the vault of stars above him, was complete, enveloping. His unnatural size, his brutal features, his heavy-boned bulk, all were hidden in the dark. From the world, from himself. In that dark moment, no one could see him and he could not see himself and suddenly, completely, he forgot his own monstrosity. He was Jochen Hübner again, not Frankenstein. He remembered the dream he had had when he had been near to death. His mother. His innocence.

When he returned to the cellar, he looked in the small shaving mirror Zombie had given him. The spell was broken; the bitterness returned. He was a monster and always would be.

It was the next day he had noticed the girl running. She was perfect. And like all of those born without flaw, she wore her perfection carelessly, thoughtlessly. It had been so long since he had had a woman, had drunk in their terror. Every day since his first sighting, Frankenstein had timed his visit upstairs to watch her run. And made plans.

He so wanted not to disappoint his guardian. Herr Mensing had done so much for him and asked so little in return, but now that Frankenstein was out in the world, free, his hunger had grown so terribly strong. He knew it was an unacceptable risk and that his guardian would not be able to forgive him, but Frankenstein would take the woman. He would grab her and drag her into the cellar. He would be able to take his time there. And afterwards, of course, he would have to kill this one.

But every time he thought it through, he realized they would find him, find his lair, perhaps even find his guardian. If Frankenstein did this, then everything Zombie had worked so hard for would be for nothing; his opportunity for revenge lost. And they would know where to start looking – the girl was clearly a creature of habit and if she went missing they would search the Stadtpark, the woods and, before long, the house.

But it had been so long . . .

It would be her decision, not his.

The next day, instead of watching from the window, he went

out of the house, leaving the door unlocked behind him. He made his way around the house and into the garden at the rear, doing his best to crouch as low to the ground as his giant bulk would allow, constantly checking that there was no one around. Some kind of old outbuilding stood at one corner of the garden. It was ruined – roofless, overgrown and crumbling, but it offered him some concealment. From here he could see the path running through the trees to where it forked. It would be *her* decision, not his. If she took the path that threaded back through the trees, he would leave her alone and never attempt this again. But if she took the other path . . .

It was a sweet, tantalizing thought. If she made that random decision to take the path that ran past the house and his hiding place, he would grab her, silence her and take her into the darkness of the cellar and his cruelty.

He felt a thrill the instant he saw her running through the dapples of sunlight between the thick trees and heading towards the bend and fork in the path. Two possibilities, two choices, two completely, drastically different futures awaited her; and it would all come down to the most casual of decisions. Frankenstein felt himself stirring in anticipation. He could hear her expensive sports shoes on the path; she was only a matter of metres away from the fork.

Do it, he silently willed her to turn towards the house. *Do it and see what waits for you.* She was nearly there. The smallest part of her brain, the briefest fluttering of neural activity, would set her on one course or another; would take her away from him or would bring her to him. But if she chose the spur that ran past him, he would awaken every neuron, every pain receptor, every part of her brain.

Do it . . .

The running woman approached the fork in the path, her strides even. Right or left. Light or dark. Life or death.

She reached the fork. Frankenstein felt something surge up from deep inside him. The anticipation was now unbearable. Without breaking step, she made her choice.

She took the spur that would bring her right to him.

He readied himself. There was no one anywhere he could see, but he would have to make sure she didn't have a chance to scream or make much noise. He had become the perfect predator and his taking of her would be as quick and quiet as a shark closing its jaws on prey and swiftly dragging it under the silencing water.

He crouched down further, losing her from sight but focusing on the rhythmic beat of her shoes on the path. She was nearly there.

Frankenstein prepared to leap and grab her as she passed.

Someone laid a hand on his shoulder.

He snapped around, ready to attack. The painfully thin, pale face of his guardian stared back at him. Zombie held Hübner's gaze and silently shook his head. There was no anger, no disappointment in Zombie's expression, just a sad concern. In that moment, Frankenstein saw once more how Zombie looked at him: as if trying to understand, seeing him as a person, not a monster. Perhaps even as a friend. In the same moment Frankenstein also realized how close he had come to ruining everything. He nodded his huge head and sank back into the undergrowth and behind the fractured wall of the outbuilding, gently pulling Zombie with him.

He heard the woman's footfalls grow louder, more inviting, then fade as she ran past them and on, back to the life she knew, unaware of the future she had nearly known.

Back in the cellar, there was no anger, no reproach. Zombie simply asked why Hübner had risked everything they had worked for; why he had ignored Zombie's instructions.

'This whole house is lying empty,' Frankenstein answered. 'With so much space above the ground, I don't understand why I have to stay down here in the dark all the time.'

'The risk of you being seen is too high. Even with the shutters closed, there would always be a chance someone could see a chink of light. All of Hamburg is looking for you, Jochen. Your picture is all over the place.'

'I know. It's just that I saw that bitch every day. Running. It's been so long . . .'

'I know. But there'll be plenty of time for that. You'll get what you want soon enough.' Zombie paused, frowning. Frankenstein thought it odd to see the wrinkling of skin usually pulled taut on his almost fleshless skull. 'You know you can leave any time you want,' he said. 'There's nothing I could do to stop you. I wouldn't even try.'

'You freed me,' said Hübner.

'Exactly. There's no prison around you any more. You could take off at any time, under the cover of night.'

'I owe you. Not just for getting me out. I will do what you ask, because I said I would. I'll do right by you because you did right by me.'

'You know that I probably won't be able to help you afterwards, don't you?' said Zombie. 'They'll have me by then. You'll have to do what you have to do on your own. But I won't give up this place. You'll be safe here because I won't tell them about it, but they'll find out sooner or later. They'll check.'

'I understand.'

'I want to give you something. You deserve it.'

'You've done enough for me. I'm sorry I nearly let you down.'

'Well, you didn't, so forget it. This is a bonus.' Zombie handed Frankenstein two photographs. Both were slightly out of focus, clearly having been taken with a zoom lens from a considerable distance. They both showed the faces of women: one was of a woman in her forties, clearly beautiful, with dark hair; the second was of a younger woman with auburn-red hair.

'My gift to you,' said Zombie. 'When you have done what I have asked, I'll tell you where to find them.'

'Who are they?' Frankenstein looked up from the photographs.

'I know you have a grudge against Principal Chief Commissar Jan Fabel. That's his woman and his daughter . . .'

37

Fabel had found fifteen other paintings stored at the back of Traxinger's storeroom, all featuring Monika Krone as the central figure. It became clear that if there really was such a thing as a muse, then Monika Krone had been Detlev Traxinger's. But, as canvas after canvas was pulled out, Fabel realized he wasn't looking at an artist's inspiration: he was looking at an obsession. These paintings had not been created for display or appreciation; their motivation was something much darker, more compelling and personal. Secretive.

Many of the paintings had simply been slightly different versions of the graveyard scene. These alternative versions had been no better nor worse executed than the one Traxinger had stowed at the very back of his collection, and the variations were barely noticeable – as if the artist had been trying to capture something very particular and had not been entirely satisfied that he had succeeded. Fabel could see that while Monika remained constant, with only the minutest alteration in the tilt of her head, the angle of a pale thigh or the brightness of the moonlight, there were slight changes in the background details.

In contrast, the non-graveyard paintings were all wildly different: Monika in period costumes, one strangely disquieting one of Monika against a background of writhing vegetation, like a moving jungle, with a whip in her gloved hands. Fabel had decided he would come back later and examine the paintings in greater detail. In the meantime he took a picture of the grave-yard nude with his cell phone before calling the Presidium to get a forensic photographer to document them all.

At eleven the following morning, Fabel assembled the whole team in the Murder Commission's briefing room. He had first emailed a report to each of them on what he had discovered at the gallery, including a photograph of the graveyard painting featuring the nude with Monika Krone's face, asking for each of them to start following a specific line of inquiry. But the significance of two major homicide investigations converging – added to a possible connection to the child-murderer Jost Schalthoff – was of such magnitude that the whole team had to be briefed together.

Fabel had instructed that both inquiry boards – the Traxinger and the Krone cases – be wheeled into the briefing room and set side by side. When he entered the room, Fabel was taken aback to see the print that had hung in Schalthoff's apartment, sitting propped up against the metal support of the incident board.

'I didn't think we'd ever be able to locate that,' he said, turning to Anna. 'I imagined it would have been disposed of along with the rest of Schalthoff's furniture. However did you manage to track it down?'

'It was in the evidence store,' said Anna.

'Evidence? But why would a picture be kept as evidence?'

Anna held Fabel's gaze, trying but failing to hide her awkwardness. 'Blood spatter,' she said flatly.

'Oh,' said Fabel. He looked again at the print but could see no hint of his two-year-old blood on it. But he knew that blood spatter could be aerosol, hardly visible to the naked eye, and simply because the picture had been tested didn't mean Fabel's blood had been found on it.

'I see,' he said. 'Well, whatever the reason, I'm glad we have it. Anna, could we have some expert look at it to tell us anything we can get on where, how and who printed it? I don't know if we can find out if it was a one-off or part of a run, but that information would be very useful if we can get it.'

'Yes, *Chef.*'

'Okay . . .' Fabel addressed the entire team. 'What we now seem to be looking at are two cases that may be connected, but are separated by fifteen years, with some possible, but so far unestablished connection to Jost Schalthoff, two years ago. Detlev Traxinger was murdered with an undiscovered weapon that we know was highly unusual and specialized. He was killed by a single upward strike with a long, thin-bladed weapon. Maybe a needle-file or something similar. Whoever killed him was confident and efficient.'

'A professional hit?' asked Nicola Brüggemann.

'I doubt it. So far we have no motive for anyone to go to the effort and expense of hiring a professional killer. And most of all, contract killers don't hang about the scene to set up tableaux. Whoever killed Traxinger wanted to make some kind of personal statement. In the meantime, let's say the killing was professionally executed – it could possibly have been a pro or it could be someone who had been planning and rehearsing for some time.' Fabel pointed to a large glossy photograph, taken in the forensics lab to where it had been moved, of the nude portrait of Monika Krone. 'And this is our connection to the Krone inquiry. A woman murdered fifteen years ago turns up in a murder two days ago.'

'It could simply be a coincidence,' said Anna. 'We know that she did pose as a model on occasion at the University of Fine Arts in Uhlenhorst, and we know that Traxinger was a student there. Maybe he painted the picture back then and the only connection is that Monika was the anonymous model who posed for his class. Maybe she made extra cash as an artist's model outside the uni – and their relationship was strictly professional. Or maybe she was a friend of a friend. It could be a very tenuous connection.'

'All that could be true. But we're talking about a painting that Traxinger treasured but hid from the world, even from his business manager. It clearly had some deep significance for him. However, I do admit there could be any number of coincidental reasons why she's turned up here, and I need you all to start looking for historical connections between Traxinger and Monika Krone. But there's coincidence, there's correlation, and there's causation ...' Fabel turned and looked at the photograph closely, before tapping it with his forefinger. 'And I smell a cause and effect here. If we hadn't found Monika's remains, I would still have found this painting and would have been surprised at its presence. But I would probably have put it down to chance. The fact is that Traxinger was murdered within days of Monika's body being unearthed. That's a coincidence on top of a coincidence.'

'So you think that the discovery of her remains was some kind of trigger for Traxinger's death?'

'It's possible. And what I *really* don't like is that it could also have been the trigger for the escape from prison of the only suspect we had for Monika's murder fifteen years ago.'

'You think Jochen Hübner maybe killed Traxinger?' Anna asked. 'What would his connection to him be? And anyway, it looks like Traxinger let his killer get close. I don't see that happening with Frankenstein.'

'Maybe not, but like I said, when the coincidences start to pile up, I look beyond chance for a correlation. But we've got to keep all investigative options open.' He turned to Glasmacher and Hechtner. 'Thom, Dirk, I need you to stay on the chronology of Traxinger's murder and his personal connections. Have you found anyone close to him?'

'We're going through his emails, cell phone records, et cetera,' said Glasmacher, 'and we're working our way through his friends, or more correctly his acquaintances. It would appear Traxinger wasn't someone who got close to anyone. I get the feeling he was difficult to like. Plus he had no close family – he hadn't spoken to his parents or brother in years.'

'What about relationships with women?'

'Well, there were a lot of those,' said Dirk Hechtner. 'But all casual. Very casual. There are some I don't think we'll ever get to, because they involve married women. It's like Traxinger actively avoided any lasting or deep relationship with a woman. There were two marriages though, both short-lived and disastrous.'

'Oh?'

'Two ex-wives, one Italian, one French,' said Hechtner. 'He apparently didn't much care for the domestic product. Both moved back to their native countries several years ago. We've arranged for statements to be taken by the local police, just to check on their whereabouts when he died. But, reading between the lines, both ex-wives were glad to put as many kilometres as possible between them and Traxinger. And I'm guessing neither will be in mourning. In both marriages, he was a drunk, unfaithful and I suspect occasionally abusive.'

'So we've got nothing of interest with the ex-wives . . .' said Fabel.

'Not directly,' said Thomas Glasmacher. 'But there is one thing that is interesting. We processed Traxinger's home. It's a huge villa out by Blankenese. For someone who was supposed to have avowedly socialist ideals, he sure liked to live well. Anyway, we found photographs of both ex-wives. I really don't know how he managed to land women like that.' Glasmacher flipped open a file and took out two photographs. He walked over to the inquiry board and taped them onto it.

'He certainly liked his redheads,' said Fabel, examining the photographs. 'Shit . . . I see why you said this is interesting.' Both women were beautiful but did not look at all like each other except for their hair colour: exactly the same shade of auburn-red as Monika Krone had had. Exactly the same colour the artist had seemed obsessed with capturing in his paintings.

'I've got the painting Traxinger did of Monika Krone down in forensics,' said Fabel. 'We need to know when that painting was done. I asked Traxinger's business manager, Anja Koetzing—'

'The one who looks like Anna?' Dirk looked across at Anna and grinned.

'Vampira? You saying I look like the Queen of Darkness?' Anna said jokingly, but was clearly a little annoyed. 'Thank you very much.'

Fabel laughed but, looking at Anna, he could see that there was a similarity in look between the two women and wondered why he hadn't noticed it before. The memory that he had been very attracted to Koetzing disturbed him and he pushed it away.

'Okay, can we focus?' he said. 'I asked Frau Koetzing if she knew when the painting had been done and she said she had never seen it before. She said that she was generally always aware of what Traxinger was working on, which would suggest the painting pre-dates her involvement in the business. Detlev Traxinger knew Monika Krone – we need to know how, where and when. We've also got this to explain . . .' He pointed to the print of the riot scene, titled *Charon*. 'Another hidden gem from the Traxinger oeuvre. Again, Anja Koetzing said that this was an old piece that never left the studio's gallery, and pre-dates her involvement with the business. She also swears blind that no prints were ever made of it, yet here we have one. And it was found in the apartment of Jost Schalthoff. Another inexplicable coincidence. Anna, where are we on that?'

'I haven't been able to find any connection whatsoever between Detlev Traxinger and Jost Schalthoff,' explained Anna. 'Traxinger and Schalthoff were both from Altona and had spent much of their lives there – in Schalthoff's case all of his life. But it's kind of like two aircraft occupying the same airspace, but at completely different altitudes. As far as I can see, their paths never crossed.'

'This,' Fabel nodded to the print, 'says otherwise.'

'Maybe the print was stolen,' said Nicola Brüggemann. 'Or found, somehow. There seems to be no direct or indirect connection between Schalthoff and Traxinger.'

'And Schalthoff comes into possession of the only print of a highly personal painting? I doubt it, but let's keep all options open. In the meantime, stay on possible connections . . .'

38

It was odd how personalities could be read through their living environments, through the subtle expressions of individuality: a language Fabel had learned to read over the years.

During the original investigation into her disappearance, Fabel had visited Monika Krone's student apartment frequently, and had indeed carried out a detailed search of its three rooms: it had been a place of disorder and chaos, the walls completely hidden behind often overlapping posters of medieval, pre-Raphaelite and Gothic art, or flyers promoting Gothic literature events and exhibitions. The tones had been dark. A modern computer desk, he remembered, had stood out incongruously and had been mismatched with a heavy, ornately carved, almost cathedra-style chair that looked like it had been salvaged from a church. Fabel had refreshed his recollection of that apartment, once more poring over photographs from the original file.

This home could not have been more different. Kerstin Krone lived in a small house in the north of Altona. It was compact, immaculate and ordered, with white walls to make the most of the limited space and bright, colourful, modern paintings hanging here and there. This was a place of light, not darkness. And everything was in its place, books ordered on shelves, the magazines on the coffee table in front of him neatly stacked.

'You live here alone? Thanks . . .' Fabel accepted the cup of tea she handed him.

'Yes,' she said, a deliberate, amused puzzlement in her expression that wordlessly but eloquently asked *and why is that relevant to anything?* She sat down opposite Fabel and placed her coffee on the low table. Again Fabel was struck by her natural elegance and beauty. It occurred to him that Kerstin Krone tried hard to tone down her looks, to distract people from them. Her hairstyle was less than flattering and she wore no make-up, which only served to accentuate the naturalness of her beauty. He found it difficult to imagine her teaching physics to a disruptive class.

'You've never married?' he asked.

'No. Why?'

'Listen, Frau Krone, your sister's death fifteen years ago may be linked to a very recent one. In fact, I have the suspicion that the discovery of her remains may even have been a trigger or catalyst for this recent killing – although I do have to point out all that is pure conjecture on my part.' He held up a hand to emphasize his point. 'Monika seems to have attracted a great deal of male attention. Infatuation, almost.'

'So you think I'm some kind of man-magnet too?' Her smile had no warmth. 'A tormentor and serial breaker of hearts?'

'If I may say so, you are a very striking-looking woman. I can imagine that you have had no shortage of suitors. But I wasn't trying to pry. I'm just trying to understand Monika, to get a handle on her relationships. You're the nearest thing I have to being able to talk to Monika directly.'

'Then you've made a serious mistake.' Kerstin's tone was flat, but not hostile. 'The problem with men, with most people for that matter, is that they cannot see past the most superficial level. I look exactly like Monika. Or I imagine we would still look as similar at this age as we did at every other. But that is where the similarity ended. There's a lot of crap talked about twins. Sure, some – maybe even the majority – have a very close bond and very similar personalities, but not always.'

'And you and Monika were one such exception?'

'We couldn't have been more unlike each other. Biologically, identical twins are clones of each other. The raw material was identical, you could say. But there was a fundamental difference . . .' She frowned and shook her head. 'No . . . not a difference. A deficit. Some twins are born and they're identical, except one of them has a deformity or a finger missing or something like that. That's what it was like with Monika. There was something missing, but you couldn't see it, something missing inside. A deficit of the soul, you could say.'

'And what form did this *deficit* take?'

'Monika believed she was at the centre of the universe, that everything and everyone else was there for her convenience or amusement.'

'Including you?'

'Especially me. I loved my sister, Herr Fabel, but she loathed me. No, that's not right either – she was incapable of hating anyone just as she was incapable of loving them. She hated what I represented. She saw me as an imperfect reflection. Weak, unambitious, introverted – everything she was not. She gave me a hard time, I'll tell you. Do you know why I didn't study at Hamburg? Why I went to Hannover to study and told no one I was a twin?'

Fabel shook his head.

'Monika used to think it was a great joke to pretend to be me. She would sleep with men, victimize other girls or get into trouble under my name. It was her way of punishing me for being her reflection. My parents always believed me – they knew what Monika was like – but no one else would buy the whole "evil twin" thing. It took me a long time before I came back to Hamburg.'

'Why did you?'

'It was tough on my parents. They felt they'd lost both daughters. I wanted to be near my mother after my father died of a heart attack. Then she got sick and died two years later. I was her main caregiver.'

'Why didn't you tell me any of this the first time round, when I asked you about Monika's death fifteen years ago?'

'I didn't think it had anything to do with her disappearance. To be honest, for a long while, I thought it was just another Monika stunt – that she would turn up on the doorstep sometime.'

'Your Schrödinger's Cat analogy?'

'Exactly. I kept her alive in my mind because it helped me, especially after Mamma and Papa died, but also because I believed there was a faint chance she really had escaped to another life. Like I told you before, Monika spun so many webs around herself that she ended up being the one trapped, or lost in a storm of her own making. It was always possible, no matter how unlikely, that she had simply chosen to untangle herself.'

'Did you ever think she could have committed suicide?'

'Never. Yes, Monika was a destructive personality – but never a self-destructive one. Whatever the situation, she would find a way out of it.'

Fabel was about to answer when his cell phone rang. He excused himself and answered the call.

'It's Anna, Chef. We've got another homicide. Another weird one.'

'Where are you?'

'At the Bruno Tesch Centre, you know, the new building the Principal Mayor opened. We don't have an ID for the victim yet.'

'How was he killed?'

'That's the weirdest thing. He was buried alive.'

39

It was an ugly building. Fabel was far from being a traditional-
ist, and even counted himself as an admirer of modern design,
but he believed that architecture should always reflect its context: topographical, architectural, historical. Just like you could
tell a lot about a person from the interior of their home, it
struck Fabel that you could tell a lot about the character of a city
or a quarter from its architecture. This jagged jumble of geometry and dark glass had nothing to do with Altona. It was like a
completely alien race had crash-landed a spaceship in the middle of the quarter.

Fabel had heard of its opening. The building had been named
the Bruno Tesch Centre which, in an ironic way, summed up the
perpetual ambiguity of German history. Hamburg had produced
two sons called Bruno Tesch, both of whom had been executed.
One – the one after whom the building had been named – was
the anti-fascist martyr of Altona Bloody Sunday in 1932,
beheaded by the Nazis; the other was the inventor and supplier
of Zyklon B gas used in the death camps, hanged by the British.

Nicola Brüggemann was waiting for Fabel at the main
entrance.

'The body was found in the main atrium,' she explained.
'Although the building was officially opened a week ago, a lot of

the completion work is still to be done. They've had teams working to get it finished.' She led Fabel into the atrium. He spotted security cameras angled towards the entrance and across the concourse. As the space opened up before him, Fabel had to admit that the building looked better from the inside – looked better, but still lacked any connection to the character of the city quarter around it. He could have been anywhere in the world, and the design style was strangely sterile, soulless. He took a moment to gaze up to where the shard-like angles of glass came together high above them. Oddly, the triangles of dark glass seemed to diffuse but not weaken the light from the sky.

'It's some kind of energy capture technology.' Nicola Brüggemann read Fabel's thoughts. 'Or so the site foreman told me. We're over here.' She nodded to the centre of the atrium, which had been cordoned off by tape. The forensics team were standing by.

'They've done their initial forensic recce,' said Brüggemann. 'They say we can have a look at the body in situ, but not too close, before they start detailed processing of the scene and removing the body.'

Impossibly, a vast marble block seemed to float in the air at the heart of the atrium. When he grew near, Fabel could see it was actually a huge trough filled with earth. There were two stepladders set next to it.

'The Floating Garden,' explained Brüggemann. 'It's based on some Japanese concept.'

'Very minimalist,' said Fabel.

'If you ask me,' said Brüggemann with mock seriousness, 'the problem with minimalism is that you can get too much of it.'

Fabel smiled. 'How's the conjuring trick done?'

'The trough is actually held up by a titanium support that's shielded by mirrors. The mirrors are angled to reflect the floor in such a way that, unless you crouch down and really look, you can't see what's keeping it in the air. Clever shit.'

'Your site foreman again?'

'Yep. To be honest I think he has a bit of a thing for me. We have a lot in common. More than he realizes – mainly that we both like women. I'll break it to him gently that we don't have much of a future.'

Fabel laughed.

'Anyway, the idea is that they were going to fill the Floating Garden with small trees, shrubs, crap like that, and you get the idea of it all kind of levitating above the ground. I'm sure it'll look quite something when it's done.'

They both donned forensic gloves and overshoes before ducking under the tape. A technician also handed them masks to prevent DNA contamination.

'This is a really weird one,' said Brüggemann, her voice slightly muffled by the mask. 'The gardeners came in this morning to start planting, one of the last phases in completion. The earth was delivered and put into the planter last week. When the gardeners started digging into it, they hit something solid . . .' She indicated that Fabel should climb the stepladder, which he did. 'The forensics boys say we're not to stand on the earth or even on the ledge edge of the marble. Lookee, no touchee.'

Fabel climbed to the top of the ladder and looked into the trough. It was big – he reckoned about three metres wide, six metres long and, from what he had seen from the outside, roughly two and a half deep. Looking into the trough, he could see where less than a metre of soil had been cleared to expose a wooden box, its hinged lid opened. Some of the earth has spilled back into the box and partly covered the naked body of a man.

His mouth was wide open and his neck arched back as if mid-scream, but the face and the open eyes were empty of any fear, of any expression at all. His arms and hands had fallen into the pose of a dog begging and Fabel noticed the fingertips were raw and bloody. He saw scratch marks and streaks of blood on the inside of the now open lid.

'*Shit* . . .' he muttered in English.

'Hell of a way to go, isn't it?' said Brüggemann. 'It's not a coffin as such, by the way. Apparently it's a wooden tool chest that was kept on site. But it had been padlocked shut and they broke the lock to see what was inside.'

'So whoever did this must have been familiar with the site and what was available.'

Brüggemann shrugged. 'Or just someone who has done their homework really well.'

Fabel looked down at the dead man's face. Death had washed expression from it, but Fabel knew that while the angling of the head and the gaping mouth seemed to speak of the terror the man must have experienced as he died, his very last moments would have been almost peaceful. The hours leading up to those last moments, however, would have been filled with unimaginable terror. There would have been intense panic, then, as the oxygen in the coffin was replaced by carbon dioxide, he would have started to hyperventilate – speeding up the process – felt dizzy, disorientated and confused. Then, when the critical tipping point in the balance between oxygen and carbon dioxide had been reached, he would have lost consciousness within thirty seconds. Then death.

Some of the earth that had tipped across the upper part of his body had spilled into the dead man's open mouth and a woodlouse crawled over the broad, pale brow. Fabel resisted the temptation to brush it away. 'People don't just allow themselves to be buried like this,' he said. 'We need to get toxicology as soon as possible. My bet is he was drugged before being placed in here. And he must have been brought here in a vehicle.' Fabel nodded across to where a closed circuit television camera was angled to take in the atrium. 'And we need the tapes from that for the last thirty-six hours.'

Brüggemann shook her head. 'I'm way ahead of you, Jan. I checked: the security camera system isn't operational yet. One of the last jobs still to be done before completion.'

'Damn it.' He looked up again at the vault of the atrium's ceiling. He imagined the hypoxic death of the victim turning from terror to euphoria and wondered if, in those last seconds, he too had experienced the illusion of floating free of his body and looking down on where he lay. 'It would have taken him hours to die. Maybe a whole day – and all in earth so shallow that if he had broken through the lid he would have been able to stand up with his head above ground.'

'But he wasn't to know that, poor bastard,' said Brüggemann.

Fabel climbed back down the ladder. 'We need to get him ID'd as soon as possible.'

40

Another briefing. Another reallocation of the Murder Commission's teams. Before the briefing, Fabel had been up to the fifth floor to ask for additional resources which had been agreed without debate. Fabel suspected the lack of resistance was due, at least in part, to the fact that the murder in the Bruno Tesch Centre had been splashed all over the media. It was hardly surprising that it was considered sexy news: the building had just been opened by Hamburg's principal Bürgermeister and the press incorrectly speculated that the victim may have been fighting for breath and trying to claw his way out of his coffin even while Uwe Taubitz had been making his speech and declaring the building open. And, of course, it had been murder by burying alive, which appealed to the ghoulish imagination of the tabloid-reading masses.

There was also a discussion about progress, or the lack of it, in the hunt for the escaped Frankenstein Hübner. He had so totally dropped out of sight that it was now believed he had had an accomplice who was hiding him somewhere.

Fabel had already cancelled one of the Living Dead group sessions because of the pressure of work, and now he called Lorentz's secretary and told her he would miss the next. He was surprised when he got a call back almost immediately from Lorentz himself.

'I'm afraid I have too much to do with work,' Fabel said, a little annoyed at having to explain himself twice. 'I am sorry, I do get a great deal out of the sessions. But you do know what I do for a living, Herr Doctor. I'm afraid that always must take priority.'

'I understand that, but I really think you should try to make it, Herr Fabel,' he said. 'This is a very important study. As you say, I knew from the start that your job is very demanding. But I also made it clear that if you were to commit to the study, you had to commit fully to it. Group studies, and group therapy, for that matter, is all about the dynamic of the group. Once that dynamic has been established, if one person isn't there, it changes how everyone else interacts with each other. I've already lost a subject and I would really appreciate it if you could find the time . . .'

Fabel sighed. 'I'll do what I can, Dr Lorentz. But no promises.'

After he put the phone down, Fabel sat in his office and tried to work out what it had been that Lorentz had said that was causing an itch somewhere in his mind. He picked up the phone again and called Nicola Brüggemann, asking her to come into his office and to bring Anna with her.

A few moments later, Brüggemann came in and sat down opposite Fabel.

'Anna's out of the Commission, but she'll be back any minute,' she explained.

'Where is she?'

'The morgue.'

'The morgue?' Fabel was puzzled. 'Why is she at the morgue?'

'She said she had something to check out. She got the

preliminaries in on the buried-alive guy and said there was something she needed to double-check. But that was well over an hour ago, so she'll be back soon. Do you want me to come back?'

'No . . . no, I'm just trying to get to something. I've just had a phone conversation with someone who was talking about group dynamics – the way people interact with each other in social groups.'

'Okay?' Brüggemann frowned.

'Stick with me here, Nicola. There was something about what he was saying, about one figure being absent from a group causing the whole inter-personal dynamic to break down. Ever since we started looking into the Monika Krone case again, I've had this nagging feeling that there is a ghost in the file – someone who makes a connection that would make sense of everything. Because we can't identify that person, we can't see the connection, we can't make it make sense.'

'And you think that ghost is Detlev Traxinger?'

'I think he could be. Or it might be someone we're not seeing yet. I need everything back on everyone who was at that party the night Monika disappeared. Instead of checking who was with who, or who knew who, I want the specific focus to be on finding out if anyone had a connection to Traxinger before or since that night. I think he's our key.'

'It's a bit of a stab in the dark, Jan.'

'With a fifteen-year-old case we're surrounded by the unknown. Everything is a stab in the dark.'

'I'll get everyone on to it—'

Anna Wolff came into Fabel's office without knocking. Fabel could see instantly from her face that she had something big for him.

She grinned broadly. 'You are not going to believe this . . .'

41

Anna taped the mortuary photograph to the inquiry board for the 'Buried Man', as he had become known. The Buried Man was now linked to the other two murders and the three inquiry boards were standing side by side, with Monika Krone's in the middle.

The photograph was a close-up of the chest, cleaned of soil, of the man who had been found buried alive in the atrium of the Bruno Tesch Centre. The tattoo was clearly visible: the initials 'DT' were interwoven and wreathed with acanthus and ivy.

'Get this sent to the whole team, Anna. I want every single tattooist in Hamburg to see this. I want to know where it was done, when and by whom. My guess is that we're looking at something between fifteen and twenty years ago. As far as the team's concerned, we are looking for a single killer for Buried Man and for Detlev Traxinger.'

'Unless of course our unidentified guy just happened to have the same initials and this was a common tattoo,' said Brüggemann.

'He didn't.'

They all turned to see the bulky frame of Thom Glasmacher come into the Commission briefing room. He was carrying a hardback book, which he held up for the others to see. The title was *The Satan Network* and the author's name was Alan Edgar.

'Good book, is it, Thom?' asked Anna.

'Actually, it's terrible. I've only read a page and a half, but I can confidently say it's shit. But . . .' He flipped open the cover and held out the back flap of the dust jacket. There was a biography of the author, plus a photograph. The author was in his early forties, unexceptionally handsome, with blond hair sleeked back from a long face with strong cheekbones. Fabel recognized it instantly as the face of the buried man.

'And the initials "DT" do not fit with "Alan Edgar". Nor do they fit with his real name – Werner Hensler.'

'Hensler?' said Fabel. 'Werner Hensler . . . I've heard that name before . . .' He turned to the Monika Krone board and searched through the names, pegged and interlinked with red ribbon, of the people who had attended the party on the night Monika had disappeared. He went over to the conference table where the files had been piled up, selected one and rifled through it. 'Yes . . . here we are: Werner Hensler, a literature student. His alibi for after the party was confirmed by a Danish national studying at the university, Paul Mortensen, and by Tobias Albrecht—'

'Shit,' said Nicola Brüggemann. 'Let me guess, who was studying Architecture.'

Fabel checked the file. 'How did you know that?'

'The Bruno Tesch Centre, where we found our literary chum, was designed by Albrecht and Partners. Tobias Albrecht's firm.'

'Right.' Fabel's tone was decisive. 'Now we're getting somewhere. That's the focus for our search for a Traxinger connection. Thom, find out if this Dane still lives in Hamburg. If not, I'll get in touch with Karin Vestergaard at the Danish National Police in Copenhagen and get her to trace him for us. She owes me a favour.'

He looked again at the photograph of the tattoo. 'If "DT" doesn't stand for Detlev Traxinger, then what does it stand for?'

42

Like all such groups, the Club of the Living Dead followed the American convention of using first names only, but combined with the German etiquette of using the formal first-person form of address. This session, it was Hanne, the bourgeois woman from Blankenese, who still tried not to look too prosperous, who was the focus of Lorentz's interrogation and, reluctantly, did most of the talking.

'You think the world goes on for ever, that you go on for ever,' she explained. 'Everything is about expectations – what people, what the world expects from you and what you expect from people and the world. I knew who I was. I knew where I fitted in. Then, one day, I was doing the things I always did. I got home from work and started making the evening meal – my husband works in central Hamburg and I'm always home before him. Our kids are all at university or working. Anyway, I was chopping onions when I got this toothache. Bad, but vague, as if I couldn't pinpoint which tooth was causing the pain. It just seemed to radiate through the whole left side of my jaw. So I took painkillers and just got on with stuff. But the pain didn't go away and was now in my back – which made no sense to me – between the shoulder blades, then in the left shoulder blade itself. I was trying to work out if I'd twisted myself and could have injured my back and decided to sit down till it passed, but I didn't make it to the chair. It was like someone had put a metal band around my chest and was tightening it, crushing it. There still wasn't any chest pain, just intense pressure. All the pain was now in my back, jaw and arms.'

'Did you know you were having a heart attack?' asked Lorentz.

'No. I don't know why but I always thought it was men that got heart attacks and women got strokes. But I knew there was something very wrong. Like I said, I didn't make it to the chair: I was on the floor of the kitchen, on my hands and knees, struggling – and I mean really struggling – to breathe. Then I passed out. Michael, my husband, found me on the floor and dialled one-one-two. The ambulance team worked on me, but my heart had stopped.'

'And that's when you had your experience?'

She nodded. 'It was wonderful. I've listened to you all and you all have had different experiences, and you know how difficult they are to describe. But for a lot of you, you felt the presence of God. I didn't. Or maybe I experienced the same thing, but just see it as something different.'

'What did you see, Hanne?'

'Everything. The whole universe. I saw how things worked at the smallest level yet I could see into the depths of the universe, across galaxies. I saw the connection between the microscopic and the cosmic. Makes me sound like a hippy, doesn't it? But it's not like that.'

'No one here makes any judgements about anyone else,' said Lorentz. 'Tell me, Hanne, if I say to you that what you saw wasn't the universe, that you didn't suddenly see across time and space, that everything you experienced was simply chemical and electrical activity in your brain as a result of being near death, would you find that difficult to accept?'

'But don't you see? It doesn't matter. I *did* see across the universe, into it. I accept that it was perhaps all just generated in my brain, but the point is it was *in* my brain. It's in all of us – this enormous knowledge and capacity to understand. The only difference between us and everyone else is that we have been given the gift of seeing it. Some of you call it heaven. Okay, maybe it is ... for you. But the fact is that we all felt there was no time in the experience. That it lasted a second, or for ever. Whether it's paranormal or just neurochemical it doesn't matter.'

'I know exactly what you mean.' It was the ex-medical student, who now wore a patch over one eye, who spoke. A vague slur in his speech, along with the unquestioned eyepatch, indicated to the others that he had deteriorated since the last session. Lorentz's group dynamic, thought Fabel, was going to be disrupted by an absence sooner or later. 'The tendrils of my tumour stimulate different areas of the brain – that's physiology – but the result is, well, spiritual.'

'Exactly,' said Hanne. 'You could be right, Herr Doctor, that the basis of my NDE was all a neurological illusion. But the experience was real, valid. It unlocked a knowledge and an understanding I didn't know I had. The mechanism is irrelevant.'

'You clearly feel changed by the experience.' Lorentz, the monastic scientist, cradled his crossed knee in his hands, leaning forward in his seat. 'What has that change meant for you?'

'I was never that bright. Or I never considered myself bright. And I was never really encouraged to have any kind of ambition by my parents. I think it was clear from a young age that I wasn't academic. I scraped through my Abitur, but that was about as far as I was ever going to go, academically. But what I saw during my NDE . . . what I *understood* . . . it filled me with this deep curiosity. This need to understand more and better.'

'So what did you do?' asked Lorentz.

'I started reading. Then I did some evening classes.' Hanne paused, looking for a moment a little embarrassed. 'And now I'm doing a full-time MSc in Mathematical Physics at Hamburg Uni. It's taught in English, so I've had to improve my level in that too.'

'And how's that working out for you?'

'Surprisingly well. I mean, it's challenging, but mathematics is the language of the universe. I'm simply learning the vocabulary to express what I saw, the answers that opened up for me.'

There was more general discussion. It was one of Lorentz's protocols that the rest of the group comment on the observations of the individual. Everyone had his or her own, very personal, perspective. But every contradiction came with agreement, every disagreement with consensus. Everyone agreed their experience was unique, but a uniqueness based on common elements and principles. And everyone agreed that the experience had been positive.

'That, I'm afraid, is not always the case,' said Lorentz, with a professionally troubled expression. 'I agree with the Strassman hypothesis that the pineal gland, buried deep in the brain, is responsible for the natural production of dimethyltryptamine. This is better known as the psychedelic drug DMT. Its natural production, which tends to be linked to the amount of light around us, has a lot to do with states of consciousness, sleep patterns and the like. It also may be what causes us to dream. I think that dimethyltryptamine is released in massive doses at the point of death and this, combined with a lightning storm of electrical activity in the brain, is what causes such convincing hallucinations, as well as the illusion of greatly heightened senses.'

'When I had my NDE, which involved a full out-of-body experience, I heard one of the nurses say something I didn't understand,' said Fabel. 'But I remembered the word – *kahretsin*. I found out later that the nurse was Turkish-German, and *kahretsin* means "shit". She remembered saying it because she knocked a tray of stuff over when they were working on me. That wasn't a hallucination. It happened.'

'I'm sure it did. And you weren't dead. You were *near* death and all of your senses were still functioning. Perhaps at a different level of consciousness, but you would still process sounds, sensations, et cetera.'

Others in the group began to chime in. They, like Fabel, protested the authenticity of their experiences. Several offered similar verifications. Fabel listened, nodded, voiced agreement, but deep inside knew that his experience had been some kind of neurological, not spiritual, episode. It was just so difficult to let it go. And maybe, as the bourgeoise Blankenese housewife-turned-quantum physicist had asserted, it didn't really matter.

Lorentz held up his hand to halt the crosstalk. 'Anyway, whether you accept it or not, there is growing evidence that NDEs are effectively psychedelic experiences generated by a massive release of DMT and other neurochemicals and hormones. You all have had positive experiences because you launched into your DMT psychedelic state with a rush of euphoria-producing endorphins being released into your system. But sometimes the mix is different. Sometimes the DMT interacts with a rush of cortisol, the stress hormone, before endorphins are released. Any recreational user of DMT or ayahuasca or even psilocybin mushrooms will tell you that you have to be in a positive and relaxed mood before taking a hit. Mostly the experience is positive, but if you have a bad trip, it can be truly horrifying.'

'So you can have a near-death experience "bad trip"?' asked Fabel.

'I have – or had – a patient whom I wanted to take part in this group, but he refused. He refused further treatment, for that matter, despite him being a professional therapist himself. His near-death experience – following an attack in which he was stabbed – was actually, like yours, a mainly positive experience, but towards the end it took a very, very dark turn. He found himself in some kind of hell filled with demons. The damage was lasting, too. I'm afraid I was treating him for Cotard's Delusion when he stopped coming to see me.'

'Cotard's Delusion?' The young ex-medical student frowned, forcing him to adjust his eyepatch, and Fabel realized it was the first time he'd seen him look troubled. 'That's bad . . .'

'Cotard's Delusion,' Lorentz addressed the rest of them, 'is a tragic personality disorder, also called Delusion of Death. It is, like in the case of my ex-patient, often caused by trauma. Sufferers believe themselves to be dead. A common characteristic is for them to turn up at graveyards and demand to be buried. Some believe they are ghosts, others that they are animate corpses, moving about but rotting away. It's tragic, but thankfully it's rare. I've only come across this case and one other in my whole career. Anyway, my point is that what you experienced at the point of death is no more or less than the same kind of psychedelic trip that an ayahuasca or DMT user experiences.'

'Unless,' said Sepp, the unexceptional business-type, 'what ayahuasca causes is also a genuine spiritual experience.'

43

Hübner had found it odd how, from their first encounter, he had opened up to Zombie. It had been like that even in the prison. Herr Mensing, as Zombie was known there, had been Frankenstein's social therapist and counsellor. There had been something in the way Zombie had looked at him – or more correctly something missing in the way he looked at him: fear. There had never been the slightest hint of it in the way Herr Mensing had dealt with Frankenstein during their sessions. No fear, no apprehension or mistrust or revulsion. He had even insisted at the first session that the guard leave them alone, which he did only reluctantly. The other thing that had set Herr Mensing apart was that he treated Hübner with respect; he was interested in what the giant of a man across the table had to say about himself, the world and his place in it.

To start with, Frankenstein had suspected their empathy had something to do with the way Mensing looked himself. His thick dark hair emphasized the sickly paleness of his complexion and his face was all skull angles, his hands skeletal, long fingers almost fleshless under the skin. At times, Hübner had felt that Mensing was only partly there in the room with him, as if some other fragment of his being was absent, or occupying some distant place. Eventually Frankenstein decided it was simply that they had recognized each other as outsiders, shunned by the world and sharing the same dark corner.

Jochen Hübner had never had friends, never had time for or wanted friends. When, from the age of thirteen, he had slowly turned monstrous, he had settled himself to a life alone, but one where he set the agenda for his rejection from society. For whatever reason, Herr Mensing – Zombie – was the only person he had trusted. The only person who had not treated him as a monster; the only person who had talked to him, tried to understand him, who had shown him kindness.

It was as if Zombie had been blind to Hübner's appearance. And that here, in this misleadingly remote house hidden in a swathe of woodland in the heart of Germany's second biggest city, Jochen Hübner had come to know friendship and had become blind to his own monstrosity.

Zombie came once a day, usually at the same time, around lunchtime. He would let himself into the house and the cellar, deliver the fresh provisions he had brought and sit for a while, talking to Hübner and sometimes sharing lunch. Today he chose to talk about the mission he had set the giant.

'What I want to know,' Frankenstein said, 'is why? You know that I'll do exactly what you've asked me to do whether you explain it to me or not. But I'd like to know why.'

'That's reasonable,' the pale wraith in the corner said. 'I'll explain . . .'

And he did. He talked for over an hour, explaining what had happened, about a night fifteen years before, a nightmare, who had to pay for it, why they had to pay for it, when and how.

When Zombie had finished, Frankenstein sat quiet, nodding. There was more than one kind of monster, he realized. And the real monsters were the ones you couldn't recognize by looking at them. The ones disguised behind a mask of normality.

'I saw things,' said Frankenstein, emboldened by Zombie's openness. 'When my heart stopped, I mean.'

'What kind of things?' Zombie leaned forward, a slow folding of cloth and bone.

'Memories, but memories I could watch. I saw who I used to be. I remembered what it was like not to be a monster.' The huge shoulders sagged. 'It was nice. Beautiful. It made me happy then, but sad now. Now that I can't go back to it.'

'Yes you can.' Zombie smiled. 'I can take you back there. Without the risk. Would you like to go?'

Frankenstein nodded.

'It isn't working,' said Hübner. 'Nothing is happening.' It had been five minutes, at least, since Zombie had injected the DMT.

'Yes it is,' said Zombie. 'Just wait.'

Hübner felt the impatience rise in him, but noticed that it was a cool, rageless impatience, unlike the restless fury he usually felt. 'I'm telling you, nothing's happening . . .'

'Just wait . . .' The voice that said it wasn't Zombie's. Zombie's mouth hadn't moved. Hübner looked around the cellar. Something else, someone else had spoken to him, but he knew it wasn't a voice in his head, it was a voice from outside his head. It was the strangest feeling: he felt completely normal, felt totally in control, yet everything was beginning to operate on a different level. He looked down at the floor of the cellar. He couldn't see through the flagstones, through the dense clay and soil beneath, yet he knew there were roots beneath him, a spider web of tendrils from the trees around the house, alive, feeding, drawing moisture and nourishment, holding the house like cupped fingers beneath it. He could suddenly smell the soil, smell the life and death in the soil, the cycle of decay and renewal; he became aware of the forest beyond the walls of the cellar: a vast, living, breathing thing. The air around him began to change: it became viscous, palpable.

Frankenstein started to fade away; his body became a concept, not a solid reality. He left his monstrousness behind.

He collapsed into himself. He remembered things he thought he had long ago forgotten and they played out in front of him. Not once did he lose his bearings: he knew he was still in the cellar, but he was also everywhere else, every time else he had been.

He was a small boy again. He was playing with his toy cars and trucks in the garden of his parents' home, creating his own imagined world, contented and unaware of the genetic predestiny within him, of the malevolent endocrinology already conspiring to turn him into a monster.

He lay down on the cellar floor, not because he needed to, but because he wanted to be closer to the roots beneath him, around him, through him; the endless web of consciousness that linked every place, every time he had ever been.

He saw his mother again. She was beautiful. She smiled at little Jochen and held his cheek in her soft, cool palm and talked quietly to him about his toys.

It wasn't that the scene changed, it was more that another level of time and place superimposed itself. It was now his fourteenth birthday. There was piano music, soft and echoing, a slow, sad waltz, and Jochen danced with his mother. Already he was big and clumsy, but his mother didn't seem to notice. He had been so happy that day and she had said the strangest thing to him: that she would always be there to look after him. To make things right.

There, in the dark cellar now and in the bright room where they danced then, two moments that occupied the same space, Jochen forgave her. He forgave her for her lie: she had left him alone. Two years later she went away and even that day when they had danced she would have known about the disease growing inside her, spreading. Taking her away from him by degrees. But he forgave her.

The experience lasted hours, maybe even a full day, most of it spent with his mother and others he could not quite see. Then Zombie guided him back, slowly, gently, as the DMT started to wear off.

When he was fully back in the now, Frankenstein checked his watch. The whole experience had really only lasted about fifteen minutes.

Afterwards, he thanked Zombie for being his guide and guardian once more, and fell into a deep, dreamless sleep.

44

It took less time than Fabel had imagined it would. It was like triangulation on a map: they now had three landmarks, reference points: Monika Krone, Werner Hensler and Tobias Albrecht. All three had been at the party the night Monika had disappeared, but Detlev Traxinger had not. But their relative positions gave Fabel's team the coordinates they needed.

He phoned Susanne and told her he'd be late, which turned out not to be a problem because she was working late herself at the Institute for Judicial Medicine. He sat in his office examining the connections the team had made that day and going through fifteen-year-old statements, letting the past come to life in his head. It was something he was good at, a natural at. Fabel had always considered that he had become a policeman by accident: he had been a gifted History student at the universities of Oldenburg and Hamburg and had always seen his future mapped out for him as a historian. But then a girl, a fellow student he had been having a casual relationship with, had been abducted, raped and murdered. Suddenly his relationship with her had no longer seemed casual and his future less clear. He became obsessed with trying to understand what had happened to his girlfriend and what led people to commit acts of violence on others. The day he finished his studies, he applied for officer-level entry into the Polizei Hamburg.

But the instincts and skills that would have guided him as a historian instead guided him as a detective – and now he used them to force an event from the past to come back to life in the present.

Going through the fifteen-year-old statements from the partygoers, he saw that three girls who had been friends with Monika had previously dated Tobias Albrecht, then an Architecture student. One of them had also dated Werner Hensler, the future horror writer. Another couple, who probably had long since parted and married other people, had attended the party together and had both mentioned in their statements that Hensler and Albrecht had been friends of sorts.

And all five referred to someone who had not been able to make the party that night. It was a detail you had to be looking for to find. Two partygoers referred to the missing person as a friend of Hensler, one stated that it had been a friend of Albrecht, and two witnesses indicated he had been a friend of both men. It had been, in the original investigation, less than a footnote. All named him as Detlev Traxinger.

During the original investigation, Traxinger hadn't even made it onto the list of Monika's acquaintances. He had been identified as an absence, rather than a presence. Was Traxinger, Fabel wondered, the ghost whose presence he had sensed in his rereading of the files?

At the end of a three-hour session of referencing and cross-referencing, Fabel set the members of his team their respective tasks. Tobias Albrecht was someone Fabel wanted to talk to personally and he asked Anna to fix up a time for them both to interview the architect.

'And Anna,' said Fabel, 'be insistent. Herr Albrecht is connected to two murder victims, one of whom was found in a building he designed. Until we can ascertain otherwise, he's a potential suspect. Explain to him his full cooperation is in his best interest.'

Throughout his career, Jan Fabel had always tried to keep personal feelings out of how he treated a witness or a suspect. Sometimes, he knew, you took a like or dislike to someone on first meeting and it was very difficult to keep those feelings from colouring your attitude. The guilty, Fabel had learned, could be likeable and charming; the innocent could be arseholes.

Fabel took a profound dislike to Tobias Albrecht the instant he met him. So profound that he was surprised by the intensity of his antipathy towards the architect.

It wasn't that he hadn't been cooperative. Albrecht certainly hadn't delayed seeing them, agreeing to meet Fabel and Anna at his offices the very next morning. His architectural practice, Albrecht and Partners, was located in the HafenCity, Hamburg's twenty-first-century interpretation of its Hanseatic traditions. Albrecht had, of course, designed the building himself and Fabel was surprised to see how elegant and restrained it was in comparison to the incongruous jangle of steel and glazing in Altona where they had found the writer's body.

Everything in Albrecht's offices was cool and elegant, including the staff, all of whom looked as if they had been recruited from a modelling agency rather than architectural college. Albrecht's sense of the aesthetic obviously extended into every part of his business. A tall, blonde and glacial assistant catwalked Anna and Fabel to where he waited for them.

Albrecht's office was a huge and mostly empty space with a

vast redwood desk sitting throne-like at the far end, the wall behind it a mosaic of slate shards. The architect stood up when the police officers entered, and smiled a vulpine smile. He was dressed in a pale grey houndstooth double-breasted suit and a black shirt, open at the neck. Albrecht's hair was almost unnaturally black against his strikingly pale complexion and his strong jaw was blued with precision-measured stubble. His eyes were a piercing blue beneath the dark arches of his eyebrows. He asked Fabel and Anna to sit.

'As Frau Commissar Wolff has already informed you,' Fabel began, 'we are investigating the deaths of the painter Detlev Traxinger and the author Werner Hensler, whose body was found in an incomplete building designed by you.'

Albrecht leaned back in his leather chair and nodded thoughtfully. 'Yes . . . yes, it's all a terrible business. Obviously I'll do anything I can to help.'

'We believe that both victims were friends of yours,' said Anna.

'No . . . not at all.' Albrecht seemed surprised by the suggestion.

'But you did know them both?' asked Fabel.

'Knew them, yes. But I hadn't seen or spoken to either for years. No . . . actually that's not correct. I bumped into Detlev at a city function, about three months ago, but we only exchanged a few words. Werner I haven't seen for years.'

'Since university?' asked Fabel. 'You were closer back then, would I be right in thinking?'

'We certainly had more to do with each other than we do now, if that's what you mean.'

'What I mean is that you were friends. We know that for a fact.'

Albrecht held Fabel in his cold blue gaze. If he was rattled, he wasn't showing it. 'Acquaintances. Not friends. Part of the same crowd. We were students at the Hamburg Uni at roughly the same time, but studied different subjects. We went to the same social events, had friends in common, that kind of thing.'

'And you all knew Monika Krone, didn't you?'

'What's this got to do with Monika?'

'Don't you find it a coincidence that within a month of Monika Krone's body being discovered, two members of *the same crowd*, as you put it, are found murdered?'

'You can't seriously be suggesting there's a connection?'

Fabel didn't answer right away, but took in the office: the wall behind Albrecht with its blue-grey shards of slate, the polished wood of the floor and the raw wood in the ceiling beams, the large windows looking out towards the elegant nineteenth-century red-brick warehouses of the Speicherstadt from one aspect, the rest of the HafenCity from the other.

'This really is a beautifully designed office,' said Fabel. 'I really like the way you've combined the natural, the organic, I suppose, with the high-tech. I also like the way you've combined the past with the present, even the future.'

Albrecht didn't answer.

'The past and the present are always intertwined,' Fabel continued. 'The HafenCity has nothing to do with the Speicherstadt, really, but if there hadn't been a Speicherstadt, there wouldn't be a HafenCity. If Hamburg hadn't been a medieval Hanseatic city, it wouldn't be leading the world in trade with emergent economies today. History echoes through everything, Herr Albrecht. I'm hearing echoes with these killings.'

Albrecht pulled his handsome features into a *maybe* expression. 'It's a hell of a stretch. Isn't it more likely that it's just a coincidence? Werner and Detlev didn't have anything much to do with each other after university either.'

'Oh?' said Fabel. 'And how would you know that? I mean if you had no dealings with either, for all you know they were in regular contact with each other.'

'I told you I bumped into Detlev at a function. I asked him then if he ever saw anyone from uni, and he said no.'

'I see.' Fabel paused again. 'The three of you were all involved, in one way or another, in the arts scene, you all went to the same university at the same time, and all three of you remained in Hamburg. Isn't it odd that you never had any contact with each other, or even bumped into each other more than you did? It's almost as if you went out of your way to avoid each other.'

'Is it?' said Albrecht. Another faintly amused but confused expression. 'People go their separate ways, that's all. Have you kept in touch with everyone you went to uni with?'

'I've kept in touch – even regular touch – with the people I was friendly with. And like I said, the three of you were involved in the Hamburg arts scene—'

Albrecht laughed loudly. 'I wouldn't call what Werner did art. And I did tell you that Detlev and I would run into each other at the occasional function. I'm sorry you find it odd if we didn't see each other otherwise. But that's as far as it goes: maybe odd, but not sinister, which seems to be what you're implying.'

'Unless, of course, there was something, some event, that made you decide not to see each other again. Like I said, the past shapes the present. It's almost as if the three of you made some kind of agreement fifteen years ago never to see each other again.'

'Of course we didn't. You're talking utter nonsense.'

'Did you know Monika Krone?' asked Anna.

'I was asked that fifteen years ago when she first went missing, so you already know the answer.'

'That's right.' Anna smiled. 'You and she were involved, weren't you?'

'For a while.' Albrecht made a show of sighing. 'But that ended months before her disappearance – again, you already know all about that. And you also know that it was a very casual involvement. She was a very beautiful girl and I had lots of relationships with lots of other female students. There was nothing deep nor special about my relationship with Monika.'

'And you were able to account for your movements at the time of her disappearance, as I recall.'

Albrecht now held Anna in his cold, blue gaze. She showed no sign of being impressed.

'I was,' he said.

'And that seems to complete the circle,' said Fabel, 'and brings us back to the late Herr Hensler, who happened to be your alibi for that evening, and you his. In his statement at the time, he said you and he went on from the party to a bar. Or several bars.'

'Where we were seen by other people.'

'Only later in the evening,' said Anna. 'No one can remember seeing you at the first couple of bars.'

'I can't help that. We didn't go out of our way to be conspicuous. We had no idea that we should be making sure people saw us to support our alibi. And if we had, I'm sure you would have found that suspicious too.'

'Maybe you could tell us where you were the nights Detlev Traxinger and Werner Hensler died,' said Anna.

This time, Fabel saw something shift in Albrecht's expression.

'I was at a dinner the night Detlev was killed. I have a dozen or more people who can confirm that.'

'And when Herr Hensler was murdered?'

'I was at home,' he said eventually.

'Alone?' asked Anna.

'No.'

'So someone can verify you were there?'

'No.'

'Why not?'

Another sigh. 'I was with someone. A woman. A married woman. I can't give you her name.'

'Herr Albrecht,' said Anna, 'you can be assured that we are very discreet. And I have to stress that it's in your best interests to cooperate. Anything you tell us will be in complete confidence.'

'No it won't – you'll have to go and talk to her to confirm that she spent the night with me. And God knows how many people will be able to find out.' He paused and gave a strange, small laugh. 'She might not even back up my story. We are talking about someone with a position to think about. So no, I can't tell you. And, to be frank, I don't see why I have to. You are treating me as a suspect yet you have absolutely no grounds to believe that I killed Detlev. Or worse still Werner, who I probably would have walked past in the street without recognizing.'

Fabel watched Albrecht for a moment. The architect still was in control of his emotions. He nodded to Anna who reached into her bag and took out two photographs. She stood up, leaned across the desk and placed the photographs in front of Albrecht. He picked them up and examined them.

'What's this?' he asked.

'This tattoo has no significance for you?' asked Fabel.

Albrecht examined the photographs again and shook his head.

'These photographs were taken of both bodies in the mortuary. Herr Traxinger and Herr Hensler had identical tattoos, in exactly the same spot.'

Albrecht shrugged and held the photographs out to Anna. When she didn't take them, he let them fall back onto the vast polished plateau of his desk.

'What's the significance of the initials "DT"?' she asked.

'I have absolutely no idea. Detlev's initials?'

'Then why would Werner Hensler have the same initials?'

'Like I say, I'm afraid I really have no idea.' Albrecht stood up to punctuate the end of the conversation. 'I have to get on. I have answered all of your questions and there's nothing more I can add.'

Fabel and Anna made no move to stand up.

'I don't suppose you have a similar tattoo, Herr Albrecht?'

Albrecht laughed as if confounded by the stupidity of Fabel's question. 'No, of course I don't.'

Fabel and Anna remained silent. Albrecht sighed and unbuttoned first his suit jacket, then his black shirt, pulling it open to reveal his chest above the heart. His chest was heavily muscled, the skin smooth and very pale. And unmarked by a tattoo.

'Satisfied?'

'Thank you, Herr Albrecht,' said Fabel.

As they made their way back to the car, Anna said, 'Well, whatever the significance of the tattoo, he certainly doesn't have one. He off the list?'

'No, Anna,' said Fabel. 'Herr Albrecht has just promoted himself to the top of the suspect list. Let me see the morgue photographs again.'

Frowning, she stopped, searched her bag and handed the photographs to Fabel.

'Look,' he said. 'These are extreme close-ups of the tattoos.'

'So?'

'You can't see anything else other than the tattoos and a centimetre or so of skin around them. There's no clue as to whereabouts on the body they are. It could be an arm, a thigh, a shoulder, anywhere.'

Anna's eyes widened slightly as the realization hit her. 'So how did Albrecht know to show us the left side of his chest?'

'When we get back, I want absolutely everything we've got on Herr Tobias Albrecht.'

45

Water was Fabel's element. He grew up by the sea, had an
instinct always to be close to it. It was an element, and an
instinct, he shared with Hamburg. The city was a paradox: a
world-leading seaport more than a hundred kilometres from
where the Elbe opened its mouth wide into the North Sea. But it
was the ocean and maritime trade routes that had shaped the
city. And there was water everywhere: the deep, broad river Elbe
that ran through it, the Binnen and Aussen Alster lakes, the web
of canals – more than Amsterdam and Venice combined – that
connected the whole city.

And sometimes, when he needed to think, he followed his
instinct to be near water and got away from the Presidium. One
of his favourite venues was a café by the Winterhuder Fährhaus,
a canal stop where small red and white ferries would pause to
drop off or pick up passengers. It was close enough to the Presidium but offered him a chance to break away from the constant
flow of paperwork, internal emails and interruptions.

This small canalside café, along with another Turkish-
German one in Ottensen, had become two of the places Fabel
went to be alone. In both places he was known but anonymous;
recognized, but simply as a regular who usually came alone, sat
alone and left alone.

Today, however, Fabel had arranged to meet Anna there and she had phoned to say she was running late. While he waited, he ordered a tea and phoned the Institute for Judicial Medicine for an update on the autopsy results from both victims. He got through to Holger Brauner.

'I think we've maybe got something for you,' said Brauner. 'Something came up in toxicology on both victims and we're in the process of isolating it.'

'The same thing in both of them?'

'Looks like, but let me get back to you. I'll give you a buzz as soon as I know more.'

Fabel had just hung up when Anna arrived. He waved to the waiter and ordered a coffee for her.

'We've checked every tattooist operating in Hamburg,' she explained. 'Not one remembers ever doing that monogram motif. Of course it was fifteen years ago . . .'

'But whoever did the tattoos did more than one.'

'That's not the point – some of the tattooists operating fifteen years ago are no longer around, for one reason or another. But we'll keep on it.'

'What about Tobias Albrecht – you get anything on him?'

'No criminal record at all . . .' Anna flicked through her notes. 'Rich parents, educated at a boarding school here in Germany and another in France. Studied architecture at the Uni Hamburg and post-grad at Bauhaus-Weimar. About seven years ago he made it onto this list – "the top ten young European architects to watch". He's an important guy in the world of architecture. But he has been in a few scrapes though.'

'Oh?'

'Basically he fucks anything that moves. I mean, he's a really good-looking guy and he obviously knows how to work the whole bad-boy thing, so I guess he wouldn't need to try hard, but it goes way beyond that. Almost pathological. Sex-addiction . . . satyrism, I think they call it. Anyway, he's left a string of broken hearts, broken marriages, abortions and Christ knows what else in his wake. He tends to go for married women to avoid the complication of commitment. It all came to a head about five years ago and he's learned to be a bit more discreet since then.'

'What happened?' asked Fabel.

'A girlfriend tried to kill him – stuck a knife in him – in a fit of jealousy and then killed herself. From what I can gather it shook him up a bit.'

'I don't remember that,' said Fabel.

'It didn't happen in our jurisdiction. It was in Bremen. I've asked the Polizei Nordrhein-Westfalen to email me copies of all the relevant files. Albrecht got a team of lawyers to sit on the press – protection of privacy, that kind of crap – but it still got a fair amount of coverage.'

'Is there any chance it wasn't a suicide?' Fabel paused; a young couple passed by their table as they left the café and he waited till they were out of earshot. 'That she stabbed Albrecht in self-defence?'

'Like I said, the details are on their way but no, from what I've been able to find out, it was pretty clearly a jealous rage thing. There was a witness, apparently – the woman Albrecht was banging when his girlfriend found them together. Believe me, getting the dirt on him has been easy, and I've only scratched the surface.'

'Anything else?'

'Just that he was holding back on us about just how close the three of them were at university. Albrecht was a hell of a lot pallier with Werner Hensler and Detlev Traxinger than he let on. I made a few phone calls and there are a couple of old university contemporaries of theirs I'd like to chat to. All three were complete arseholes, from what I can gather, and they all were pretty busy with the female students. Obviously Albrecht was busier than the others.'

'So the three of them were all friends together, not just Traxinger and Albrecht?'

'If anything, it seems like Albrecht and Hensler were closer. But yes, the three of them, plus the Dane who was interviewed at the time of Monika's disappearance. Paul Mortensen.'

Fabel nodded thoughtfully. 'So, Hensler is Albrecht's alibi, and vice versa. Let me guess . . .'

'Yep,' said Anna. 'Mortensen and Traxinger provided each other with an alibi for Monika's abduction and murder. You think the four of them were acting in concert?'

'I think it's a distinct possibility. And it looks a hell of a lot like the discovery of Monika's remains has been the trigger for two of them being ticked off a list. What I don't know is if Albrecht is on the list or is the person holding it. Whatever is going on, he and this Dane are both suspects and potential victims.'

'Unless we're reading this all wrong,' said Anna.

'But if we are reading this wrong, what is the motive for killing two university compatriots who haven't seen each other for years? And why the symbolism? We need to talk to the Dane, Mortensen. Do we have anything on where he is now?'

'Thom Glasmacher checked him out. He left Hamburg after his studies and went back to Denmark. Copenhagen, Thom thinks.'

'I'll get on to Karin Vestergaard—'

'There's more,' Anna interrupted. 'Just by chance, as well as the ex-students I got on the phone, one of the SchuPo commanders based here went to Hamburg at the same time, studying law. She got in touch with me because she knew we were looking into the case again. She said everyone knew, or at least knew of, the "Gothic set", as they were known.'

'The "Gothic set"?'

'It was apparently their thing – Traxinger, Hensler, Albrecht, Mortensen and – wait for it – Monika Krone. There were others, of course, maybe about twenty of them. They all revolved around a literature professor – Thorsten Rohde – who had set up an informal Gothic Studies club. '

'Damn it,' said Fabel. 'I read something about that in the files. Not as specific as that, just that there was some kind of Goth thing going on. I didn't take it seriously – just thought it was dressing up, that kind of crap.'

'It seems to have been much more serious. I mean more academic and literary. Not just a bunch of losers listening to death-metal.'

'You're being very scathing, Commissar Wolff. I thought you were into that kind of thing yourself, at one time.'

'Me? You're kidding. Punk was my thing . . .' She frowned, reading something in Fabel's expression. 'What is it?'

'It's just that these two killings . . . there's more than a touch of the Gothic about them. The *Picture of Dorian Gray* thing that was going on at the Traxinger scene – then the Edgar Allan Poe-type premature burial of Werner Hensler.'

'You think it's a serial killer with a literary bent?'

'No, it doesn't feel right. There'd have to be another murder before it's officially serial anyway, but this is more personally invested than that. It all lies in the connections between them . . .

and with Monika Krone.' Fabel sipped his tea and looked across the water to the park on the other bank, the spire of the Sankt Johanniskirche in Eppendorf piercing a sheet of blue-white sky above the tree line. The season was changing and Fabel could feel it. 'There's a connection we're just not seeing.'

'Dare I say it, *Chef*, that connection might be Frankenstein. He's still on the loose and there hasn't been a single sighting of him.'

'Even if he did abduct and murder Monika, why would Jochen Hübner want to kill Traxinger and Hensler? No, it's something else . . .'

Fabel was not long back in his office when there was a knock at the door and Henk Hermann came in, something dark in his expression.

'How's it going with the seniors' home thing?' asked Fabel.

'Confusing.'

'Oh?'

'I don't mean the processing – the state prosecutor's office has agreed that Georg Schmidt will never be competent to stand trial. His mental state is deteriorating so fast that it's unlikely he will ever remember what he did, far less why he did it. I mean the background. I've been reading through Schmidt's diary and there's a lot of stuff that doesn't make sense. At the end of the day I suppose it doesn't make a difference, but I'm going to check something out before I sign the case off. I'll get back to you when I've got a handle on it. But that's not what I wanted to see you about.'

'Oh?'

'There was a call from the Danish National Police headquarters in Copenhagen – a *Politidirektør* Vestergaard. She wanted you to know she got your email and she'd like you to give her a call.'

Fabel thanked Henk and when he had left dialled Vestergaard's number. When he had first met her, Karin Vestergaard had been a tough character to get to know. Fabel had worked with her a few years before and the Danish officer had been edgy and defensive. But despite a frosty start, they had got on well, even though Germans had not been high on her list of favourite nationalities. Fabel had joked with her that he was a Frisian, and there were Frisians in Denmark and the Netherlands, not just Germany.

He got through to her straight away. English was their chosen language of communication. They both spoke it perfectly: Fabel because his mother was Scottish and he'd spent some of his youth in Britain, and Vestergaard simply because she was a Dane. There was the usual small talk and catch-up chat, which was neither Fabel's nor Vestergaard's forte, before they got down to the case.

'If you don't mind me saying, Jan, your email was a little confusing – do you consider Professor Mortensen a suspect in your case, a witness, or a potential victim?'

'That's my problem: he could be any of the above. *Professor* Mortensen, you say?'

'Yes. You've picked not just a Danish citizen, but one of our most notable Danish citizens. Paul Mortensen is one of the world's leading experts on blood cancers.'

'I knew he had studied medicine. Have you located him?'

'That's the thing – he's on tour at the moment.'

'On tour?'

'Yep – he's the Mick Jagger of the haematology world. A lecture and conference tour. Which is why I wanted to get in touch with you quickly. He's in Paris at the moment, then Amsterdam tomorrow. His last stop before returning to Copenhagen is Hamburg. There's a conference at the CCH at the end of the week.'

'Do you know where he's staying?'

'Not yet, but I'd guess one of the hotels near the congress centre.'

'There's one hotel attached to it but over a hundred in the area,' said Fabel.

'I'll check with his wife – she knows his arrangements.'

'Mortensen is married? How long?'

'Yes, he's married . . .' Vestergaard sounded puzzled. 'He has a ten-year-old daughter and a son about seven, why?'

'Happily married?'

'I have no idea, Jan. I guess. What's this all about?'

'You've met his wife?'

'No, but I know of her. She's a city politician here in Copenhagen.'

'I know this sounds a weird question to ask, but what colour is her hair?'

'Blonde. A touch lighter than mine. What the hell has that got to do with anything?'

'Obsession. And whether Mortensen has an immunity to a particular strain of it.'

'Jan, you know that I'm not one to be afraid to step on toes, but Professor Mortensen is a very important guy up here. A little international diplomacy would be appreciated.'

'Of course, Karin. Do let me know if you find out which hotel he'll be staying in.'

46

As he drove to Ochsenzoll, in the north of the city, Henk Hermann felt a little aggrieved that he had been doubly lumbered. He was out of the main cases – both the historical Krone inquiry and the current murders that could be related to the cold case. Instead he was stuck with the paperwork of the seniors' home killing. And he had been saddled with nursemaiding the new guy, Sven Bruns.

But he didn't let his annoyance show. Henk Hermann was an easy-going, friendly type and, in any case, the new guy couldn't help being the new guy. Henk reminded himself that it hadn't been so very long ago that he'd been the new guy himself and Anna Wolff had been doing the nursemaiding. But it had been different back then: back then, Henk had been filling a dead man's shoes.

He had been stationed in Norderstedt, in the north of Hamburg. Because of old borders, Norderstedt, though considered a part of metropolitan Hamburg, didn't fall under the jurisdiction of the Hamburg police. Therefore Henk had been a uniform commissar in the Polizei Schleswig-Holstein, not the Polizei Hamburg. That hadn't prevented Fabel from recognizing Henk's keen instincts and eye for detail, and he had recruited him directly into the Murder Commission. In one fell swoop, Henk's every ambition had been fulfilled.

It was only after he had joined the Commission that Henk realized he had been recruited as a replacement for Paul Lindemann, a long-standing member of the Commission team who had been shot and killed while on duty. Anna Wolff, who had been the dead police officer's partner, had been openly resentful at the speed with which Fabel had replaced him. Henk hadn't understood why Anna had given him such a hard time until he had seen a photograph of Lindemann and noticed there was a considerable physical similarity between them. For a while Henk had felt as if Anna and the others were all seeing Paul Lindemann's ghost every time they looked at him. It had caused him to wonder, at the time and since, if his superficial similarity with Lindemann had played a part in Fabel's decision to recruit him. After all, it was human nature to expect similar personalities in people who looked alike.

As they made their way to the hospital, Henk made an effort to chat to Sven Bruns, but the lanky Frisian was quiet to the point of dour, and Henk eventually fell into silence too.

Georg Schmidt was being kept in a secure psychiatric wing of the Klinik Nord in Ochsenzoll and Henk and Sven were kept waiting for some time before the consulting psychiatrist, a short, balding man carrying too much weight for his height, turned up. He introduced himself as Dr Gosau.

'And why, exactly, do you want to interview my patient again?' Gosau had a high-pitched, thin voice that seemed to emphasize his supercilious tone.

'There's a couple of things we'd like to clear up . . .' Henk held up a plastic document folder as if in explanation. 'A question or two we'd like to ask.'

'Things you'd like to clear up?' Gosau overdid the incredulity in his tone. 'You do realize that Herr Schmidt is well beyond being able to clarify anything for himself, far less for you?'

'I understand.' Henk hid his dislike for the doctor behind a smile. 'But I was led to believe that he had some periods of lucidity. It's just that there is an inconsistency I don't understand. If he could clear it up, then that would be great. If he can't, then we'll leave him alone. I do appreciate that Herr Schmidt is very ill, but he did kill a man and I'm trying to understand why.'

'I cannot allow you to take advantage of his condition so that he incriminates himself.'

'There's no question of that, Herr Doctor,' said Henk, keeping the smile locked in place. 'We have more than enough evidence that Herr Schmidt committed the murder – but there's no question of him ever facing trial for it. That's not why we're here.' Henk held up the evidence bag he was carrying. In it was the notebook journal they had found hidden in Schmidt's room at the Alte Mühle Seniors' Home – locked away in a drawer that had been opened with the key they had found on a chain around the old man's neck. 'There's something in here doesn't make any sense. If there's any chance of him explaining it, then I'd be grateful. If not, then we'll have to chalk it up to a mystery.'

Despite himself, Gosau looked intrigued.

'And, of course, Herr Doctor,' said Sven Bruns, 'if you had the time to sit in on the interview, we'd really appreciate it. It means you can be assured your patient's rights aren't being compromised – and we would greatly value your professional insight.'

While Gosau made a show of thinking over what he had said, Sven looked over to Henk and smiled. Maybe, thought Henk, Bruns was okay after all.

'All right,' said Gosau, 'but if I say the interview is to end, it's to end. Clear?'

'Perfectly, Herr Doctor,' said Henk, holding his hand out in an 'after you' gesture.

There was a kind of day room at the far end of the ward and Gosau arranged for them not to be disturbed. It was on the third floor and above tree level, so the windows were large sheets of sky and the room was bright.

Georg Schmidt was smaller than Henk imagined he would be. He had seen old photographs of the seniors' home killer: one as a tall, athletic-looking youth with a shock of thick blond hair, one of Schmidt dressed in military uniform, another in his mid-sixties, the hair darkened, thinner and flecked with grey but the robustness and vigour of youth still lingering.

The frail, small figure sitting uncertainly at the table seemed to be the time-eroded ruins of the man; the original architecture only just recognizable. The once-broad shoulders were slumped and bird-boned, the hair had thinned to a white web combed over the dome of his skull, and his skin was mottled with freckles and liver spots. The eyes that watched Henk and Sven guilelessly had retreated into their orbits and the cheeks were sunken. Georg Schmidt was by far the most unlikely murderer Henk had ever dealt with.

Dr Gosau spoke to Schmidt first. Henk was surprised to see the arrogant veneer and superciliousness evaporate from the psychiatrist. He spoke quietly and soothingly to Schmidt, asking how he was today, if he could remember what he'd had for lunch, what day of the week it was. When he was finished, Gosau introduced Henk and Sven as 'visitors' and made no reference to their official capacity. But when he turned back to the policemen, his expression was warningly protective. Henk acknowledged Gosau's look with a nod.

'Herr Schmidt,' he said as he and Sven sat down opposite the old man, 'I'd like to ask you a few questions, if I may.' Placing the plastic document folder on the table in front of him, Henk took out Schmidt's diary and laid it on top of the folder. Schmidt looked at the leather-bound journal without any signs of recognition.

'Do you remember when you were younger? Do you remember before the war?'

Schmidt nodded.

'You knew Helmut Wohlmann back then, didn't you?'

'Helmut?' The dull eyes brightened a little. 'Where is Helmut? We play chequers, you know.'

'Yes,' said Henk gently. 'I do know. But can you remember Helmut before the war?'

'Yes,' said Schmidt. 'He was my father's apprentice. He lived with us for a while. He was like a big brother to me.'

Henk nodded, taking a moment. He laid his hand on the diary. 'Do you remember when the three of you stopped living together?'

'Helmut moved out . . .' Schmidt frowned, as if confirming the fact to himself. His expression hardened. 'Yes, Helmut moved out. My father and I were anti-Nazis and Helmut joined the SA. So he had to move out, you see. There were lots of rows, arguments. My father said he couldn't have him under the same roof.'

'But you played – you *play* – chequers with Helmut.'

'He is my friend. He was my father's apprentice, you know. He lived with us. He was really like a big brother to me . . .'

'Yes, you told me,' said Henk without impatience, but Gosau shook his head in warning.

'Tell me, Herr Schmidt, you were in the Wehrmacht, weren't you, later in the war?'

'Me? No. Because I was the son of a known communist, I was sent to a camp for a while, for "re-education". Later I was conscripted into the merchant navy. But I was never a soldier. Never.'

Henk nodded. 'Can you remember what happened to your father?'

'My father?' Again there was a struggle to recall, then the old face set hard. 'My father was murdered. By the Brownshirts. Or the Polizei Hamburg. Altona Bloody Sunday, nineteen thirty-two.' Another frown, confused this time. 'Helmut?'

'Do you remember seeing Helmut Wohlmann that day?'

'He was so proud – of his uniform, of marching with the others.' Georg Schmidt smiled. 'They jeered at him. The others in Altona. The Communists. Then, when they were in the heart of the Altonaer Altstadt, Helmut and the others took their belts off, wrapped them around their fists and used the buckles . . .' Another confused frown.

'Where were you?' Sven Bruns asked. Schmidt looked at him as if startled by the question.

'I was at home. My father told me to stay at home. So I did.'

Henk laid his hand on the diary on the desk, thought for a moment, then smiled. 'Thank you very much, Herr Schmidt. You've been very helpful. Dr Gosau, might we have a word with you?'

Gosau nodded. 'Let me get Herr Schmidt back to his room and you wait here. I'll be back in a few moments.'

Gosau led the bent-backed Schmidt out into the hall and into the care of an orderly.

'What on earth was that all about?' Gosau's imperiousness was back in place when he returned to the day room. 'If there was a point to these questions, it eluded me.'

Henk nodded, his expression faintly sad. 'I understand your confusion, Herr Doctor. Trust me, I do.' He laid his hand flat on Schmidt's notebook journal, which still sat on the table. 'We have three narrators to the events and the motive that led up to the murder of Helmut Wohlmann. Unfortunately, all three narrators are unreliable and all three tell a different story. My problem is that all three also happen to be Georg Schmidt.'

'Go on . . .' Gosau sat down at the table, in the seat vacated by the elderly man.

'We have Herr Schmidt's current testimony, which is at best unreliable to the point that he can't be held responsible for his actions in killing Herr Wohlmann. Then we have the diary he kept at the seniors' home, which tells of the events of Altona Bloody Sunday and describes Schmidt witnessing Wohlmann murdering his father, presumably getting away with it because no Nazis were ultimately held responsible and Communist scapegoats were beheaded a year later for all the deaths that day. That's the motive for the killing.'

'And the third?' asked Gosau.

'The third is still unreliable, but less so than the other two.' Henk opened up the document folder and took out a buff file. 'This is Georg Schmidt's personal record, which is full of gaps. But what it does tell us is the opposite story from the one we have just heard. Georg Schmidt's father was murdered during Altona Bloody Sunday, all right, but not in the way he described and certainly not by Helmut Wohlmann. My guess is that it would most likely have been, like most of the deaths, the result of a carelessly fired police round.'

'How can you be sure it wasn't Helmut Wohlmann?' asked Gosau.

'Because I have Helmut Wohlmann's personal record too. But let's stick with Herr Schmidt for the moment . . .' Henk took some photographs out of the buff file and laid them, as if dealing cards, in front of Gosau.

'I don't understand . . .' said the doctor, picking up each picture in turn. 'I thought he said he never fought in the war?'

'He did. But it was Helmut Wohlmann who was sent to the concentration camp, then forced to serve in the merchant marine. It was Helmut Wohlmann who was the life-long anti-Nazi.'

'But Schmidt's father?'

'Schmidt's father turned *him*, not Wohlmann, out of the house for being a Nazi. Wohlmann was Schmidt senior's apprentice all right, but also shared his political beliefs. Georg Schmidt was a bright kid, and his father had had hopes for him, but then it all went south.'

Gosau laid the photographs out flat on the table once more: Georg Schmidt as a youth; in an SA uniform; in the last, he stood grinning with a group of friends leaning against a Kübelwagen jeep, an unidentified flat, empty landscape behind them. All of them, including Schmidt, were wearing SS uniforms.

'Do you understand why I wanted to interview Schmidt again? I just can't make any sense of the killing. And I wanted to see how much he believed the fiction in the diary. And it looks to me like he believes it totally, even if the detail changes all the time.'

'This . . .' Gosau pointed to the photographs. 'Tell me about this.'

'Helmut Wohlmann didn't kill Schmidt's father, that's for sure. But it wasn't Schmidt, either. There is a chance that he

279 | CRAIG RUSSELL | 279

took part in the march, but he was only thirteen at the time and, although he was a big lad, he would have been a follower, not a member of the SA. Maybe he did witness his father's death, I don't know. The experience didn't dampen his enthusiasm though. He was a member of the Deutsches Jungvolk, obviously without parental consent, then the Hitler Youth from age fourteen. Full indoctrination. He just segued his way into the SA, then the SS. He fought in Russia and was arrested in Hamburg after the war, suspected of participating in war crimes. Like so many, there were huge gaps in his history and he had to be released without charge. He set up a bookstore after the war and kept his head down.' Henk held up his hands in a 'that's it' gesture. 'I think you can understand my confusion.'

Gosau thought for a moment. 'And Helmut Wohlmann – his history is effectively the opposite.'

'As far as I can see, yes. Working class, vehement anti-Nazi before the war, "inner exile" during, and lifelong SDP supporter after. Became a marine engineer, eventually. So why, in his diary, does Schmidt paint himself into Wohlmann's picture?'

'It's not that surprising. Or uncommon. We are all revisionists when it comes to our personal histories, and I would think that Schmidt felt some collective responsibility for his father's death. Being Wohlmann, and Wohlmann being him, would offer a much more attractive retrospective.'

'But you've seen it,' said Sven Bruns. 'You've heard him yourself. He completely *believes* it.'

'Again that doesn't surprise me,' said Gosau. 'You clearly want my professional opinion. Well, it's pretty straightforward: Georg Schmidt has for whatever reason – guilt, shame, desire for acceptance or simply fear of discovery – coveted his childhood friend's blameless history. Maybe for years, for decades. But of course there was nothing he could do about it. You are who you are. But then they both end up in a seniors' home together and the details of their previous lives have become loose and inter-mingled. Dementia condemns you to live in the now – a confusing now that sometimes feels more past tense than pres-ent. Our memories play us all false, at times. Georg Schmidt's memories have become so malleable that he's twisted them into a new shape.'

'So there's no truth in any of this?' Henk held up the diary.

'It's all true, in its way. But objectively, of course, it's not . . . Helmut Wohlmann was murdered for a passionately held motive that was true to Georg Schmidt but, sadly, to no one else. He died because of Schmidt's desire to escape from one life into another.'

47

The day was undecided, trying out different seasons in turn. Between the clouds, it was quite sunny, but fresh. After attending another session of the Club of the Living Dead, Fabel needed the light and the fresh air. Before starting the session, Dr Lorentz had informed them all that Ansgar, the former medical student with the brain tumour, had suffered a major seizure that had effectively shut down all his functions and left him paralyzed, blind, probably deaf and certainly cognitively compromised. In keeping with the instructions Ansgar had given covering such a situation, no heroic measures had been taken; nourishment and hydration had been discontinued.

'He would have drifted away peacefully,' Lorentz had explained. 'But it is no less tragic because of it. Such a waste of a young life.'

The rest of the session had been a subdued experience, with the absence of one of their number filling everyone's thoughts and a single empty chair dominating the room.

After the session, Fabel felt the need to take a few minutes for himself. It was something that he had tried to do every day in the two years after the shooting.

Throughout the months of recuperation that followed Fabel's near-fatal wounding, he had felt imprisoned by the well-intentioned company of others. There was always someone with him: first it was doctors, nurses, specialists; then therapists of all kinds; then, when he returned home, Susanne had taken compassionate leave to tend to Fabel, and there had been a constant stream of visitors and well-wishers. He had been ashamed of his hidden ingratitude, the fact that he had felt stifled, smothered by their relentless goodwill.

He had said nothing but, ever since, he set aside a few minutes each day just to be alone.

When Fabel had moved in with Susanne four years before, he had given up his apartment in Pöseldorf. That too had been a reluctant surrender of solitude, and he had missed the bars and cafés in the area; but, he had to admit, Altona had grown on him. It had a completely different atmosphere and feel, but that somehow had suited him. After the shooting, as soon as he had been free to spend some time alone, he had found this small, unpretentious café near Ottenser Marktplatz. It was the kind of place that served its immediate neighbourhood and not somewhere passers-through or tourists would have call to visit. It was small, bright and clean without being sterile. An older man, whom Fabel guessed was Turkish-German, ran it most days and was friendly and chatty without being inquisitive, which suited Fabel perfectly. He guessed that the owner, and his pretty daughter who sometimes worked with him, would have noticed Fabel to start with, but as he became a more frequent face, they would probably have assumed he lived or worked somewhere in the immediate vicinity. It was exactly what Fabel needed: here, like at the café at the Winterhuder Fährhaus, he was just the anonymous blond middle-aged guy in the English tailoring who drank his coffee by the window, idly watching the people and cars go by on Holländische Reihe.

Fabel had no idea what the Turkish owner and his daughter would think he did for a living, if they even gave it a thought, but he guessed that a murder detective would be at the bottom of the list. That suited him too.

But today, this unlikely refuge was tarnished: as he had come into the café he had noticed one of the Polizei Hamburg's posters in the window next to the door, Jochen Hübner's grotesque face glaring out at him.

He tried to put it out of his head and, ordering a coffee, sat in his usual spot and watched the world slide past the window. Try as he might, the face of Frankenstein continued to haunt him. It chilled Fabel to think of a predator like Hübner unbound, in hiding, making plans.

An expensively dressed woman walked past on the street outside and their eyes met through the window for a second, then she was gone. He noted that he had found her instantly attractive: she had been dark-haired with blue eyes, just like Susanne. He had a thing for brunettes; always had. Why, he thought to himself, are we attracted to 'types'? Why had he always felt drawn to dark-haired women more than redheads or the locally abundant blondes? Fabel had always had this theory that people work on the principle of archetypes: that individuals are seen, for superficial reasons, as belonging to a particular genus. In its most extreme, he had seen serial killers target victims for the most tenuous or superficial similarity. The deaths of Traxinger and Hensler seemed to be the same thing in reverse. They shared an obsession with redheads that, in turn, had stemmed from their obsession with Monika Krone. But they were the ones who had ended up dead.

He sighed in annoyance at himself: there he was again, despite his best efforts, thinking about the case in his set-aside time.

Where the hell was Hübner? There hadn't been a single sighting since his escape. First Monika Krone's body is found; Jochen 'Frankenstein' Hübner, one-time favourite suspect for Monika's murder, escapes from Fuhlsbüttel prison; and since that escape, two men connected to the Monika Krone case are murdered. It was this chronology, this perfect syzygy of events, that gave Fabel a bad feeling. It reeked of cause and effect.

His thoughts were interrupted when his cell phone rang: it was Holger Brauner, the head of the forensics team.

'We've isolated that "something" I was talking about. I could tell you that both victims had enough tranquillizer in them to knock out a horse, but you might think I was just being metaphorical.'

'Holger, I don't have time—'

'Horse tranquillizer,' Brauner said. 'Xylazine hydrochloride, to be exact. It explains how they seem to have been killed without a struggle, or in Hensler's case, how he allowed himself to be tied up and placed in a box without a struggle.'

'You said both? Traxinger too?'

'The wine glass – and what we were able to recover of the spilled wine – tested positive for xylazine. My guess is that he ingested some but not enough to flatten him. It can create a weird zombie-like state where you're effectively out for the count but still on your feet. It would explain how Traxinger was killed with a single strike from the Empress Sisi-type weapon.'

'So it doesn't follow that he knew his attacker after all?'

'That's your province, Jan. I just do the chemistry.'

'But would it sedate someone enough that they wouldn't react to someone stabbing them?'

'No problem. Like I say, it's a very powerful central nervous system suppressor; vets use it on cattle and horses when they want to sedate them heavily but still keep them on their feet. Especially while they're having dental work or when horses are being castrated. So yes – your painter guy wouldn't have seen it coming. There is one other possibility, however ...'

'Oh?'

'An overdose of xylazine, even a slight overdose, can bring on bradycardia and myocardial infarction. A heart attack. Maybe that's what your killer was hoping for with Traxinger – and that it would be put down to natural causes – but ingestion wouldn't work quickly or even that well. Could be that he realized he'd have to finish the job off with the blade.'

'I doubt it. If he had wanted to cover up his tracks he wouldn't have dragged the painting through from the storeroom. How easy would it be to get your hands on xylazine?'

'Again, I wouldn't know. It's a restricted drug, so not that easy, but it isn't really used illegally, except, bizarrely, in Puerto Rico where it's known as the "zombie drug". You certainly don't get a high from it and God knows why anyone would want to use it recreationally. But to answer your question, I suppose if you had the right contacts, you wouldn't find it too hard to get your hands on some.'

'So do you think Hensler's was slipped to him in a drink too?'

'No . . . he was given a discrete dose, from the traces I'd say just enough to keep him under long enough to bury him. I found a puncture mark in his neck – done crudely and with enough time to cause bruising around it. Looks to me like it could have been done from behind. But that's speculation on my part, not something I have enough evidence to put into the report.'

'Okay. Thanks, Holger.'

'There's one more thing,' said Brauner. 'It may be nothing . . .'

'What?'

'You mentioned just now that the killer dragged the painting through to the studio from the storeroom. Well they didn't – the only scratches on the floor were where the picture was adjusted, pushed into place. That was a very heavy frame on it and you would struggle to carry it all the way through. That means one of three things: either the killer was strong—'

'Like Frankenstein Hübner . . .'

'Like Frankenstein Hübner . . . The second option is that there were two or more people involved in the killing and they moved the painting between them. Or, the third option is that they used something in the studio to move the picture. So what we did was check everything. It's a huge place and it's taken until now to process it all.'

'Just the headlines, Holger . . .'

'Okay. The picture frame was covered in fingerprints and as you know, it's very difficult to tell the new from the old; but there were smudges that suggested someone wearing gloves had handled it recently. Then we found a two-wheeler hand barrow right at the back of the studio, where it wasn't normally kept, according to Frau Koetzing. My guess is that the barrow was used to shift the painting. We found no prints on it – and I mean *no* prints. Someone had taken a great deal of time to wipe it down, which doesn't make sense if they were wearing gloves. Earlier in our sweep we had found an extraneous partial – an odd-shaped part of a thumbprint – on the reception hall door. It's entirely possible that the killer was wearing latex gloves and they tore a little without him noticing when he was holding the picture frame. Then, when he was putting the hand trolley at the back of the studio, he saw the tear and felt the need to completely wipe down the trolley, to be safe.'

'So you think the partial is our guy?'

'It's a stretch, but it's a possibility. The problem is we haven't got much of a pattern to go on, but we're doing our best to see if we can get a match. Even if we do, we won't have enough comparable points for it to stand up in court.'

'Okay, thanks, Holger. By the way, make Jochen Hübner's prints your first port of call.'

48

Even after two decades living in the city, Fabel could still be surprised at how quickly, driving out from central Hamburg, you found yourself in a rural environment. It had only taken him and Anna just over twenty minutes to get to Tatenberg, officially still part of the Bergedorf quarter and Metropolitan Hamburg, but a century or two distant in feel.

The house sat next to the Dove Elbe, a tranquil spur of Hamburg's lifeblood river. Most of the area was given over to one of Hamburg's nature reserves and everything here was green: thick swathes of broad-leaved trees, hedgerows and gently rolling fields, all dotted with ponds, small lakes and with the sedate Dove Elbe running through it.

'It's beautiful here,' said Anna as they drove along the narrow ribbon of road on the Tatenberger Deich, past the yacht marina.

'Yes it is,' said Fabel. 'But I wouldn't have thought it would have been your kind of thing. I thought you were into the whole bar and club scene in the Kiez. A city girl, through and through.'

'Maybe I'm getting old. Like you.'

'You should be more respectful, Frau Wolff.'

'Respectful my arse. Although I've heard there's a rumour that you might be on the way up. *Capo de Capo*.'

'Oh?' said Fabel, although he knew very well the rumour to which she referred. 'And the expression is *Capo di tutti capi*. I'm going to start recruiting officers with broader cultural references.'

'It's true though, isn't it? You're going to be offered Leading Criminal Director when van Heiden officially retires?'

'No one has approached me about it at all, Anna. It's just people speculating. Like you said, a rumour, that's all.'

'But it's not groundless. Everyone knows you're the best choice to lead the whole State Criminal Office. Frankly, I don't see you as a paper-shuffler and pen-pusher. Are you going to take it?'

'Anna . . .' said Fabel, annoyed, 'I've told you – no one has asked me. And Berger over at Organized Crime is as good a candidate as me—'

'He's an arsehole,' said Anna contemptuously. 'And he's from Frankfurt. He's an arsehole from Frankfurt . . . is that tautological?'

'What is this thing you've got about Frankfurt, Anna?'

'Haven't you *ever* been there?' She turned and looked out of the passenger window at the passing trees and the sparkle of water between them. 'They make Parisians seem warm and welcoming. You'd make more eye contact at an Asperger's self-help meeting.'

'Anyway,' said Fabel. 'Being an arsehole doesn't diminish your abilities. Berger's very capable.'

'You're more than his equal.'

'As an officer or an arsehole?'

'The former always, the latter occasionally. You haven't answered my question: will you take it?'

'Ah, here we are . . .' said Fabel in a 'saved-by-the-bell' manner.

He turned into the drive that led to a long, low, one-and-a-half storey thatch-roofed *Reetdachhaus* of the typical, traditional rural North German style.

'Very nice,' said Fabel as they pulled up on the drive outside the house, which was surrounded by a large, well-tended garden and a wall of trees. 'Maybe I should have stuck with the academic world after all.'

A man in camel-coloured moleskin trousers, a dark green sweater and checked shirt appeared at the door and waited for them. From first impressions, Fabel estimated that Professor Thorsten Rohde, although having retired from the Uni Hamburg the year before, could only have been in his late fifties or early sixties. His hair was grey-blond and combed back from a broad-browed, long face and an aquiline nose that gave him the look of an aristocrat rather than an academic.

'Thanks for agreeing to meet with us,' said Fabel after he had introduced Anna and they shook hands. 'And sorry for the intrusion.'

'Not at all – I welcome the company. My wife has gone to . . .' He paused, frowning. 'She's gone out but she'll be back soon. Anyway, I hope I can help, Herr Fabel. This is about Monika Krone? I heard that they discovered her body. After all this time. It's tragic.'

'That it is, Herr Professor,' said Fabel. 'But there are some other things, possible connections, we are looking at.'

'Oh, sorry . . .' said Rohde, suddenly aware they were all still standing at the threshold. 'Please come in.'

The interior of the cottage was surprisingly modern, the decor bright to make the most of the light from the small, thatch-shadowed windows. The living room was large and open plan to the kitchen, whitewashed wooden columns breaking up the space. Fabel noticed a large American-style refrigerator in the kitchen, covered with more than a dozen handwritten yellow and orange sticker notes.

Rohde invited them to sit on a soft-toned cambric-covered sofa. A beech coffee table in front of them was piled with books, most of which looked like academic publications and all of which seemed to deal with Gothic literature or studies. Fabel noticed Rohde's was the author name on several. From the cover of one Boris Karloff, made up as Frankenstein's monster, stared obliquely and menacingly at them.

'May I offer you tea . . . coffee?' said Rohde.

'No,' said Fabel, once they were all seated. 'But thank you. We won't take up too much of your time, Herr Professor. We're looking into a specific group of friends, fellow students who shared an interest in Gothic literature and attended your extra-curricular lectures on Gothic fiction. They were known informally by other students as the "Gothic set".'

Rohde laughed. 'Everyone I come into contact with can be called that. And the students who went out of their way to attend my elective lectures all had a specific interest in the Gothic.'

'But this would be a group including Monika Krone,' said Anna. 'You remember Monika Krone?'

'Of course I remember her. And what happened to her. The police came to talk to me back then as well. In any case, Monika Krone was not the kind of student – or woman – one forgets.' Rohde suddenly seemed to remember something and made to stand up. 'Where are my manners? Can I offer you something – tea or coffee?'

'You already—'

'No thanks, Herr Professor . . .' Fabel cut Anna off. Rohde's early retirement and the score of handwritten notes on the refrigerator suddenly made sense. 'We won't keep you long. Do you remember the crowd Monika went around with?'

'Some more than others. They were more deeply into the Gothic than the rest. By that I mean not just the literature, but the history, the leading figures, the architecture, the philosophy, the culture – for many that's what the Gothic is: not just a literary movement, a culture. It's a way of seeing life.'

'Seems to me more like a way of seeing death – but would you say Monika and her friends were particularly into Gothic culture?'

'I wouldn't say all. Some of them – a hard core, if you like, including Monika – certainly took it very seriously indeed. Like the others, they had a very deep intellectual interest in the movement, the literature, but for them it went beyond that and into their way of looking at life. Or living it.'

'So this hard core comprised mainly literature students?'

'Actually, no. Not exclusively. Obviously, the majority of those who came to my lectures were literature students – there were those who were studying German Lit and were interested in the German Schauerroman development of Gothic fiction, then there were my own Gothic Studies students and students of English, who were looking to boost their understanding of the genre. But I got students from all disciplines and not just the liberal arts – including a lot of science and medical students.'

'I wouldn't have thought that it would have attracted many from the sciences.'

'That's where you'd be wrong. Gothic fiction is inseparably connected to the history of science. Mary Shelley's *Frankenstein* is a science-fiction novel as much as anything else. You have to remember that Victor Frankenstein animated his monster by using electricity, which in Shelley's time was the biggest area of scientific study and moving from the theoretical to the practical realm. Just as today there are writers speculating about the moral and existential threats posed by computing and artificial intelligence, in Mary Shelley's day people had the same worries about the magic of electricity. It's ironic that the real Castle Frankenstein, which inspired her to use the name, sits above Darmstadt, which later would become the very first city to have a faculty of electrical engineering at its university. You could also say *Frankenstein* was the first novel to raise bio-ethical issues. So it's no surprise that there were science students interested in the Gothic. But to answer your question, the group that seemed to be associated with Monika came from an unusually broad range of disciplines.'

'There was a medical student in particular,' said Fabel. 'A Dane by the name of Paul Mortensen – do you remember him?'

Rohde pursed his lips as he thought. 'Sorry, can't say I do.'

'How well did you know Monika Krone?' asked Anna.

'Well. Or at least as well as she would allow anyone to get to know her. I was her tutor and had her in my formal classes as well as her having an almost hundred per cent attendance at the elective lectures. As an educator, the names and faces of most of your students over the years fade into the background, but there are the few bright stars – the ones who stand out and whom you remember. Monika was one such star.'

'Professor Rohde . . .' Fabel leaned forward, resting his elbows on his knees. 'I hope you understand that I have to ask you this: were you ever in any kind of intimate relationship with Monika Krone?'

Rohde smiled, a little sadly and resignedly. 'I knew you would ask me that. Yes, I had an intimate relationship with her. But not in the way you mean, not sexual or romantic. And it's very difficult to put into words . . .' Rohde thought for a moment, drawing a breath. 'Listen, Herr Fabel, I have devoted my life to studying and teaching the Gothic movement. Every aspect of it. I want you to imagine that I am an archaeologist, dealing with dusty artefacts and obsessed with, say, the Mycenaeans. Imagine what it would be like for that archaeologist to meet, not buried bones, but a living, breathing person who had lived through that time, who had known Agamemnon, who could give a first-person perspective. It was like that with Monika. I have never encountered another student, or anyone else, who so perfectly understood the Gothic, who so perfectly *embodied* the Gothic. You could say that I learned more from her than she from me.'

'If you don't mind me saying, it sounds like you were a little in love with her.'

'Perhaps. More fascinated, more in awe of her. And, truth be told, a little afraid of her.'

'Afraid?'

'Monika Krone had a presence – not just physical, but intellectual and emotional – that is very hard to describe. I said she embodied the Gothic for me, well, she did. Hers was a very dark presence.'

They talked about Monika for a while longer, Rohde explaining more about the personality of his long-dead student. After a while, they moved on to the other members of the Gothic set.

'I do remember Werner Hensler was involved,' said Rohde. 'He most certainly was someone who was in love with Monika. I was shocked to read about his death. Werner was a pleasure to teach and he had a real passion for Gothic literature – Poe, in particular. But he made the fatal mistake of comparing himself to his hero – measuring his writing against Poe's – which was always going to lead him to disappointment. I read one of his novels not that long ago. It was tripe. I got the feeling that he had sold out believing he was capable of less than he really was.'

'What about Tobias Albrecht, the architect?'

'I remember there was an architecture student, but can't recall the name. He was what people used to call "devilishly handsome" and clearly saw himself as some kind of Byronesque character – you know *mad, bad and dangerous to know*.' Rohde used the expression in English. 'I got the impression his involvement was more about the usual student search for a style or an identity, rather than any real interest in the Gothic form.'

'Was he involved with Monika?'

Rohde laughed. 'Of course he was. They all were at one time or another, I think. And those that weren't desperately wanted to be. Like I say, Monika was a dark presence – but a dark presence that formed the heart of the group. I actually wonder if some of them really were that interested in Gothic literature or were simply trying to ingratiate themselves with Monika.'

'Do you remember the painter Detlev Traxinger being part of the set?'

'Yes I do.' Rohde frowned, suddenly perturbed. 'I forget . . . didn't I read something about his death too?'

'I'm afraid you did.'

'So *that's* what this is all about. Not just Monika?'

'We're investigating possible connections, yes. That's why it's important that you try to remember anyone else in particular that was part of that set.'

Rohde laughed, bitterly. 'I have no problem remembering stuff from back then. It's this morning, yesterday or last week I struggle with. There was someone else . . .' He frowned. 'It'll come to me – eventually.'

'Was this someone who was involved with Monika?'

'No . . . damn it, I wish I could remember his name. He was one of those poor peripheral people. You know, the hangers-on and wannabes whom no one really notices. That's probably why I can't remember too much about him. Maybe he was the Danish medical student you mentioned.'

'I understand that Gothic literature is a serious subject – academically, I mean,' said Fabel. 'But what I can't get my head around is why a group of young people would become so obsessed with it. I mean, especially Monika Krone, Traxinger, Hensler and Albrecht. They were all in their early- to mid-twenties. Why should the literature of death and darkness be so appealing to such young people with such bright futures?'

'That's where you've got it wrong, Herr Fabel. The Gothic belongs to the young and vital. It's all around us in teenage culture – Goth fashions, death-metal music . . . Teenagers and young people flooding to watch movies and television series about vampires and zombies.'

'But we're not talking about teenagers,' said Anna. 'We're talking about serious students in their middle twenties.'

'Gothic literature is and always has been the literature of youth. Mary Shelley was still a teenager, only nineteen, when she wrote *Frankenstein*. Her husband, the poet Percy Bysshe Shelley, who was her model for Victor Frankenstein, sang loud and sweet but was silenced when he was only twenty-nine. Polidori, who wrote the first real vampire story, died when he was twenty-five. Even Byron, who blazed so bright that he scorched all who got too close, eventually burned out at only thirty-six. The

Romantic and Gothic movements speak with the irrepressible and vibrant nihilism of youth.'

'You don't think a youthful obsession with death is unhealthy?' asked Anna.

Rohde smiled. 'When you're young, your vigour allows you to see Death – with a capital "D" – as a concept, as something that exists in its own right. Something you can romanticize about . . . even personify. But as you get older, death becomes a much more lowercase affair. You begin to realize that just like the dark doesn't exist but is merely the absence of light, death doesn't exist and is simply the absence of life, and that makes it all the more terrifying. It is no longer something you conceptualize, no longer a presence but an absence. It becomes an event. An endpoint just around the corner. Death becomes a hell of a lot less romantic the closer you get to it.' He turned to Fabel. 'I'm sure, with your experience, you'll agree.'

'My experience?' Fabel was taken aback for a moment.

'I mean as a homicide investigator. You encounter death, or at least have to deal with it as part of your day-to-day routine. What did you think I was referring to?'

'Nothing. I see what you mean and yes, death holds no romance for me.'

'And as for a group of young people, riven by sexual rivalries and jealousies, to be held together by the Gothic is far from new. As everyone knows, Polidori wrote *The Vampyre* in the same place, the Villa Diodati, and at the same time as Mary Shelley started *Frankenstein*. Both at the instigation of Byron. And everyone at the Villa Diodati was trying to get into everyone else's bed. And if there's one thing that the Gothic's about as much as death, it's sex. It seethes with sex.'

'Sex and death,' said Fabel thoughtfully. 'It's a potent mix.'

'As I'm sure you've encountered in your work, dealing with people who have killed for physical gratification, the lines between sex and death can blur. Venereal diseases haunted both the Romantic and Gothic genres. One could argue that vampirism was a metaphor for syphilis. One could even extend the argument that HIV/AIDS was an epidemiological revival of the Romantic Gothic. Have you noticed how zombieism and vampirism have dominated television and movies for more than two decades? Sex, infection and death. The Gothic is still with us, will always be with us, as long as sex and death remain part of the human experience.'

Fabel reached into his inside jacket pocket and took out the photograph he had brought with him. He handed the photograph to Rohde, who placed it on the table while he searched for his glasses.

'Sorry,' he said when he returned with a pair of gold-rimmed spectacles balanced halfway down the aquiline nose. 'I'm always forgetting where I put them.' He examined the photograph.

'Does that mean anything to you?' asked Fabel. 'Both Werner Hensler and Detlev Traxinger had these Gothic-styled tattoos on their chests, just above the heart.'

Rohde looked across at Fabel. 'Is this . . .'

'It's a post-mortem picture, yes.'

Rohde examined it again, then shook his head slowly. 'The initials mean nothing to me, nor the overall design. But this motif – the interlacing ivy and acanthus – that maybe has some symbolism.'

'Like what? I've heard that the acanthus was associated with death.'

'That's not strictly true,' said Rohde. 'The acanthus leaf is the most common motif used in Corinthian and Greek architecture.

A lot of Roman too. You'll see it used in funerary symbolism too – but it doesn't mean death, it means the *survival* of death. Life beyond the grave, if you like. Even immortality.'

'And the ivy?' asked Anna.

'That too has a similar symbolism. Immortality, endurance – particularly enduring love or friendship. If you're asking me if I feel this tattoo could be linked to the so-called Gothic set, then yes – I can't imagine two more Gothic symbols than ivy and acanthus.'

Fabel nodded, processing what Rohde had said. 'Can you remember the name of the other person?'

'What other person?' Rohde looked puzzled.

'You told us there was someone else involved with the so-called Gothic set, but you couldn't remember their name.'

He thought for a moment. 'Wait a minute . . . there *was* someone else. Yes, yes, I remember now. There was a male student, not one of mine, not literature. Damn it, what was his name? That's the problem: he was one of the orbiting planets, minor planets, and not one of the stars at the centre. You know, the kind of poor soul who desperately wants to be part of something but is condemned to the sidelines. He was always at the extra-curricular lectures I gave. I really got the impression that he was there simply to be near Monika – although he did have a real interest in Gothic influences in film, that kind of thing.' Rohde's eyes brightened and he snapped his fingers emphatically. 'Mesling . . . Messing . . . something like that. And he was a Sociology student. That was it.'

Rohde saw them both to the door of the cottage.

'This is a really nice place you've got here, Herr Professor.'

'Thank you. It's quiet here, which suits me. I eke out my university pension by writing the odd piece on the Gothic for periodicals. At the moment I'm writing an autobiography on Ann Radcliffe, one of the very first ever Gothic novelists. You know her work?'

Fabel shook his head.

'I think you would enjoy her, Herr Fabel. Forensically, I mean. She was a great believer in the rational resolution. Her stories revolved around supernatural goings-on that her investigators always exposed to have nothing at all to do with the supernatural but which had a rational, real world explanation.'

'Just like *Scooby-Doo* . . .' Anna said, smiling. Fabel shot her a warning look.

'It's really a pity you missed my wife,' said Rohde, again frowning. 'Where was it she said she was going? Anyway, she'll be back soon.'

Fabel shook Rohde's hand. 'Thank you for your help, Herr Professor.'

As they got into the car and Fabel started to drive off, he had to brake to allow through a Land Rover coming in from the drive. As she passed, the female driver eyed Fabel and Anna curiously, almost suspiciously.

'You've got to be fucking kidding me . . .' muttered Anna.

'So that's Frau Rohde,' said Fabel as he moved off again. In his rear-view mirror he watched the woman make her way over to Rohde and kiss him on the cheek, then look again in Fabel's direction, clearly asking her husband who had been visiting. She was at least fifteen years younger than her husband, well-dressed and attractive without being beautiful. She stood watching Fabel's car make its way back to the main road, the late summer sun picking out bright highlights in her shoulder-length, rich auburn-red hair.

49

'Have you come to probe me for a second time?' asked Anja Koetzing. Like the last time they had spoken, Traxinger's business manager was dressed in a black skirt suit but this time her blouse was open-necked and when she again stood too close to Fabel, he could smell her scent, hot, musky and sweet. He laughed a little uncomfortably and stood back, feeling the heat in his neck and cheeks. Once more, Fabel found himself discomfited by his own reaction to her.

'Oh I'm sorry,' she said coyly. 'I've made you blush. Do you know some psychologists consider that a blush is a "redirected erection"?'

'Why do I feel I need a chaperone whenever I question you, Frau Koetzing? An armed chaperone?'

'But you didn't bring one, did you? Fair game, I say.' She moved even closer.

'Frau Koetzing . . .' Fabel injected his tone with authority. 'This is a serious matter. I am investigating the murder of your business partner and I would appreciate your proper attention and cooperation.'

She laughed, her deep hazel eyes flashing darkly. 'Anything you say, Herr Principal Chief Commissar. I was only playing with you. How can I help?'

'I'd like to talk some more about Herr Traxinger. But I'd also like to have another look at his paintings.'

'Sure. What do you want to know?'

'Is there anything – *anything* – you can tell me about Traxinger's private life?'

'Detlev's life was an open book – but as I'm sure you know, anyone whose life is an open book is hiding more than everyone else. He rejoiced in scandal and saw himself as some kind of *bête noire* of the artistic world. Truth is that rejoicing in a little scandal is good PR and goes a long way to boost sales. People buy the artist as much as the art. Underneath it all Detlev was as much a conformist as anyone else – just that he was conforming to the non-conformity that was expected of him, if you know what I mean.'

Fabel nodded. 'Have you heard of Tobias Albrecht?'

'The architect? Of course I have.'

'Did Herr Traxinger ever talk about him, or mention knowing him?'

Koetzing thought for a moment then shook her head, red lips pursed. 'I can't say he ever did. Which was odd.'

'Odd? Why?'

'Because architectural practices are great buyers and renters of original art. I've got clients across Germany in the architectural sector, but not Albrecht and Partners. I just couldn't get an appointment. I guessed that he didn't like Detlev's work so I let it go. And I can't remember Detlev ever mentioning Albrecht.'

'They were friends at university,' said Fabel. 'And I know that they crossed paths at arts-related functions, at least two or three times.'

'Not any I was also at, I can tell you that. You telling me that Detlev knew Tobias Albrecht is complete news to me. I mean, I told Detlev I was chasing Albrecht and Partners for business. He didn't pass any comment even then.'

They walked through to the gallery and storeroom side of the studio, Anja Koetzing leading the way. Fabel, despite his best efforts, found himself watching her body as she walked ahead of him. She was like a small cat: sleek, dark, sensually elegant. The truth was he didn't like her flirting with him because he really was strongly attracted to her.

'Here we are . . .' Koetzing unlocked the door to the storeroom, leaned in and switched on the light. 'I'll leave you to it.'

'If you don't mind, I'd like to ask you about some of the paintings.'

Koetzing arched an eyebrow and smiled. 'All this time have you just been trying to get me alone in a dark storeroom?'

'Frau Koetzing . . .' Fabel again tried to inject warning into his tone, but it sounded feeble.

'Okay, okay . . . I'll behave. Your virtue shall remain untarnished.'

Fabel went to the back of the storeroom and pulled out the series of paintings featuring Monika Krone. The original painting, the one Fabel had found first, was no longer there but being examined by the forensics department, who were trying to work out roughly when it had been painted. The pictures that remained disturbed Fabel. There was some bright, cold cruelty that Traxinger had clearly sought to express in his depictions of Monika.

'Why was Detlev Traxinger so obsessed with Monika Krone? Most of these works were done long after her death.'

'I honestly don't know. Like I told you, I didn't see most of these paintings until you showed them to me. She appeared in a lot of his stuff I did see, but at that time I just assumed it was some sort of idealized redhead. I always knew he had a thing for redheads, I just didn't know that it was more that he had a thing for one *particular* redhead. He had a muse I didn't know about.'

Fabel pulled out another of the larger canvases. Again it was Monika Krone, this time dressed in dark green velvet and what Fabel guessed to be seventeenth-century fashion. Her hair was still partly in the style of that time, but snake-like strands of it, swept by wind, coiled and writhed their way free of pin and clasp. Her hands were sheathed in riding gloves and held a black, plaited-leather horsewhip gathered in loops. Again her eyes burned with the cold emerald fire that Traxinger had sought to capture in all of his paintings of her. He had signed the painting with the monogram DT, using the same design as the tattoo both he and Hensler had borne above their hearts. This time, however, he had also added a title, small and in dabs of black paint as if written with quill and ink, next to the monogram. It was difficult to read and Fabel leaned close to make it out.

'*La Quintrala . . .*' he said, stepping back to look up into the cold, cruel green gaze. 'What does that mean?'

Koetzing didn't answer for a moment then said, 'It's Spanish. It was the nickname of Catalina de los Ríos y Lisperguer. She was a Chilean landowner in the time of Spanish colonial rule. In fact she became a symbol for all that was wrong with colonial rule.'

Fabel turned to her. 'You're remarkably well informed . . .'

Koetzing grinned and held up her smartphone, screen towards him. 'No, I'm remarkably well connected to the internet.' She examined the screen again, the smile fading. 'It would appear that *La Quintrala* was a monster. Extremely beautiful, extremely clever, and extremely fucking crazy. According to this she was a female serial killer. Apparently she used that whip of hers to beat her . . .' She frowned at the screen. 'Her *inquilinos* . . .'

'Indentured workers – basically slaves.' Fabel recalled the Spanish term from his days as a history student. He stared at the painting. Traxinger certainly had had a particular talent for capturing cruelty. 'What else does it say about her?'

Koetzing read for a moment, holding her phone close. 'Well, she was quite a gal . . . apparently the nickname *La Quintrala* was given to her because of the colour of her flaming red hair. The name comes from some kind of mistletoe called the quintral that grows in Patagonia and has bright red flowers. She was part German, by the way, which explains the Lisperguer bit of her name, I suppose. She was a sexual adventuress – well, can't blame a girl for that – and prolific murderer of her own family, a priest and anybody else who pissed her off, basically.' Koetzing fell silent for a moment while she scrolled through and read the information. 'But it was her taste for killing servants that earned her her reputation. Some say she killed forty, others say the true figure was in the hundreds. Same old story though: no one cared about the plebs, but she stood trial for the murders of her more noble victims. She got away with it all, of course.'

'Do you think that's really how Traxinger saw her? Monika, I mean?'

'I don't know. It could have been just some kind of joke. Detlev's extremely ornate version of a caricature.'

'And you say he never mentioned Monika Krone to you?'

'Not once.'

As he stared up at the painting, Fabel thought about how Kerstin Krone had described her sister – the cliché of the evil twin made real. Two men dead: two men linked to a young woman who had disappeared off the face of the earth fifteen years before. Not just linked, obsessed with her. And one of them had painted her over and over again in Gothic-themed paintings: a figure of death, of sexual, physical and mental torment. A beautiful monster.

50

Sleep kept promising itself to Fabel, but stayed teasingly just out of reach. His body was exhausted but his mind flashed and fluttered with thoughts, ideas, disjointed images, fragments of things people had said. Susanne slept soundly beside him and he tried to will himself into a sleep that refused to yield. He slipped out of bed and went through to the kitchen, pouring himself a glass of milk and sitting at the small table, staring blankly at its surface, trying to shut out all thoughts of work.

But it wasn't just Fabel's caseload that had kept him awake: an undecided future taunted him every time he neared sleep. As Anna had pointed out, Leading Criminal Director Horst van Heiden, the officer in charge of all of the City State's investigative branches and Fabel's immediate boss, had been on sick leave for three months and was due to retire. The Police President had been filling van Heiden's role as well as her own and the search was on for a permanent replacement. The rumour was that, at the moment, the search hadn't extended any further than Fabel. The truth was that the idea of becoming Leading Criminal Director in charge of the whole State Criminal Office had started to have its appeal. The life of a bureaucrat and administrator would perhaps result in fewer sleepless nights and fewer vivid nightmares when he did sleep.

But, he told himself, the bad dreams had paradoxically become fewer since the shooting. His close encounter with death had brought him a strange peace, a contentment which he hadn't known before. But tonight, for a reason he didn't fully understand, that peace eluded him.

Taking his milk through to the living room, he switched on the television, the volume turned down, flicking through mute channels.

He stopped at one channel. He recognized the movie that was showing as *Nosferatu*. Max Schreck shadowed his long-fingered way menacingly across the screen and through the streets and alleys of a monochrome Bremen. Fabel switched it off.

Rohde had been right, he thought. If you have come close to death, then the literary romanticizing of it became vacuous. The Gothic did belong to the young, whose relationship with death was a long-distance one. When you were young you felt immortal, and when you were immortal you could play and tease yourself with the idea of death.

But, that Saturday night fifteen years before, something had happened to make Monika Krone's relationship with Death suddenly close-up and personal. And now people connected to her were dying.

He switched the television off and went back to bed. The sleep that had eluded him claimed him and he fell into a dream he would not remember when he woke. A dream about a beautiful red-headed woman who was trapped beneath the ground.

Fabel called Anna through to his office as soon as she came in the following day.

'You look like shit,' was her opening statement.

'Why thanks for that, Anna. As a matter of fact, I didn't sleep too well last night.'

'Me neither,' she said. 'There's something really weird going on with the whole Gothic set thing and it just kept going round and round in my head. What do you think is going on with Albrecht?'

'I don't know. There's every chance he's been telling us the truth – that he really was with some married woman the night Hensler died. Have you checked out his alibi for Traxinger's death?'

'Yep, and it holds up. It's not airtight – there are gaps that can't be verified, but it doesn't look likely that he could have got all the way across town, killed Traxinger and got back to where he was next seen.'

'Mmm . . .' Fabel sipped his coffee. 'That would kind of rule him out. It's pretty clear that both killings were the work of the same perpetrator.'

'That doesn't mean that Albrecht isn't involved. This whole Gothic set is beginning to look like a cultish thing. A secret society or some crap like that. Maybe he's working with a partner – or more than one.' Anna sat down opposite Fabel. 'Maybe Monika Krone was killed by them all. Everyone working together in some kind of secret society ritual. Maybe that's what the whole tattoo thing is all about.'

'Maybe. But Albrecht doesn't have the tattoo – even if he did know where he would have it if he did – and there's no evidence of him having had any meaningful contact with the victims since they left university.'

'That we know of . . . The whole point of a secret society is that it's secret. Maybe the lot of them got together every second

Tuesday to prance around naked and whip each other with ivy and acanthus.'

'Sometimes, Frau Wolff, your imagination worries me. But I take your point. And there's his convenient mystery woman whom he claims was with him the night Werner Hensler was murdered.'

'Who could be a lot of bollocks.'

'Or maybe he really has been messing about with someone in the public eye who can't be identified. Unfortunately we don't have nearly enough evidence, even circumstantial, to push him on it. But I really do think there's something more to Albrecht's involvement with all of this. If you're right and this is some kind of secret society or cult thing, then someone is killing members one by one, and the trigger has been the uncovering of Monika Krone's body. Maybe it's another member, or maybe it's someone who knew about their club but wasn't a member—'

'And they didn't know *for sure* that she was dead – that the others had killed her – until the body was found . . .' Anna finished the thought for him.

'Exactly,' said Fabel. 'So we're left with someone on the periphery and not completely in the know.'

'What was it Rohde said? "One of the orbiting planets, minor planets, and not one of the stars at the centre"?'

'Rohde's forgettable student, and maybe my "ghost in the file". I need you to get people on that right away, finding a sociology student around the same time with the name Messing or Mesling . . . anything similar sounding.'

'That's if Rohde got the name right, Jan. Or if there really was such a student at all. What was his deal? Rohde, I mean?'

'I don't know . . . early onset Alzheimer's, I'd guess. Poor bastard. I wouldn't hold my breath for that biography to be finished.

But if my understanding of it is right, then it's his short-term, not long-term memory that's the problem. He said as much when we were there.'

'And what about his wife? The mini-Monika lookalike? By the way, I'm going to dye my hair red – it seems to get men going.'

'Not all men,' said Fabel, a little awkwardly. 'But yes, there's something very odd going on there and I think Rohde was maybe more involved with Monika Krone than he let on. But in the meantime, let's focus on Tobias Albrecht and this sociology student.'

'What about Frankenstein Hübner?'

'He has to stay in the frame too, but we still haven't had a single sighting on him in the metropolitan Hamburg area. He could be long gone by now. And one of these murders was committed in the middle of Altona. I would have thought *someone* would have noticed a hulking presence like Hübner's before or after commission. But it's by no means certain that he isn't involved. In any case, he's a hidden quantity, Albrecht isn't. I'd like eyes on our architect chum for a couple of days. Nothing round the clock, just to see what he gets up to.'

'Or who he gets up to. You want me to take it?'

'If you don't mind. No more than two teams tied up on it – and make sure you stay out of sight. He'll recognize you if he spots you.'

'Not if I become a redhead.'

'I think that's exactly when he would notice you ...'

51

The sharks were circling.

Men could be pathetic, thought Anna Wolff as she sat at the bar sipping her tomato juice. She had dressed appropriately for the venue: a skirt short enough to show off her legs but not so short as to look desperate, and a blouse that fitted snugly at the waist and accentuated the swell of her breasts. Her short, thick dark hair was styled more softly than usual and she had spent more time than usual applying make-up.

It was like tossing raw chum into the water.

One of the circling sharks – fat, middle-aged and wearing a grey business suit and a few too many Scotches – decided to try to take a bite. Anna smiled sweetly and declined his offer of a drink politely but firmly, explaining she was waiting for someone. It was the way Jan would want her to do it, so she did it his way instead of hers, which would have been to ask the business-type how he could think she could possibly be interested in a fat pig like him and to tell him to fuck off.

Instead she turned back to her drink and, with a shrug of his shoulders, he swam back through the shoals of singles in the bar to try his luck elsewhere. To be fair to him, almost everyone there other than Anna was there to get laid.

The wine bar in Ottensen was a moderately glitzy place and

probably had evolved into a singles bar, rather than that having been the original intent. It was ideal for the job, though: the decor trendy, the furnishings plush, the music smooth, and the lighting soft enough to give the homely a fighting chance. There remained, however, a lingering atmosphere of quiet desperation.

It was a large space to cover. From where she sat at the bar with her back to the lounge, Anna could see most of the seating and standing area reflected in the smoked glass behind the bar counter. Occasionally people would stand between her and her target, but she couldn't risk making herself too obvious by turning around. After all she had, as Fabel had pointed out, been there when they had interviewed Albrecht and she was counting on him not recognizing her in this get-up. However, it was best to stay inconspicuous. Added to which, she didn't need to take risks: she was the team leader, not the close surveillance.

She turned around, keeping her back to the booth in the furthest corner of the bar where Albrecht sat. At the opposite end of the lounge, standing near the door at a chest-high table, the tall, muscular Thomas Glasmacher was almost unrecognizable. For Anna, the almost perpetually scruffy Glasmacher had always brought to mind some non-urban type – a Kiel trawlerman or a fruit farmer from the Altes Land. He habitually dressed with no coordination in jeans and battered-looking T-shirts or sweaters, to the point of being teased about it by his partner, the small, dark and impeccably tailored Dirk Hechtner; but tonight Glasmacher was wearing a grey sharkskin suit that emphasized the breadth of his shoulders, with black shirt open at the neck; he had gelled and combed his thick, curly and usually unruly blond hair back from his face. He had already, that Anna had seen, been approached by three women. Another case of too much raw chum in the water.

From where he was standing Glasmacher would have a clear view of Albrecht, who had arrived alone but now sat in the far booth with a tall, slender woman with black hair. The woman's skin had a dark tone and from her brief glimpse of her Anna wasn't sure if she was of mixed race. The relief team had arrived: Dirk Hechtner, who looked very much as if he was in his natural environment, was immediately behind Anna and stood talking to a younger, attractive blonde, Sandra Mau, who was one of the Commission's junior officers. Anna realized she should have teamed Glasmacher up with a female undercover officer too, and the idea of Thom as a babe-magnet made her smile.

'You look happy . . .'

Anna turned to see a man at her side. He was attractive: reasonably good-looking in a rough-at-the-edges kind of way and, like Glasmacher, had the kind of breadth across the shoulders you only earned at the gym; his nose and cheeks had the kind of geometry you only earned in a boxing ring. Or some less legal context. He was reasonably well-dressed, his shirt and suit well cut and not cheap, but not top-designer expensive. An instinct told Anna he was some middle-rank thug. This was a diversion she could do without.

'I'm waiting for someone,' she said and turned back to her drink.

'No you're not,' he said and leaned an elbow on the bar and his face close, too close, to Anna's. 'You're here to meet someone all right, you just haven't decided who. I've been watching you. You've been eyeing up the big blond guy over there by the door, but take my word for it, he's not what you're looking for.'

'And let me guess . . . you *are* what I'm looking for?'

'I'd like to be. Can I buy you a drink?'

'I've got one.'

'Then let me buy you another.'

'I'm good.'

The boxer-type made no sign of moving. Instead he rested his other hand on the back of her bar stool.

'Why are you being so stand-offish?' he said.

'Oh, am I?' she said with mock apology. She let the expression fall. 'It's my natural demeanour with creeps. Now fuck off.'

He straightened up. Anna readied herself for unpleasantness. That's all she needed, to have to slap this guy down, create a scene and blow the cover of the entire surveillance team. Instead, the boxer held his hands up.

'Okay . . . I'm sorry you feel like that. I didn't mean to bother you . . . I just thought you looked like someone who would be interesting to get to know.'

'Oh sorry,' said Anna, affecting the same sarcastic tone, 'I've gone and hurt your pride. And you were so confident and all . . . Never mind, I'm sure you'll find someone who'll fall for the sensitive ape routine. Now, if you'll excuse me, I'm going for a piss.'

She got up and headed to the women's bathroom. She passed Glasmacher and they exchanged a look.

There was a hallway between the door to the main lounge and the bathroom. Anna was waiting for it and she heard it: the door had just shut behind her when she heard it open again.

'Hey . . .' It was the ape's voice. And now it was his hand on her shoulder.

Without taking the time to turn, Anna cupped her right hand and swung it back and up into his groin. He doubled over and at the same time she jabbed her elbow back and upwards to meet his downward-headed face, doubling the force of the impact. She swung around and kicked out at the still bent over figure and he slammed into the wall. Anna became aware of Thomas Glasmacher coming into the hall. He drew his Glock and aimed at the boxer who had slid down the wall and now sat bent over, his nose bleeding, one hand cupping his bruised testicles. He looked from Anna to Glasmacher and back.

'Cops?' he asked, his voice strained through the pain.

'Cops,' said Anna. 'And you've probably screwed up an important operation. Why the hell couldn't you just take no for an answer?'

He reached out his other hand; it held Anna's clutch bag.

'You left your purse on the bar. For a cop you're very careless with your personal property.' He grimaced as he eased himself up. 'With my personal property as well.'

'Fuck!' said Anna. Glasmacher reholstered his sidearm and helped the boxer straighten up.

'I'm sorry,' said Anna. 'You're entitled to make a complaint.' She nodded to Glasmacher. 'Get back out there, Thom. I need your eyes on the subject.'

She took her clutch bag from him, found a handkerchief and handed it to him. 'Are you all right?'

He wiped his face, looked at the blood on the handkerchief then back at Anna. 'I think I'm in love . . .'

Glasmacher reappeared at the door. 'Anna . . . he's on the move.'

'I'll be right there. What's your name?' Anna asked the bloodied guy leaning against the wall.

'Marco Tempel.'

'Here's my card, Herr Tempel. If you want to make a complaint, get in touch. Are you sure you're okay?'

'I've had worse.' He looked at the card. 'Anna.'

Back out in the bar, Anna caught up with Glasmacher.

'They've left. Dirk and Sandra are on his tail. We can catch up. You okay?'

'I'm fine. But maybe we can keep this little incident to ourselves.'

'Okay . . . but he might make a complaint.'

'I doubt it . . . But if he does I'll deal with it then.'

Anna phoned Dirk Hechtner who told her they were heading south, towards the river.

Anna drove.

'You know where we're going?' asked Glasmacher.

'My guess is that they're heading for Albrecht's place. He's got a penthouse apartment overlooking the river.' She sighed. 'It's going to be a long night.'

'You think it's him? Albrecht?'

'The *Chef* says we should keep an eye on him, so we keep an eye on him. But no, I don't. But he's hiding something, that's for sure.'

'Enough to warrant a four man surveillance?'

Anna shrugged. 'We need to change faces. Albrecht's not stupid and, if he does have something to hide, then he'll be watchful.'

They arrived just in time to see the tail lights of Albrecht's Lamborghini as it tipped into the downward access of the private garage beneath his building. Anna saw that Dirk Hechtner had already parked further down the street.

She called Fabel on his cell phone. 'Looks like it's going to be a long night. Albrecht picked up a woman and he's taken her back to his apartment.'

'Do you think she's the mystery woman who he claims can give him an alibi for the night of Hensler's death?' asked Fabel.

'Doubt it. Looks more like a casual pick-up. Do you want a team parked on him all night?'

Fabel thought for a moment. 'No. Leave it. Send Dirk and Sandra home, but you and Thom stay put until I get there, then you can clock off.'

'You going to watch him all night?'

'No. If it looks like his guest is staying the night, then I'll leave it at that. But I'd like to make sure.'

52

Fabel sat in his BMW, parked across the street from the building Tobias Albrecht had designed and now lived in. Again he found himself grudgingly admiring the architect's work and wondering why the Bruno Tesch Centre in Altona had been so dissonant with its context. Fabel knew that Albrecht had bought this building outright when it had been a derelict grain store, similar to those found in the Speicherstadt. Once he had renovated and extended the original building, Albrecht had rented out the luxury apartments, retaining the penthouse for himself.

Hamburg was famed for its brick architecture, including the Polizei Hamburg's own Davidwache, the world's most famous police station and a protected monument. It was said that Hamburg architects could knit with brick; Albrecht had acknowledged his debt as an architect to predecessors like Hans and Oskar Gerson or Fritz Höger by restoring to its former glory the red brickwork of the original grain store. The twenty-first century made its presence felt through the huge windows that offered the apartments impressive views over the Elbe. It was the kind of home and view you paid through the nose for and Albrecht, Fabel realized, was a rich guy in a rich city. Germany's richest city.

Albrecht had done well for himself, all right; he had

everything that he could have wanted. Traxinger had had all he could have wanted. Werner Hensler had had all that he wanted. Yet all three seemed to have had an inexplicable emptiness in their lives. And Fabel was beginning strongly to suspect that the source of that emptiness was Monika Krone. Perhaps that emptiness came specifically from their involvement in what had happened that night when Monika had disappeared, fifteen years before.

The question Fabel asked himself was whether he was sitting outside the apartment of a killer or a potential victim.

His cell phone rang. The caller ID displayed the Murder Commission's number.

'Hi, *Chef*, it's Anna.'

'I thought you were heading home.'

'I was, but there was something I needed to check out. I did, and now you need to know something.'

'What?'

'There was an incident during the surveillance tonight. I didn't think it was important or even relevant—'

'What kind of incident?'

'A guy came on to me and I brushed him off. Then I thought he was going to assault me—'

'Oh shit, Anna, not again. Was he hurt?'

'Nothing that an icepack wouldn't sort out. Anyway, it turned out to be my mistake and he was returning something I'd left on the bar. But that's not important. The other thing is he looked like some middle-rank thug, so I thought I'd check him out.'

'And?'

'And he's anything but. His name is Marco Tempel and he's a doctor. He lives in Bremen.'

'He's come a long way for a night out.'

'I wish that's all that's going on with him. Do you remember me telling you about the incident five years ago that caused Albrecht to tone down his womanizing – or at least be more discreet and careful with it?'

'The woman who stabbed him and committed suicide?' asked Fabel.

'That's the one. Her name was Lara Tempel. My dance partner's sister.'

'Shit.' Fabel looked up at the penthouse. There were no lights on that he could see. 'And if he's a doctor, he'll have access to drugs. Maybe he carries around a supply of xylazine. Do we have an address for him here in Hamburg?'

'Nope. I'm assuming he's staying in a hotel somewhere. But my concerns are more immediate.'

'You think he's after Albrecht?'

'I think it's a hell of a coincidence that he was in the same bar as the guy his sister tried to kill, and that he clearly knew Thom Glasmacher was working the surveillance with me. I'm beginning to think the little act he put on was to distract us and get us off Albrecht's tail.'

'The woman . . .'

'Exactly. She's maybe in it with him. A honeytrap.'

Fabel was already out of his car and crossing the street. 'Get here as quickly as you can, Anna. And bring back-up.'

53

The front door of the apartment building was locked and there was no sign of anyone in the foyer. Fabel kept his thumb down on the button for Albrecht's penthouse apartment; when he got no answer he pressed the buzzer for the concierge. Through the glass door, Fabel saw a young man in a dark green uniform appear from a side door into the hall. He had a flop of blond hair above an expressionless, slightly girlish face. When he reached the main door, he made no attempt to open it, instead gazing blankly, silently and unsmilingly at Fabel through the glass.

For a moment Fabel thought of using the door intercom to explain the nature of his visit, but annoyed by the concierge's arrogance, he held up with one hand his police ID for the young man to see, while thumping heavily on the glass with his other fist. The concierge jumped, then pressed a buzzer to admit Fabel.

'You . . .' Fabel said flatly. 'Take me up to the penthouse and let me in to Herr Albrecht's apartment.'

'Don't you . . . I mean, shouldn't you have a warrant or something?' The flustered concierge scrabbled around for the scraps of his authority.

'I have reason to believe that someone in this building is in immediate danger. Do as I say. Now.'

The journey up in the elevator was silent, the previously arrogant young concierge looking more than a little afraid.

'When we get up there, let me in to the apartment,' said Fabel. 'Then get back down to the lobby right away. I've called for backup and I need you to let them in as soon as they arrive. Got it?'

The concierge nodded.

It was like coming up and out into the night sky. The elevator doors opened and Fabel and the concierge stepped out into a wide landing like a huge summerhouse encapsulated on three sides by glass walls, the other wall marble with an oak door set into it. With the exception of the elevator's winding house above them, the roof too was glazed and the moon-edged shadows of clouds slid across it. Fabel counted two glass doors out onto the roof terrace. Beyond the glazing he could see Hamburg sparkle in the dark. For a moment he felt disconcerted, remembering another time he had watched from an elevated position as Hamburg sparkled below him. He shook the feeling off.

Crossing to the glass doors he tried them, rattling the handles. They were locked. He leaned into the glass, shielding his eyes with cupped hands, and peered across the roof terrace. It was difficult to see clearly in the dark but suddenly the terrace was lit up. He turned to see that the concierge had turned on the roof lights from a switch next to the penthouse door. Fabel nodded his thanks and went back to searching the shadows for anyone lurking. It was clear.

He went across to the penthouse door and pressed the buzzer. No answer.

'Did you see Herr Albrecht go out again this evening?' he asked the concierge. 'Or see his female guest leave?'

'No . . . but that doesn't mean they didn't. All the residents have access to the underground garage. Sometimes they come and go all day, taking the elevator down to the basement. I have a monitor at my desk, but if I'm not there, I don't see them.'

'So similarly someone could have got in that way too?'

'Only residents. Unless it was someone who went in through the garage and had a code for the elevator. It only works by code from the basement.'

Fabel tried the door to the penthouse, but it was locked. He nodded again to the concierge and drew his service automatic. At the sight of the gun, the young man froze, the colour draining from his face.

'It's all right,' said Fabel, less harshly. 'Unlock the door, then go down to the lobby and wait for the others to arrive.'

The concierge did as he was told. Once the penthouse was unlocked and the young man was back in the elevator, Fabel swung the door open and called out into the darkness.

'Police! This is Principal Chief Commissar Fabel of the Polizei Hamburg. Herr Albrecht? Can you hear me, Herr Albrecht?'

Darkness and silence.

Aware that he was a target framed in the doorway and illuminated by the landing lights, Fabel stepped into the apartment and immediately sideways, cursing as he knocked over a low table and sent the lamp it held crashing to the floor. Keeping his gun pointed into the darkness of the apartment, he skimmed the wall with the flat of his hand until he found a light switch. The apartment lit up. There was no one there, no sign of a struggle, nothing out of the ordinary.

'Herr Albrecht?' Fabel called out once more. Nothing.

He scanned the apartment again, taking a wider sweep. It was exactly what he would have expected from Albrecht: chic, cool, oozing a quiet, restrained but obvious expensiveness. Strangely, it was also completely devoid of personality.

The living area was a huge room with a double-height ceiling. Across from where he stood, Fabel could see his own faint ghost reflected in the vast windows that looked out onto the Elbe and Hamburg beyond. The kitchen and dining areas, both large enough to be rooms in their own right, were open-plan to the living room. There were three doors off the open-plan area. Bedrooms and a bathroom, Fabel guessed, and again was transported to another time and another search of a suspect's apartment where he had tried to guess what was behind a closed door.

He turned and saw the painting on the wall by the entrance.

Life-size, framed by writhing ivy and acanthus and her nude body pale-skinned and ethereal in the moonlight, Monika Krone stared at Fabel from the graveyard in which she stood. Despite his situation, Fabel was momentarily distracted by Monika's cruel, beautiful, green-eyed gaze. Her hair blazed deep red around her head and her lips were slightly parted as if shaping a word or a kiss.

Shit, he thought, *that's why he agreed to see us so quickly at his offices, he didn't want us to interview him here.* Albrecht had denied that he had had any significant contact with Detlev Traxinger since their days at university, but the picture on the wall was clearly, unmistakably a Traxinger original. And it was also a very clear indication that Albrecht, like the painter, had been obsessed with Monika Krone.

Again Fabel felt haunted by memories of a different, much more modest apartment, but another in which a Traxinger picture had looked completely out of place with the decor.

Tearing his gaze from the green eyes that had held him fixed, Fabel snapped his attention back to the apartment. He called out for Albrecht again, once more identifying himself as a police officer. He could hear approaching police sirens, outside and below. Fabel crossed the room and swung wide the first door, which opened up on the glistening onyx and marble of a luxurious bathroom. Empty. The second room was empty too: a largish bedroom that had been converted into a study.

Fabel crossed the main area of the penthouse, this time to the third door on the far side. Again he called out for Albrecht but noticed that he automatically trod lightly as he crossed the polished redwood floor.

He swung the door open. It was a bedroom suite with a short hall leading to the bedroom itself; a marble and glass cave of a bathroom to one side of the hall, a dressing room to the other. All the doors were open, all the lights were on.

Fabel moved slowly along the hall, his gun held in both hands, sweeping as he went. The dressing room and bathroom were empty. When he reached the end of the hall, he snapped around the corner, checking there was no one lying in wait for him in the main bedroom.

But there was no one in the bedroom. No one living.

It was another huge room: the bedroom, en suite and dressing room perhaps slightly out of proportion, too big in comparison to the rest of the penthouse. For Tobias Albrecht the bedroom, it would seem, had been the most important room in the apartment; the focus in his life. Not that he would be using it any more.

Fabel heard the sounds of footsteps from behind him in the main living area, then Anna Wolff's voice as she called out.

'In here . . .' he called back without turning around. His attention was fully focused on the bed.

Anna Wolff, Thom Glasmacher and Dirk Hechtner walked into the bedroom.

'Oh shit . . .' he heard Anna say as she came to stand beside him. Glasmacher and Hechtner joined them and the four formed a row at the foot of the huge, low bed.

Tobias Albrecht lay on top of the covers. He was naked, his legs together, his hands neatly set at his sides, as if he had been laid out by an undertaker. His pale skin was even paler than it had been in life. It was normally a sign of post-mortem lividity, all of the body's blood sinking to and empurpling the low-gravity points in the body, the rest bleached of colour. But Fabel didn't need a forensic expert to tell him that that wasn't the reason for Albrecht's pallor. Arced and stretching up the wall behind the bed, like a single, wide-spanned crimson wing, a spume of arterial blood had spattered across the expensive wall-paper. The pillow and bedding on the right side of his neck was black-red where the last leachings of blood had soaked into the fabric as arterial pressure had diminished. A chilled, shuddering end.

In all of his years as a murder detective, Jan Fabel had never been able to get beyond the gut reaction to blood. Something deep in the oldest part of your brain responded to the sight of it, no matter how often you saw it. As he looked at the spray on the wall, Fabel found himself thinking back to Helmut Wohlmann, the murdered centenarian in the seniors' home, and how little blood there had been.

But even the blood-splashed wall and bed weren't the most disturbing aspects of the scene: a thick shaft of wood, about twenty centimetres long and eight centimetres in diameter, had been rammed into Albrecht's chest. There was practically no blood around the stake, which jutted nauseatingly from just below his sternum.

'Shit . . .' Anna repeated. 'It's like he didn't move. The blood's a single spatter pattern. Unless he was restrained, somehow.'

She nodded, her face distorted in disgust, to the stake embedded in Albrecht's chest. 'From the lack of blood around that, I'm guessing it was done post-mortem.'

'It's symbolic, not the cause of death,' said Fabel. 'We're supposed to derive some sort of meaning from it. Or maybe the meaning is purely personal to the killer. And my guess would be that the restraint that kept him motionless while his artery was severed was pharmaceutical, rather than physical. I'll lay odds we find xylazine in his system.'

'You think it's the same guy?' asked Glasmacher. 'The modus is completely different.'

'It's the same guy – or maybe the same guys, plural. He or they maybe kill in different ways, but this is all to do with a single agenda. He kills for the same reason. And this is his third victim, and that qualifies him as a serial.'

'But if Marco Tempel is behind this, what's his motive for the other two killings?' asked Anna.

'I'd like to ask him that in person. Get in touch with the Polizei Niedersachsen in Bremen and tell them to get round to his home, just in case he heads back there. In the meantime get as many people as you need onto finding out where he's staying in Hamburg.'

'Yes, *Chef.*'

Back down in the apartment building's foyer, the young concierge stood talking to a uniformed SchuPo. The youth was white-faced, his eyes darting in that exhausted-agitated way Fabel had seen in so many witnesses and bystanders to murder. Even though the concierge hadn't seen the body, a murder had been committed in his building. Fabel had seen the sequence so many times before: shock causing adrenalin and cortisone to flood the system creating what felt like an inappropriate but deeply unpleasant excitement, then the withdrawal, the crash, as the initial buzz faded and the stress and the disquiet remained. Murder, he had learned, was only a concept to most people: vague, indirect. But when murder came too close, it shook the world beneath their feet.

Fabel went over to him and smiled. 'You okay, son?'

He nodded behind a weak smile. Then shook his head, giving up the pretence. 'I can't believe it. Herr Albrecht was our most important resident. He designed this building. He used to talk to me whenever he passed. I just can't believe it.'

'I know,' said Fabel. 'Herr Albrecht had company this evening – an attractive dark-haired woman – you're sure you didn't see her?'

The concierge shook his head.

'Did Herr Albrecht have any other visitors over the last few days? I know you said they could come and go through the base-ment garage, but if they came here alone – I mean without Herr Albrecht bringing them – then maybe you saw them as they passed through the foyer.'

'Herr Albrecht had lots of visitors. He tried to be discreet about them, but I did see them occasionally. On the monitor.'

'I take it we're talking about female visitors?'

'One of the things we're taught about in training is to be dis-creet. Not to pry or talk about the residents' affairs. But you can't help noticing things. Herr Albrecht was one for the ladies, if you know what I mean.'

'Anyone in particular? Or anyone you could identify for me?'

The young concierge frowned. A lock of dark blond hair fell

across his face and he palmed it back. Fabel knew he had something to say, but didn't want to say it. Again, years of experience told him to be patient.

'Yes,' said the concierge eventually. 'There was one woman who came often. I saw them arrive and leave together a couple of times.' He nodded towards the reception desk. 'On the monitor, like I said.'

'And you know who this woman was?' asked Fabel.

Another frown creased the girlish brow. 'I don't want to get into trouble. We're not supposed to—'

'You'll get into much more trouble if you withhold evidence in a murder case,' said Fabel, his tone still friendly.

'Yes,' the concierge said decisively. 'I do know who she was. And I can give you her name . . .'

54

The office was the same, but the figure behind the desk was very different. Fabel had spent more time than he would have liked up in the Presidial Suite, on the fifth floor of the Presidium – but as head of a major wing of the investigative service, bureaucracy and politics were something that came hand in hand with the role.

For fifteen years, nearly all of Fabel's service in the Commission, it had been Hugo Steinbach who had served as Hamburg's Police President: an avuncular, open man who had started out as an ordinary patrolman and had worked his way up through every rank and every department. The fact that Steinbach, immediately before transferring to Hamburg, had been head of the Polizei Berlin's Murder Commission had made him someone Fabel had found very easy to deal with; someone who understood the very particular pressures of Fabel's job.

Steinbach had also been still in office when Fabel had returned to duty after his shooting and had made it clear that he would do anything to support him, including the offer to free him from his Murder Commission duties.

But now Steinbach, the bottom-to-top policeman, was gone. Negative press over a mishandled human-trafficking case, Steinbach's often too-direct manner with media and public, political pressure from the generally hostile Principal Mayor's office and a shot-across-the-bows minor heart attack had guided the Hamburg Police President into early retirement.

Now, in his place, someone new sat behind the huge presidial desk.

Petra Gebhardt stood up when Fabel entered the room, came round the desk and greeted him with a smile and a handshake. She was a tall, slim, unremarkable-looking woman in her early forties, with blonde hair and pale blue-green eyes. She was dressed in a dark blue trouser suit with a pink blouse: an outfit that made her look more corporate than municipal.

Not that Fabel felt there was anything wrong with Petra Gebhardt, or her appointment as Police President. She was likeable, amenable and very supportive of Fabel and his department, which was not in itself surprising: under Fabel's command LKA411 – the official designation of the Hamburg Murder Commission – had become a resource increasingly tapped into by other state police forces across the Federal Republic. It became known that Principal Chief Commissar Jan Fabel was the *go-to guy*, as the Americans would say, if you had a multiple killer on the loose, particularly if there was some kind of complex or psychological agenda behind the murders.

Petra Gebhardt, unlike her predecessor, had joined the police at officer entry level – there again, so had Fabel. Gebhardt, however, struck Fabel as more management, more a professional administrator, than a policewoman, and much of her experience during what had been an accelerated rise through the ranks had been behind a desk. But Fabel had resigned himself to that being the way things were now, and that hers were probably exactly the skills that a modern chief of police needed.

Moreover, Petra Gebhardt, again very unlike her predecessor, had proved herself to be a very political animal: adept at dealing with politicians, the public and the media. And that was exactly why Fabel had asked to see her.

'Sit down, Herr Fabel, please,' she said, taking her place once more behind the huge desk. 'I'm so glad you asked for this appointment. I was about to arrange one with you myself.'

'Oh?' *Here it comes*, thought Fabel.

She leaned back in the leather chair. 'As you know, Leading Criminal Director van Heiden is due to retire at the end of this year.' Gebhardt referred to Horst van Heiden, Fabel's immediate boss. As Leading Criminal Director, van Heiden was in charge of all officers in the LKA – the investigative branch of Hamburg's police force.

'Of course,' said Fabel. 'I'll miss him, we have worked together for a long time.'

'Quite. Anyway, it would be grossly unfair of me if I weren't to offer you first refusal of the promotion.'

Fabel smiled. 'That's an interesting way of putting it. Why do I get the idea you want me to refuse it?'

'Because I do. I really don't want you to move. I cannot imagine anyone else taking over from you and maintaining the Murder Commission's reputation as a national centre of excellence. But you deserve the promotion, and I know you would do as good a job as commander of the whole investigative branch as you do in charge of the Murder Commission.'

'Thank you,' said Fabel. 'But I think you're overstating my gifts. There's any number of very capable officers both inside the Polizei Hamburg and in other forces who could take over the Commission. Nicola Brüggemann, for example. Come to that, there are other officers who are qualified to take over the Leading Criminal Director role – like Freddy Berger from the Organized Crime Commission.'

'I'm not sure that Herr Berger has the . . . the *people* skills for the role. He can be abrasive.'

'He's an excellent officer,' said Fabel.

'The truth is that if you don't take over as head of the investigative branch, we'll probably recruit from outside the force. I already have my eye on a couple of potential appointees. And as far as head of the Murder Commission is concerned, Frau Brüggemann would perhaps be my first-choice replacement if you *do* take over as Leading Criminal Director. But you know as well as I do that you have a very special level of experience and set of skills that would be hard to match. And anyway it's more than that – you have this unique understanding of what drives and motivates a killer.'

Fabel smiled. 'Thank you, but I'm really not that special. People always seem to be surprised to find out that I'm a very ordinary kind of guy – that I'm not some tortured soul struggling from one existential crisis to the next because of my job. And that I don't have any special gifts or insights.'

'Come on, Jan,' said Gebhardt. 'Enough false modesty. You know you've got something special going on.'

'Not really. In many ways, my job is very straightforward. And if you're working a difficult case, you use the skills you've got. Adapt them. As you know, I studied history – if there's no easy solution to a case, I start to think like a historian. A murder is an event, a point in time, with a chronology before and after. All I do is examine that history. It's a process, a technique, not some deep, nearly psychic attribute. Others have their own routes to it. Far be it from me to say, but I'm not as indispensable as you think.'

'Are you saying you want to make the move? As I remember, you were pretty emphatic with Herr Steinbach that you wanted to stay at the Murder Commission when he offered you the chance of a transfer before.' Gebhardt paused for a moment, reaching into a desk drawer and taking out a file. 'Like I said, it would be unfair of me to hold you back, so the Criminal Director's job is there for the taking. However . . .' She handed the file to Fabel. 'This is my counter-proposal. Right at the start when it was suggested that the Commission took on a consultative role with other forces, the proposal was that you be promoted to the rank of Criminal Director while still staying in charge of the unit. It was never followed through, mainly because of your concerns about the Commission becoming swamped with outside cases.' She nodded to the file in Fabel's hands. 'That proposal includes your immediate promotion not just to Criminal Director but to Leading Criminal Director while still remaining head of the Murder Commission. You will be equal, and not subordinate, to the new Leading Criminal Director. Effectively, the Murder Commission becomes an autonomous unit with potentially a Federal Republic-wide brief. You'll see that the proposal also gives you an additional two teams. Four new officers, whom you are free to recruit yourself from any department or rank.'

'That is a quite some proposition . . .' Fabel nodded as he flicked through the proposal.

'It's my way of keeping you where you are, while still treating you fairly. That said, I expect you to *build our brand*,' Gebhardt used the English expression, 'across the Federal Republic.'

'I won't accept outside cases if our Hamburg caseload has us fully committed,' said Fabel.

'It goes without saying that the Hanseatic City remains your absolute priority, but that's why you'll be allocated extra human resources. Take your time and think about it. But not too much time, I have to get the wheels in motion sometime next month.'

'I will.'

'So what was it you wanted to see me about?' asked Gebhardt.

Fabel's expression darkened. 'Something you're not going to like. It's maybe going to make you reconsider your offer . . .'

Petra Gebhardt sat silently watching the sky for a moment, her leather chair turned to the window and tilted back slightly. She had maintained the position and the silence while Fabel had gone through all of what he knew about Tobias Albrecht's potential involvement with the murders, and his actual involvement with Birgit Taubitz. Birgit, Fabel had explained, had been the mystery woman Albrecht had wished to shield, even though she could provide him with an alibi for the night Hensler was killed.

'Are you absolutely sure about this?' asked Gebhardt. 'After all, we just have the word of a lobby boy.'

'I'm sure. It fits with Albrecht's reluctance to name her. And we've done our own enquiries—' Fabel held up a hand to halt Gebhardt's coming protests. 'We were very discreet, I assure you. Anyway, we have enough to suggest there really was something going on – although it has to be said that Albrecht and Frau Taubitz took great care to cover up their tracks.'

'Was she the one who was with Albrecht the night he was killed?' she asked.

'No, we checked. Frau Taubitz was at an official function with her husband. The woman the surveillance team saw Albrecht with looked like a casual pick-up from the bar. I'm sending a team in tonight to see if any regulars or staff in the bar can shed any light on her identity.'

'Do you think she was the killer?'

'I honestly don't know. We watched the place but missed her leaving. And we have at least two strong leads that would take us in another direction. However, we're looking for a man whose sister committed suicide because of Albrecht. There's always a chance that the woman in the apartment was at least an accomplice.'

'I take it you're going to interview Birgit Taubitz?'

'I'm afraid there's no way around it, Frau Police President.'

'I trust you to be *delicate* in your handling of the interview.'

'Naturally. As I would whatever the status or celebrity of the witness.'

Gebhardt smiled, taking Fabel's point. 'Okay,' she said. 'Could you keep me regularly up to date on progress? I mean in my role as acting Leading Criminal Director more than Police President.'

'Of course,' said Fabel, but he knew very well that her interest in the case was political, rather than investigative. He picked up the file on the proposed Super Murder Commission and stood up.

'And you will let me know your decision about which promotion you decide upon? Carrying Herr van Heiden's workload as well as my own has been difficult. I'd like things decided as soon as possible.'

'Certainly, Frau Police President.'

55

When it came to real estate, the Elbchaussee wasn't just the most expensive street in Altona, it was the most expensive street in Hamburg. Probably in Germany. You had to count your change in millions to own a property of any size here.

The house was a huge, white, Jugendstil affair, taking up, Fabel reckoned, almost five hundred square metres of a two thousand square metre lot. Like Traxinger's studio and Albrecht's apartment, it had views out over the water. The gardens were immaculate, with an in-ground pool flanking the house and a fringe of trees shielding it from its equally imposing neighbours. This was a world Fabel occasionally had to move in, but he did so like an explorer on an alien planet. The people who lived here were those who made Hamburg Germany's richest city. This was the milieu of the Free and Hanseatic City's seriously, incomprehensibly wealthy.

Fabel was surprised that it wasn't a servant who answered the door to him, but Birgit Taubitz herself. Her unexpected appearance made her beauty all the more striking, and he made a real effort not to let its impact on him show. Like Monika Krone, even like Kerstin Krone, the wife of the Principal Mayor of Hamburg wasn't just beautiful, she was intimidatingly beautiful. *Caligynephobia* – it was a strange word and a strange time for it to fall into his recall. He remembered reading about it once: the fear of beautiful women. At the time he found it hard to believe that any such phobia existed, but Susanne had assured him it did, and was often, like many phobias, the result of some deep trauma. Standing there at the threshold of the huge Taubitz villa, held in the imperious gaze of Birgit Taubitz, Fabel suddenly found it less difficult to believe in caligynephobia.

Frau Taubitz's hair was exactly the same tone of vibrant auburn-red as Monika Krone's had been and she shared the same emerald green eyes as both the Krone twins. She was dressed very casually, in jeans and a sweater, but Fabel could see at first glance that the ensemble would have cost more than he made in a week.

Fabel introduced himself and offered his hand.

'We're in the front study,' she said without taking it and turned to lead the way. Fabel followed her, wondering how many studies they had that they had to be described by their position in the house.

The front study was a bright room with white paintwork, art deco French windows out to the garden and some original art hanging on the pale cream walls. Fabel found himself checking that there wasn't a Traxinger hanging among the other paintings. There wasn't: this was a much more select artistic crowd. A tall, thin twist of dark metal stood on a plinth in one corner and Fabel recognized it as a Giacometti. Birgit Taubitz indicated Fabel should sit with a wave of her hand.

'I expect you and your department to handle this situation with the delicacy and discretion it deserves. I have agreed to meet you only on that basis and I will only answer questions I deem relevant. I spoke with the Police President about this this morning.'

'I see,' said Fabel smiling. 'Of course we will be discreet.'

'I'm glad to hear it.'

Fabel leaned forward in the chair, resting his elbows on his knees. The smile dropped. 'I think I should make myself perfectly clear: it is my job to be discreet in all investigations and in all situations like this, Frau Taubitz, whatever the background of the witness. Your status, such as it is, has no bearing whatsoever. And as for the questions you'll answer – *I'll* decide what's relevant, not you. And you will answer everything. If I am not entirely satisfied that you have, then I will take you into the Presidium and we'll continue the questioning there – in which case it will be a hell of a lot more difficult to keep your involvement out of the media. You maybe have been speaking to Petra Gebhardt, but I know that she'll have told you in no uncertain terms that your best policy is to be as open with me as possible. I will do my best to keep your involvement out of the papers, but you may well end up as a witness in court. The secret to discretion in this situation, as you put it, would have been for you to have chosen your fellow adulterer with more caution. Have I made myself perfectly clear, Frau Taubitz?'

Birgit Taubitz sat glaring at Fabel, wrapping a tight-lipped silence around her rage before nodding briskly.

'Your husband,' said Fabel. 'Have you told him that you were involved with Tobias Albrecht?'

'Of course not.'

'It's not my place to advise you on marital matters, but I don't think his knowledge of your involvement can be avoided.'

'You'll tell him?' The defiance suddenly left her demeanour. 'Why would you do that?'

'I have no intention of telling the Principal Mayor at the moment. We are following specific lines of inquiry and hopefully one of these will bear fruit. However, if they don't, then, at the end of the day, your husband has a pretty strong motive – perhaps one of the most common motives – for committing murder: killing his wife's lover out of sexual jealousy.'

'You can't seriously be suggesting that?'

Fabel held up a hand. 'Like I said, we have other lines to follow first. And your cooperation in following those lines is key. Do we understand each other?'

Another nod, this time with less rage behind it.

'How long were you sexually involved with Tobias Albrecht?'

'A year and a half, roughly. We met at a function.'

'And the affair was conducted where?'

'His apartment, mainly.' She held Fabel's gaze determinedly, as if trying to prove she wouldn't allow the indelicacy of the subject to faze her. 'A hotel room on a couple of occasions, but that was too risky and only when we met away from Hamburg.'

Fabel placed a mortuary photograph of the tattoo on the desk in front of Birgit Taubitz. She stared at it for a moment.

'Do you recognize this tattoo?'

'I don't understand,' she said. 'This can't be from Tobias's body – he didn't have any tattoos.'

'That's not what I asked you. This isn't Albrecht. Do you recognize this tattoo?'

'No . . . but I recognize the motif.'

'Oh?'

'It was used as a monogram at the bottom of that God-awful painting. The one he had hanging in his apartment despite the fact it didn't go with anything else. *The Silent Goddess*.'

'Sorry, what did you say?'

'*The Silent Goddess*. That's what he called the painting. Or at least he called it that once.'

'When?'

'The strange thing about Tobias was that he was moderate in most things, apart from sex. He wasn't a big drinker, but one night he'd had a little too much. Not drunk, really, but he let his guard down so I asked him about the painting. You know the one I'm talking about – have you seen it?'

Fabel nodded.

'Anyway, I hated that picture and I asked him what the hell it was meant to be, and he said it was the Silent Goddess. Then it was like he instantly felt he'd said too much and he dropped the whole thing.'

'Why did it annoy you? This particular painting?'

'I was jealous of her . . .' Birgit Taubitz shook her head, as if annoyed with herself. 'The woman in the painting. I was aware of the similarity with me and I often suspected that she was the *great love*' – she exaggerated the phrase and crooked her fingers in the air to mime quote marks – 'of Tobias's life and that he had chosen me as some pale substitute. She made me feel like second best. That's not an emotion I'm used to.'

'But he never told you the identity of the woman in the picture?'

'He never even admitted that she was a real person, or anything other than an artist's idealized creation. But every painting has a model, someone real on whom the fantasy is based, and I knew that it was someone Tobias had some kind of connection to.' She shrugged. 'Don't ask me how, I just knew.'

'The artist who painted the picture – Detlev Traxinger – did you know him?'

'I bumped into him once or twice at functions, that kind of thing.' She made a disgusted face. 'And I mean bumped into him. He was a fat pig and a creep, always pawing at women. And a drunk.'

'Did he ever try to paw you?'

'No . . . but he still gave me the creeps. Every time our paths crossed he would stare at me. Not leer, just stare. I wondered even then if it had something to do with my similarity to the woman in the painting.'

'And you never got a hint from Albrecht who the Silent Goddess was or why she was called that?'

'No . . .' Taubitz frowned. 'What is it? Is it significant?'

'I don't know,' said Fabel, but there was a beat's pause before he asked his next question. 'Before his death, Herr Albrecht was a suspect, albeit not a leading one, for the death of Werner Hensler. He claimed he was with you all that evening, but wouldn't give up your identity. Is it true – was he with you?'

'Yes, we talked about it afterwards. He seemed genuinely upset. I had no idea that he knew Werner Hensler, but then he told me he had gone to university with him.'

'Did he say they were close?'

'No, just that they were contemporaries. But I got the feeling he was understating it. Like I said, Tobias seemed very upset by Hensler's death.'

'Were you ever aware of Albrecht having an interest in the Gothic – in Gothic literature or art?'

Birgit Taubitz looked taken aback for a moment. 'It's odd that you should say that. As an architect, Tobias was a modernist – which I believe is paradoxically considered old-hat these days. All of his buildings were about clean lines and geometry, some of them almost minimalist. But one day he had some drawings out on his desk – you know, the mini-studio in his apartment.

They were beautiful, pencil and ink, as if they'd been done on a drawing board, rather than on a computer. I asked him about them and he said they were stuff he had done when he had been an architecture student. It's odd, he seemed embarrassed by them, but they really were beautiful, in a dark sort of way. Anyway, they were all Gothic. There were designs for a fountain, a mansion of sorts and then some kind of ornate building that looked like a cross between a mausoleum and a temple.'

'And these were just studies – not for any planned real building?'

'That's what he said, but I noticed that the sketch for the mausoleum-temple thing had a location written at the bottom.'

'What was the location?'

'Sorry, I can't remember. It was in Hamburg though. Maybe the sketches are still in his apartment.'

They talked for another hour. Fabel went through times and dates, connections, friends and acquaintances. As the conversation went on, he got the impression that the Principal Mayor's wife was regaining some of her previous confidence and arrogance. The suggestion that her husband could end up a suspect had been a bluff on Fabel's part and he suspected she was beginning to see through it.

But he was simply going through the motions now. There was one thing he was going to take away from the interview. Two words slipped between lovers in a moment of tipsy carelessness.

Silent Goddess.

56

The Institute for Judicial Medicine was in Eppendorf, to the north of the city. If you died in Hamburg without an appointment, this is where they brought you. All the autopsies were carried out at 'Butenfeld', which was police shorthand for the institute's morgue and referred to the street it sat on. It was also somewhere you could find an expert on almost any aspect of forensic science. Over recent years the institute had become a world-leading resource and its expertise had been sought by police forces around the world. It was, Fabel reckoned, the kind of model Petra Gebhardt had in mind for the Polizei Hamburg's Murder Commission. Fabel had driven there straight from the Taubitz villa, stopping off to pick up coffee from a stall down by the fish market, and left his BMW in the car park in front of a double storey block. This was where Susanne worked and he had arranged over breakfast at the flat that he would call in.

'I brought coffee,' he said as he entered her office, placing two takeaway lattes on the desk in front of her. 'Have you had a chance to do that profile I asked for?'

'I thought I'd save that for pillow talk,' she said, sipping at her coffee. 'Nothing gets a girl going in bed more than talking about the mindset of the dead. Like I told you this morning, you didn't need to come up, I would have emailed it to you.'

'I'm in a bit of a hurry,' he said. 'I need to find this Dane before he gets the Gothic treatment. And the truth is I'm desperately trying to understand what the hell is going on. Whatever it is, it all revolves around Monika Krone. I'm more convinced of that now than ever. I'm not asking you for something that'll stand up in court, I'm just trying to get my head around who and what she was.'

'I've told you that it's nigh on impossible to do a psychological post-mortem on someone. All you've given me is second-hand accounts and vague observations from her sister – who's unlikely to be objective one way or the other – and others she encountered at university.'

'Nigh on . . . but *not* impossible. Even I've been able to build some kind of picture of her from what others have said. Anyway, I can tell by the preamble that you've got something for me.'

'I could be totally wrong, Jan. I can only offer at best a half-informed opinion.'

'But?'

'But it strikes me, as I'm sure it does you, that Monika Krone was a highly manipulative individual. Supremely egocentric and with little or no empathy for others. She used men *for* sex and she used sex *against* men – as a means to control them. She also seemed to have had difficulty balancing her highly organized scheming with her tendency to be unpredictable and impulsive. I think you know where I'm going with this . . .'

'A sociopath?'

'It's the picture that's emerging. Don't tell me that you hadn't already put it together yourself. Bear in mind that one per cent of the population can be classed as clinically sociopathic. And of that one per cent, the majority manage to lead normal lives without any criminal behaviour. Some say it's even an advantage in the business world, which says a lot: the less you care about people the better capitalist you're likely to be. And, it has to be said, it's mainly a male thing.'

'But you think Monika Krone was a sociopath. Do you think she could have been violent?'

'I think there was maybe the potential for violence, considerable potential, but she wouldn't have found it necessary. Criminal sociopaths use violence as a means of exerting their will over others. Monika Krone had other, more powerful weapons in her arsenal: she used her beauty and sex to get what she wanted. The other thing is that I've been through her academic records – both school and university. She had problems at the start of her school career but an educational psychologist was called in and sorted her out. Got her back on the rails, so to speak.'

'What was her problem?'

'Her problem?' Susanne laughed. 'Monika Krone's problem was that she had an IQ that was off the scale. Her records also note that she had an incredibly encyclopaedic knowledge. Intelligence plus knowledge plus beauty is a highly potent mix. Add sociopathic ruthlessness and it becomes explosive. But her academic performance fluctuated, as that of the highly gifted usually does. She would be able to out-think, out-manoeuvre just about anybody she came in contact with.'

'Except the last person she came into contact with,' said Fabel.

'Brute strength and violence, Jan. Not the same thing. She could control everyone around her, except herself. And whoever killed her was either a complete stranger, immune to her powers, or someone whom she had pushed to breaking point. Sometimes violent passions distil down to simple violence.'

Fabel sipped his coffee, deep in thought. 'Would someone

with the type of personality you're describing manipulate others exclusively to get what they want – to achieve definite goals – or would they do it for its own sake? Just to see how far she could make others go?'

'I'd say either . . . or both. Sociopaths like to see how powerful their wills are, compared to others'; to see just how far they can push.'

'Anything else?' asked Fabel.

'There's one thing that came to mind: you told me what her sister Kerstin said to you – about how she suspected that Monika had maybe trapped herself. That she'd maybe built so many webs around her that she couldn't escape and she perhaps welcomed her killer.'

'I think that was just emotional talk . . .'

'I don't think it was. I know that Kerstin and Monika seem like polar opposites, but they weren't. No twins really are. What Kerstin said about there being something missing with Monika . . . that was true too. Sociopaths don't have something the rest of us are missing. Quite the opposite – it's they who are missing a part. Most of the qualities you see in Kerstin as a person would have been there in Monika too, and vice versa. In Monika's case, however, she would have greatly diminished empathy for others, or perhaps no empathy. Plus her sociopathy would deny her control of her impulses or her ego, which would have become supreme. But, contrary to what many people believe, sociopaths are capable of introspection. In Monika's case, there would always be the possibility of self-loathing. Part of her, deep down inside, would have always wanted out, wanted to escape the vortex of chaos she had created. The only problem with that is that you can never run away from yourself.'

'You seriously think that she could have been suicidal?' asked Fabel.

'It's a trope that sociopaths don't commit suicide because they're too self-centred to be self-destructive. They do get depressed, and they do commit suicide – just for different reasons than normal people, mainly because they've lost the one thing they crave: control. More often than not a sociopath takes his or her own life because their actions, their manipulations of others have left them isolated or their situation untenable. I'm telling you, Jan, if Monika Krone's body hadn't been so clearly deliberately hidden, I would not have ruled out suicide.'

'So you think she maybe did welcome her killer after all?'

'No. Not her killer or however she met her death. But extinction – freedom from the mess she'd made of her life – perhaps.'

Fabel was about to say something when his cell phone rang. It was Karin Vestergaard.

'I got your message. You said it was urgent,' she said. 'By the way, I've got the details you wanted on Paul Mortensen.'

'That's why I was phoning. And why it was urgent. We've had another killing – another fellow student of Mortensen's. I'm beginning to suspect we have a shopping list and your countryman is next to be ticked off.'

'He's in Hamburg now,' she said. 'His flight got in late last night. I have his cell phone number but he may have it switched off – he's attending this haematology conference at the congress centre, and he'll be in and out of seminars all day. I have his hotel details, I'll text them to you, but I think your best bet is definitely to try to get him at the congress centre between events. Is there anything else I can do, Jan?'

'Thanks, Karin . . . not at the moment but I'll get back to you if there is.'

'Jan?'

'Yes?'

'He's one of ours. Don't lose him.'

'I'll do my best.' After Fabel hung up he leaned over the desk and kissed Susanne. 'I've got to go.'

'Everything okay?'

'I hope so. Thanks for the evaluation. See you later.'

On the way out to the car Fabel phoned Anna Wolff and asked her to meet him at the congress centre. 'And bring a few bodies, Anna. We need to find Mortensen quickly.'

It was a huge expanse to cover, unless you knew exactly where to find who you were looking for. The congress centre was a vast building, not in height – it was mostly over three floors with a five storey central complex – but in area. It sprawled over its city centre site, the only high rise element the soaring tower of the adjoining hotel.

Fabel arrived on site first, but Anna arrived a minute or two later. A Mercedes Sprinter minibus and a patrol car, both in the silver and blue livery of the Polizei Hamburg, pulled up behind Anna's car and ten uniformed officers decanted from them. It was followed by a red Opel Astra saloon and Dirk Hechtner and Thom Glasmacher joined the knot of police officers. All were armed with the photograph of Mortensen Karin Vestergaard had emailed Fabel, along with the details of the seminars he was due to attend.

'Okay,' said Fabel. 'We know who we're looking for and where he should be. There's no way we can check every square centimetre of the building, so we just have to hope that Professor

Mortensen is exactly where he's supposed to be which is . . .' Fabel checked his notebook. 'The haematology conference in Hall Six, which is one floor up from the entrance level. His seminar is supposed to start in fifteen minutes. If by chance you see him anywhere in the crowds, secure him and notify me. Tell him it's for his own protection. I want two uniforms at the main entrance. Anna – we'll take four uniforms and go in through the west entrance. Thom, Dirk – you take the other four and go round to the east.'

Fabel called Mortensen's cell phone for the third time, and for the third time got his voicemail service.

'Shit,' he said, putting the phone back in his pocket. He nodded and Glasmacher, Hechtner and four uniforms headed around to the east entrance. He led Anna and the rest in through the main entrance foyer. It was a vast hall of marble floors and polished stone pillars, and it was filled with hundreds of people milling about, moving from one hall to another, or gathered in knots, talking about whatever business they were in, whatever product they were going to hear a presentation on. There were two more levels above them. 'This place is huge. Hall Six . . . let's go.'

Fabel led the way up the escalator, a dozen business-types staring at the blue uniformed SchuPos following him.

When he reached the top, he saw Hechtner, Glasmacher and their escort emerge from the other escalator. There were throngs of people in the foyer, obviously waiting to get in for the next seminar.

'Shit, that's him . . .' Anna said at Fabel's side. He turned to her.

'Who, Mortensen?'

'No . . .' Anna laughed disbelievingly. 'It's Tempel. The guy we're looking for. The one whose sister tried to kill Albrecht before topping herself. Christ – do you think he's here to do Mortensen?'

Fabel looked across to where a group of men dressed in suits and wearing name badges stood talking. One of them was medium height and athletic-looking. His hair was buzz-cut and his face angular, his nose showing signs of an earlier break. Fabel could see why, in a different context, Anna had suspected him to be some kind of thug.

Marco Tempel looked across and saw them. He seemed puzzled for a moment, eyebrows raised, then he waved to Anna who was already moving purposefully towards him, her hand resting on the grip of her service automatic. Fabel trotted to catch up with Anna and placed a restraining hand on her arm.

'Take it easy, Anna . . .' he said in a low voice. 'This isn't the place for a takedown. Anyway, he's making no move to flee.'

'It's *him*.'

'I know, but let's get him out of here quietly and with no fuss.' He turned to the uniformed officers and indicated with a jerk of their head that they should follow.

'Hello.' Tempel smiled at Anna when she and Fabel reached him. 'Are you here for the seminar on blunt force trauma?' He turned to the others. 'Trust me, that's her speciality.'

Fabel took Tempel by the elbow and eased him away from the group. The doctor's colleagues suddenly seemed to become aware of the presence of uniformed police. Fabel leaned in and spoke quietly.

'I'm sure you don't want to make a scene, Herr Doctor Tempel. You are under arrest. I need you to come with us now.'

'Arrest? What for?'

'On suspicion of murder. If you resist, things could get very unpleasant and very public. Please come with us and keep your hands at all times where I can see them.'

'What?' Tempel pulled his arm free from Fabel's grip. 'Are you crazy?' He laughed uneasily and looked across to Anna, who had unholstered her pistol and held it against her thigh, out of sight of the small group of watching doctors. Two of the uniforms took a step forward.

'What's this all about, Marco?' asked one of the other doctors.

'We need to talk to Herr Doctor Tempel,' said Anna, without looking away from her charge. 'That's all.'

Shaking his head, Tempel allowed himself to be led through the foyer and out to a waiting blue and silver patrol car. Before guiding him into the back seat, Anna held out a pair of handcuffs.

'You're kidding me, right?'

'Just play nice,' said Anna.

'Which way do you like it, Anna?' said Tempel, his face hard. 'Front or back?'

'In front is fine.'

Tempel held his wrists out in front of him and Anna snapped the handcuffs in place. 'Where's Mortensen?' she asked. 'I take it we're not too late?'

'Mortensen? Professor Mortensen? He's about to give his lecture. The one you've just stopped me attending. What the hell is this all about?'

'Take him in,' she said to the driver, shutting the door on Tempel's confusion.

'We better get back in there and find Mortensen,' said Fabel. 'What is it?'

Anna watched the patrol car disappear. 'It's just his wounded innocent act – it seemed more genuinely wounded innocent than act.'

'Well, we have him now and can get to the bottom of things one way or the other.'

'It's not just that,' Anna said mournfully. 'He was kind of cute.'

When they went back into the conference centre, Fabel led Anna up the escalator once again to the foyer for Hall Six. It was nearly time for Mortensen's lecture and Fabel had to shoulder his way through a crowd of name-tagged suits to get to the entrance door. A congress centre member of staff, a woman with an Eastern European accent, stood at the entrance to the hall, holding a walkie-talkie in her hand and clearly waiting for the go-ahead to admit the audience of physicians. She looked startled to see Fabel and his entourage.

'We need to get into the hall,' said Fabel. 'But everyone else has to stay out here.'

The woman nodded and let the police officers in. At Fabel's request, she came in after them and locked the door behind her. It was a large space with seating for around four hundred with a sound stage at the front. It looked to Fabel like something more suited to a rock concert than a haematology lecture. But there had been hundreds of doctors waiting outside, so he decided that Mortensen must really be someone important in the field.

He led everyone down to the stage. It was empty. No Mortensen setting up for his lecture. He turned to the female staff member.

'There's a room off to the side.' She read his intent. 'Maybe the professor is in there. It can be used to set up audio-visual, computer presentations, that kind of thing.'

She walked them across and unlocked the side door. The room was empty.

'*Shit* . . .' Fabel said in English. He took out his cell phone and tried Mortensen's number: again it went straight to voicemail.

'Hotel?' asked Anna.

Fabel turned to the uniformed officers. 'I need four of you to stay here and search the centre as best you can. I'll try to get some more bodies sent.'

Fabel led his team and the remaining SchuPos out of the hall and through the puzzled expressions of the doctors gathered outside.

'He's not in the congress centre hotel,' Fabel said to Anna and the others. 'According to Karin Vestergaard he likes boutique-type hotels. She says that Mortensen's staying in the Hotel Kirschner, opposite the Hamburg Messe, on Schröderstiftstrasse. Let's go.'

The hotel was small and sat with one aspect facing and dominated by the soaring presence of Hamburg's television tower. Fabel told Hechtner, Glasmacher and the uniforms to wait while he and Anna checked if Mortensen was there.

'No need for us to create a scene,' he said. 'Anyway, Mortensen may be between here and the congress centre. His not being there could be as innocent as a late taxi.'

The girl behind the reception desk explained that she hadn't seen Mortensen leave and that housekeeping had told her that there was a 'do not disturb' sign on his bedroom door, so his room hadn't yet been serviced. Anna and Fabel exchanged a look.

'Get Dirk and Thom,' he said and Anna rushed out. He turned back to the girl. 'I need a key to get into Professor Mortensen's room.'

The girl hesitated, looking uncertain and a little scared.

'Now.'

She handed him a pass key from behind the desk, her hand shaking slightly.

'It's room thirty-two. Third floor.'

'Thank you,' he smiled reassuringly. 'Everything will be fine.'

Fabel took the stairs with Anna, Glasmacher and Hechtner at his back. As the receptionist had said, a 'do not disturb' sign hung from the handle. Fabel knocked loudly on the door.

'Herr Professor Mortensen? This is the Polizei Hamburg, Principal Chief Commissar Fabel. Could you open the door please?'

Silence.

As he placed the key in the door, Fabel turned to Anna. She nodded, resting her hand on the handle of her service automatic. Fabel swung open the door. The hotel room was empty. Mortensen's bed was unmade and Fabel noticed a cell phone, watch and wallet on the bedside nightstand. A rollercase sat in the rack by the door. Mortensen's laptop lay, closed, next to a notebook and folder on the desk under the window. The window faced out over the street and towards the trade-fair conference halls of the Hamburg Messe across the wide dual carriageway, but the feature that dominated was the Heinrich-Hertz-Turm television tower.

'Check the bathroom,' Fabel instructed Anna. He craned his neck to look out and up to the huge disc near the top of the tower, like some alien spacecraft permanently hovering over Hamburg.

He heard Anna open the bathroom door and draw a sharp breath.

'Oh Christ . . .'

57

There were several guises in which the guilty dressed their culpability; Fabel had seen them all, and had seen through most of them. The most common was indignation: a bluster of overdone outrage. Feigned confusion came next, where the accused made clear his or her bewilderment at the stupidity of the police in getting it all so very wrong. Then there was the overly cooperative 'of course I'll do anything to help' strategy. And there was the defiant: a stonewall challenging of the police to do all the talking and all the proving.

When he walked into the interview room, Fabel couldn't tell if Marco Tempel was employing no guise, or a subtle combination of them all. It looked for all the world as if the doctor was genuinely at a loss to understand why he was in police custody.

'I've been waiting here for nearly two hours,' he said in an even, calm tone. 'I have been taken away from an important seminar – arrested in plain view of my colleagues – and told I am suspected of murder. It seems to me that the only reason for all of this is that I was assaulted the other evening by one of your female officers. I think it's perhaps time I got my lawyer involved.'

Fabel sat down opposite Tempel. He had told Anna that given her scuffle with Tempel in the bar it would be best if she didn't sit in. He had thought of asking Nicola Brüggemann to partner him but had decided to keep his interrogation of the doctor low-key. For the moment. He switched on the recorder and stated his name, the date and time and who he was interviewing.

'Herr Doctor Tempel, if you wish to suspend this interview until you can have your legal representative present, then you are fully entitled to do so. Your rights under Article one hundred and thirty-six of the Federal Criminal Procedure Regulations have been already been explained to you?'

'Yes . . .'

'Then you'll also know that you can refuse to answer any or all of our questions and that no inference of guilt can be drawn from such a refusal. You understand that also?'

'Yes . . . I also know that if I don't answer, or if I wait for my lawyer, I'll be stuck here even longer. Right?'

'It would be good if we could get things sorted out now. I would be very grateful for your cooperation, Herr Doctor.'

'You're very polite for a policeman.'

'Have you had many encounters with the police in the past?'

'I dare say you've already checked that out and you'll know that I haven't.'

'I'm sorry that you've been kept waiting. But I've been attending a crime scene, you see. A pretty gruesome crime scene.' Fabel allowed a beat for a response; when there was none, he continued. 'You're a haematologist, I believe.'

'That's right.'

'As was Professor Mortensen.'

'He is much more than just another haematologist. Professor Mortensen is arguably the most important figure in haematology alive today. He leads the world in research into blood cancers, especially the rarer kinds. He's one of those one-in-a-generation figures in a particular field that sets the agenda for decades.'

'Then I'm afraid the world has just got poorer.'

Tempel frowned, then gave a confused laugh. 'You're telling me he's dead?'

'The crime scene I've just come from. Someone has indulged in a little poetic whimsy – the world-leading haematologist has been bled to death in the bathtub of his hotel bathroom. Do you use xylazine in your work, Doctor Tempel?'

Tempel didn't answer for a moment, instead looked away from Fabel, his eyes focused on nothing, shaking his head. 'Mortensen's dead?'

'Do you?'

'What? Do I what?'

'Use xylazine in your work? Medically, I mean?'

'Xylazine?' Tempel looked at Fabel as if he had said something profoundly stupid. 'Xylazine hydrochloride isn't used in human medicine. It's a veterinary sedative. What's that got to do with anything?'

'Just that it looks very like Mortensen was rendered incapable before someone opened up his arteries. It's exactly the same modus employed in the killing of Tobias Albrecht, except this time there was no stake through the heart. The symbolism of that we'll let go for the moment, but I suspect it was a reference to him being a vampire – someone who metaphorically if not literally sucked the life out of the women he used. Women like your sister.'

'Wait a minute . . .' More confusion on Tempel's face. 'Tobias Albrecht is dead too?'

'Yes, Herr Doctor, Tobias Albrecht's dead. That's why you are here. We have reason to believe that you may know how he died, where and when.'

'I haven't the slightest idea what you're talking about.'

'Then let me spell it out. You just happen to be in the same bar as Albrecht, who just happens to be the man your sister tried to kill before taking her own life. As if that isn't coincidence enough, we just happen to be mounting a surveillance of Albrecht in that very bar and, somehow, out of all of the women in the bar, you hit on one of the surveillance officers. A scuffle ensues which serves to distract the two surveillance officers, while your female friend gets Albrecht on the move. Next thing, Tobias Albrecht is found drugged, bled to death and with a chunk of symbolic joinery in his chest.'

'I know nothing about any of this.'

'You're denying it was you in the bar?'

'No . . . but I'm saying that it is a coincidence. Or at least partly a coincidence. I promise you I had nothing to do with Albrecht's death. Or the woman he was with.'

'Then why were you in the bar, Herr Doctor Tempel?' asked Fabel. 'I'm sure you can see that that stretches coincidence beyond credibility . . .'

Tempel sighed. 'Lara – my sister Lara – was a troubled woman. She was bipolar and had episodes of paranoid schizophrenia. That doesn't mean I don't hold Albrecht responsible for his actions – he treated her terribly and caused her to do what she did. But the truth is it could have happened with someone else, sometime else. The man was a shit, but he learned his lesson when Lara tried to kill him.'

'That still doesn't explain your presence in the bar.'

'I know this doesn't sound good for me, but I followed him there. I don't mean that I came all the way to Hamburg to find him – I was going to be here anyway for the haematology conference. It's just that while I was here, I wanted to see him. Maybe even talk to him. I've had a hard time coming to terms with Lara's death ...'

'I see,' said Fabel. 'You're right to say that that doesn't sound good for you. Basically, you came to spy on and possible confront Albrecht and within a matter of hours he's found dead.'

Tempel shrugged, an expression of hopelessness on his rugged face. 'I had no intention to confront Albrecht. Or at least I think I didn't – I just didn't know how I'd react to seeing him. But the truth is I *didn't* confront him. And I certainly didn't kill him or act as an accomplice to the woman he was with.'

Fabel leaned forward, resting his elbows on the table, his expression thoughtful. 'After your encounter with my officer last night ... where did you go?'

'Back to the hotel. I really did need to get a cold compress on my ... on my *injury*. No witnesses, I'm afraid.'

'Did you see Professor Mortensen at all?'

'No, of course not. He only arrived late last night – or early this morning.'

'And you know that how?'

'Through his schedule.' Tempel's tone was shifting: moving through the impatient to the indignant. He was either genuinely blameless or a skilled actor. 'The details of his lecture tour have been publicized through the medical journals. I travelled from Bremen to hear him – of course I knew when he'd be here.'

'Where were you this morning?'

'The hotel and then the conference centre.'

'And people can verify that?'

'Obviously. But maybe not down to every last second.' He

sighed. 'Let me get this absolutely straight: you think I killed both Tobias Albrecht and Paul Mortensen?'

'We're just trying to make sense of what is happening. You're the only person we can link to both victims, at the moment. Plus you have a motive to murder Albrecht – he drove your sister to suicide.'

'And Mortensen? Why on earth would I want to kill him?'

'What we're looking at is a series of murders that seem to be linked to a fifteen-year-old case. We also may be looking at more than one killer. It's entirely possible that you've made some kind of deal: someone has helped you do your killing on the understanding that you help them with one of theirs. Maybe more than one.'

'Are you insane? Don't you see, it's my job to save lives, not take them.'

'I am something of a specialist in serial murderers,' said Fabel. 'If you break down serial killers by occupation, by far the largest single group is the medical profession. Your business, it could be argued, is as much about death as it is about life. Unfortunately, for some of your colleagues, observing and experiencing the moment of death of others becomes an obsession. Gives them a feeling of power.' Fabel gave a small laugh. 'It's funny, since I've been working these cases the Gothic keeps cropping up. It's amazing just how Gothic the concept of medical profession serial killers is: Angel of Death nurses, doctors taking lives for the sense of power it gives. Death with a capital "D", as someone said to me recently.'

'And you think that's the type of physician I am: some kind of Doctor Death?' Tempel seemed genuinely angered by the suggestion. 'You don't get it at all, do you? Whoever killed Mortensen took more than one life. Because Paul Mortensen is no longer in the world, research into the whole spectrum of blood cancers had been put back years. Not many years: others will pick up his research and develop it – it's all there in the academic record. But even if it takes only, say, two years to regain his insight – that's two years' delay in research, two years' delay in development and testing. Two years' delay in bringing new treatments to the medical front line. Do you have any idea how many people will die in those two years? Professor Mortensen's killing wasn't murder, it was mass murder, and if you think I could ever have had anything to do with it you're mad.' He stood up. 'You know what? I'm finished with this. Either you charge me with something or let me go. And if you're not letting me go, I want my lawyer right now.'

Fabel stood up. 'Okay, thank you, Herr Doctor.'

'I'm free to go?'

'Not for the moment, I'm afraid. If you want to see your legal representative, we'll arrange that for you. In the meantime, I think you need a refreshment break and then another officer will take full details of your movements over the last few days. But once they've been checked out, and once we've finished the forensics process at both scenes, then we'll take you back to your hotel.'

Fabel was at the door when a thought hit him.

'There's one thing . . .' He turned back to Tempel. 'Would you mind opening your shirt?'

'My shirt?'

'If you don't mind. I need to check your chest for something.'

Tempel sighed and shook his head. After a moment he stood up abruptly, unbuttoned his shirt and pulled it open. His chest was smooth, tanned, muscular and blemish free. No tattoo.

'Satisfied?'

'Thank you, Herr Doctor Tempel.'

Out in the hall, a troubled-looking Anna Wolff was waiting for Fabel; she had been watching the interview on the closed circuit screen in the next room.

'What is it?' asked Fabel.

'I think he's clean,' she said. 'I think we've screwed up. Or more correctly, I've screwed up.'

'I take it you're referring to more than your love life. Maybe you can take him out on an apology date. Anyway, it's too soon to write him off.'

'You still think he's maybe had something to do with it?'

'I honestly don't know. We're in the dark so much here. And his distracting you while the woman got Albrecht out of the bar . . . If you and Glasmacher hadn't been changing shift with Dirk and Sandra, it would have worked. Get people over to Tempel's hotel and ask if anyone remembers seeing him with anyone else, particularly anyone fitting the description of the woman you saw Albrecht with that night.'

Nicola Brüggemann, carrying a document, came along the hall towards them.

'You were right,' she said, handing the printed-out email to Fabel. 'Forensics have confirmed xylazine in Albrecht's system. A lot of xylazine. They're rushing through tests on samples they got from Mortensen, not that there could have been much blood left in his body.'

'Thanks, Nicola.'

'There's more,' she said, nodding to the stapled pages in Fabel's hands. 'Take a look at the photograph over the page . . .'

He flicked through the pages until he found a mortuary

photograph, clearly of Albrecht's chest. The wooden stake had been removed and the hole gaped raw into the chest cavity. Someone had circled an area on the photograph in red marker, close to the chest wound.

'What's this?' asked Fabel.

'You can't really see it that clearly on the photograph, and we wouldn't have seen it when Albrecht showed you his chest – but the pathologist confirmed that there are hypopigmentation spots on the skin. Albrecht's skin tone was light anyway, so they would be difficult to notice . . .'

Fabel looked meaningfully at Anna. 'Laser tattoo removal?'

'That's what the pathologist reckons.'

'Shit,' said Anna. 'So he *did* have a tattoo.'

'And in exactly the same place as the others.'

58

Beyond the windows of his office, the sky above the Winter-huder Stadtpark had turned to a shade of pewter, as if the rain that had started falling had washed any colour out from it. Against his will, another day when the sky had been the colour of pewter pushed its way into his recall and a knot tightened in his gut.

He called Nicola Brüggemann in and asked her to round up the whole team and get everyone in the briefing room in ten minutes.

'Sure, Jan – you think we're getting close?'

'We're close,' he said. 'But close to what, I don't know. There are so many potential routes I'm worried that we'll head off in the wrong direction again. We've got so little forensic evidence from any of the scenes that I'm beginning to think we won't be able to pin any suspect down. Anyway, I want to discuss something else with the team as well.'

Henk Hermann appeared at the door. 'I just wanted you to know that I'm free, *Chef*. I've finally got all the paperwork done on the Alte Mühle Seniors' Home thing. I'm guessing you need all hands on deck.'

'You're guessing right. We're having a briefing in ten minutes, and if you and Sven Bruns could be there, it would be good.

What was the confusion? You said something about the Alte Mühle case having some kind of mix up?'

'Oh, nothing that confusing,' said Henk with a wry smile. 'Just that the killer was the victim and the victim was the killer.'

'What do you mean?'

Henk ran through what he had found in Georg Schmidt's diary, his interview with the old man and the discussion with the psychiatrist, Gosau, that had followed.

'So Schmidt killed Wohlmann in revenge for sins *he* had committed, not Wohlmann.'

'So it would appear. Herr Doctor Gosau seemed to think that Schmidt, once his mind and his memory started to fail him, escaped from his own history and slipped into the life he had always coveted.'

Fabel thought for a moment, then turned to Brüggemann. 'Nicola, do me a favour – get onto custody and tell them to hang on to Marco Tempel. I don't want him leaving the building until I talk to him again. But I don't want him to know why he's being delayed. I need to speak to him after the briefing, but without him getting a lawyer involved.'

'That sounds like thin ice . . .'

'Trust me. I'll see you in the briefing room in ten minutes.'

'Okay, is everyone here?'

'Anna's been delayed,' said Nicola Brüggemann, 'but she shouldn't be too long. Something important she needed to check up on, she said.'

'Fine,' said Fabel. 'Obviously I want to go through where we are with the so-called "Gothic" murders. It's become pretty clear that the murders of Detlev Traxinger, Werner Hensler, Tobias Albrecht and Paul Mortensen are all connected. The last two employed the same form of killing – bleeding the victim to death, probably while they were sedated and immobilized by a large dose of the horse tranquillizer xylazine hydrochloride. That seems to be the one thing common to all the killings. There's little doubt, as far as I'm concerned, that all four killings are connected to the disappearance and murder, fifteen years ago, of Monika Krone. However, before we go over where we are with the cases, there's something else I need to discuss with you all . . .'

Fabel paused as Anna Wolff came into the briefing room.

'Sorry I'm late, *Chef.*'

'Now that we're all here . . .' Fabel addressed the room. 'I have something to tell you. It will affect you all, so I wanted you to know about it and I want to hear your honest opinions. I have been offered one of two jobs. The first is as Leading Criminal Director in charge of the Hamburg LKA. If I accept, it would take me away from the Murder Commission, but as head of the whole investigative branch I would definitely have a say in my successor here. The second opportunity I've been offered is to stay on here, but in the rank of Leading Criminal Director and for the Commission to become a semi-autonomous unit within the LKA.'

There was a buzz of voices and Fabel held up his hand to halt it.

'This isn't just a choice for me. All of you here are officers I hand-picked for the Commission. As individuals, I consider each of you to be among the very best officers on this force; collectively you are the best investigative unit in Germany. Any success we have achieved has been more down to you than to me. I wanted you all to know, before I make it official, that I have decided to accept the Police President's offer and develop the Commission. What that'll mean for us all is that we'll be called in more and more to help other forces, if they ask us, with complex cases or when they have a serial offender active in their area. I should point out that if we do go down this route, we'll be given more resources and more people. And, because we'll be accepting consultative roles at a federal level, the Polizei Hamburg will get some funding from the federal government to help develop the Commission. But I want you all to be assured that our focus will remain Hamburg, first and foremost. This additional role will involve some of you being called away to other parts of the Republic, sometimes at short notice. I want you all to think this through and if, as a team, you're unhappy about the new arrangement, I want you to elect a spokesperson and let me know before I formally accept. If any individual officer wants to transfer, I will understand. I won't stand in your way and you'll be guaranteed a report that will put you at the top of any department's wish list.' Fabel paused, holding his palms up. 'Any questions?'

'I don't know about the others, but personally I think it's great,' said Anna Wolff. 'If there are any cases in Berlin, let me have them. Or Cologne. Oh, yeah . . . and Munich. Anywhere, really. But not Frankfurt . . . anywhere but Frankfurt. Fuck that.'

Everyone laughed.

'Are we covering only the German-speaking world,' asked Dirk Hechtner, 'or will we be taking cases in Baden-Württemberg too?'

More laughter.

'I'm glad you're all taking it so seriously,' said Fabel. 'Okay, think about it and if any of you wants to discuss it further, my door's open. In the meantime, let's get back to the case in hand.' He turned to the incident boards, now side by side and interconnected with pins and red thread.

'We've got a clear sequence of events,' he continued, 'starting with Monika Krone's remains being accidentally uncovered. Whatever else that event signifies, it seems to have torn the scab off a fifteen-year-old wound. Think about it – a new development needs a rerouted water supply and the trench cuts through the exact corner of a mini-market car park where Monika Krone has lain undisturbed for fifteen years. Her remains could have stayed hidden there for decades longer if it hadn't been for that single turn of fate . . .'

Fabel went over to the incident board to where Jochen Hübner glowered from a custody mugshot.

'But by chance or not, once her body was discovered all hell breaks loose: Jochen Hübner – aka Frankenstein and the only solid suspect we had fifteen years ago – escapes from Santa Fu prison and disappears off the face of the Earth. Then, in quick succession, four men – Detlev Traxinger, Werner Hensler, Tobias Albrecht and Paul Mortensen – are all murdered. All four men were involved to one degree or another with Monika Krone, who seems to have left them all deeply marked. I mean, Detlev Traxinger was completely obsessed with her – and probably Tobias Albrecht too, just that he was better at hiding it. And two of the four men had the same tattoo, the significance of which we've yet to establish, but I'd bet a month's pay that it had something to do with being members of this so-called Gothic set, which is looking more and more like a cult or secret society. And it's pretty safe to assume that the fourth man, Albrecht, had the same tattoo because we've just established that he'd had laser surgery to have one removed from exactly the same spot as the others.' Fabel paused.

'So who's killing former members of this secret student society? There are two strong possibilities – there's actually a third that only came to me today, but I need to think it through. But the first obvious possibility is this: that Jochen Hübner *did* kill Monika Krone fifteen years ago and the discovery of her remains has prompted him to escape from prison and, for some reason, start killing men who were close to her. Incidentally, forensics have told me that the partial thumbprint retrieved from Traxinger's studio isn't good enough for significant identification purposes, but it *is* enough to eliminate Jochen Hübner. Significant differences in morphology, apparently. But that doesn't, by any means, exclude him as a suspect.'

'But what's the motive?' said Nicola Brüggemann. 'I mean, I get it if he abducted and killed Monika – that would fit with his twisted sexual agenda and hatred of women. But we've only just discovered, through hard investigation, that these men were all connected to Monika. How would Hübner know?'

'He wouldn't. Jochen Hübner has been on the run for three weeks. He's not called Frankenstein for no reason – he has got to be the most conspicuous fugitive in the history of Hamburg manhunts. Yet there hasn't been a single sighting of him. I mean, this guy's appearance literally stopped traffic when he made his break from the hospital, yet no one has seen him since.'

'An accomplice . . .' Brüggemann nodded.

'An accomplice. Someone who helped him escape for a price. There is a fifth man – my ghost in the files – who was involved with the Gothic set. He was a ghost even back then – someone on the periphery of the group. Maybe he's the one who knows all the connections and sprung Hübner to do his dirty work. But maybe not. Which brings me to another possibility: that this fifth man is acting alone and killing his former associates.'

'Motive?' asked Dirk Hechtner. Fabel paused before answering: a young woman in uniform had knocked on the glass door of the briefing room. She leaned in and gestured towards Anna, who nodded.

'Excuse me, *Chef*,' she said. 'I need to see to this, it's relevant . . .' Fabel nodded and Anna went out into the hall and spoke to the uniformed policewoman, who started to guide Anna through a file of papers she had brought. Fabel turned back to Hechtner.

'Motive? We have two possibilities. One is that our mystery man is Monika's killer and the other four knew his identity. Maybe they didn't know for sure that he *had* killed her. The other possibility is that the reverse is true: that Traxinger, Hensler, Albrecht and Mortensen acted together in the murder of Monika Krone, and our fifth man has always suspected but never knew for sure. Then the body is found . . .'

'And your third possibility?' asked Nicola Brüggemann. Fabel noticed that Anna had come back in, clutching the file the uniformed officer had brought her. Anna's face was pale, her expression set hard.

'That's a long shot, Nicola . . . In fact it's so improbable I find it difficult to believe. In any case, I need time to think it through before sharing it.' He turned to Anna. 'What is it, Anna?'

'Your fifth man. I've got him. And this is big, *Chef* . . .'

'You don't look happy about it. Who is he?'

'The reason I don't look happy is that I've found a sixth man, too . . .' She walked to the front and handed Fabel a photograph. It was another morgue shot, again a close-up of the tattoo: the DT monogram circled with acanthus and ivy.

Fabel looked up and across to Anna, shrugging.

'Jan . . . I checked this out on a hunch. Trying to find a connection. That photograph is from the autopsy of Jost Schalthoff – the man who shot you two years ago.'

59

It wasn't yet full evening, but the dense trees around the old forester's house were already blotting out the light. Zombie had arrived twenty minutes before and had sat in the cellar, in that motionless way he had, and had quietly gone over what was to happen, how it was to happen and when. As he described the horror to be unleashed, he did so without emotion, without passion. Nevertheless a dark excitement had still risen in Frankenstein's chest. Now, their plans agreed, they stood in the dusty hallway.

'It's nearly time,' said Zombie. He handed Frankenstein a photograph and the keys to the white van. 'This is the revenge we've waited for. They will take me now.'

'I know,' said Hübner.

'They'll catch you too, you know that?'

'I won't let them. I'll kill as many as I can before they kill me.' Frankenstein turned his eyes, small and black, almost lost in the huge architecture of his face beneath the bulging brow. He rested his too-heavy hand on Zombie's too-light shoulder. 'Thank you. For everything.'

Zombie smiled. 'We'll both be free now.'

After Zombie had left, Frankenstein stood alone in the gloom of the dusty hallway and looked down at the photograph Zombie had given him.

He would wait until dark. Until the exact time he had been given.

60

'Jost Schalthoff?' Fabel stared at the photograph as if it could yield the answer. The briefing room was silent.

'It explains why we found that print – the one of Traxinger's painting – in his apartment.' Anna still looked worried. 'Are you okay with this?'

'What?' Fabel looked up, frowning. 'Sure . . . I'm fine. Yes, it explains the painting but nothing else. I just don't understand . . . Wait a minute.' He beckoned over to Sven Bruns. 'Sven, the architectural drawings I asked you to look for in Albrecht's apartment. Did you find them?'

'Yes, *Chef*, I put them on your desk.'

'And the book I asked for?'

'The dictionary . . . yes, it's there too.'

'Anna, Nicola – come with me. The rest of you wait here. I need to get something sorted out, then I'll assign duties.'

Once they were in the office, Fabel pulled the drawings from their cardboard tube.

'Birgit Taubitz told me about these.' He unrolled them flat on his desk. The top drawing was of a fountain. The style was totally different from that which Fabel associated with the architect: ornate, rich in detailed flora. Gothic. He shuffled through the drawings until he came to the one he wanted. It was the mausoleum-cum-memorial that Birgit Taubitz had described.

'It's beautiful,' said Nicola Brüggemann.

'A bit overdone for me,' said Anna.

Fabel stabbed his forefinger at the legend at the bottom of the page. It read: PROPOSAL FOR MEMORIAL AT JEWISH CEMETERY, ALTONA. He went through his desk drawers, almost frantically, until he found the file he was looking for. He placed a photograph of the painting of Monika Krone standing in a graveyard, surrounded by ivy and acanthus, on his desk next to the architectural drawing. In the background of the painting they could see tilted or broken headstones. The legend on some was in German, but in Hebrew on others.

'This is the place,' said Fabel. 'Whatever happened that night fifteen years ago, it happened here. And that's our link with Jost Schalthoff. He has absolutely no other connection with the others. He never went to university, but he did have an interest in Gothic literature. And God knows there was more than a touch of the Gothic about Schalthoff. He was all about death.'

'I still—' started Anna.

Fabel interrupted her: 'Schalthoff worked for the Hamburg state monuments department ever since he left school . . .'

Realization lit up Anna's expression. 'And the Jewish cemetery is a Hamburg monument . . .'

'My guess is Schalthoff was allowed into their little secret club because he had the keys to their playground. Nowhere is more Gothic than a graveyard.' He turned to Anna. 'So tell me . . . Schalthoff is our sixth man, but who is the fifth? Who's my ghost in the file?'

'I did a search for the guy Professor Rohde said was always

loitering in the wings of the Gothic set. Well, the name wasn't Messing or Mesling – it was Mensing. Martin Mensing.'

'Do we know where to find him?' asked Fabel.

'Oh yeah . . . and this is where it gets really good. He studied sociology, all right – then he worked for Hamburg state as a social worker but had some kind of breakdown which was attributed to post-traumatic stress. I checked out what the trauma had been and was told that Mensing had been stabbed, near fatally, in a street attack. I dug out the records. Guess when he was stabbed? Fifteen years ago, on Saturday, eighteenth of March. The exact same night that Monika Krone went missing.'

Fabel stared at Anna for a moment. 'Shit . . . that was quite a punchline, Anna.'

'That's still not the punchline. There was a mystery as to how he had ended up dumped outside the main entrance to the Asklepios Klinik Altona – especially because it looked like someone with at least some medical expertise had tried to patch him up long enough to get to the hospital without bleeding out. But after the attack Mensing was in a coma and in no condition to talk for weeks. Then his statements about the attack were so garbled and contradictory that no one knew where to start looking – they put his confused state to him having been in a coma. Anyway, there were never any arrests and Mensing made a recovery, at least physically. He went back to work for a while, but there were continued problems and he had a complete nervous breakdown. Started to believe he wasn't really alive – that he had died during the attack and was a walking corpse—'

'Cotard's Delusion?'

Anna looked surprised. 'Yes, as a matter of fact that's exactly what was diagnosed. Anyway, he made a recovery, went back to work and he retrained in a speciality within social work. And this is where we hit the jackpot. He became a social therapist for serious and sexual offenders. He has a two-day-a-week placement at Fuhlsbüttel prison. And I think you can guess who one of his clients there was . . .'

'Shit . . .' Fabel unfolded his arms and straightened up from where he'd been leaning against the wall. 'Jochen Hübner?'

'In one.'

'All the pieces are finally beginning to fall into place,' said Fabel. 'But the picture they're making still doesn't make any sense.' He looked at his watch, it was eleven thirty a.m. 'Get on to Santa Fu, Anna – tell them that Mensing is not to leave the prison until we get there.'

'I'm way ahead of you – today isn't one of his consulting days. He's not due in until Thursday and has been off sick for the last week. That's not an unusual event, apparently. He still has health issues – both physical and mental – mainly as a result of his stabbing. But despite that, the JVA investigators don't like his absence this time – they were already getting twitchy about him after Frankenstein's escape. When I phoned they were already trying to find him to interview him. Mensing seemed to be the only person in the whole system, staff or prisoner, who Frankenstein seemed to get on with. But I've got an address for him.'

'Let's get the team briefed . . .'

61

All the vehicles pulled up out of sight of the apartment's windows. Fabel had three Murder Commission teams with him, but had also arranged for an MEK mobile support unit to deploy with them. It wasn't that they expected much resistance from Mensing, who had been described as physically very frail, although there was always the possibility he would be armed. But the real threat – and the real prize – would be Jochen Hübner. And Frankenstein would take a lot of bringing down.

They moved in single file, pressed against the wall of the building as if magnetized by it, the MEK team in their heavy black body-armour leading the way. An old woman walking along the pavement froze at the sight of the officers and their weapons and the MEK commander gestured with a gauntleted hand for her to move on. Henk Hermann broke rank and dodged over to the woman, taking her by the shoulders and reassuring her quietly as he guided her past the officers.

The apartment, they knew, was on the third floor and the tactical officers moved swiftly and quietly up the stairwell, two men flanking each side of the door while the commander assessed its strength. He pointed to two spots on the door and a sixth MEK officer swung a small black ram where the commander had indicated. The locks shattered and the door burst inwards.

Fabel and his team followed up the stairwell but were stopped from entering the apartment by the MEK commander.

'Wait until we give the all-clear.'

There was shouting. The tactical team barked orders, yelling at someone inside the flat. Fabel rested his hand on the handle of his gun. Shouts of 'Clear!' from different parts of the apartment, then one of the team re-emerging from the doorway.

'It's all clear,' he said.

'No one home?' asked Fabel.

The MEK man laughed. 'You could say that . . . but yes, we have your suspect in custody. I just don't think he knows it yet.'

'No Hübner?'

'No Hübner.'

Fabel and Nicola Brüggemann went into the apartment. It looked as if it was unoccupied, with hardly any furniture, no pictures, no decoration of any kind, except that the walls had been amateurishly gone over in black paint, which had dried in streaks and patches.

The MEK officers were in the living room, again darkened by the patchily blackened walls. The only colour was a blood-red 'DT' that had been daubed in metre-high letters over the black paint.

'I just love what he's done with the place,' Brüggemann muttered beside Fabel, and grinned. 'Must get him round to do mine . . .'

The only furniture in the room was a single chair and a small coffee table. The body-armoured MEK men were gathered in a circle around a figure kneeling on the naked tiled floor. Martin Mensing's appearance shocked Fabel: he was wearing only underpants that looked oversized on his frame, which was emaciated to the point of being skeletal. Mensing had large, blue eyes that seemed sunk into their sockets and his cheeks were hollow and drawn. He had a shock of thick black hair that somehow accentuated the skull-like appearance of his face. To Fabel, Mensing looked like someone in the end stages of a terminal disease, or recalled grainy black-and-white images of concentration camp victims.

And there it was, on the corrugated chest of rib and skin: the same tattoo that Traxinger and Hensler had had. *DT*.

The MEK officers had handcuffed his hands behind his back, but Fabel could see that Mensing was probably unaware of the fact. He was singing quietly – not songs or recognizable melodies, but tones, sometimes with long gaps, as if he was singing along to some radio station no one else could hear. As he sang, he swayed, his eyes following objects and movements in the room that only he could see. There was a hypodermic syringe sitting in a saucer on the floor next to him.

'We need a doctor here right away,' Fabel said to Brüggemann.

'I'll get on it. What is it? Heroin?'

'No . . .' Fabel watched Mensing as he swayed. A smile would break out occasionally, white and toothy in the skull face, suddenly to be replaced with a look of surprise or awe. 'Something else – and we need to find out what. We're not going to get any sense out of him until it wears off.'

While Brüggemann called for the police surgeon to attend, Fabel walked through to the kitchen. It was as empty as the rest of the apartment, with the barest minimum to sustain a life in the way of utensils and food. He snapped on latex gloves and opened the cupboards. Most were empty, but in one he found two rubber-capped fifty-millilitre pharmaceutical bottles. He read the label: *Xylazine Hydrochloride 100mg/ml. For veterinary use only.*

'The doctor's on his way.' Nicola Brüggemann came into the kitchen. Fabel nodded towards the bottles. 'Is that what he's on?' she asked.

'No. This is what was used to sedate the victims. And from what I've heard, what Hübner used to fake heart failure.'

He opened another couple of cupboards. One contained a small amount of canned food, the second was again empty except for a plastic bag containing a white crystalline substance that looked almost like salt.

'Bingo,' said Fabel. 'We'll get that analysed. Whatever it is, *that's* Mensing's ticket to the moon.'

'I'll check the bedroom . . .' Brüggemann left Fabel and he went back through to where Mensing knelt, still rapt in a universe visible only to him.

'Can we get him up into the chair?' asked Fabel, and two MEK officers eased the jumble of bones up and into the room's sole chair. Seeing him there, Fabel thought back to Monika Krone's remains lying abandoned in red clay and how hard he had found to link them with anything human. Martin Mensing, through his own devices, was well on his way to the same place.

'Jan!'

Fabel turned and as soon as he saw Nicola Brüggemann's face he knew something was wrong.

He followed her into the bedroom. Again there was practically nothing in the room save a single bed dressed in only a mattress with a single sheet over it. And like the rest of the apartment, there were no decorations. Except for one, slightly blurry enlarged photograph that had been taped to the otherwise naked, black-painted wall.

'Oh no . . .' Before he turned and charged back out into the stairwell to start barking orders at his team, Fabel stood for a moment and stared at the photograph.

'Susanne . . .'

62

Susanne sat alone in her office. She knew Fabel was going to be working late so she decided to do the same and use the time to catch up on some of the case reports that had been building up.

It was late, she was tired, and every time she fixed her attention on the report she was writing, her focus seemed to dissolve and with it her professional objectivity. She was working up a background on an eighteen-year-old male who had sexually assaulted at least four girls between the ages of six and ten. Despite there being a very clear dynamic at work in the youth's background and specific deficits showing up in the psychometrics, Susanne was tempted to fill the conclusions section with: *he's a sick fuck and always will be.*

But it wasn't just that it had been a long day that caused her mind to keep drifting from the task at hand: Fabel's proposal kept creeping into her thoughts. If you could call it a proposal – it had been more a declaration of intent, which was a typically Jan Fabel thing to do. He was a good man. In fact, if she were to be asked if there was a single phrase that summed Fabel up, it would be that: a good man. Her quiet hero.

And she loved him. She had known that for years but hadn't known just how much she had loved him until the day he had been shot. Sitting in that hospital corridor, waiting for one of two possible futures to open up, she became aware of the chasm his absence would leave in her life if he died. He had been so good for her and, if she were honest with herself, she had been good for him. But marriage . . . She knew it was just a piece of paper, a change in legal status, but it was also so much more.

She remembered how he had nearly packed it all in. A year or two before the shooting, she and Fabel had been out for dinner when they had met Roland Bartz, with whom Fabel had gone to school in Norden. Bartz, who had remembered Fabel as the brightest in the school, could not believe that his classmate had ended up a murder detective – the least likely of all possible futures. Bartz himself had become a highly successful owner of a multinational business and had, after a few discussions, offered Fabel a job. It would have meant more money, better hours and less worry – for both Fabel and Susanne. It had taken him a long while to come to a decision – so long it had tested Bartz's patience. But, like everything else in his life, Fabel had had to think it through from every angle. Eventually, however, he had said no.

Fabel didn't know it, had no idea, but Susanne had never forgiven him for his decision.

But then there had been the shooting and everything changed. Fabel changed: fewer nightmares, less seriousness, more ease in how he handled life.

He said she didn't need to rush to give him an answer, or even give him an answer at all; but she knew that she would have to.

She shook the thoughts out of her head. If she couldn't concentrate, she was as well going home. She looked at her watch: it was nearly eight.

Her office door sat open and she heard a sound from down the hall – someone else was obviously working late. She heard heavy footsteps coming along the corridor towards her office.

Her cell phone rang and the caller ID told her it was Fabel.

'Hi . . .' she said. 'I'm just about to head home. How much longer—'

'Susanne, where are you?' Fabel's voice was strained, anxious. Susanne could hear a siren loud in the background.

'I'm at the institute, in my office,' she said. 'I was just about to leave.'

'Is there anyone else there with you?'

'No, I'm alone . . . Well there's obviously someone else here working late because I can hear them.'

'Susanne, I want you to go right now and lock your office door.' Fabel spoke with a deliberate clarity that alarmed her.

'Why? What's going on, Jan?'

'Do as I say! Right now. I'll stay on the line.'

As she ran across to the door, she heard the footsteps in the hall louder, nearer. She slammed the door shut and turned the snib lock.

'Jan, what is this all about?'

'Have you locked the door?'

'Yes . . .'

'I want you to get the heaviest thing you can move and put it against the door. I'll be there in five minutes, but I need you to secure that door.'

Susanne was about to protest again, but she knew that she was in a serious situation. She scanned the room. The cabinets were filled with files and too heavy to move. Her best bet was the desk itself. She grabbed it by the edge and pulled. It too was heavy and moved only a little.

She heard the lever handle angle down as someone tried to open the door. When it didn't, the person on the other side started to rattle the handle, the lever jumping.

'Is he there?' asked Fabel, his tone low.

'There's someone trying to get in,' she said, her voice shaking.

'Stay where you are. Block the door. I'm nearly there.'

The handle stopped moving. Susanne went back to the desk and this time managed to drag it in grudging spurts across the floor. As she did so, the cables that connected her phone and computer were pulled taut and tugged them from the desk. She heard the computer screen crack as it toppled off and hit the floor.

The door lever started to jump again, this time more agitatedly. Panting and grunting, and finding a strength she didn't know she had, Susanne got to the other side of the desk and shoved it against the door. Another couple of heaves and she had the desk as tight to the door as she could manage. The lever of the door handle now bounced off the desk's edge whenever it was tried, meaning the action could now no longer be fully turned.

The handle stopped moving. She could hear nothing from the other side of the door and glanced nervously around. The window. If he went outside and round the building he could maybe get in through the window.

She leaned over the desk and held her head close to the door, listening. She jumped back with a cry when the person on the other side banged on the door with their fist.

'They're outside the door . . .' she whispered into the phone. 'They're trying to get in.'

'Stay calm, Susanne . . . I'm nearly there.'

More thumping on the door.

'Frau Doctor Eckhardt?' A deep male voice from behind the door. 'Frau Doctor Eckhardt, are you all right?'

'Who is it?' she shouted, trying to mask the quivering in her voice and sound authoritative.

'Are you all right, Frau Doctor? Let me in . . .'

'Who are you?'

'Security . . .' the voice boomed deep and resonant. 'I'm Lars, from security.'

'The police are on their way. They'll be here any minute.'

'The police? What's the matter? Please open the door.'

Susanne heard the approach of police sirens. More than one car. The door shuddered as a massive shoulder slammed into it and she jumped. The desk started to move.

'Please hurry, Jan . . .' she breathed into the phone.

'I'm right outside . . . I need to hang up now, but I'll be right there.' The phone went dead and Susanne suddenly felt completely alone. The desk budged again and the door opened a crack. Huge, thick fingers curled around the door edge and began pushing.

Voices. Commands barked out. The fingers disappeared and there was a shouted exchange between the deep voice outside and others. Then quieter talk.

A knock on the door.

'Susanne, it's Jan. Open the door.'

She dragged the desk only partly clear of the door, the strength suddenly gone from her arms. Fabel edged his way into the room, looked at the desk; at the shattered computer on the floor.

'Are you okay?' He put his arms around her.

'I'm okay.'

He guided her out through the narrow crack in the door and into the hall. Anna Wolff was there with some of Fabel's team and a couple of uniformed officers. A large man with a shaven head stood in the hall, looking a little stunned. He was wearing the white shirt, black jumper and trousers of a security uniform.

'This is Lars,' said Fabel. 'He's from security.'

'I'm sorry, Frau Doctor Eckhardt, I didn't mean to scare you. I thought there was something seriously wrong.' He looked around at the others. 'It's my first day . . .'

On the way out to the waiting police cars, Susanne asked Fabel, 'What the hell was that all about?'

'I think that might have been a diversion. I have an awful feeling we've been had.'

rm. John question. Can you fix everything up in an hour? I have

63

Henk Hermann told Fabel that his daughter Gabi had been
located, picked up from her student digs by a patrol car and
driven across town to Fabel's apartment. Two uniforms would
stay there with her and Susanne until such time as Jochen Hübner was safely back in custody.

Between them, the police surgeon and forensics had identified the drug that had taken Martin Mensing temporarily off
the planet: dimethyltryptamine had been found in his system at
much higher than naturally occurring levels. Fabel recognized
it as the same compound that Dr Lorentz had described as being
involved in the creation of near-death and out-of-body experiences. As he sat in his office, waiting to get the all-clear from the
doctor to interview Mensing, Fabel wondered if the DMT really
had just taken him to the same place Fabel had been, two years
before.

The phone rang and Anna told him that the medic had confirmed that it would be okay to interview Mensing in an hour,
but that he may still be tired and unresponsive.

'Whenever you get a chance, or whenever he's capable of
understanding,' he told Anna, 'remind Mensing that he can
have a lawyer present when I question him. I want you and
Nicola to observe on the closed circuit, but I'd like to fly solo on

this interrogation. Can you fix everything up in an hour? I have something to do . . .'

'Sure,' said Anna.

Fabel hung up, one hand resting on the receiver, his other on the German–Latin dictionary he had got Sven Bruns to find for him. Another answer was in place, but the idea that had led him there now seemed too abstract, too unlikely. They had Mensing and they were hunting Frankenstein Hübner. They had found xylazine, the drug used to incapacitate the victims, in Mensing's apartment. He had his killers.

But there was one conversation he knew he had to have.

Kerstin Krone sat with the same quiet grace as the last time, as every time Fabel had talked to her. It was a composure that hadn't faltered when she had answered her door to find Fabel there. She had offered him tea, but he had declined and now she sat down facing him. Her hair had been cut since the last time he had seen her and it was now even shorter. She was dressed in jeans and a T-shirt with a blue striped shirt over it. The haircut and the clothes style were both deliberately androgynous, but again it seemed only to emphasize her femininity and the perfect, fine-boned architecture of her features.

'There's a couple of things I wanted to discuss with you, if you don't mind,' Fabel said.

'Of course I don't mind. I'll do anything I can to help you find who killed Monika.'

Fabel watched her for a while, his expression blank; hers calm, patient. The ember of an idea still burned in some dark corner of his mind; a dim glow that illuminated nothing. But it was there.

'I appreciate it.' He smiled. 'I need to ask you again about the phone call you got that night. The one we found on Monika's phone records, from her cell phone to yours. It was an hour or so after she left the party and, as I'm sure you're tired of hearing, the very last contact she had with anyone, other than her killer.'

'Okay.' Kerstin still made no sign of being impatient. 'I don't know what more I can add. I've gone through it so many times – not just with the police, but myself, in my head. Over and over.'

'And you say she effectively just phoned for a chat?'

'To talk, yes. Monika was never one for chat. But there was nothing about the conversation that suggested she was in any danger or trouble.'

'So there was absolutely nothing out of the ordinary about the conversation?'

'No, nothing out of the ordinary.'

'You see, I find that strange. Firstly, it was a very strange time of day – a very strange time of *night* – for her to call, simply to catch up. Secondly – and I'm sure you don't mind me saying this because you've said as much yourself – you and Monika were never close. You weren't close even for ordinary sisters, far less twins. In fact, throughout her time at the university, Monika never so much as hinted to anyone that she had a sister, far less a twin sister. And you told me she had practically no dealings with you over those last two years – almost as if she was actively avoiding contact with you – and vice versa. Do you see why I find it strange that she phoned you out of the blue?'

'Of course I do. I found it strange myself, but that's the way it happened. Monika was a strange girl. A troubled girl.'

'But it's more than strange . . . To me that last call suggests a cry out – a call for help to the only person who maybe truly understands her.'

'I'm sorry, Herr Fabel, I don't know what you're getting at.'

'I don't know if I know myself.' He sighed. 'If I were honest with you, your sister's disappearance has haunted me for fifteen years. An investigation like this should be all about the facts – about information and pieces of evidence. Books and movies would have you believe we're creatures of gut instincts and cases are solved on hunches. But it's not like that at all. I once explained to someone that there are no such thing as hunches, only your unconscious processing data that your conscious hasn't access to. That sometimes you know something but you just don't know what it is yet.'

'And what is it you think you might know about Monika's murder?'

'That's what I'm still trying to work out, I'm afraid. There are events in history, in life, that are either significant or insignificant in their own right, but they set in train other events, start a sequence. The discovery of your sister's remains seems to have been one such event. Four men dead. Four men who were closely involved with her killed almost immediately after her body is recovered.'

'But why would Monika being found cause that?'

'Something happened the night Monika disappeared – and these men were all involved. Maybe they acted together and, once Monika's body was discovered, someone else is avenging her death.'

'And that's what you think is behind it all? And I'm guessing you have suspicions as to who this avenger would be.'

'I have a couple of ideas.' Fabel paused, little more than a heartbeat. 'But it could be the opposite. It could be that Monika's killer is behind these other deaths.'

'Why?' Kerstin frowned. Beautifully. 'I mean, why now, after all this time?'

'I have this odd feeling that whoever killed Monika believed their identity was safe as long – as you put it before – as the box remained unopened and no one knew for sure what had happened to her. It could be that each of these four suspected each or all of the others of Monika's death. Maybe these four men had to die simply because they were pieces in a jigsaw that the reopening of the case would – and has – put together.'

Kerstin Krone watched Fabel for a moment. 'And what picture do you get from the pieces?'

Fabel gave a bitter laugh. 'That's the something I know . . . but can't reach yet. But I do know it has to do with this . . .' Reaching into his jacket pocket, Fabel took out two photographs and laid them side by side on the coffee table in front of Kerstin. One was a close-up of the monogram Traxinger used on his paintings, the other of the tattoo on the painter's chest.

'You've shown me these before,' she said. 'I have no idea what it means.'

'I struggled with it myself. I mean, to start with we assumed the DT stood for Detlev Traxinger, but then we found the same tattoo on the others. And I assumed that when it was at the bottom of a painting it was his signature. But that was a mistake I made once before: I saw the name *Charon* at the bottom of one of his paintings and thought it was a signature, but it wasn't. It was the subject. All of those paintings Traxinger did of Monika had that at the bottom, but it wasn't his initials, it was the subject. Monika was "DT".'

Kerstin made a confused face.

'I couldn't work out what it meant. Then someone who was *intimate* with the architect Tobias Albrecht said he had let slip the words "Silent Goddess" when referring to the paintings of your sister. *DT* stands for *Dea Tacita*, the Silent Goddess. The female personification of Death.'

'I'm sorry, I still don't understand . . .'

'I think Monika lost her way. I think she perhaps went too far in finding out how much she could manipulate the men around her. Push them.'

'So you think one of them killed her? And it has something to do with this *Dea Tacita* thing?'

'I don't know. But I believe the so-called Gothic set took things a little too far – with Monika the high priestess of her own little death cult. Something happened the night she disappeared, the night she called you. Something from which there was no going back. I think she made that call because she needed a way out.'

'Why do I feel you're skirting around something, Herr Fabel? That there's something that you want to say, but you're afraid to say it?'

Fabel gave a small laugh. 'There's this other case we've been working on – an old Nazi in a seniors' home murdered an old anti-Nazi. But he killed him because he got confused – the roles became reversed. He believed his actions were justified because he was killing a man who was guilty of crimes that in truth he had committed himself. A very sad case.'

'I really don't understand what this has to do with Monika.'

'Just that I think that night, the night she phoned you out of the blue, Monika would have given anything to do exactly the same thing – to slip into another life. Even into the life of her twin sister. Like you said, escape the storm of her own making. There's another odd thing,' he said, leaning forward and resting his elbows on his knees. 'We've uncovered a link between Monika and a man called Jost Schalthoff – you'll remember I asked you about him before. And we know she had a sexual affair with the architect, Tobias Albrecht. Schalthoff worked for the City Council; Albrecht was at that time an architecture student and had done a work placement with the City Planning Office. It's entirely possible that, fifteen years ago, either or both men could have known about the development and building work on the site where the remains were buried.'

'So that makes them suspects?'

'In the original killing, yes. But, as I know only too well, Schalthoff died two years ago – and unless he has risen from the grave, there's no way he can be behind this current spate of killings. And Albrecht has ended up a victim himself.'

'I don't understand your point . . .'

'Simply that Monika perhaps knew about the site herself.'

'What?' Kerstin frowned to emphasize the effort of following Fabel's logic. 'She went there, committed suicide and lay down where she knew her body would be hidden? That's absurd.'

'Absurd and physically impossible. Monika lay in tight-packed clay. She was buried after her death. Deliberately and by someone else.'

'I still don't understand what you're getting at.'

Fabel paused. There was the sound of a car passing along the street outside, the ticking of the clock out in the hall. He remembered sitting in another room full of expectant silences, fifteen years ago. *This is mad*, he told himself, *the parents must have known. She couldn't have hidden it from them. They would have been able to tell.*

'I had an experience,' he said eventually. 'A couple of years back. And it involved Jost Schalthoff. He shot me before he was gunned down himself.'

'I'm sorry to hear that.' She sounded genuine.

'The fact that Schalthoff was involved isn't the point. The point is that I came as close as you can come to death and still come back from it. I saw things, experienced things. I went through the whole near-death experience. When I go back to the Presidium, I'll be questioning a man we've been looking for in connection with this most recent spate of killings. Martin Mensing. Is that name familiar?'

Kerstin shook her perfectly sculpted head.

'Mensing knew Monika at university and was a member of the *Dea Tacita* crowd along with Traxinger, Hensler, Albrecht, Mortensen. The very same night that Monika went missing, he suffered a near-fatal stab wound to the chest, missing his heart by millimetres. And if our chronology is right, he was stabbed sometime shortly before the time you had that telephone conversation with your sister. His account of how he got the wound doesn't fit with the injury itself, and he couldn't explain how he had got to the hospital, but that was all let go. Anyway, that's not why I'm telling you about him. My point is that Martin Mensing had a near-death experience the same way I did after I'd been shot. Except he came out of it believing he *hadn't* come out of it – that he had really died and all he is now is an animated corpse. Cotard's Delusion, they call it.'

'I see . . .' Kerstin said, still patient.

'The funny thing is that I really can understand why he believes he's dead. When you've gone through an experience like that, it changes you. Completely. It changed me – to the point that sometimes I feel like I am a completely different person to who I was before. Sometimes people close to me find it difficult to adjust – they see the *old* me, the person before the event. But inside, I know I'm different. Maybe to the extent of being someone else. And, yes, there are nights when I lie in the dark and I wonder if I really did die back then, and everything I have experienced since has just been an illusion created by the last-second flutterings of my dying brain.'

'That's a terrible thought.'

'I don't believe it, of course. I'm just saying that you have moments, when you've been through a life-changing experience like I have. Like Mensing has . . . Like you have.'

'Me?'

'Losing your sister like that. Losing half of a genetic identity, an alternate you.'

She held him in her gaze. Her expression remained the same, but something changed in the eyes. An emerald glitter like the one a painter had fought so hard to capture.

'I suppose so . . .' she said. 'Are you fully recovered now, Herr Fabel?'

'I am. But sometimes I like to get away for a while. Go somewhere for a coffee or a drink where no one knows who I am, what happened to me, or what I do for a living. Just a time to be someone else, I suppose. Just for a while. Have you never been tempted to do that, Frau Krone?'

'I can't say I have. I'm content with the life I have.'

A silence stretched between them.

'Anyway . . .' Fabel stood up with a 'that's it' gesture. 'Thanks for your time. By the way, I was sorry to hear about the suicide of your boyfriend – the one who confirmed you were with him in Hannover the night Monika disappeared.'

'Thank you, it was very sad. But we had split up by then. Is that all, Herr Fabel?'

'It is. Thanks again. I'm sorry we're no further forward.' He paused, holding her gaze. 'I want you to know that I *will* find out what happened to your sister that night. I promise you that. And I'm never going to stop looking for who killed these four men. Incidentally, have you ever met a doctor from Bremen, a haematologist called Marco Tempel?'

'No . . . not that I can remember.'

Fabel nodded. 'Thank you for your time, Frau Krone. I'm sure we'll see each other again soon.'

She stood up and smiled. 'I doubt it, Herr Fabel . . .'

64

No one was calm when they had been arrested. Not even the most experienced and hardened criminals. Arrest brought with it its own form of claustrophobia: the awareness that you were restricted, confined, stifled; not free to go about your business, to move around the world as you wanted. Added to that was the anxiety about what would happen next: dark projections into a future you could not control; imaginings of an even more claustrophobic prison cell, of the unnatural and frightening life of a prisoner.

No one was calm. No matter how hard they tried to hide it, there was always a tell-tale fidget, a tick, a bouncing knee, restless fingers on the metal tabletop.

Except now.

The closed circuit camera was mounted in the corner of the interview room, slightly above and facing Martin Mensing, who sat at the table with complete calm, as if he were waiting for a bus or a fast-food delivery. The T-shirt and coveralls supplied by the Polizei Hamburg were loose and baggy on the prison social therapist, as almost all clothing would have been, and it made him look even more insubstantial.

As he, Anna and Nicola Brüggemann watched the unnaturally thin, unnaturally pale face of Martin Mensing on the monitor, Fabel could see that he was totally at ease. No fear, no anxiety, no impatience.

'He's waiting,' said Fabel.

'Waiting for what?' asked Brüggemann.

'That I don't know, but I wish to hell I did. But I think it's no coincidence he was off his head with DMT just as we came to arrest him, meaning we couldn't interview him for nearly two hours. Then there was the chase across town to get to Susanne ... It's like he's been playing us. Delaying tactics.'

'There's no one left to kill,' said Anna. 'At least that we know about. So why would he deliberately delay us?'

'I don't know. You're right, everyone else we know about who was involved with the Gothic set is dead ... except him.' Fabel shook his head.

'What is it?' asked Nicola Brüggemann.

'I don't think it was him.'

'What?'

'I know it makes no sense, but I don't. Just like I don't think it was Hübner either. All we've got on them so far is suspicion, some circumstantials, and a sequence of events that would lead you to an obvious conclusion. We don't have a single forensic trace or witness to place either him or Hübner at any of the crime scenes.'

'That doesn't mean they weren't there.'

'I know ... but there were no signs of struggle at any of the scenes. The painter Traxinger was killed with a weapon that you had to get up close to use. It suggests he was killed by someone he knew. If you saw Frankenstein Hübner coming for you, wouldn't you make a run for it?'

'It was maybe him ...' Anna jutted a chin towards the figure on the monitor. 'Traxinger knew him and he's certainly not the type that would scare you into flight.'

'True, but I just don't believe he's behind the killings. It's like he's deliberately stringing us along. Whatever he's guilty of, it hasn't happened yet.'

'But if he's innocent, then he has no reason to string us along,' said Anna.

'Yes he does. Look at him.' Fabel nodded towards the monitor. 'He's waiting. He's waiting for something to happen and he wants us to be looking the other way. And that something is to do with Jochen Hübner . . .'

Fabel watched the perfect stillness of the figure sitting at the interview table.

'Time to commune with the dead.'

'Where is Jochen Hübner?'

Zombie stared at Fabel, his drawn, pale face motionless, his eyes large and watery in their sockets. There was no hostility in the eyes; no anxiety, no impatience, no concern. No interest.

'Herr Mensing, you work as a social therapist in prison. You know what life can be like in there. You helped Jochen Hübner, an extremely dangerous prisoner, to escape. For that alone you will go to prison. But if he kills any more people, then you'll be spending the rest of your life behind bars.'

Zombie laughed quietly, as if Fabel had said something stupid.

'Where is Jochen Hübner?' asked Fabel again.

Mensing looked up, his pale, too-thin face calm, a smile on his lips.

'Where is Hübner?' repeated Fabel.

'There's nothing you can do to me, Herr Fabel. No threat you can use, no promises you can make, no deal you can offer, that will have the slightest effect on me. These are all things of the living. I am dead, I remain dead. What happens to my body is inconsequential. I don't care if I'm in my apartment, if I'm here or if I'm in prison. It makes absolutely no difference to me.'

'Okay, maybe you don't care about yourself, but you know what Hübner is capable of doing – the pain and terror he'll spread because he's at liberty. If you have any decency left in you, you'll tell me where he is.'

'You have no proof that I helped Hübner.'

'We found xylazine hydrochloride in your apartment – the drug used to fake illness and get Hübner into a civilian hospital. Incidentally also the drug used to sedate each of the victims, but I'll come back to that. And, if you don't mind me saying, you are not the biggest or most robustly built man, Herr Mensing, yet we have found internet transactions for oversized clothing and boots – in the kind of sizes that can only be sourced from specialist stores.'

Silence. Peace. Stillness. Mensing's eyes, his expression, remained empty, except for a moment when he seemed to look past Fabel.

'Okay, Herr Mensing – what about the killings? Traxinger, Hensler, Albrecht, Mortensen . . . Why did you kill them? Or why did you have Hübner kill them?'

Silence.

'You admit you had them killed?'

Silence.

Fabel responded in like. The two men sat mute, staring at each other for a moment. Fabel had been there before – suspects engaging him in a silent staring contest, but this time it was different. This time there was no defiance or stubbornness in the gaze that met his. Mensing's eyes were empty of anything. For a moment Fabel could almost believe there was nothing living behind those eyes.

'I know so little about what's going on here.' Fabel broke the silence. 'But I do know that it has got something to do with that night fifteen years ago when Monika Krone died. The same night you were attacked and nearly died yourself. I know that those two events were connected, I just don't know how. Why don't you give me at least that much? Why don't you tell me what happened that night?'

Again Mensing said nothing, his pale, skull-like face empty of expression. But once more Fabel thought there was a temporary flicker in the eyes as Mensing looked past him, then back.

'You want me to cooperate and I will. I'll tell you what happened that night. I'll tell you that and a whole lot more. But not now.'

'Why not now?'

'Because I'm tired. I need to rest first. Can I go back to my cell?'

'Why don't you tell me now, get it over with? Get it off your chest?'

Mensing fell silent again. Fabel sighed and stood up.

'I'll have an officer escort you back to your cell. We'll reconvene in thirty minutes.'

'That should be fine.' Mensing smiled.

Before calling for a uniform to take him back to the holding cells, Fabel let Mensing sit alone for a moment while he rejoined Anna Wolff and Nicola Brüggemann in the next room. Again he watched the silent, implacably patient figure on the screen.

'Do you see?' said Fabel. 'He's looking at the exact same spot again. He kept looking past me during the interview and he's looking at the same thing again.'

'So?'

'It's the clock. He's sitting there watching the clock. That's what he's waiting for. He knows something is going to happen and he knows when.'

'I don't see how that helps us,' said Brüggemann.

'He doesn't have a watch,' said Anna. 'While he's in his cell, we could put the clock forward, not much, but maybe twenty minutes or so. But we'd have to do it with any clock he might pass between the cell and the interview room. Your watch as well.'

'It's a good idea, but it wouldn't work,' said Fabel. 'We can only keep him in his cell for half an hour tops, or whatever he has planned will have happened before we talk to him again. Anyway, his internal clock would tell him if we'd almost doubled the time.'

'Ten minutes then,' said Anna. 'Bring him out ten minutes early and have the clock set at the time you've already told him you'd resume the interview.'

'It's worth a try, Jan,' said Brüggemann.

'Okay. You two listen to the interview here and as soon as you get a hint of what it is that he's been waiting for, don't wait for my instructions, just get our people there fast.'

'Okay, *Chef*.'

Fabel gave the custody team their instructions: after exactly twenty minutes they were to bring Mensing back to the interview room, but before that they were to make sure that any clock or watch that he might be able to see in passing should be advanced ten minutes.

Fabel was waiting for him, seated in the interview room, when they brought him back.

'Are you rested?'

Mensing nodded. Another glance past Fabel.

'Are you ready to tell me where Hübner is?' he asked.

'Nearly,' said Mensing. 'In a while. But you asked me what happened that night, fifteen years ago. I'll tell you about that first. Maybe then you'll be able to put it together for yourself.'

Fabel made an open-handed gesture, inviting him to continue.

'I loved her, you know,' said Mensing. 'I really, truly, completely loved her.'

'Monika Krone?'

'Of course, Monika Krone. But so did all the others. But she was cruel, you know that, don't you?'

'So I've gathered.'

'Some monsters – the very worst monsters – are often pleasing to look at. Monika was at the one time the most beautiful woman I have ever known and the ugliest. It was just that all of her ugliness was in the inside, hidden from the world. She played us, one off the other. She wanted to see how far we would go to please her. We all thought there was this great sadness in her. An emptiness. But it was more a black void where the rest of us have emotions.'

'Were you all members of the *Dea Tacita* society?'

'You know about that?' A flicker of surprise.

'The tattoo on your chest. You all had the tattoo. It took me a while – and a Latin dictionary – to work out the significance. Monika Krone was your *Dea Tacita*, your Silent Goddess, right?'

'She was. Right from the start she led us. Led us right into the dark.'

'So what was it? A sect? A death cult?'

'It started out innocently enough. More a student society than anything else. We were all fascinated by Gothic literature. Me too, but my special interest was mainly movies – the Gothic influence in German Expressionism. Although the truth is I think we were all more fascinated by Monika. To start with there were four other girls in the society, but Monika marginalized them, belittled them until they left. Truth is, I think they tired of the men all being focused on Monika.'

'Were there any other members? I mean other than Monika, you and the four who are dead?'

'Like I said, there were the four girls and another three male students to start with. But at the beginning it was a laugh – nothing to take at all seriously. But Monika did. She knew from the start what she wanted the society to be. Traxinger and Hensler maybe took it a little more seriously.'

'Albrecht?'

'Tobias Albrecht was just playing a part. It was a game of dressing-up for him. Paul Mortensen was the least into it. He was a serious, quiet guy: a Dane, studying medicine. I think it was all just a joke for him to start with, but he was as hypnotized by Monika as the rest of us. He was all reason, except when it came to her. He would have done almost anything for her. We all would.'

'But something happened to change that, didn't it? They killed her, didn't they?' asked Fabel. 'And that's why you killed them, or had Hübner kill them . . .'

Mensing laughed, shaking a skull-head that looked too heavy for the thin neck. 'You're being impatient, Herr Principal Chief Commissar. You've asked me to tell you what happened that night, so I will. But I'll do it in my own time. And I'll do it in a way that means you will understand.'

'Go ahead . . .'

'We started to meet regularly. Once a week, sometimes twice. It started off with readings of poetry or from Gothic novels. Werner Hensler, even back then, was an incredibly knowledgeable Poe scholar and he would start every session with a reading from Poe in English. But then we started to focus on German works.'

'I thought the Gothic was an almost exclusively English-language form,' said Fabel.

'Its Golden Age, perhaps, but Germany is the true Gothic land,' Mensing explained. 'The literary form was born in the English Gothic novel, which became the French *roman noir* and the German Schauerroman. But it was in the Schauerroman that Gothic literature came home, you could say. Home to our dense, dark forests and our dense, dark souls. No nation, no people, is more haunted by its own ghosts. Through the Schauerroman the Gothic became darker, more horrific – filled with violence, blood and death. And that was what we – our little group – started to explore. What we didn't realize is that we were all just children playing with fire. All except Monika, who knew exactly what she was doing. Did you know she was an enormously talented writer?'

'No I didn't.'

'It was her writing that turned our little literary club into a pagan-Roman cult. It was her story that changed everything. It was the summer before – we went away for a weekend, the six of us. I didn't think I'd be invited: I was never the most confident of people and some of the others treated me like a hanger-on. But Monika . . . Monika asked me to come. We all clubbed together and rented a house near the bay at Gelting.'

'In Schleswig-Holstein?'

'Yes . . . Angeln, you see. It was one of our pretentiously clever in-jokes: we thought the original homeland of the English language would be the ideal place to celebrate one of its greatest literary forms. A truly Gothic weekend.'

'What happened?' asked Fabel.

'What happened? We had a wonderful, beautiful time. The last truly good time we had together. We drank and talked and watched the sun come up over the water. Monika had this idea that we could do the same as the original Gothics at the Via Diodati – you know, each of us write a ghost story. She cast herself as Mary Shelley and Albrecht as Byron. In Mortensen, the medical student, we even had our own Dr Polidori. So we all tried writing stories. They were all crap except, of course, Werner Hensler's. Detlev Traxinger was too drunk or stoned or both to write anything coherent, so instead he illustrated Monika's story.'

Mensing paused and for a moment Fabel saw something like emotion fleet across the thin features.

'Anyway, we sat on the sand, around the fire we had lit, and listened as she read us the story she had written. She had called her story *Dea Tacita*. It was painfully sad, beautiful and graceful; it was also so very dark and terrifying. It was the most perfect Gothic tale. It was the story of the Silent Goddess – a Roman personification of Death. In Monika's story, Dea Tacita was the most beautiful of all women and all men loved her. She endlessly wandered the ages and the world seeking love. But because she was immortal and man is mortal, whenever she found love, found a man she wanted to be with, her very first touch would end his life. In the story Dea Tacita sees a young girl by the sea, singing contentedly as she mends fishing nets. It was the way Monika described the goddess's feelings – her terrible longing

for a simple, carefree life like the fisher girl . . . It was so beautifully written. Heartbreaking.'

'And that's what she became to you? *Dea Tacita*?'

'We all knew it was her own story. Monika was the most
completely destructive personality I have ever known. But the
truth is that we all wanted her touch, even if it meant death.
That was when we got the tattoos. Detlev sketched it out and we
took it to a tattoo parlour we found in Eckernförde, on the way
back to Hamburg.' Mensing paused, his thoughts for a fleeting
moment in a different place and time. 'After that night in
Gelting we were all completely hers. We would do anything for
her, but we had to constantly prove that we would do anything
for her.'

'Like what?'

'We became less like a literary group and, like you said, more
like a religion, a cult. But the truth is none of us took it that seriously. Only Monika, and we didn't know just how seriously she
was taking it. But we started to get sucked into it. She knew the
tools to use . . . Sex, mainly, then as time went on, she used drugs
more and more. She said that as a civilization we couldn't connect any more – get in touch with the other side of reality. With
the gods. She explained that there were gods and angels and
monsters residing in us all.' Mensing shrugged. 'I know it'll
sound ridiculous to you. It even sounds ridiculous to me . . .
now.'

'As a matter of fact,' said Fabel, 'I don't find it ridiculous. Go
on . . .'

'You have to understand that we were caught up in this thing
and although we didn't take it that seriously to start with, we
began to lose sight of reality, of normal behaviour. Everything
was dictated by Monika. Anyway, she started to introduce potions,

I suppose you'd call them. Entheogens – hallucinogenic drugs designed to make you have spiritual experiences. Shaman drugs. And, like I said, there was the sex. Monika would use it as a tool to control us. She would choose one of us to make love to her, some more often than others. It was a reward we all wanted to win. But there was also her wrath, which terrified us all.'

Mensing paused to drink from the plastic cup some of the water Fabel had brought in for him; as he did so the angular knot of his Adam's apple jumped sickeningly in the scrawny neck.

'About two months after the weekend by the Baltic, Monika started to demand we had meetings at midnight – naturally – in places like graveyards. Graveyards were perfect because part of the original Roman religion of *Dea Tacita* was to make offerings to the dead.' Mensing laughed. 'Truth is, we were chased out of a couple of cemeteries. It was then that this guy suddenly appeared. Monika had found him. He was some kind of ditch-digger or something for the City.'

'Jost Schalthoff? Was his name Jost Schalthoff?'

'Yes. He just didn't fit in with the rest of us. He was obsessed with the Gothic, all right, but Gothic horror. He seemed to be every bit as obsessed with Monika, but in a different way. He was a pleasant enough looking guy, but there was something very dark about him. I knew, whatever it was, it had to do with death. It was only years later, when I read that he had been shot by the police, that I found out he had been a child-murderer. Anyway, Schalthoff was our caretaker, if you like. He arranged it so we could meet at the Altona Jewish Cemetery. That's where Monika wanted us to have our little rituals.'

'What form did these rituals take?'

'It all became about death. Instead of us making offerings to the dead, it started to involve death itself. We had to make, well . . . *sacrifices*. Birds. Small animals. It got sicker and sicker . . . We resisted at first, but everyone wanted to please her. And between Monika's manipulations and the effects of the peyote or whatever the hell it was she had us drink, we were all beginning to lose our minds a bit. Every gathering had to end with the taking of a life. Instead of a Roman religion or Gothic games, it started to look a hell of a lot more like Black Masses.'

'And you never once thought that it was becoming extreme? That it was ridiculous? Mad?'

'It was mad. But it was a creeping madness. We'd drifted out from the shore of what was sane and normal in slow centimetres. Before we knew where we were we had lost sight of what was normal, barely even remembered what was normal. All that existed for us was Monika and the storm around her. Each gathering, each ritual, became more and more extreme. We became afraid of her, afraid of each other. But the main thing was she kept mixing cocktails of entheogenic drugs into the wine. We got lost in the madness.'

He paused and again looked past Fabel to the clock on the wall.

'I was the weakest. I would have done anything for the Silent Goddess. She said that we had all been bound together by Death, but the bonds weren't strong enough because the deaths we'd offered weren't big enough, significant enough. There had to be a human sacrifice. Someone had to become the husband of the Silent Goddess – had to know her true touch.'

'You?'

'None of us really believed she'd go through with it. We were caught up in her frenzy and half off our heads with drugs, but I think we all thought it was some kind of symbolism – or that she was just testing us all to see how far we'd go for her. We had no idea how mad she was. It was that night after the party. We had all arranged to leave the party separately and gather at the Place of Broken Stones – which was her name for the cemetery. When we got there she was wild, her eyes were insane. Like before, she made us all drink something. Again it was wine, but there was something mixed into it that was stronger than the stuff she'd given us before.'

'DMT?'

'No. This was different. Similar, but different. Mescaline, maybe. I suspect I was given a bigger dose than the others. Everything started to . . . *scintillate*. It was like the whole world, the entire universe was a vibrating string. But it was the real world – I didn't start to hallucinate. The others were pretty wild on it too. But there must have been something extra in mine because my muscles went weak. I was fully conscious, but I had no control of my body.'

'Was Jost Schalthoff there?'

'Outside. Keeping watch. He was only allowed to take part in some ceremonies.'

'What happened?'

Mensing paused. His dull eyes lit up with something as memories played out behind them. 'Monika transformed. She changed. I would have sworn she truly, totally became the Silent Goddess. Death. Her eyes . . .' He looked at Fabel as if urging him to understand. 'Her eyes were like green fire in the torchlight. She ordered the others to hold me down on one of the broken headstones. They did what they were ordered, but I could see that Mortensen and Albrecht, despite the drugs and the excitement, were getting uneasy. I mean I don't think any of them believed she meant to go through with it – but I did. I became scared and started to scream for help, but they still held me down. Monika slipped off her robe and stood there in the torchlight naked. She was so beautiful and so terrifying. I think it was Albrecht who saw it first – the knife. She held it above me and screamed. It was like some trapped animal screaming. All of a sudden it was no longer about anything that had brought us together, there was no hint of it being a joke. It wasn't even about worshipping the Gothic, or a Roman goddess or even Death any more. It was sheer insanity.'

He paused again, and Fabel noticed the almost fleshless fingers shaking on the table's surface.

'She brought the knife down. Everybody started yelling and screaming and they let me go. Albrecht lunged at her and tried to grab the knife. He knocked her off target and she missed my heart with the first strike. The pain was incredible – more painful still when she pulled the knife out: white hot and filling my entire chest. The others wrestled the knife from her before she could strike again. But it was too late. That was what killed me.'

'But, Herr Mensing, you are not dead . . .' Fabel sighed. 'What happened next?'

'All of the screaming and shouting brought Schalthoff running. I saw his face when he saw me lying there, dying. He grinned. He was as bad as she was. Every bit as mad and obsessed with death. He took charge of Monika while the others took care of me.

'Because he was a medical student, Paul Mortensen did his best to treat the wound. He and Hensler kept a compress on it while Albrecht and Traxinger got me into the car. They took me to the hospital, leaving me at the emergency entrance. They begged me not to give their names, but by that time I was slipping in and out of consciousness. I heard afterwards that they supported each other's alibis for that night.'

'I don't understand,' said Fabel. 'They saved your life. Why would you want to kill them?'

'No one saved my life. I was supposed to die that night. That was my destiny and I did die. But ever since that night I have been condemned to walk around among the living, while my corpse rots and stinks of death.'

'So that's why you killed them? Because you should have died? Because they denied you your peace?'

Again Zombie looked past Fabel. He was looking at the clock again. He was checking. Suddenly, an expression swept over his face, like a sudden breath of wind across a becalmed sea.

'No, Herr Fabel, I didn't kill them. They were my friends. They were lost in the same madness as me, that's all, but they saw through it and tried to save me. I just haven't been quick enough to save them.'

Fabel frowned as a thought flashed into his head. 'If the others took you in the car, then Monika was left alone with Jost Schalthoff, the council worker?'

'Yes.'

Fabel thought it all through for a moment. 'So Schalthoff murdered Monika?' he said, but the statement sounded wrong in his mouth, in his head.

'No. Schalthoff didn't kill her.' Mensing checked the clock again. He smiled: an ugly baring of too-large teeth by too-thin lips. He leaned forward. 'Time flies, doesn't it? Time is a preoccupation with me. What happened to me that night left me dead, yet I've been condemned to walk amongst the living. I am, truly, literally, a zombie. It's a state of waiting, and when you spend so long waiting, you learn to measure time.'

He knows about the clock, thought Fabel. *He's delayed me again.*

'I waited all this time. I could never know for sure, but when they discovered the body – then I knew for sure. I knew who it was in the ground and why she'd been put there.'

'Please,' said Fabel. 'If Schalthoff didn't kill Monika Krone, who did? Was it Hübner?'

Mensing shook his head. 'You're too late. It's all too late now.'

'Who killed Monika Krone?' Despite himself, Fabel was shouting. Mensing's elaborate plan to spring Hübner, the months of preparation, the deliberate delaying tactics to keep the police occupied – it had all been leading up to this moment. Fabel knew something terrible was happening and he didn't know what, where, or when.

Mensing smiled more broadly than ever. A victor's smile. 'You just don't understand, do you? No one killed Monika Krone. Monika Krone didn't die.'

'What do you mean she didn't die? What makes you think that?'

'I saw her. Years later. Here in Hamburg. I was walking along the street and there she was: my Silent Goddess. She had changed her appearance, but she couldn't hide her beauty. I saw her and I knew it was her, hiding in another life.'

'No . . . that wasn't Monika, that was—' Fabel broke off as a thousand thoughts seemed to fall suddenly onto him. He had nearly given it voice himself: that thing he had known all along, but hadn't realized he knew it. He felt his heart pick up a pace. He turned and looked at the wall clock behind him.

Mensing smiled his skull smile again. 'Now you see. Now you understand. You see through the deceit. You see through the mask.'

'Why did you help Jochen Hübner to escape?' Fabel asked, though he already knew the answer.

'He is my instrument. My Golem. My monster.' Another look at the clock. 'You're too late, Fabel. It's done. What had to be done has been done. It's too late for you to stop it.'

Fabel jumped up from his seat and turned to the closed circuit camera.

'Kerstin Krone! Get units over to Kerstin Krone's apartment now!'

65

She lay in the bath, allowing her headache and her tiredness to soak out of her body and into the warm water. It had been a long day. The thing about being a teacher was that your environment stayed the same, the same room, the same view through the window, but the characters who peopled it changed throughout the day: a constant stream of humanity.

Today seemed to have been more mixed than others. A boy in her first class, sixteen years old, had begun crying for no reason at all. Kerstin guessed that there must have been something wrong in his life that his classmates knew about, because there was no sniggering, no joy at his distress. Instead a couple of the girls comforted him and looked expectantly over at Kerstin.

That moment, that look, had been the most challenging experience she had faced in a long, long time. Something had been expected of her. It was a call to her, but a call in a foreign idiom. It was a language of empathetic responses she would never fully understand – even if she had studied it for so long now that she could generally answer appropriately.

She had nodded to the girls and they had escorted the boy out of the class. But it had troubled her for the rest of the day: should she have gone with them? Was that what had been expected of her?

There had been no further incidents in her other classes, but again she had found it difficult to cope with the peaks and troughs of ability; the vagaries of personality and variations in emotion. She always, however, dealt with every class and every pupil with the same equanimity. No one had ever seen Frau Krone lose her temper, or even her cool. The boys were easiest because they worshipped her. The girls did too, in their own confused manner. There was always the occasional adolescent pushing of boundaries, but she could crush those with a look. There was some instinct common to all others that recognized something to be feared in that look. Someone, a long, long time ago, had told her she was an archetype: a real person who mirrored a figure buried in the common unconscious. He had struggled so very hard to try to capture that archetype with his art.

All she wanted now was peace. Calm. A return to the dull ease of her life.

It hadn't just been the school day that had tired her so.

She hadn't come straight back to her apartment after school. First thing that morning, she had filled her car with petrol, also filling a small plastic canister. After school, instead of driving home she had followed a circuitous route through the city then, once she was sure no one was following her, out of Hamburg and along the north shore of the Elbe. She had found a quiet stretch of beach and had gathered the things she had brought – an expensive dress, a brunette wig, an empty plastic bottle that had held fake tan, a box of veterinary sedatives – and arranged them in a pile, doused them with petrol from the canister and put a match to them. There had been a long, thin needle-file too, and she had walked to the water's edge and had thrown it as far out as she could. Afterwards, she had sat on the sand, hugging her knees, watching the pile burn. It had made her think of another beach bonfire, a long, long time ago. And a story she had once told by firelight.

Now she lay in the calm and peace of her bathtub. But she knew it wasn't over yet.

He would be back, she knew. She may not have been fluent in the language of emotions, but no one knew how to read men the way she did. They were much simpler than they thought they were: just different variations on a handful of themes. Fabel was different because he had encountered death through his own journey, had come face to face with his own Silent Goddess. He would be persistent: he had an instinct, a suspicion he couldn't prove. That he would never, ever be able to prove. But that wouldn't stop him coming back.

She would transfer to another school, another city. She had done it before: the years spent away from Hamburg after that night. The falling into a new but familiar life had been easier in a distant place. Now she would again take this life with her: the life her sister had given up for her.

If only the remains hadn't been found. If they hadn't been found she wouldn't have been forced to act . . . Of them all, it was Detlev's face she remembered most: his expression on seeing her once more. She hadn't taken his life, he had given it up.

She smiled. There was no one to speak against her now. It would only have been a matter of time before they had put it all together; before they had come out from behind their fear of exposure and realized what had really happened. But now they were all silenced. Only Mensing remained, and everyone knew he was mad. No one would listen to him.

She had got away with it, got away with it all.

The water had cooled and her skin began to prune. She rose from the bath, towelled herself dry, pulled on her robe, stepped out of the bathroom and into the hall.

He was waiting for her there, in the hall. Filling its space with his bulk and his darkness.

In the second it took for him to close the distance between them, for his oversized hands to fasten on her, the thought flashed through her mind that he wasn't human. He was too big, too horrific.

That he was a monster she had once read about.

Discover another unmissable thriller
from Craig Russell ...

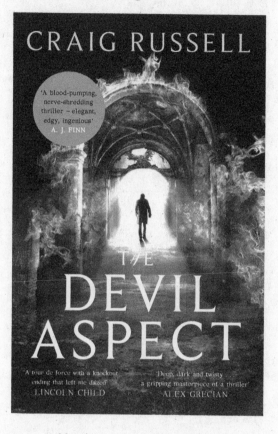

CRAIG RUSSELL

'A blood-pumping,
nerve-shredding
thriller – elegant,
edgy, ingenious'
A. J. FINN

THE
DEVIL
ASPECT

'A tour de force with a knockout
ending that left me dazed'
LINCOLN CHILD

'Deep, dark and twisty
a gripping masterpiece of a thriller'
ALEX GRECIAN

'A blood-pumping, nerve-shredding
thriller – elegant, edgy, ingenious'
A. J. Finn, *New York Times* bestselling author

Turn the page to read the opening chapter of *The Devil Aspect* ...

The appearance of that voice, of that dark personality, was like some terrible black sun dawning, filling the castle's tower room with a shining darkness and sinking with malice deep into the dense, thick stone of its ancient walls. Despite the patient being securely fastened to the examination couch, Viktor felt strangely isolated, vulnerable. Afraid. What he was hearing didn't make sense. It could not be.

Viktor realized this voice was not simply some fragment of his patient's splintered personality. This was something else, something other. Something much worse.

'I can sense your fear,' said Mr Hobbs. 'I am attuned to the fear of men. It is the energy which renews me and you renew me now. You have sought me out, and now you have found me. You want to know what I think, what I feel. Well, let me tell you: when I killed them – when I killed all those people, did all those terrible things to them – I enjoyed every second of it. I did what I did because of the dark pleasures it brought. Their pain and their fear were like fine wines to me.

'I especially liked it when, at the end, they begged for their lives: when they did that – and they all did that, eventually – I would pretend to hesitate and see in their eyes the glimmer of a faint, final, desperate hope. I let them have that, for an instant, then I took it away. It was that – that extinguishing of their very last hope – that I savoured more than anything, more even than the extinguishing of their lives.

'You see, Dr Kosárek, it was at that moment that they would feel the presence of the Devil and beg God to come and deliver them from him. And it was at that moment that I made them see – that they finally realized – that God had been there all along.

'It was then they realized that the Devil is just God in his night attire.'

CHAPTER ONE

*J*n the late autumn of 1935, Dr Viktor Kosárek was a tall, lean man in his twenty-ninth year. He was handsome, but not that unexceptional handsomeness that most of the Bohemian race possess: there was a hint of ancient nobility about his long slender nose, high-angled cheekbones and hard, blue-green eyes beneath dark-arched eyebrows and raven-black hair. At an age where many still looked boyish, Viktor Kosárek's rather severe features made him look older than he actually was: a guised maturity and accidental authority that aided him in his work. As a psychiatrist, it was Viktor's professional duty to unfold inner secrets, to shine a light into the most shadowed, most protected corners of his patients' minds; and those patients would not release their closest-held secrets, deliver their darkest despairs and desires, into the hands of a mere boy.

It was night and it was raining – a chill rain that spoke of the seasons turning – when Viktor left his rented apartment for the last time. Because he had so much luggage and his provincial train was leaving from Masaryk Station on Hybernská Street rather than Prague main station, he had taken a taxi. Also because he had so much luggage – a large trunk and two heavy suitcases – and because he knew how difficult it could be to secure a porter, he had timed his arrival at the station with three-quarters of an hour to spare. It was just as well because, once paid, the dour taxi-driver simply deposited the luggage on the pavement outside the station's main entrance and drove off.

Viktor had hoped his friend, Filip Starosta, would have been there to see him off and to help with the luggage, but the increasingly unreliable Filip had called off at the last minute. It meant Viktor had no option but to leave his baggage where it was and go off in search of a porter, which took him a good ten minutes. He guessed that the absence of porting staff had something to do with the commotion inside the station – the urgent shouts and cries that Viktor could now hear but which were out of his sight. Eventually he secured a young station attendant of about sixteen in an oversized red kepi who, despite his slight build, swung the trunk and cases onto his porter's trolley with ease.

They were heading into the station when a Praga Alfa in police colours pulled up into the rank that Viktor's taxi had just vacated. Two uniformed officers leapt from the car and ran across their path and into the station.

'What's going on?' Viktor asked the boy porter, whose shoulders shrugged somewhere in his loosely fitted uniform jacket.

'I heard a lot of shouting,' he said. 'Just before you called me over. Didn't see what was going on, though.'

Following the boy and his luggage into the station, Viktor could see right away that some significant drama was unfolding. Over in a far corner of the concourse, a large crowd was clustering like iron filings drawn to a magnet, leaving the main hall almost empty. Viktor noticed that the two newly arrived policemen had joined a number of other officers trying to disperse the crowd.

Someone concealed by the cluster of people was shouting: a male voice. A woman, also hidden by the throng, screamed in terror.

'She's a demon!' yelled the man's voice, hidden by the curtain of onlookers. 'She's a demon sent by the Devil. Satan!' There was a pause then, in an urgent tone of frightened warning, 'He is here now – Satan is here! Satan is come amongst us!'

'Stay here . . .' Viktor ordered the porter. He walked briskly across the station hall and shouldered his way through to the front of the crowd, which had formed in a police-restrained semicircle. As he pushed through, he heard a woman whisper in dark excitement to her friend: 'Do you think it's really him? Do you think he's Leather Apron?'

Viktor could now see the source of the cries: a man and a woman. Both looked terrified: the woman because she was being held from behind by the man, who had a large kitchen knife to her throat; the man terrified for reasons known only to himself.

'She's a demon!' the man yelled again. 'A demon sent from hell! See how she burns!'

Viktor could see that the woman was well dressed and prosperous looking, while her captor wore a working man's garb of battered cap, collarless shirt, coarse serge jacket and bagged corduroy trousers. At first glance it was obvious they were not a couple and he suspected the woman had been seized at random. The wild, darting, wide-eyed gaze of the young man indicated to Viktor the existential terror of some schizophrenic episode.

A single police officer stood closer than his colleagues to the couple, his hand resting on his undrawn pistol. Keep it holstered, thought Viktor; don't add to his sense of threat. He pushed through the front rank of onlookers and was immediately restrained by two policemen, who seized him roughly.

'Get back!' a Slovak accent commanded. 'Why can't you ghouls—'

'I'm Dr Viktor Kosárek, of the Bohnice Asylum,' protested Viktor, wriggling to wrest his arms free from the policemen's restraint. 'I'm a clinical psychiatrist. I think I can be of help here.'

'Oh . . .' The Slovak nodded to the other officer and they both released their grip on Viktor. 'Is he one of yours? An escapee?'

'Not that I know of. Definitely not one of my patients. But wherever he's from, he's clearly in the midst of a psychotic episode. Paranoiac delusions. Schizophrenia.'

'Pavel!' The Slovak called over to the policeman who stood with his hand still resting on his gun holster. 'There's a head-case doctor here . . .'

'Send him over,' said the officer without taking his eyes from captor and captive.

'I need you to disperse this crowd,' Viktor said quietly to the Slovak policeman as he stepped from the throng. 'They're hemming him in. The more anxious he gets, the more threatened he feels, the greater danger the young lady is in.'

The Slovak nodded and, with renewed urgency and determination, he and his fellow officers pushed and cajoled the crowd into a retreat from the drama.

Viktor went over to the policeman the Slovak had addressed as Pavel.

'You the headshrinker?' asked the officer, without taking his eyes from the knifeman.

'Dr Viktor Kosárek. I'm an intern at the Bohnice Asylum . . . well, I *was* an intern at the Bohnice Asylum,' he corrected himself. 'I'm actually travelling to the Hrad Orlů Asylum for the Criminally Insane to take up a new post.'

'Thanks for the curriculum vitae, Doctor – but we do have a bit of an urgent situation on our hands here.' The sarcasm dropped from his tone. 'Wait a minute – Hrad Orlů? Isn't that where they've got the Devil's Six locked up? In that case, this should be right up your street. Can you help?'

'I'll do my best, but if he's seriously delusional, I don't know if I'll get through to him.'

'If you don't get through to him, then I'm afraid I'll have to.' The policeman gave his leather holster a tap.

Kosárek nodded and placed himself squarely in front of the woman and her captor. He looked directly into the woman's eyes first.

'Try not to be afraid,' he spoke to her quietly and evenly. 'I know this is very difficult, but, whatever you do, don't struggle or scream. I don't want him more emotionally aroused than he is at the moment. I need you to be brave for me. Do you understand?'

The woman, her eyes wide with terror, gave a small nod.

'Good,' said Viktor. He noted that the sharp edge of the knife creased the skin of her neck right above the jugular. It wouldn't take much – the smallest of movements – for her deranged captor to sever the vein. And if he did, within seconds she would be so far from the shore of life that there would be nothing anyone could do to save her.

He turned to her captor, looking over the woman's shoulder and again directly into his eyes. He was a young man, perhaps even a couple of years younger than Viktor. His eyes were no less wide and no less afraid than those of his captive, his gaze scanning the space around them, not focusing on, not even seeming to see, the now moved-back police and agitated crowd. Instead he seemed to be watching horrors unfold that were invisible to everyone else. It was something Viktor Kosárek had already seen many times in his brief career: the mad inhabiting a different dimension mentally, while remaining in this one physically.

'My name is Dr Kosárek.' Viktor's voice was again calm, even. 'I'm here to help you. I know you're afraid, but I'm going to do everything I can to help you. What is your name?'

'She is a demon!' cried the man.

'What is your name?' Viktor repeated.

'A fire demon. Can't you see? They are all around us. They feed off us. She's been sent here to feed off me. She's been sent by the Devil . . .'

The young man broke off and looked as if he had suddenly heard a sound, or smelled a strange odour. 'He is *here*,' he said in a forced, urgent whisper. 'The Devil is here, now, in this place. I *sense* him—'

'Your name,' said Kosárek quietly, kindly. 'Please tell me your name.'

The man with the knife looked confused, as if he couldn't understand why he was being distracted with such trifles. 'Šimon,' he said eventually. 'My name is Šimon.'

'Šimon, I need you to keep calm. Very calm.'

'Calm?' asked Šimon incredulously. 'You ask me to be calm? The Devil is among us. His demons are here. She is a demon. Don't you see them?'

'No, I'm afraid I don't. Where are they?'

Šimon cast his gaze like a searchlight over the marble floor of the railway station. 'Don't you *see*? Are you blind? They're everywhere.' He suddenly looked more afraid, more agitated, again seeing something that only he was witness to. 'The ground – the floor – it's *sweating* them. They ooze up out of the stone. Lava from the bowels of the Earth. Then they bubble and froth upwards until they take form. Like this one.' He tightened his grip on his captive, the hand with the knife twitching.

'Šimon,' said Viktor, 'don't you see you've got it all wrong? This woman is nothing but a woman. She's not a demon.'

'Are you mad? Can't you see? Don't you see the fire horns curling out from her head? The lava of her eyes? Her white-hot iron hooves? She is an elemental demon. A fire demon. I am so terribly burned from just touching her. I have to stop her. I have to stop them all. They are here to feed off us, to burn us all, to take us into the lake of fire where there will be no end to our torment.' He thought about his own words, then spoke with a sudden, but quiet and considered resolve. 'I've got it: I have to cut her head off . . . . That's it, I have to cut her head clean off. It's the only way to kill a demon. The only way.'

The woman, who had been doing her best to follow Viktor's command and remain quiet, let out a desperate cry. Kosárek held up a calming hand to both captive and captor. He realized he was dealing with a delusional schizophrenic paranoia of massive dimension; that there might be no way of reaching Šimon's tortured mind before he killed his captive.

He cast a meaningful look in the direction of the police officer, who gave a small nod and quietly unbuttoned the flap on his leather holster.

'I assure you, Šimon, this woman is no demon,' said Viktor. 'You are unwell. You're unwell in a way that makes your senses deceive you. Close your eyes and take a breath.'

'It's the Devil who deceives. The Great Deceiver has blinded everyone but me. I am God's instrument. If I close my eyes, the Devil will sneak up on me and drag me to Hell.' He lowered his voice; sounded pained, afraid. 'I have seen the Great Deceiver. I have seen the Devil and looked into his face.' He gave a cry of terrible despair. 'He burned me with his eyes!'

'Šimon, please listen to me. Please try to understand. There is no Devil. All there is, all you're experiencing, is your mind. Your mind – everybody's mind – is like a great sea, a deep ocean. We all live our lives, every day, every one of us, sailing on the surface of that ocean. Do you understand me, Šimon?'

The madman nodded, but his eyes remained manic, terrified.

'But beneath each of us,' continued Viktor, 'are the great dark fathoms of our personal oceans. Sometimes frightening monsters live in those depths – great fears and terrible desires that can seem to take real form. I know these things because I work with them as a doctor all the time. What is happening to you, Šimon, is that there is a great storm in your ocean; everything has been stirred up and swirled around. All of those dark monsters from the deeps of your mind have been awoken and have burst through the surface. I want you to think about it. I want you to understand that everything that is frightening you at this moment, everything you think you see, is being created by your mind.'

'I am being deceived?' Šimon's voice became that of a frightened, lonely child.

'You're being deceived,' repeated Viktor. 'The woman you hold is an ordinary woman. The demon you think you hold is a demon of your imagination. The Devil you fear is nothing but a hidden aspect of your own mind. Please, Šimon, close your eyes—'

'I am being deceived—'

'Close them, Šimon. Close them and imagine the storm passing, the waters calming.'

'Deceived . . .' He closed his eyes.

'Let the lady go, Šimon. Please.'

'Deceived . . .' He let his arm fall from around the woman's shoulders. The hand that held the knife eased away from her throat.

'Move!' The policeman hissed the urgent command at the woman. 'To me, now!'

'Deceived . . .'

The woman ran, sobbing, across to the policeman, who ushered her beyond the police line; a woman from the crowd folded comforting arms around her.

'Please Šimon,' Viktor Kosárek said to the young man, who now stood alone with his eyes still closed, 'put the knife down.'

Šimon opened his eyes. He looked at the knife in his hand and again repeated: 'Deceived.' He looked up, his eyes plaintive; his hands, the knife still in one, held out beseechingly.

'It's all right,' said Viktor, taking a step towards him. 'I'll help you now.'

'I *was* deceived,' said Šimon, suddenly angry. 'The Great Deceiver, the Guiser, the Dark One – *he* deceived me.' He looked directly at Viktor and gave a small laugh. 'I didn't recognize you. Why didn't I recognize you? But I know who you are now.' Šimon's eyes became suddenly hard and full of hate. 'Now I know! Now I know who you are!'

It happened too fast for Viktor to react. Šimon launched himself at the young psychiatrist, the knife raised high and ready to strike.

Viktor froze and two sounds filled the space around him,

reverberating in the cavern of the station concourse: the deafening sound of the policeman's gunshot; and Šimon's screaming, as he lunged at the young doctor, of a single word.

'Devil!'